TRUE NORTH

ALSO BY ANDREW J. GRAFF

Raft of Stars

TRUE
NORTH

A NOVEL

ANDREW J. GRAFF

ecco

An Imprint of HarperCollins*Publishers*

TRUE NORTH. Copyright © 2024 by Andrew J. Graff. All rights reserved. Printed in the United States of America. No part of this book may be used or reproduced in any manner whatsoever without written permission except in the case of brief quotations embodied in critical articles and reviews. For information, address HarperCollins Publishers, 195 Broadway, New York, NY 10007.

HarperCollins books may be purchased for educational, business, or sales promotional use. For information, please email the Special Markets Department at SPsales@harpercollins.com.

Ecco® and HarperCollins® are trademarks of HarperCollins Publishers.

FIRST EDITION

Designed by Alison Bloomer
Lake illustration © Aksol/Shutterstock

Library of Congress Cataloging-in-Publication Data has been applied for.

ISBN 978-0-06-316141-2

23 24 25 26 27 LBC 5 4 3 2 1

For the river, and for family.

TRUE NORTH

FOR SALE: WOW! Don't miss this! Woodchuck Rafting Co., very established business. All rafts, gear, shuttle buses, and boat barn included. Dedicated, perennial guide staff. Owner stays on for 1993 rafting season (May through Sept) to show the ropes to new owner/operator ready to LIVE THE DREAM! Bring the whole family. Life-changing opportunity. WOW!

MAY

ONE

THEY WERE HALFWAY THERE. THEIR NEW HOME IN THE WOODS. SAM
Brecht pulled the brand-new twenty-three-foot Winnebago Brave to the
gravel shoulder of County Road A. Darren needed to pee. Sam stepped
out into the long grass with his son and took a deep breath. Even the
ditches up here smelled the way ditches should, just the way he remembered them smelling, sweet and sandy, with pine in the air. There were
pines all over this far north, white pine and jack pine and spruce bor-
dering leaning barbed-wire fences, abandoned cow pastures Sam knew
would fill with goldenrod and Queen Anne's lace by summer's end. The
setting sun made a perfect orange-and-purple sky behind all that fresh
northern pine. The sun would rise over it too. New horizons.

Sam stepped into the tall grass with Darren. At ten years old, the
boy had only known the city, and was a bit shy at first about peeing roadside. North of Green Bay, Sam had had to set the example and go first.
The camper had a toilet, but Darren didn't want to use it while driving,
and as long as they had to stop, Sam thought they may as well conserve
the water tank. "Let her rip," he said, and Darren smiled and did so.
This move up north was going to be good for him. Sam had purchased
Darren a folding green compass that the boy wore around his neck. The
compass swayed on its lanyard as Darren leaned forward over the ditch
grass. There was so much to show the boy and his little sisters.

Sam finished first and buckled his belt. "See those shoots growing
there?" he said. "You know Queen Anne's lace is really a wild carrot?
You can dig down and pull up a little clump of carrots. Your great-uncle
Chip from Woodchuck taught me that when I was a kid. Can't wait for
you to meet him."

Darren pushed his lower lip out and raised his eyebrows, looking
at the wild carrot shoots and pulling the waistband of his sweatpants
back up.

Swami leaned out the high passenger window of the Brave.

"Check for ticks," she said.

"No ficks!" yelled Dell, Sam and Swami's three-year-old daughter, standing with her hands on her hips at the open side door of the camper. Dell had her mother's dusty blond hair. Darren had his father's red. The new baby had a tuft of strawberry-colored fuzz.

Darren strode toward the door, shaking his head at his little sister and knotting his pants back up. "No Dell. Ticks with a *T*," he said. "*T. Tuh, tuh*. Ticks."

"No ticks!" shouted Dell, and then made *T* sounds—*tuh, tuh*—as Darren corralled her back up into the camper. Swami peered out the window again, irritation on her face, her arms looped around the baby, pulling the child in close to nurse. "We need to get there, Sam. The kids are going to need supper and bed."

Sam nodded, took another deep breath, and trudged up the ditch. It smelled good. Sam hoped someday soon Swami might like to stand out in one of these fields with him and smell the sweet grass and pine and agree how wonderful it was. They could be in love again, the way they were in the summer of '79, when they both had summer jobs as raft guides down in West Virginia. This journey north was a bit of a last chance for them, and more than Swami even knew. The thought of what was at stake made Sam feel like holding his breath, like he had swum out to water too deep and the silty bottom was no longer there. He reassured himself that they had fallen in love near a river, and maybe another river could make everything right again.

Sam walked around the front of the idling Brave. Its new motor idled smoothly. It was nice to have something in his life that worked. Sam ran his hand across the warm, truncated hood as he passed, brushing a peppering of dried mosquitoes from the smooth paint. The paint job was incredible. Sam loved it. Darren loved it. Dell loved it. DeeDee loved it, even though she couldn't lift her head or talk. The Brave was tan with teal and blue stripes, plus a hot pink dealer-installed water splash decal that ran up along both sides. It looked like something right out of one of those Juicy Fruit commercials. Driving it made Sam feel

younger and more fit, like an extreme skier carving down the freeway in bright ski pants. He'd carved up from Chicago, through Milwaukee, up through Green Bay, onto Highway 41—*up past the palm
and thumb and up to the fingertips of Wisconsin, straight north, true
north*, as he explained it to Dell. Darren showed his little sister which
way north was on his compass, the big *N*.

"What's at the fingertips?" she asked her dad.

"Marigamie County," he said. "Forests and rivers and sky."

"And deers?" she asked.

"So many deers," he said.

"Baby ones?"

"Baby ones too," he said, and Dell smiled at him.

Sam opened the driver door and pulled himself up into the cab.
Swami had the baby pulled up into her breast.

"Do you want me to wait?" he asked. They had car seats, and Sam
usually insisted on them.

Swami shook her head. "It's okay," she said. "I'm buckled, and I've
got her." She looked tense, like she always did when she nursed, like the
world beyond her baby bothered her, Sam included. "The kids are going
to get overtired."

Sam pulled the Brave into gear. "Off we go! Home to the woods!" he
called back to his kids, hopefully. He was speaking of the campground
where they planned to stay May through August. What Swami didn't
know was that he'd actually booked it beyond summer—as a precaution
only—all the way until the park closed in late October.

"Home to the woods!" shouted Darren, too loudly. His little sister
echoed him. They both sat on the bench at the fold-out table in the galley, eating a stack of flaxseed crackers Swami had chosen for them.

"It's not home, you guys," Swami corrected them. She looked right
at Sam. "It's camping, and only for a few weeks until we can figure out a
more permanent situation."

Sam winced. He knew Swami didn't like him filling the kids' heads
with ideas, but Sam couldn't resist their enthusiasm. He liked watching
them light up when they asked him about how long they could stay up
north, or the baby deer, or if the river could really tear a raft in half. He'd

just give them a wide-eyed shrug that they knew meant, *Who knows? Maybe. Probably.*

"It gives them false hopes," said Swami. "Don't say it if it's not true." Swami had studied geology in college. She knew about fixed layers of rocks, the way they formed and the way they didn't. Sam was an art teacher with a degree in ceramics. He knew about clay.

"Well," he said, peering toward the shoulder to read a road sign. "We could live in the woods forever if we wanted to."

"We don't," she said.

"But we could," he said, and Swami just looked at him and then at the road.

Jack pines and white pines marked several silent curves in the road. Dogwood grew in the ditches and sumac atop the sandy bluffs. Sam's seat belt fluttered in the breeze of the open window. He hoped this would work. He needed this to work.

"Swami?" Sam asked in a quiet voice.

He waited for her to look at him. She did, hunched over their youngest.

"I love you," he said.

Something softened in her neck and she looked out the window.

"Thank you," she answered.

County Road A seemed narrower in the dark, just a faded yellow line, a grass shoulder, and cedar trees in the headlights. Sam muscled the Brave through a few slow curves. It wasn't far now. The older kids turned the light on at the galley table behind them. Sam and Swami and the baby sat in relative darkness in the cab.

"Hey, Dell?" Sam called back.

Dell looked up from a travel brochure Darren had picked up from a gas station in Crivitz. Sam had gotten a look at it while they pumped gas, a trifold of images of river bluffs and bridges and creeks, people riding tractors and snowmobiles and horses.

"What, Dad, what?" she said.

"You want Daddy to take you to your uncle Chip's deer farm this week?"

Darren looked up. "What's a deer farm, anyway?" he asked.

"What, Dad?" Dell yelled. She spoke a lot of words for her age, more than Darren had when he was three, but Dell was working on volume control. She either whispered secrets or yelled.

"It's like a petting zoo," he said. "But with deer in it. You can pay a few quarters for alfalfa pellets and feed the deer. You guys want to feed the deer?"

Darren pushed out his lip and nodded.

Dell screamed, "Yay!"

"Don't get her riled up before bed," said Swami. She held the sleeping baby now. The baby's name was Deidra—DeeDee—after Swami's mom, but it had taken Swami four weeks to name the girl. She'd insisted on getting to know the child. Sam had insisted it was hard to know a child without a name, and still found himself referring to her as "The Baby." The baby hung in Swami's arms now, like a plump rag doll, her belly full of milk, her mouth hanging open in bliss.

"I'm not riling her up," Sam said. "I just want her to see a baby deer. My uncle still has the deer out at his place. I'm not sure if it's still open to the public. I went there as a kid."

"I hole a baby deer!" Dell shrieked with glee.

"I know, Dell," Sam said. "Stop yelling, honey."

Darren said, "Not *hole*, it's *hold*. D. Duh. Duh.*"

Dell yelled, "*Duh! Duh!*"

Swami gave Sam a cool look. Sam looked away from it, out at the road ahead. The sky had been red behind the pines, and now it was black, the moon hanging in it. Sam sank in his seat. He knew what Swami's look meant. It meant, *You are not doing a good job.* That's the way it felt, anyway. Those looks started coming not long after the first teaching job, then their first baby and lack of sleep, more opportunities to disagree, Sam's worsening anxiety and bad moods. Swami's raised eyebrows made Sam's body tense. There had been too many fights. Sam promised himself there would be no more fights. Fresh starts. Home in the woods. He could hear the kids yelling now, and feel Swami's gaze growing more intense.

"Mom, Dell's poking at me!" yelled Darren.

"No!" yelled Dell.

Sam looked into the rearview mirror just in time to see Darren whack Dell with the travel brochure, and then Dell lean in to try to bite Darren, her mouth wide as a shark's. Then Swami huffed, and Darren whacked Dell again, and Dell howled, and then the baby squawked. Sam looked up in the mirror and took a deep breath to bark at the kids.

And then the deer jumped out.

Sam gripped the wheel, instinctively stomping the brake as the animal leapt from the shadows into the light. The deer's mouth hung open, its leaping body stretched out in flight, crossing the path of the Winnebago, its black-and-white eye wide, angled unnaturally backward and downward at the charging headlights of the Winnebago.

The kids' crackers slid from the galley table. Swami reached out for the dash with her free hand. A set of nested pans slid from a shelf. It was them or the deer, Sam knew, and so instead of swerving he clipped the animal midflight, its rear quarter, and watched the animal spin violently off into the shadows. He felt the collision in the steering wheel as much as he heard it, and his heart sank as he maneuvered the Brave to a rolling stop on the thin gravel shoulder.

His left headlight was out. The short hood steamed. Sam looked at the temperature gauge, and watched the needle spike to boiling and then fall dead. He shut the motor off.

Dell was crying, but Sam knew she was more startled than hurt. He'd seen her plop off the bench to the carpeted aisle the way she sometimes slid from a kitchen chair. It was a gentle enough bump. Darren stood gripping the table.

"What happened?!" he asked.

Swami pursed her lips and shook her head. The baby was crying, and she bounced her, looked back at Darren and Dell. "Sam, get Dell!" she demanded.

Sam twisted from his seat and began to step over the carpeted center console in time to see Darren jump over his crying sister and dart forward.

"What happened!" he asked again, peering through the windshield.

Sam couldn't get past him. "Darren, move back," he said.

"Did we hit a car?" Darren demanded. He was as wide-eyed as the deer.

"Sam!" demanded Swami.

"I'm trying!" Sam yelled, one sandaled foot still held midstep over the console. Maps and a foaming soda can and crackers were all over the floor. "Darren, back up!"

Dell cried even harder, really screaming now. The baby yelled. Darren craned his neck to try to get a view out the windshield. The Brave smoked. Swami smoked. Sam smoked. He brushed past Darren and scooped up his screaming daughter. She was pure, sobbing weight. He pulled her to his shoulder and bounced her and said, "Shhh," as much to himself as to her.

Darren was standing on the center console, arguing with his mom about wanting to see, and Swami was saying something to Sam at the same time, and Dell shuddered and shook, and it was all too much noise now, the way the art class mess and lunch duty and bad teacher coffee and pay and life itself all made too much noise. Sam felt it rising, a hot fog threatening to burst from his mouth, so he quickly unlatched the side door and escaped into the cool night air.

The moon was large and round and the stars were bright, and something about stepping out into that darkness and sweet-smelling air made Dell stop crying immediately. She picked her head up from his shoulder and sniffed and looked out at the dark cedars. She held her head really still as she heard the singing frogs. She looked at the moon and then at the glow of the headlights, her wet cheeks shining.

"You okay? Are you hurt?" Sam asked her, and she buried her head in his neck again to dry her face on his T-shirt. She shook her head.

The Brave gave a sharp hiss. A final shot of steam burst into the air.

"It broke, Dad?" she asked him.

Sam walked closer to the front end and groaned.

"Yeah, sweetie. It's broke," he said, and the two of them just stood there in the dark for a time, staring at how broken it was. It smelled hot. Like rubber and steam.

"Fix it, Dad," she said.

Sam surveyed the sizzling Winnebago, the dented hood and shattered headlight. Inside the cab he heard Swami and saw her make a grab for Darren's arm while she clutched the baby to her chest. Darren bolted, and Swami made to chase him but remembered the baby. Sam knew she couldn't see him holding Dell just outside the beam of the headlight. She slumped back in her seat and clenched her eyes shut.

"Fix it," Dell said again.

As Sam stood there, only feet from his wife, but so far away, while their potentially permanent home smoked on the side of a dark road, he couldn't bring himself to tell his daughter he would fix it. He didn't know if he could. What his family didn't know was that he wasn't entirely certain his teaching job would be there for him after this summer break. The week after they purchased Woodchuck, the school board and superintendent announced that arts funding was "being reviewed." Arts and metal shop might be cut. Sam still hadn't received a contract for fall. His throat felt too tight to speak. Sam felt that familiar fog in his body, that looming shadow of frustration and fear that Swami's looks had a way of amplifying. The fog became even thicker when Sam held one of his crying children, because he knew that child depended on him to tell them life would somehow work out and that they would be happy.

Sam looked at Dell and nodded his head. He looked up at his wife, leaning back in the passenger seat. For the space of several breaths, Sam just closed his eyes too.

•••

BACK IN JANUARY, WHEN SAM first brought up the idea of buying his uncle's whitewater rafting company in northern Wisconsin, Swami was washing a few dishes. The winter night was cold beyond the window, and the dishwater felt warm on her hands. Swami was eight months pregnant.

Sam held a clipped ad from Thunderwater Realty. His uncle had mailed it to him, he said, the listing circled, the first time Sam had heard from him in years. It was snowing heavily outside in the streetlights. The bushes still held Christmas lights Sam failed to take down even though it was three and a half weeks after New Year's. Swami stopped washing. Sam had had these bad ideas before. He was always dreaming, coming up with some "new vision," instead of just living in the present and helping to live well where they were. Like the *blueberries*. The previous fall, Sam came home from work after visiting an apple orchard with the school, and already had a plan to start a pick-your-own blueberry farm. He had it all written out, his art teacher math scribbled in the margins. *We could plant next spring,* he said, *find the land, move out there. There aren't many blueberry farms near Chicago because the soil is too alkaline. But,* he said, *I looked into that today too, and if we bring in a truckload of sulfate per acre—probably twice every season—we should be able to yield about ten pounds of berries per bush.* His eyes widened, as if what he'd say next would knock her over. *That's ten grand an acre, Swami.*

Swami didn't know what to say to him then or now. After they'd had Darren, Swami's annoyance with Sam's dreaming had grown exponentially. Sam's annoyance at her refusals grew too. She'd watch him wrestle the garbage cans out to the road and stare at the sky, shake his head at the air, mope for days. When they first met, Swami liked to play along. She never thought he was serious, but she'd humor him. The summer after his first year of student teaching in college, Sam mused over a bottle of beer that he wanted to move to West Virginia near the New River and sell pottery from a van in winters and raft in summers. They could live in the van, he said, in Fayetteville. Swami stole his beer and took a drink. *I'll be your pottery model,* she said, and they laughed, and then they stopped laughing and made love instead. It wasn't like that anymore. Swami had lost her ability to humor him. They couldn't daydream about living in vans.

Swami scrubbed a cutting board beneath the warm dishwater. Her back ached. She'd sit down soon and Sam could finish.

"Just think about it," he said. "All I'm asking is to think about it. We could go up there for one summer, get it really rolling again. It's an investment. We could resell it. This is me thinking of our future," he said.

"And what about Darren's school year, and yours? You can't leave in May."

"I'll take some vacation. And we can take Darren out early just once. It'll be educational. My uncle is off-loading this place cheap. I already spoke with him."

Swami spun around. "You *already* spoke with him?" she asked.

"Well, I wanted to know details," said Sam. "Before I talked with you."

Swami shook her head while he tried to say more, turning back to the sink. She heard Sam shift his weight for a moment. He stood and walked away to the living room, where Dell begged him to read a book. It was bedtime. Darren was reading in bed. Dell had brushed. Swami looked out the window at the Christmas lights, drained the sink, listened to Sam read the story to Dell too quickly and tersely.

"You're skipping, Daddy," Dell said. "Don't skip."

The next morning, Swami called her mother to talk it out.

Her mom sighed. "Oh, honey," she said. "I watched your father do this. It was always this or that. Don't let it grow. You were only seven, but you remember. Don't let *California* happen to you too."

Swami remembered. It was fun until it wasn't. Her dad convinced their mother to sell their home and move the family to Encinitas when Swami was seven. He wanted to surf, he said, wanted his family to have sun on their backs. He turned them poor instead. They moved back to Chicago when the money dried up. Swami wished it was different with Sam. But it wasn't. Sam wanted to go. Needed to go. He was thirty-five and already wilting in his teaching job, no longer the guy she'd met down in West Virginia, happy as a wet dog shaking river water out of his shaggy hair. Maybe rafting in summer would do him good, keep him grounded in winters. Maybe saying yes would be like a controlled burn to prevent the coming of a larger fire. It wasn't California. It was just a summer business.

"Listen," her mom said, after a long conversation. "I wouldn't entertain it. I entertained your father when I was expecting you, let him start subscribing to surfer magazines, and it landed us in a hut we couldn't afford and took us twenty years to build back what we left behind."

"But there were sea lions," Swami tried.

"No," her mother told her. "You've got a baby coming. Just tell him no."

Swami could hear the woman shaking her head on the other end of the phone, and her mother was still shaking her head when they packed the new camper later that spring. *Brave*, it read, in bright teal letters. Swami didn't know quite what made her say yes to Sam—it was almost a whim—but two weeks after the baby came in February, something in the little girl's gray eyes, the very gift of them, opened Swami momentarily to other possibilities. Something about the sleeping face of her new baby allowed her to say yes to Sam. He kissed her lips when she did.

Sam unwilted, busy each night after putting the older kids to bed, planning what they'd need for the summer, ordering river gear from catalogues, a new paddle, a helmet, life vests for the family. The day he leapt from the brand-new camper in their driveway, arms held wide with pride, Swami quickly carried DeeDee into the house to take a few breaths. Maybe her mom had been right. Sam sold his car and used some of their retirement savings to make down payments on everything. He reassured her that the moment they returned in the fall, he'd sell the RV and put the money back where it belonged. He said something about a tax write-off covering depreciation—*basically half the camper is free*, he beamed. By fall, they'd have the extra income from a season with the outfitter. Swami kept breathing deeply for several days, held her baby very closely.

Swami took one last walk around their home before they left, inside and out, while Sam double-checked the bikes strapped to the back of the idling camper. Sam seemed nervous, eager to get there. Swami was nervous about leaving things behind. The lilies by the foundation had their full leaves now and were just beginning to push up bulb-tipped stems. It was a shame she'd miss them this year.

"I put all the houseplants in the tub," she told her mom as she handed her the keys.

Her mom folded the keys into her crossed arms and gave a stern look at Sam as he climbed the steps of the Brave. He didn't notice. He leaned out from the steps and waved like a sea captain leaning out from the rigging. Swami's dad clapped his hands, waved at the kids looking out the sliding side window. "Living the dream!" her dad called to them. He still had a long gray ponytail. "Wish I could come with you!" he said to Swami.

"You'll visit, Dad," Swami said. "You know the campground where we'll be."

"We're coming," he said.

"Maybe," her mom added. She looked at Swami, tried to smile, softened a bit.

Swami hugged her. "Wish me luck," Swami whispered into her mom's perfumed, dyed hair.

Her mom hugged her back, only a little of the old fear in her eyes. "Call if you need me," she said.

"I will," Swami said.

•••

"DAD, WE HIT A *DEER*!" Darren yelled, plowing into Sam in the darkness.

"What, Dad? What?" asked Dell.

Sam shook his head, told Darren to wait, just wait a second, which was all too often his automatic response when he felt overwhelmed. He tried to hear the frogs again. He hoisted Dell farther up his side and gave her a squeeze. The way Dell trusted and loved so freely often made Sam feel like crying—Dell the shining miracle with glitter in her hair. He loved her.

"Dad, a car is coming," said Darren.

Sam walked to the road and watched the approaching headlights illuminate the mound of deer lying in the road fifty yards back. It was a big pickup truck on tall tires. It slowed, drove around the deer, and came to a squeaking stop beside them. Sam peered up into the open passenger window. Two young men in their late teens or twenties sat inside with a huge dog between them. The cab smelled like beer. The radio was loud.

"You cream that buck back there?" said the driver, more an acknowledgment than a question.

The passenger smiled and lifted a can of beer from between his legs and took a sip. The dog shifted in its seat, a big Siberian husky.

"We did," said Sam.

"What, Dad?" asked Dell.

"Nothing, sweetie," Sam told her. "We're in a bit of a bind," he said to the men. "Any chance you know of a tow truck in town?"

The driver leaned forward to take a look at the steaming front of the Winnebago. He winced. "Oh—buggered your rig!" Sam heard a hint of accusation in the words, as if he were the negligent owner of some lame horse. He didn't know how to reply. Darren asked his dad what the man meant.

Then the driver adjusted his ball cap. "Well, hey," he said. "I got some tow chains in back. How far you headed?" the driver asked.

"Thunderwater," Sam answered. "But really, if you could just let me know of a tow driver in town."

The driver opened his glove box, grabbed a big Maglite, then stepped from his cab. He rummaged around in the bed of the truck for a moment and came back around front holding two beers. He smiled a warm smile. Sam relaxed a bit.

"I'm your only tow at this time of night," said the driver. "Coldie?" he asked.

"What?" asked Sam.

"Want a coldie?" the man asked him again, and held out one of the beers.

"Thanks," said Sam, reaching out for the beer with a free hand. He didn't want to be rude, even though he didn't drink much anymore. Swami didn't like it, unless it was a craft cider or maybe some red wine, and then no more than two or three ounces. Sam held the unopened beer in one hand and his silent daughter in the other. Dell just watched everything, quiet, wet eyes blinking.

The man turned to Darren. "Hey, bud, hold this for me, eh?" The man handed Darren his open beer, turned his ball cap backward, and lay down beneath the front of the Winnebago with his Maglite. He wore Carhartt coveralls with grease on them, boots with mud, and Sam hoped that maybe this man scooting around on the gravel was a mechanic. Darren stared up at his dad with a wondering grin on his face, holding this stranger's beer in the darkness.

Then the man in the cab turned the radio up a bit more. It was Def Leppard, "Pour Some Sugar on Me." The man bobbed his head a few times, cracked open another beer.

"You gonna want that buck?" he called from the window.

Sam didn't know what he meant.

"That buck you hit. You want him? My name's Pete. That's Randy. And this is Bear," he said. "She's a good girl, husky mix," he said, ruffling the dog's thick mane. Pete held his hand out the window to shake. He was brown-skinned, a bit older than the other man. He wore a flannel and had two long black braids of hair trailing from his camouflage hat. Sam shook, introduced himself, and reassured Pete he didn't want the dead deer. The huge dog nuzzled Pete to be pet again. Pete ruffled her hair again. The dog was massive, colored like a husky but thicker, taller. Sam saw Dell just stare at it with wide moonlit eyes.

"What kind of mix is . . . Bear?" Sam asked.

Pete shrugged. "Wolf," he said. "Uh-oh—*Radio drink!*" He chugged his can of beer as he turned up the knob of the stereo. His bobbing head got away from him, and he spit foam on himself before barking along with the chorus. He turned it back down again and chuckled. "Every time that song says 'sticky sweet,' you gotta drink," he said. "Hey, Randy!" he shouted out his window.

Randy didn't answer from underneath the Winnebago. Pete went on.

"This guy says—What'd you say your name was?—Sam says he don't want that buck back there." Randy shouted something from under the camper. Pete leaned farther out of the cab. "I said we gotta get that buck back there! Sam don't want him!"

Swami leaned her head out the cab window above Sam at this point. "Sam?" she said. She was worried. Sam could hear it. He didn't blame her.

Randy popped up from under the Winnebago and dusted himself off with his cap. "We can tow her," he proclaimed. "She's got some solid frame down there. Man, this is a beauty," he said, patting the hood. "Brand-new?"

Sam nodded.

Randy whistled in admiration, and then he reached down to Darren for his beer. "Didn't drink her all, eh, bud!"

Sam heard Swami give a gasp.

Darren just stared at these men, in fear or wonder or admiration. Something new in the galaxy was being revealed to the boy. Darren had the same look on his face the first time he saw the full T. rex skeleton in the Chicago Field Museum.

"Sam." It was Swami's voice, both stern and worried now.

Pete and Randy looked up at her.

Sam nodded. He didn't know how to speed this along. "This is my wife, Swami," he said. "And this is Dell and Darren. So how far of a tow would this have to be?"

"Swami," Pete said slowly. He paused for a moment as if adding her name to the list of possibilities. His galaxy was expanding too. "Where you guys from?" he asked.

"Chicago."

Pete gave an unimpressed nod. His dog just stared. "Well, welcome to the Northwoods." He said the word *North* as *Nort*. If it had been Dell who said it, Sam knew his son would be correcting him.

"Swami, you need a coldie up there?" Randy asked. When she didn't answer, Sam told him she could share his coldie. Randy shrugged and drank. Sam felt so incredibly helpless, so at the mercy of the night, the steaming camper, Swami's frustration, and these two good old boys. He could only imagine Swami's reaction if she knew the whole truth about the possibility of his job being cut. Sam was too afraid to tell her. The rafting company, Sam hoped, would be a bridge, a financial buffer. Sam wanted to save their family. He wanted to save their marriage. He just didn't know if he could do it, and now he cursed himself for creating this much of a mess. The summer, he knew, would take a miracle.

"Holy smoke!" Randy yelled, tipping his beer back down. "Would you look at that *moon*! Oh, wow!"

The husky barked. Sam looked up. And above him he saw Swami look up, the profile of her face lit bright. Darren stared up. Dell was silent. The moon seemed so incredibly enormous and bright and full. It hung above the pines like the bright, calm palm of a hand. Sam felt himself take a full breath. If only a hand that large could hold it all, guide it, take over. He had to admit, for a moment, he felt hope that everything could come together.

"All right, then!" said Randy, tossing his can into the back of the truck and digging for another. "Let's roll. I'd tow you to Smitty's, but he's closed up till next week, unless you got another mechanic in mind. Smitty's right in Thunderwater."

"How far is the state park?" Swami asked him.

Randy shook his head. He did seem slightly more sober than Pete. Sam was thankful for it. "They close the gate after ten."

"What about Woodchuck Rafting?" Sam asked. "You know where that is?"

"Know it!" laughed Randy. "I *work* there! Me and Pete were just doing a beer run. Pete here works for the power dam. River's up. You guys coming rafting tomorrow?" His voice was bright and happy as he asked it.

"Actually . . ." Sam hesitated; he didn't want to explain it all right now, so he just said, "Yes, we are," which wasn't really a lie. He hoped to be on the water as soon as possible.

Swami was silent at the mention of Randy's employment at Woodchuck.

"Sounds good," said Randy. "I'll get you hooked up, you put your blinkers on, and we'll give 'er. Woodchuck ain't far. I gotta warn you, though, the guides are having a sort of bonfire tonight, so I'm gonna park you off in the alfalfa instead of up by the barn. It'll be quieter for your family."

"Gettin' tuned up!" said Pete.

Sam nodded. "We just need a place to go."

Randy gave the general scene a thumbs-up and hopped back into the cab. Sam stepped with Dell and Darren back to the shoulder of the road, while Randy rumbled the truck down through the ditch, spinning mud, and chirped the tires back up onto the pavement. He roared back to the dead deer, got out with Pete, thumped the carcass onto the tailgate, and roared back in front of the Brave. Randy hooked up the chains while Sam got back in the Brave, situated Dell in a car seat, Darren in a seat belt.

"I do *not* want these men pulling us," Swami hissed as he climbed up front. DeeDee had fallen back to sleep. Swami had her buckled into her car seat on the floor between her legs.

"We need a tow," said Sam. "They'll go slow. And I can still use the brakes."

"And *these* guys work for Woodchuck?"

Sam hesitated. "Well, one of them does. You remember how raft guides can be. We just haven't been around them in a while. And besides, *we* are the owners, right? My uncle Chip will be there. It'll be fine."

Sam waited in silence with the cold, unopened can of beer between his legs, waiting for another of Randy's thumbs-ups. Sam flashed his blinkers, the chains grew taut, and with a gentle jerk, they were back out on the road, rolling. Pete leaned out his passenger window, laughing and waving Sam forward. Swami glared ahead, gripping the handle of the baby seat. Randy's truck gently weaved between the centerline and the gravel shoulder, attached to the camper with a rusted chain like an old tugboat. In the illumination of the Brave's flashers, the truck showed all its rust and spray paint, gray primer patches. The truck's rear window revealed a shotgun rack with a canoe paddle and a rifle in it. The window glass wore a big silver *Metallica* sticker, a sparkling trucker girl silhouette, and an NRA decal the size of a dinner plate. The dog kept turning in its seat, pausing to look out the rear window with its big paws on the backrest. In the truck's bed—Swami's mouth gaped open in horror for the first half mile—were a dozen empty beer cans, a chain saw, and the roadkill deer carcass with its hind leg up in the air, its stubby antlers in velvet.

Randy did drive slowly. Incredibly slowly.

"How much farther?" Swami finally managed to say. She sat with her eyes closed tight.

"Not too far," said Sam.

"Can I see the deer again?" asked Darren.

"What deer?" said Dell.

"Stay buckled up," said Sam, quietly now.

Randy's diesel pickup whistled and burped black smoke as it chugged up a long hill. Its taillights illuminated Swami's face a deep red as the vehicles coasted down the other side. They soon passed a row of small houses leading into the town, and Randy slowed. Sam recognized the houses, but they'd aged. Their paint had peeled. Porches drooped. The trucks in their driveways rusted and sagged on their springs. In one yard Sam could make out in Randy's headlights a collection of cardboard election signs. Several faded ones read *Clinton/Gore*. One with a black ribbon read: *We'll remember you, Sheriff Patcher, Marigamie Co. Sheriff, 1957–1993*. Several shiny new ones read, *Quit whining and start the mining!*

Thunderwater, Sam knew, had always been a paper town, its small collection of square homes trailing like a tail along the riverbank downstream of the pulp mill that built them. Things had changed since he was a kid. It looked rougher. Like hard times had come, or a river flood. But then Sam caught a glimpse of the river shining blackly through a few of the trees. The river hadn't changed, nor had the broad rock bluff along its far side. The pines on the bluff's top blocked a few of the stars. And there was the giant moon too, more permanent and older than all of it.

One last bend and Sam saw the town's official entrance, but he didn't triumphantly shout out their arrival as he'd envisioned he would. The kids didn't cheer, and Swami didn't smile at him. The kids stayed quiet, and Swami's eyes stayed closed. A single streetlight illuminated a big, faded sign hung between two poles, painted with images of pines and a river, a tiny pulp mill dam, and a huge copper-colored musky chasing a spinnerbait. Beneath the musky in yellow letters the sign read:

WELCOME TO THUNDERWATER. POPULATION 284.

TWO

SAM FIRST HAD THE THOUGHT HE WANTED TO MARRY SWAMI DURING a rainy shore lunch on the banks of the New River in West Virginia. They were both on summer break from college, 1979, training to be river guides for Valley Rafts, a newer operation with a handful of neoprene boats and blocky, bright orange life vests. Sam was holding a sodden bologna sandwich on white bread, still shivering from the adrenaline and cold beneath a green canopy of dripping oaks, when Swami—he knew her name now, two weeks into guide school, Swami from Illinois with the bright green helmet and dusty blond pigtails, eyes as blue as the rafts—looked at him from where she sat in the wet gravel and said one word.

"Good," she said, and smiled at him, which made Sam feel less afraid of the river that had nearly killed him, less afraid of life, and he had the thought he wanted her to look at him and smile and say *good* forever.

During the first week of guide school, seasoned guides steered the rafts, pointing out river features, drilling the trainees with the names of rapids. They taught paddle strokes, the draw and the pry. They taught rope throws and knots and "live bait" rescues, the trainees taking turns leaping out into rushing water and bear-hugging fake victims, dragged back in by shore crews. Morning and afternoon, the rafts drifted and spun and beat their way downstream between steep green hills and over steep green waves. Sam paddled, ate, swam, then wrapped himself in his damp sleeping bag before the sun went down and studied the names of rapids. Thread the Needle had mild whirlpools. Lower Kaymoor had a deadly hydraulic named Teacher's Pet. A bright-bearded guide named Lucas who kept a bag of candy in his helmet said, "If you go out of the boat in Kaymoor, swim left or die." A guide named Peaches said, "Swim right at Pig-Farmer's, and at Beury's Hole." A Valley Rafts founding

guide named Goddess, in her fifties with two silver braids sticking out
of her helmet, told them to not swim too far right at Beury's. "Too far
right and you'll suck under Vulture Rock," she said. "Lights out."

Beneath all of these warnings, Sam could always sense a sort of
veteran's mirth. Lucas and Peaches enjoyed scaring them, acting like
old salts. But no one ever joked about Keeney's. They spoke of that rapid
with reverence. It was the river's gatekeeper. It had a house-sized pile
of submerged rock to avoid, a sieve named Meat Grinder that let water
through but not trees or rafts or bodies. One day Lucas sat in the back
of the bus with the trainees during the ride up the narrow switchbacks
from the takeout. Sam sat with his helmet on his wet lap. Lucas cracked
open a beer and ate a leftover bologna sandwich, pointing out things
through the windows—where to get a cord of wood from a man named
Rob, where to hunt deer if you knew who to ask.

"You guys know the difference between a raft guide and a Sas-
quatch," Lucas asked. "One is big and furry and smells like hot garbage, and the other is a mythological creature." And then he guffawed,
and the bus bounced, and he spilled a little beer on himself. Someone
a few seats up asked Lucas if he ever saw anyone go into Meat Grinder.
Lucas's face stiffened. He stopped chewing his sandwich, rolled his
tongue around inside his mouth for a second, nodded.

"I seen it once," he said, and then slouched back up to the front to sit
with Peaches and Goddess.

In the second week of training, it rained. The river rose, angry, erratic, milky, new. The rafts bobbed downriver each day like tiny corks
connected by some invisible coil, their proximity expanding and con-
tracting as they snaked their way through currents and eddies, popped
over waves. Goddess called an all-girls boat one morning, which
launched in front of Sam's. Sam watched their bright helmets bobbing
back and forth between the white tips of waves as they paddled expertly,
in perfect unison. Sam especially watched the girl in the green helmet.
She first caught his eye the day he saw her stand next to a beached raft
and squeeze river water from her braids. He didn't mean to stare. It was
just the way her eyes sparkled. She seemed so sure of herself here in the

mountains, a bit too much sun on her freckled skin, the river itself in her laughter and movement. Her name was Swami. Looking at her felt to Sam like looking at a massive wave about to break over the bow of a raft.

It was clear to all the guides and trainees that Swami possessed hints of what Goddess had in full, a certain poise or grace on the river, a sort of givenness out there on the river. On an evening off, Sam and some of the other trainees watched a VHS guide tape in the boathouse. They pulled a raft close to the TV and sat on its tubes with beers. The tape revealed that even the guides like Peaches, who had been at it a few seasons, weren't above a certain degree of panic out there. A wave would push them off course, and Peaches would overcompensate. You could see him hollering too many paddle commands, first one way and then the other, like a driver trying to muscle his way out of a skid. But then Goddess would drop into that same rapid, her toes barely tucked under the thwarts, her eyes bright at the splashes, her silver braids flashing in the sunlight. She'd lightly pick her way down invisible paths amidst class-five pillows of water, explosions all around her. She looked as calm as a woman eating a muffin on a park bench.

"How does she do that?" said Billy, a trainee from South Carolina who spoke in a slow Southern drawl. "*Dang*," he said, sipping a beer in the blue glow of the TV.

In his art classes, Sam felt competent. He loved the term *confidence of stroke*, and was always after it, even achieved it sometimes. But usually he just ended up trying to control his paintings, and when he couldn't they'd fall flat. So far, Sam rafted like he painted.

Dan nodded too. Dan was a Methodist seminarian who everyone called Preacher. He lowered his beer and pointed it at the set. "It's the numinous," he said.

Preacher had the tape on slow motion now, the VCR ticking frame by frame, Goddess sliding her raft up the face of a twelve-foot-tall wave.

"Noomi-what?" asked Billy.

"Numinous," said Preacher. "Divine presence. Burning bushes. The ocean. A naked woman. Moses. *That*." He tipped his beer can toward Goddess on the TV. They rewound the tape. Watched it again. Sam recognized the need for artfulness in the water. And it was more than art too. It was composure. The greatest guides, the silver-bearded and silver-braided, possessed a composure amidst any circumstance that Sam could not imagine. They rode waterfalls. He drank his beer down, stood up, and hiked down the hill to the Coal Chute, Valley Raft's log cabin bar and grill.

"Tell me how to do it the way you do it?" Sam asked Goddess, feeling himself leaning a bit too heavily on the bar. Goddess was eating dinner with a Budweiser. Swami sat at the corner of the bar with a girl with dreadlocks named Laura. Sam tried his best to be polite as he interrupted Goddess's meal, but the alcohol made him stumble over his words and come across a bit too adamantly. The bartender smirked and wiped a glass. Everyone knew Goddess was like the river, benevolent until she wasn't. There was a story of a time a hungover rafting guest didn't want to listen to the "girl guide." This went on for five or six river miles. Then Goddess stopped the trip, pulled her raft over, and walked the man into the forest. Those who saw it said the man's face was drained white and that he listened precisely after Goddess walked him back out.

"I mean," Sam went on, "I've listened to *everything* you've said—angles, momentum, back ferries, eddy lines, undercuts—I'm not here just to hang out in the tents and drink. You might think I am, but I'm not."

Goddess had been eating a chicken leg, and slowly put it down on her plate. She wiped her mouth, took a drink from the white can of Budweiser. She looked at Sam just long enough to make him wither. Sam's eyes met Swami's, and he felt his face get red. Swami looked down at her taco and smiled.

"You've been watching the guide tape?" Goddess asked.

Sam nodded.

"Well, what'd you learn?"

"That you don't flip rafts out there, and I do. I panic."

Goddess smirked, looked at Swami and Laura now too.

"You guys want to know the one thing that makes a good guide?"

They all nodded.

"A good guide holds his angle in the holes. There's one half second. It's that moment the raft is buried, and you're up to your neck in water, punching through the horizon of a big wave. Think of the wave as east and west, the centerline of your raft as north and south. If you can hold your angle squared up and due north through that one half second, keep your stick in the water instead of panic, you'll become a good guide."

"But how do I not panic?" Sam asked.

Goddess looked at him, then at her beer. She lit a cigarette.

"The river will teach you that. I can't. You remember how ferrying felt the first time you pulled it off, the way those invisible forces just seemed to show up, send you across?"

Sam nodded. He remembered pulling hard to rudder the nose into current, then the eddy forming downstream of the raft, the raft rocketing across the river like a ship tacking into wind.

"It'll feel like that when it shows up. One day you'll be halfway down a waterfall or down in a hole and you'll suddenly realize you feel calm, you'll see it all slowly, you'll see *through*. It will feel like a path opening that was there all along but you couldn't see it."

Everyone sat very still. Sam swigged his beer. Laura spoke up.

"Do you, like, always talk about it like that?" she asked.

Goddess laughed at herself, blew out a jet of smoke. "I have spent many years alone in a tent in the forest."

"The river will teach me," Sam said.

"The river and time," she said, and then she put out her cigarette and left a ten on the bar and got off her stool. "Speaking of which," she said to everybody. "Time to stop drinking. Try to sleep. All the rain they got upstream is going to arrive in the gorge tomorrow. Biggest water you've seen so far."

Sam watched her go. Looked at Swami. Slid his half-finished beer across the bar.

•••

THAT NIGHT, SWAMI COULDN'T SLEEP. She left her tent, took a deep breath of night air, then strode up the gravel path out of the guide camp. The frogs had grown louder. It was late enough now, or early enough, that mist had begun to collect on the trees and drip, a small microclimate beneath the canopy. Swami had been studying in the sciences. Her early life in Southern California—and the rest of it near Lake Michigan—had made her become interested in the ecotone between water and land. She liked beaches, marshes, the way river carved rocks. Here, copperheads sunned themselves on riverbanks, and the land was thick with pine, oak, laurel. The New River was the world's second oldest. Swami liked the thought of rafting that water. The river guides were interesting too, shaggy, unwashed, intoxicated by all things. She found them beautiful the way she found other wild things beautiful, admired their freedom from a distance.

When Swami told her mom over the phone about her new summer job, her mother said river guides sounded like surfers and told Swami she'd mail a pepper spray. Swami had spent most of her life in the Midwest but was named after that famous surf beach in Southern California. When her father had an early midlife crisis, he moved them—drove the family, *took it captive*, as her mom told it—from Chicago to Encinitas. The man bought a brand-new VW bus—it was 1965, and Swami was seven, which proved her father had been daydreaming of beach breaks well before her birth—and drove out across the plains and mountains and deserts, and then parked the VW next to a one-bedroom love shack three blocks from the ocean. He had dreams, *vision*, he called it. He said he wanted Swami to grow up running across the hard-packed sand, dreamed of her running around with a pail, collecting shells, the sea lions barking, the air filled with gulls. He worked at a surf shop for six months, until the money dried up, along with his wife's patience. They drove back across the deserts and mountains and plains. Swami remembers driving east more than she remembers driving west, how her parents were silent across the width of a continent.

Swami hiked out of the camp down a misty gravel path, until she arrived at a ledge of rock that hovered above Keeney's Rapid. She quickly swept the rock ledge with her flashlight before turning it off and letting her eyes adjust again. No snakes.

Swami took off her sandals and stepped out onto the rock. The

stone felt warmer than the air. She stepped carefully in the moonlight—
the black mountains, the vivid stars, the river pounding below. A second river, one of fog, snaked its way through the canyon. Somewhere
very far off, a train whistled across the dark, coal-wrinkled skin of
Appalachia.

Swami closed her eyes and took a deep, slow breath of the stars
and tree frogs and river rocks, and then sat down with her legs crossed.
She stared at the river. It moved in an easiest path, piled up against a
bank, and then straightened and flowed downriver again. It yielded to
what was. Something rose in Swami. Some insight right on the tip of
her tongue. She wanted to say that the tree frogs yielded too, to the day
and the night, and the earth yielded in its orbit. The mountains yielded
to the continents she'd driven across with her silent parents. Swami
sighed. She wanted to be more like the river, just flowing through life,
like her dad. But she was much more often hard-driving, like her mom.
Swami paddled hard in guide school, too hard at times. Her problem
wasn't that she couldn't hold her angle. Her problem was she wouldn't
let her angle go. Goddess told her in the raft that she fought the river
and paddled harder than she needed to.

Swami heard a snapping branch behind her, and then a flashlight
swept the ledge and caught Swami in its glare.

"Sorry!" said a man's voice.

Swami shielded her eyes.

"Turn your light off," she scolded.

"I didn't expect anyone to be up here," said the man. It was Sam
from the bar.

"Neither did I," said Swami, with a bit more venom than she in-
tended. Being interrupted like this felt like someone blundering into
your dorm room when you were on the edge of sleep, or, even worse,
plopping down on the other side of a library study carrel and eating
chips—Swami's pet peeve.

Sam shifted his weight.

"You can sit," she said, and immediately Sam plodded over and sat
with his backpack, cross-legged, just a few feet away.

"I came out to see what Goddess was talking about," he said. "Wild stuff."

Swami looked at him. He wore a flannel and shorts and flip-flops. Swami could smell his deodorant. He'd showered and seemed to have sobered up a bit.

"Me too," she said.

"Well, what's the river saying."

"I think it works better if we're quiet," she said.

"Right," he said. "It's Swami, right?"

Swami looked at him.

"I'm Sam," he said.

"Sam."

"Uh-huh."

"Shhh."

He nodded. A new current of fog piled up in the canyon. It rolled over the top of a giant boulder, rolled down river, turned. Swami smiled to herself in the starlight. She liked telling Sam to be quiet. She liked that he listened. She took a long, deep breath of the river and rocks again, Sam's deodorant too.

"You know," said Sam, reaching into his pack and rattling his hand into a bag of pretzels. "I think I am learning more from that mist than I am from the river."

"What?" Swami huffed. Sharp frustration sparked within her, the way it did when someone aced a test she did not.

Sam crunched a pretzel, swallowed it. "The mist," he said. "The way it moves. That feels important, yeah?" He rustled his hand in the bag again. "You know, in my ceramics class—"

"Are you eating *pretzels*?" Swami asked, incredulous.

Sam looked at the bag, then at her. "You want some?"

Swami was already standing, brushing off her shorts. Swami picked up her flashlight. "Pretzels!" she said. She turned on her light and blasted him with it. But then something made her freeze. There was his flannel. The pretzels. The gray rock. But something else too. She fumbled to turn the light off.

"Sam, don't move!" she said. "Do not move, Sam, not an inch."

"Why are you so mad?" he said.

"Sam, there is a snake in your lap."

Silence.

"What?" he whispered.

"I'm going to turn my light back on for a second, okay?"

"Okay," Sam said.

She clicked it on and off again. In that split second of light, she saw Sam holding his yellow bag of pretzels in the air with both hands, a big tense frown on his face. A half-coiled snake nestled under and over his lap, diamond-patterned, wide head.

"Swami?" Sam hissed in the dark.

"It's a copperhead," she said. The air stiffened at the very mention. A copperhead was the worst possible snake to have in your lap. Peaches had given them the rundown on some local snakes their first night in camp. The copperhead venom caused necrosis. Peaches hadn't used that word. *Necrosis* is what Peaches meant when he said, "A copperhead'll make your leg plump up hard as a pecker. And then your leg'll die right off."

"Swami," Sam whispered. "What do I do?"

The snakes weren't aggressive unless aggravated. The best course might be to do nothing. Let the snake move. She whispered as much to Sam.

Sam very rigidly shook his head. "I'm warmer than the rocks," he whispered. "It might sit here all night. I can't hold my arms like this forever."

Swami clicked her light on and off again. The snake hadn't moved. It held its head held just an inch or two above Sam's left thigh.

"Please stop doing that," Sam said.

"Do you want me to do something? I could stamp my feet, or maybe brush it off with some ferns?"

"No, no, no."

Swami felt the way she did in the back of the raft sometimes, needing to make a decision with a boulder ahead, wanting to charge out of its path without knowing which way is best.

"Swami?" Sam's voice trembled a bit.

"I'm here," she said.

"My arms. I really can't hold my arms up like this." He had his bag of pretzels over his head now. Sam's arms trembled, and the bag of pretzels rattled, and before Swami really knew what she was doing, she crept behind him and gently closed her arms around his arms. She tightened her grip as she felt him yield a bit of his weight.

"Does this help?" she whispered.

"Yes," he whispered back.

And that's how they stayed for a very long time, without speaking. Swami, Sam, and the snake, just waiting together on the ledge above the river and the fog, holding up the bag of pretzels in the starlight.

"Swami, where are you from?" Sam whispered.

She told him. Told him about California. About college. How her mom was in real estate and her dad had a ponytail. And Swami learned that Sam was from Michigan, lost his father young in a car accident, and that his mother had given him the watch he wore. Sam liked art class. Liked to glaze pots. When they ran out of things to talk about, they looked out at the mist and the river again, felt each other breathe, felt the shared warmth of their close bodies. Swami held Sam for what felt like hours, his head starting to nod. And just as the sky began to show the slightest hint of morning, Sam's head jerked and he mumbled, "Swami."

"Shhh, I'm right here," Swami said gently. She didn't want him to startle awake. Sam lifted his head again, and the light grew brighter, and then Swami looked down into Sam's lap and saw the snake was gone.

A bird sang in a tree. Sam groaned as he woke and Swami let his arms down. He shivered in the blue light. They sat close together, quietly, unsure what to say about what had just occurred. Swami could still feel Sam's body against her own. Below them, the river thundered under a total blanket of fog. Goddess was right: the rain upstream had arrived, swelled the gorge.

"Well," said Swami, and Sam nodded, and they gathered their things and walked back together.

Later that morning, Sam and Swami both took a bad swim. The rafts flipped in Keeney's, above Meat Grinder. Swami watched Sam get sucked from the boat, then went down herself. She came up cough-ing, grabbed at the raft. A handle was ripped from her hand, and the next two minutes were darkness and light and swimming hard. Yellow rescue ropes coiled out overhead. Whistles blew. No one ate much lunch after that, except for Peaches. Sam and Swami and Laura sat in the wet gravel, leaning against a boat. Sam held a bologna sandwich in a shak-ing hand.

"I just don't know if I can get in the boat again," he said. "I don't know if this is for me. I tried, you know?"

Swami was surprised by how badly she didn't want him to leave. If you don't get back in the boat, you're done, washed out of guide training. That was the rule.

Laura tried. "You flipped in the worst possible place at the highest possible water. And you're still here," she said brightly. "Sort of."

Preacher plopped down in the dirt next to them. He leaned against the tube of the raft and lifted a shaking hand for them all to look at. His face was ashy white. His eyes were jumpy. Too much adrenaline. His words came out slowly, and his breath was sour.

"I just spent the last half hour throwing up and crying behind that bus over there," he said. "And if any of you quit, I'm quitting. So you can't quit, 'cause I need this money."

"Twenty rapids," Laura said. "We gotta do one more run through twenty rapids, and then we have two days off. I'll buy you a beer to-night."

Sam looked around at his friends. Swami could tell he was scared. But Laura was right: it hadn't killed him. It was just a bad swim. "We're all between swims" is what Peaches said.

Sam nodded. "Okay," he said. "Twenty rapids."

Preacher deflated. "I hoped I could quit and blame you," he said, grinning.

"Yay, Sam and Preacher," said Laura. She gave Preacher a playful push, and he fell over on the gravel and stayed there.

Swami just said, "Good." She meant it as much as she'd ever meant anything. And Sam looked at Swami, and Swami looked at Sam, and she didn't look away and neither did he.

THREE

SAM WOKE IN THE WINNEBAGO TO SOUNDS OF CANS CLATTERING around outside. He sat up in the early light coming through the blinds, careful to not wake his family sleeping in a heap on the camper's one queen mattress. They all had to sleep on it sideways to fit. Dell slept with her mouth wide open, her blond hair plastered to her warm face despite the cool air. Swami slept with DeeDee on her chest. Darren burrowed next to her. Sam peeked through the blinds, and then slipped quietly from the bed. He slipped on his flip-flops and hugged a thick flannel around himself and shivered, surprised how cold it could get here this late in May. All was quiet. He was so glad to be here. And then he heard the cans again.

Sam stepped outside along a rotted wooden fence marking an overgrown gravel parking lot next to the old barn. There was a muddy dirt bike leaned against the door, a white Honda with knobby tires and a torn seat. Around him in every direction were fields, bright, dewy carpets of new alfalfa surrounded by a distant border of hardwoods. The sun rose above the trees and turned the sky from orange to golden. A single weedy driveway led from the two-lane highway to the property's lone barn. Sam saw it now in person for the first time since he was a kid. The barn had a steep, rounded roof of rusting tin, which sloped down toward vertical, where it met a leaning stone foundation. The barn boards were weathered and peeling, almost still red. High on the barn's wooden face sat a peeling sign that read *WOODCHUCK RAFTING CO.*, with a logo that looked like a big beaver in a bike helmet smiling in a raft. Below the sign was a tall rolling door, locked with a chain. The place needed work, but Sam had known that going in. He was game for this. He and Swami would make this place thrive again. And then it wouldn't matter if his school decided to cut the arts. They'd be rolling in river cash out here in the sweet alfalfa field. Way up north, on the fingertips of Wisconsin. *Yes.*

Sam heard cans clatter inside the barn, and then something heavy slammed the rolling door from within, hard enough that it rocked outward on its track, snapping tight the locked chain. Someone inside moaned. The door fell to rest again. Sam stopped walking and looked back at the camper, then back at the barn again.

"Hello?" he called.

There was silence, and Sam was about to call again when he heard the voice. It sounded old and dry and sad.

"You know I'm in here, Randy," it said. "I'm locked in here."

Sam approached the door, lifted the chain from a rusted slot, and just as he did so the yellow plate of a raft paddle blade shot through the gap, pried, and flung the door open on its squealing rollers in one great heave.

A giant man with a great gray beard, arms outstretched wide as if to capture someone in a bear hug, came staggering out at Sam in a clatter of beer cans.

Sam jumped back and tripped in the weeds. The giant man staggered forward into the light, tilting one way and then the other, and then lost his footing and face-planted in the hard driveway. Sam heard the man's forehead connect with the earth—*THOCK*—which is when Sam realized the man's predicament. His arms were held out wide and duct-taped to the shaft of a blue-and-yellow rafting paddle, like a man crucified on only a crossbeam.

"Oh, wow," the man moaned, lifting his head from the dirt and then deciding to set it back down. He panted. Dust puffed from his breath. "Oh, wow, it hurts."

Sam was on his feet again. He moved to help the man, but then second-guessed it. "Are . . . are you going to hurt me?" is all he could manage to say, hovering over the giant.

The man smacked his dry mouth, looked warily at Sam with bright red eyes. He shook his head. "You ain't Randy," he said. "I'm only gonna hurt Randy. I'm so *thirsty*."

"I'm going to try to sit you up, okay?"

The man nodded.

Sam pulled him up by the paddle shaft, which made the man groan again. He had the beginnings of an egg on his forehead from where he'd hit the dirt, but it wasn't bleeding. The man slouched as he sat, hands dangling from the ends of the paddle shaft. He winced at the sun coming over the treetops, and then at Sam. And then he gagged as if he might throw up. He swallowed it back.

"You here for the rafting trip?" he asked. "Welcome to Woodchuck. Don't worry about this. Just a prank is all."

"I'm Sam," said Sam.

"Sam?" said the man, and then he brightened. "Sammy Brecht? Sammy!"

"Oh my God," whispered Sam. He could see it easily now, through all the extra pounds and the sun wrinkles and the massive unkempt beard. "Uncle Chip."

Sam heard the camper door shut behind him. He turned to see Swami walking toward him, both daughters held tightly in her arms. She had big questions on her face.

The man saw her and the children and struggled to his knees in the gravel. Sam helped him to his feet. Swami watched him. Dell watched too, wide eyed and clinging to her mother. Baby DeeDee's head wobbled like Chip's did. Darren hopped down from the camper steps and gaped.

"Kids," said Sam, "Swami. This is Uncle Chip."

The man stood to his full towering height now, stared at things as if to make sure he wasn't going to fall again. He was thick as a bear—a giant, gray-headed bear. His tanned belly stuck out from under his stained sleeveless T-shirt. His cannonball shoulders were silvered with hair.

Chip nodded in agreement. "Owner-operator of Woodchuck Rafting Company for twenty-five years," he said. "Friends call me Chip. Brought the whole gang, eh?" Chip's breath was sour, and it looked like it pained him to speak. He squinted at Darren. "Kid, you wouldn't happen to have a knife in that camper, would ya?"

Darren nodded, bolted back inside.

Swami pulled her daughters more tightly to her body and looked away for a moment, out at the clean fields. Chip stared at the ground and breathed. It was quiet enough they could hear Darren rustling around in the utensil drawer inside the camper.

"So," said Chip, blinking his glassy eyes, "you guys have a good drive up?"

Silverware crashed to the floor inside the van. Swami handed Dell to Sam and jogged back through the grass with the baby.

"Listen, Uncle Chip," said Sam in a quick whisper.

"It's so good to see you. Such bright days ahead for Woodchuck. I'm so proud." And then looked right at Sam. "I'm sorry I missed your ma's funeral few years back. I wanted to come, but your stepdad and me, we didn't—"

The funeral was four years ago, and Sam had other things more pressing than old family wounds. He shook his head as his uncle spoke. "All of that is fine. Listen, Uncle Chip—"

"Just *Chip*. We're partners now."

"Chip. Listen, I need today to go well, okay, all of this. We had a long night, and I'd really like my wife to be able to be excited about this. *Why* are you duct-taped to a paddle?"

Chips eyes narrowed. "Why ain't she excited about Woodchuck? What's wrong with her?" he asked conspiratorially.

"What? No, it was just a big ask to get my family here, and it'd be good if things went a bit—smoother," Sam said, gesturing toward Chip and the general disrepair of the place.

Chip rotated and draped a paddle shaft and arm across Sam's shoulder. His breath was hot and awful.

"I gotcha, buddy," he said. "We'll ease her into it. Just wait till she meets the rest of the crew." Chip winked at little Dell. "Woodchuck is real family-friendly. You'll be glad you bought it. Kids are gonna love it. Wife's gonna love it. Just like your aunt Mary used to love it before she left."

Sam stared at him. "Aunt Mary's not here?"

Chip shook his head.

Darren and Swami emerged from the camper. Swami told Darren not to run.

"Daddy bought a Woodchuck!" exclaimed Dell.

"No, no, honey. Daddy didn't buy an actual woodchuck. Let's talk about something else."

The boy handed his dad a bread knife, and Chip tilted his body down toward his hands.

"This arm first," he pleaded. "I can't even feel it."

Sam slipped the bread knife between his uncle's hairy arm and the paddle blade.

"Oh, this hurts," said Chip.

Sam sliced carefully.

"How long have you been like this?" Sam didn't know if he was asking about the duct tape or the general disrepair of his uncle and the grounds. The place used to be well mown, bustling with guests, his uncle tanned and fit and tall. At least that's how it was in Sam's memory.

Chip looked up at the sky. "Is it Saturday?" he asked.

"Yes." The tape gave way a bit.

"Just for one night, then," Chip said, and then craned his neck to look up at Swami. "We just had a little bonfire last night. Sort of kicking things off before the opener. Guides can be a bit of practical jokesters. Not always like this. We are a *very* family-oriented business. I see you got a cute baby there. What is he, a year? Year and a half?"

"She's three months," Swami said.

"Ah," said Chip. The tape sliced free, and Chip moaned an awful moan as he unwound his body and lowered his arms to his sides. He stood there panting, rolled his neck, the paddle still taped to one of his big arms.

"Sam, I need to know if there's water we can plug into," said Swami.

Sam looked at Chip.

"Water," she told him. "A hose. I could use water for the camper." Swami had taken Dell back into her arms. "Kids need breakfast."

"There's no well here," said Chip. "But there's a fridge in the loft with some milk jugs Randy fills out at his ma's place. It's good water. Real good water. Cold."

"Sam, could I speak to you for a moment?" Swami asked.

Sam handed Chip the bread knife, turned to Swami.

Just then, a noisy open-top Jeep, bright yellow with a teal roll bar, downshifted on the highway and turned onto the rutted driveway. The Jeep revved and carried in it a blond woman in massive sunglasses. She bumped the Jeep down the lane and turned to a dusty stop between the barn and the camper.

"*Heyyyy*, guys!" she beamed, hopping out and pushing her sunglasses onto her head.

She looked to be in her late twenties. She wore teal-strapped sandals and very short running shorts and a very tight tie-dyed midriff T-shirt. She had about thirty bracelets, star tattoos up one of her thighs. She strode into their circle and lifted her arms at them all, smiling. Sam smelled patchouli oil.

"Friends!" she said, and then she frowned at Chip, who was busy slicing his other arm free of the tape. "Oh, Chip," she said. "Not again."

"Hey, Moon," Chip said, grinning. "Glad you made it." And then he started cutting the tape again. "It was Randy—I told him he better not, but he did."

The woman wrapped Chip in a huge hug that made him wince. "I'm sorry I missed the bonfire. I got a flat in Iowa, but there were these really cool old farmers who helped me out. We ate carrots from their garden and sang folk songs all night. They had a fiddle and I played the bell." Then she dug out from her shorts pocket what appeared to be a pink rock. She kissed Chip on the forehead and gently pressed the stone where she'd kissed. It was a big crystal.

Chip paused for the blessing, sliced the rest of the paddle away, and tossed it in the weeds.

"Guys," Chip said. "Meet Moonwind, your lead guide."

"Call me Moon," she said.

"Moon, these are the new owners," Chip said. "Sam and—"

"Swami," said Swami. "Sam's the new boss. I and the kids will just be in and out."

Sam looked at Swami, and she didn't look back at him.

"*Great* to meet you," said Moon. "And here I thought you were customers. Chip, what's the trip at today?"

"Sixteen custies," said Chip. "Pete said the river was at three grand yesterday."

"*Nice,*" said Moon, pushing her charms higher up her wrist. Then without warning she hugged Sam and Swami both, with Dell and the baby too. The patchouli was overpowering.

She held them for what felt like a long time. "I am feeling *really* promising energy with you guys," she said. Her face had deep smile lines, bright blue eyes. "For luck," she said, and then quickly stamped the crystal on Sam's forehead and then on Dell's, and then Swami's and Darren's too. Swami angled the baby away before Moon could quite get to her.

Darren frowned and wiped his forehead where she'd pressed the stone, and then looked at his fingers and sniffed them. Dell saw him do this and did the same.

"You guys," said Moon, "this is going to be *such* a good season for you."

"Sam," said Swami. "Could we talk?"

Sam nodded. "Chip," he said, "I didn't know there was a trip this morning."

Chip rubbed his wrists. "It's the opener, bud. Not much of one, but it's something. We got competition now." He squinted up into the bright sky. "Guests should start pulling up in thirty minutes or so. *Oh*, I need water."

"Moon!" called a happy voice. It was Randy, jogging down from behind the barn in the same work boots he wore the night before. But now he wore blue surf shorts and a wrinkled Woodchuck logo T-shirt.

"Randy!" cried Moon, delighted.

"I *warned* you, Randy!" bellowed Chip, and ran at the younger man, picking up steam like a bull through the weeds.

Randy bolted. Chip chased him. The two disappeared around the corner of the barn, where a tangle of old lilacs grew, old sneakers hanging from the limbs by their laces, beer cans tucked into all the nooks.

"Don't hurt him, Chip!" Moon laughed. "I need him on the river today!"

Randy bounded into the sun through the alfalfa field, hopping the taller grasses and cackling. Chip howled after him, Swami's bread knife glinting in the sun.

Swami took a very big breath. "Moon?" she asked.

Swami's voice was calm, but Sam could see the frustration in her eyes. It was a look that meant, *I am going to speak, and you are going to not speak.* There was a time Sam admired that glare. She'd once used it on a tollbooth operator who didn't want to accept nickels as payment. They'd paid with nickels. Now, though, after having had that look turned on him too many times, it only made Sam shrink, regardless of its aim.

"How far away is Governor's State Park?"

"Three minutes," Moon said, nodding down the highway, and then she brightened even more. "Are you staying there? *I'm* staying there, all summer!"

"Could you tow us there—me and the kids in the camper—right away, this morning?"

Moon tilted her head. Sam winced.

"Maybe you could use Randy's truck, if your Jeep can't tow it?" Swami added.

"We have the opener this morning. Boats to blow. Paddles to set out."

Swami calmly shook her head the entire time Moon spoke.

"Sam can blow boats. My children and I can go to the state park."

Sam recoiled at the "my children" part, but given how things looked around Woodchuck, and how the morning was going, maybe it was best if Swami got out of here until he got a handle on things.

Moon looked at Sam, and he nodded. "I'll blow the boats. And if Randy doesn't mind your using his truck . . ."

Randy was way out in the field now, nearly to the wood line. Chip was bent over now with his hands on his knees.

"I'll get the truck," Moon said. She shrugged, hopped in her Jeep. "Be right back," she said.

Swami gave Sam a very quick pleading and tired look, then walked in a straight line back toward the camper with her daughters in her arms and Darren jogging behind her, glancing back once at his dad. Sam stood very still in the bright light rising over the bright fields. He heard Randy's truck come to life behind the barn. He heard Randy guffawing in the fields. He heard Dell ask as she bounced up and down with Swami's hard stride if Daddy *did* buy a woodchuck and when would she get to see it.

•••

RANDY'S TRUCK RUMBLED AND RATTLED as it pulled out of sight, leaving Swami standing alone, contentedly, at a wooded campsite at Governor's State Park. Moon had offered to help her set up camp, but Swami assured her she'd be all right, that she'd prefer to just take her time and explore awhile. Dell had since climbed onto a picnic table while Darren snooped around the bushes and fire pit.

"Careful, Dell," said Swami. Her daughter lay on the tabletop and peered down through the cracks toward the grass.

"I am, Mommy."

Swami made herself exhale. This was better. The roads into Governor's, and even the paths leading to campsites, were paved with fresh black asphalt. There were family bathrooms with sinks and showers and flushing toilets. The grass was mown, and there were neat signs at all the intersections—*Beach—Showers—Ranger Station*. The park's orderliness helped Swami shake off the chaos of the morning. She shuddered to think what Darren had learned this morning. Sam had told her about the Woodchuck he knew as a kid, the happy families toweling off after a day on the water, lilacs and coneflowers around a bright red barn, smiling guides, *money pouring in like river water*, he'd said. Swami sighed. She stepped into the camper and leaned against the tiny sink. She was here now, at least until the camper was fixed. The Winnebago was daunting to drive, but she was proud of herself getting towed in here, muscling that big camper wheel, calling out the open window to Moon—"Further, a little more now!"—as her son gripped the back of her seat and peered over her shoulder, wide-eyed. Swami smiled. Darren didn't know what his mom was made of, yet.

The campsite was a circle of clean gravel and a concrete parking slab bordered by poplars, cedars, spruce, and what appeared to be either blackberry or raspberry bushes. Site twenty-two was like a decent backyard in a wooded neighborhood. Swami could hear a few neighbors stirring, a camper door, some pots and pans, children. Through the trees she could see the bright surface of Timbrel Lake.

Swami clapped her hands by the screen.

"Okay, kids," she said, in the same way she'd said *a little farther now* about that camper, "swimsuits and buckets and bikes! Let's go to the lake!"

"I want breakfast first," complained Darren, who had been poking a stick at something in the bushes.

Dell looked up from the table.

"Mom, I want breafast first too," she echoed. She always missed the *K* in breakfast, and always smiled so sweetly when she said it, and had to be reminded about saying *please*.

"Get your swimsuits on," Swami said. "We'll take granola."

Dell cheered and Darren moaned.

"I want eggs," he said.

"Yeah, eggs!" said Dell, changing her mind.

"Granola," said Swami. "Right now." Darren dropped his stick and slouched toward the van. Dell dangled her legs from the table, dropped to the ground, and skipped to the camper.

The path to the lake was paved, and shadows of sunlight played on it. The kids swerved, beelike, on their bicycles, Dell pushing with her feet in erratic starts and stops, and Darren pedaling through big swooping arcs, shirtless, with his beach towel draped over his neck, the ends of it trailing beneath his armpits. Swami watched his bony back as she walked behind them, and smiled at the way Darren tucked his chin down when he was after speed. He was getting so big. Swami could still picture him—still smell him—the way he was the week she'd brought him home and laid him on a blanket next to Sam in the sunlight of the backyard of a home they'd rented. The universe simply shrank away to the size of a baby boy. He was just a wisp of a thing in his baggy onesie, his gray eyes looking at whatever was before him. Swami remembered patting his bottom and eating an apple. She could still taste that apple, still feel the sunlight, still see and feel Sam's smile.

And now here was Darren, ten years old, bony and hard, his messy hair beautiful as he careened through the dappled light from one edge of the path to the other, still looking at things, peering into the campsites they passed. Swami looked too, the way one might glance into the open garages of neighbors' houses. In one campsite, there was a younger couple, laughing inside a tiny tent still zipped up against the morning light, wet swimsuits draped across rocks. In another site, an older couple sat beneath an RV canopy, sipping coffee, each reading their own paperbacks. In another, a family with young kids raced about their morning routine, the husband saying something to the wife about cereal while holding a crying baby, the wife telling him the melted ice in the cooler had ruined the cereal while she chased down a naked toddler.

Swami patted Dell's back, who had stopped in her tracks, to get her moving again.

"Mommy, she's *naked*!" exclaimed Dell, who said it as if she'd just discovered the most wonderful thing.

Swami corralled her forward, and Dell scooted off toward Darren, who was circling a holding pattern at the next bend. Dell pushed herself on one of Sam's creations from early in their marriage: a twelve-inch bike with the top tube cut out and the pedals removed. Swami and Sam were already starting to argue back then. Dell had just transitioned to semisolid food. Sam was on summer break from his teaching job, sleeping later than Swami thought a grown man should sleep and then tinkering with bikes or lawn art in the shed. That was the summer she and Sam began seeing a marriage counselor. The balance bike was brought up.

"And how do you think that made Sam feel," the counselor asked, "how you reacted after he finished the balance bike for your daughter?"

Swami crumpled the Kleenex in her hand again.

"Maybe," the counselor suggested, "Sam felt hurt. Sam, did you feel hurt?"

Sam nodded.

"And, Sam, Swami says she felt unloved that day."

Swami glared at the carpet. It had been a long session.

"But that doesn't make sense," protested Sam. "What's so unloving about making a gift for a child? Why can't a dad make a gift for his child?"

The counselor waved his hands in the air.

"It doesn't matter if the other makes *sense*," he said. "What matters is that you *validate* Swami's experience."

Swami waited.

"I validate that you felt unloved," Sam said.

"I don't believe him," said Swami.

Sam threw his hands in the air.

"Talk to each other," said the counselor.

"I don't believe *you*," she said to Sam.

"Without using *you* language," the counselor reminded them.

Sam didn't make sense to her either. That was their main problem. They didn't make sense to each other, and how long could a person go on validating a thing that didn't make sense? It felt like agreeing the sky was a color it wasn't.

It had been simple with Sam, long ago. It wasn't so complicated when they were river guides. She remembered a day they bought sandwiches and a gallon of orange juice from a gas station and rattled Sam's old truck down the switchbacks to the base of the Highway 19 bridge. They ate. They swam. They sat on warm rocks, watched the rafts come down. Swami was happy. They spent all their off time together, and Sam would send her postcards if they were apart for more than a day. He'd buy them from the gift shop when he returned from an overnight river trip, tuck them into the back of her mail slot in the office. She'd wake up for a river trip and find it there, smile, think of him sleeping in his tent up the hill. She'd write a note back, and put the card back in his box. They sat closer and closer during nights at the fire until their need for nearness became so strong their clothes were a hindrance. The first time they made love was out there on the ledge rock of Condor Point, with the mist and the rattlesnakes, the frogs howling from the trees.

Memories like that didn't seem to belong to them anymore. The water had grown too muddy. Swami couldn't understand exactly how or why it had become so. She could point to a few specifics—Sam's anxiety and restlessness, her own dark moods, dinners ruined by arguments, whole weekends lost in tension—but none of the parts seemed to equal the whole. It didn't make sense. They'd just changed, subtly as weathering rock. Swami still hoped it was just a season, that warmth would return as mysteriously as it had left—flower blossoms from bare tree limbs. Other times she worried it might not. Like the night she found out she was pregnant with DeeDee, alone in the bathroom with the pregnancy test, the hot water running and steaming the mirror. A nine-year-old Darren charged down the hall, laughing at some mischief he'd caused, Sam chasing after him while holding a crying toddler, Dell.

"Swami," he called through the closed door. "Swami, I need you."

She felt her throat get tight. Sam was already a tired middle school art teacher. Swami was a tired mom. They'd been married less than a decade, and it had not been happiness. It'd been hard, financially, emotionally. Swami felt scared.

"Swami?" Sam called through the door again. "Where are you?" he pleaded, more urgent this time.

Swami turned off the water, wiped her face. "I'm right here," she whispered, just as she had the night she'd held his arms above the copperhead all those years ago. The difference was it didn't feel the same—electric—not anymore.

Timbrel Lake now came into view as Swami plodded the downhill path behind her rolling children, clutching the baby. There were a good-sized sand beach—empty at this early hour—a handful of picnic tables beneath tall pines, and a floating diving dock set a ways out in the water. The lake itself was the shape of a large crescent, and Swami could see only half of the curve. The kids hooted, dropped their bikes, and sprinted for the lake. They stopped halfway.

"Wait, the buckets!" cried Darren, and the two bolted back toward their mom for the stack of plastic buckets and small dip net. Swami smiled. She loved when they played well together. A lake and buckets seemed to please everyone. Swami held DeeDee to her shoulder and walked to the water across the cool sand, waded to her shins. The water was clean and cold.

"Do you want to try?" she asked, and DeeDee kicked her legs excitedly in the water as Swami dipped the baby's toes in it. Swami looked across the lake at the cottages and docks lining the shore and tucked behind trees, a colorful jumble of flagpoles, paddle boats, canoes dragged up on grass, a Jet Ski or two. Down the shoreline, a family did morning cannonballs together. Swami watched as the husband scooped up his wife and fell backward, his wife laughing on the way down, the kids shrieking with joy as their parents splashed from the floating dock.

"Hey there, site twenty-two! Good mornin'!"

Swami turned to see a big woman with a heavy stride coming down to the beach. She wore a bright orange helmet with a face shield and ear protection, a khaki shirt, and ranger-green pants, huge boots. The woman carried a weed-eater over her shoulder and a can of gas.

"Ranger Bonnie," she said, smiling as she introduced herself and held out her hand. Her voice was friendly and bright. She had high bright red cheeks.

Swami shook her hand. "Hello," she said. "I'm Swami and this is DeeDee, and those two over there are Darren and Dell."

"Mommy, Darren caught a bluebird!" Dell exclaimed, pointing at the bucket half-sunk in the water.

"A bluegill," corrected Darren. "*Guh*. Gill. Bluegill," he said.

Ranger Bonnie waved at the kids, then smiled at Swami again. "I always like to introduce myself to our long-termers. Looks like you'll be with us through Labor Day?"

Swami nodded. "It's a beautiful park," she said. "Very clean."

Bonnie was clearly pleased by this. "It's a bunch of work, but I like it." She set down her weed-eater on the picnic table and started topping it off with gas. "Hard thing is Marigamie County's sheriff just passed away—a good man—and I and a few other rangers have been asked to assist the constable until they can bring in an interim, and I hope it's soon. I like weed-whacking and skiing and meeting nice people, but I'm no peace officer and that's the truth. *Don't like conflict*," she said conspiratorially. She screwed the gas cap back on. "Anyhow, what brings you two up north?"

"Business, I guess," Swami said. "My husband is taking over Wood-chuck Rafting." It felt good to Swami to not include herself in it.

"Oh yeah, Chip's outfit? Say, it's supposed to be a rainy summer, so I suppose that'll be real good for a rafting business?"

"You know Chip?" Swami asked.

Ranger Bonnie gave a big nod. "Everybody up here knows Chip. A real character. Say, you'll have to get these kiddos out to his deer farm." Then she sighed and looked around at some weeds poking up around the legs of the picnic tables, narrowing her eyes at a few bushier places. Swami liked this woman. This woman was kind, and liked order. "It won't be an easy summer keeping up with mowing, though. Swami, if you need anything at all, let me know up at the station. Water, sewage, camp activities for the kiddos, *and* if you meet any problematic raccoons or black bears."

"Black bears?" Swami repeated.

"They're just big raccoons, really. Only interested in trash cans. No full trash cans, no bears."

Swami would remember that, and thanked the woman.

Ranger Bonnie smiled and tugged down her face shield and ear-muffs and yanked the pull start on the weed-eater. It sputtered. She fiddled with something on the motor, yanked it again, and it spun to life with a cloud of blue smoke. Swami covered her daughter's ears as she cradled her head. Ranger Bonnie revved the motor and the smoke cleared out.

"Two-stroke!" Ranger Bonnie beamed and yelled over the whine. "See you around, Swami!"

Swami smiled and waved as the woman turned toward a far table and started attacking the weeds, rocking back and forth on her sturdy hips. Swami walked over to her kids, waded into where they held the bucket. She thought of what the ranger had said, about a rainy summer and good business. *May it pour and pour*, Swami thought. She felt the weight of DeeDee on her shoulder. There was so much riding on this.

"Mommy, the bluegill is camping." Dell giggled.

"It's his campsite," said Darren.

Swami gave a weak smile and looked down. There, in the little green circle of net, swam a tiny fish the size and shape of a silver dollar, its black hackles raised, flitting about, ready to fight, wanting to run. Darren placed a small piece of tree bark in the bucket with the fish. "That's his camper," he said.

The bluegill stopped flitting about the pail. It hovered now, its mouth opening and closing as if taking purposeful breaths, making a plan. Swami looked out across the water again. The cottages and trees and flagpoles shone in the light. A purple-hulled Jet Ski skipped across the water. Bonnie weed-whacked. The kids giggled about the bluegill trapped in its campground net. Swami would tell Darren to release the fish the moment she knew she could do it without crying in front of the kids.

"It's fine," she whispered to DeeDee, bouncing the tiny girl and squeezing her tightly. "Everything is going to be fine."

FOUR

SAM PUSHED OFF IN THE KNEE-DEEP, TEA-COLORED WATER. THE
blue twelve-foot raft glided away from the put-in. Uncle Chip sat up
front, lighting a joint in his cupped hand. Sam leapt into the back of
the raft and paddled into the current. Chip blew a lungful of pungent
smoke into the air. It trailed overhead as if they were a rubber tugboat,
with Chip as the heavy forward engine.

Sam watched his uncle smoke for a moment—his silver-haired
back and suntanned shoulders, his paunchy bulk, his big arms. Sam
worried about just how much the success of Woodchuck relied on this
man. Sam didn't even know what to tell customers when the phone
rang in the basement of the rafting barn. After Swami left, Chip and
Randy returned. They strode into the barn as the phone rang, talking easily together about the day ahead, how many boats to blow, the
fifteen-footers. Chip handed Sam back his bread knife and picked up
the phone.

"Woodchuck," he rasped. "We're better on the water."

Sam watched Chip wrinkle his face and rub his sore head, phone
to his ear, as he scratched names off the clipboard nailed to a post. Half
of the morning's big opening trip was canceling last minute. Chip gave
them a full refund—even though it wasn't policy—because they were
longtime customers. They'd come every May for the last ten seasons.
Chip knew them by name, gave them special treatment from time to
time, like an extra run through the gorge or allowing them to bring a
few beers on the trip. Sam hung life jackets back up on the yellow throw
rope, where they dried in front of an oscillating metal fan.

"Well," said Chip. "Guide run, then. Me and you. I show you the lay
of the land."

Randy and Moon would run the river trip by themselves today,
Sam and Chip hanging back in their own raft. Sam nodded, eager to get
on the water, learn the rapids, get to business.

Chip blew another hit of smoke across the river. "Good day to get out," he said.

He offered the joint back to Sam, and Sam shook his head, so Chip held the joint between his lips and puffed while helping paddle the raft out to the middle of the river. Sam leaned into his strokes. It felt good to stretch and work in the morning sun after all the tension of arriving here. Randy and Moon were already far downriver with the customers, a church group from Minnesota. Money was being made.

"It is good," Sam said.

On the left bank of the river, a granite bluff rose two hundred feet, a handful of tenacious cedars growing from its crags and ledges, sun-bleached sumac clinging to the bluff's very top. On the right bank, the small homes of Thunderwater lined the road by the high and grassy shoreline. They were all a similar size and shape—small two-story homes, short chimneys, concrete block porches. They looked to be in even rougher shape now in the daylight: peeled paint, unfinished pink foam board here and there. The bluff and the town stretched downriver together for half a mile, before the bluff dove downward and took the river and level land with it. Behind them, upstream of the put-in, sat the square wall of the old hydroelectric dam. It was the only profitable portion left of the defunct paper mill. Water poured down around its three massive metal gates before tumbling down a natural rock face.

"Used to be the first rapids," Chip said, nodding at the dam. "It's what gave Thunderwater its name. Old Iroquois word. Now the first rapid is a half mile downstream. It's called Sand Portage." Chip loosened the top of a throw bag and dumped the yellow rope inside onto the floor of the raft. He began repacking it one handful at a time. He stopped and spread his arms a moment. "So, welcome to Thunderwater," he said expansively. "The land, the bluff, the river. Everything you see used to be covered in old-growth pine, hemlock. This river is where Menominee Indians once paddled birchbark canoes and harvested wild rice. It's where French fur traders and robed Jesuits once traveled, and then where loggers arrived with their songs and spiked boots and dynamite, pushing rafts of pine down to Lake Michigan. A dam was built here, right there, and then a mill, and then houses. And through all of that history, the river's always been the river. Was here before and will be here after. And today's your day to ride it, *see* it, say you were there. There's nothing more worth doing in life than getting on a river and messing about in a boat." He looked right at Sam, snugged the packed throw bag up tight. "That's my little history speech I tell the customers. That last part about boats is from *The Wind in the Willows*."

Chip beamed.

Sam nodded, smirked. "Pretty good speech," he said. "You've read *The Wind in the Willows*?"

"Hell yes," said Chip. He spun on the tube and let his bare feet dangle in the water. "First part, anyway, with that river rat. Very wise. Rest of the book gets pretty long."

The raft floated. Sam watched the high bluffs drift past, the green shade and thick ferns at their base, their reflection in the dark, smooth water.

"So, this part of the river we call *the flats*," Chip went on. "We let the custies swim here if they want, vests on, helmets optional—some of 'em can't swim good, even if they say they can. But don't let anyone do any diving from the boats. Between those two rock points coming out of the trees up there, it's real shallow all the way across. Moon had this old lady do a dive once when her back was turned to impress her friends. Bam! Knocked herself out on the river bottom." Chip pointed, quick, at the riverbank. "*Otter!* See him? Ah, he's gone."

A black ripple fanned out from the shore. On the bank above the otter, an old woman sat on the back cement steps of a yellow house and smoked a cigarette. Young kids and a few plastic cars peppered her lawn. A boy not much older than Darren spun and popped a water balloon on his sister's forehead. The girl shrieked, her shirt already soaked. This had not been the first balloon in the fight, but she stood stock-still as the water drenched her again, mock-offended for a moment before resuming the chase after her cackling brother, nailing him with her Super Soaker. Sam watched the kids disappear around the corner of the house, thought of his own. He felt for this town. He wanted this town to thrive again, the way he wanted his family to thrive. He lifted his hand in a wave to the woman. She lifted her hand in return, unimpressed, as the raft drifted past.

"Sally Meyer," Chip said, twisting the cherry from his joint into the river and putting the rest back into his dry box. "Takes care of her grandkids. Parents are no good." Chip waved at her, and she waved back. "Sally's one of the old union widows. Used to be good money here. There were guys who operated the same paper machines their grandpas made their livings on. But it's cheaper to make paper in China. Less regulation. Investors bought it up and shipped it all overseas. The river did get cleaner here when the mill went. Thunderwater got clean river water and went broke all at once. You could buy a house here for twelve thousand dollars the year the mill went. Didn't sell many either."

"What about the mining signs?" Sam asked. "I saw them coming in last night. Stop whining and start mining. What's that about?"

"NorthSky," Chip said, and then shrugged. "No one knows too much yet. There's gonna be some town halls. It's some Canadian company wants to mine the riverbanks, promising big salaries, the area's next big move, paper town to mining town. Some people want it. Others want the land left alone." Chip smirked. "Guess which side Moon is on?"

Sam could guess.

"I try to stay out of it," Chip said. "There's already enough people in this town don't like the rafting business, don't like the city people it brings here in summer."

Sam was thinking about a small town in West Virginia that had reinvented itself. It was after its local coal mine shut. The town went green instead, became a place of outdoor pilgrimage. Mountain biking, rafting, fly-fishing, bed-and-breakfasts. Sam looked at the small homes again. There were some nice old brick buildings left in Thunderwater too. It could really be something.

"Maybe people could change their minds," he said. "Maybe rafting could be the next big move."

"People here don't tend to do that," Chip said. "But maybe. It'd be something, hey?"

They drifted beyond the houses, and the riverbanks became wooded,

old gnarled cedars leaning out over the water. "Moon should be dropping the falls about now," said Chip. "Good water too. See the rock up
ahead? That's a good gauge for what's downstream. That or you just
call Pete if he's working the dam, and he'll tell you what's releasing. I
keep the dam's number on the clipboard by the phone."

"Which rock?" asked Sam. Along the narrow shore near the bluff's
face lay a rubble of boulders—the size of TVs, and cars, and small
houses. Some lay in the ferns on the bank. Some sat in the river. It must
have been a sight to watch some of them fall, the boom and the wave,
fish and birds scattering like fireworks.

"The big one that looks like a slice of cake on its side."

"I see it," said Sam.

"When it's buried right up to its middle like it is today, then the
whole gorge is good to go downstream, smooth going right over the top
of rocks. If the water's down lower, the pour-overs show up. It's bony."

Sam just nodded. It'd been a few years since he'd been in a raft, let
alone guided one.

"And if the water's all the way down to the gravel plate that rock sits
on, it's bob and weave and run away all day long."

Sam watched the boulder as they drifted past. He could see water
marks higher up too, on rocks behind it farther in toward the cliff face.

"You ever see it up there, over the riverbanks?" Sam asked.

"Once," said Chip. "The whole river changes then. Dam opens the
floodgates and it just rips. Holes move. Some disappear. Some just keep
getting bigger and bigger. I once saw this river swallow a sixteen-foot
raft with twelve customers in it—*whoosh*, gone—for five whole seconds.
When it gets that high, we gotta cancel trips. Sort of like farming, this
business. Hoping the rain is right."

The bluff was beginning to drop in elevation, and the flats were
coming to an end. Sam could see tiny white sparks of waves a few hundred yards off.

"Chip," said Sam, "I wanted to talk to you about that today."

"About what?" said Chip. He was looking downstream now, where a
bright green bus had pulled into a clearing behind the trees.

"About Woodchuck. I know you showed me all the numbers this

spring, but I hoped this afternoon we could go over the books again, take a look at this season, get a plan going."

Chip just nodded, but his attention was fixed on the bus. The bus had a trailer behind it filled with rafts, and a team of people in hot green shirts unloading them.

"All right," said Chip.

The raft drifted closer. The bus was beautiful, lime green, parked on a fresh gravel roundabout. It looked waxed, the way the reflections of leaves and sky shimmered across its paint. It rode on a fresh set of knobby off-road tires, bright black, as did the trailer, stacked four high with matching bright green boats. The bus and rafts were marked on the side: *X-treme Outdoor Adventures*. The *X*s were made out of crossed rafting paddles.

Sam sat very still in the raft. Chip just leaned forward in the raft, his lips tight, staring.

The X-treme river guides looked as sharp as their bus, every one of them sandy blond, wearing matching neon shirts with hot pink *X*s across the back. They were fit, laughing, loosening ratchet straps, adjusting their Oakleys or pulling on bright mesh aqua socks. They looked like they came straight out of a Juicy Fruit commercial, but here in real life, in Thunderwater. Sam looked down at his own sodden pair of Converse, with their yellowed double-knotted laces. And Chip didn't even own river shoes. He rafted barefoot.

As the raft drifted close to the bus, Sam heard a cheer come from inside it with many voices—"Three, two, one, X-treme!"

"Oh, real cute," said Chip.

And then the trip leader, a man with a thick mane of hair more blond than the rest, swung down the steps of the bus followed by customers wearing the latest-model life vests and helmets, all bright blue with matching paddles. The trip leader whistled to his guides, and two of them hustled over carrying a cooler and began handing out iced bottles of Gatorade to each customer.

"Whoa," said Sam.

The trip leader ran his hands through his hair and began tying it into a ponytail. He turned toward the river, paused, then lifted his chin when he spotted the raft.

"Chip," he said.

"Duncan," said Chip.

Duncan looked at Sam then, seemed to assess his gear and his shoes in one look—the river-stained and faded orange vest, the dated plastic helmet, the wooden paddle. Sam felt like the kid at school in the secondhand clothes. It was a feeling Sam remembered all too well.

"Big trip today, Chip?" Duncan gloated, scanning the empty river for other boats.

Chip's throat grumbled. Customer after customer filed from Duncan's bus.

"We're booked all week," said Duncan. "Didn't think our opener would be *this* strong. Had a group of twelve add on just this morning."

Chip stiffened when a customer stepped from the bus, caught sight of Chip, and waved.

"Chip!" said the man, genuinely happy to see him. "How's it going?"

Chip forced a grin and lifted his hand.

The man glanced at Duncan, and then his face colored just a bit. "Figured we'd try the new kids on the block this year, see how they stack up against Woodchuck. These guys have zip lines! Have you tried them?"

"Nope," said Chip. "Duncan, you know this ain't the put-in," said Chip. "Rafts need to put in at the public landing a mile up. You're on old mill land."

Duncan finished tying his hair back. "Nah, buddy. X-treme just bought this land for access rights. From town to First Ripple." Duncan pointed. "We're about to buy some downstream too. Figured if we start here, we can probably get in three trips per day instead of two. Maybe some riverside cabins? More runs, more fun!"

"X-treeeeme!" called out one of his guides, making an *X* with his arms in the air. Others echoed him. Duncan smirked while his guides turned back to topping off air chambers with hand pumps.

Chip's eyes flashed.

"That rapid is Sand Portage, *not* 'First Ripple.' You can't just come in here and rename rapids. They are not yours to name. Maybe you could rename the river next?"

Duncan just shrugged, as if he'd consider it. Then he turned his back as Chip and Sam drifted past, back to the silent river.

Chip wrestled with his dry box, cupped his hand over his lighter, and puffed furiously at his half-smoked joint. He tried to speak, didn't, and continued smoking instead.

"Who was that guy?" Sam thought his voice sounded small. He knew.

Chip let out a rattling breath of smoke. "Your mortal enemy," he said. "Duncan showed up late last season. Scouting the river. Apparently, he guided the Yough in Pennsylvania for a couple of seasons, class-three stuff. Has a degree in 'outdoor recreation management,' whatever *that* means, along with a tycoon uncle bankrolling him. Brand-new bus, new riverfront raft barn, zip lines."

"Those rafts," said Sam, still reeling from the implications of all this. "I've never seen bright green boats before."

"Hypalon," Chip answered.

"What's Hypalon?"

"Exactly. It's the latest in raft material. UV-resistant, abrasion re-sistant, lightweight, and fast too, real slippery on a wave face. It's basi-cally the best raft money can buy."

Sam's feeling of envy turned to dread. He thought of Woodchuck's own "welcome center": a patch of weedy gravel with a peeling barn, a clipboard, and a grubby phone nailed to an old post.

"Chip," Sam said. "These guys are going to smoke us."

Chip's face tightened. He held a fist to his chest like a man with in-digestion. Then he took a deep breath and looked up at the bluff, sloping now toward the gorge. Downstream, sunlit licks of whitewater leapt behind the horizon line of Sand Portage. Chip exhaled.

"You wanted to talk business," said Chip. "Well, here's the long and short of it. Every August, there's a Boy Scout jamboree up here, troops from all over the Midwest. And every year one of the things they do is come rafting, usually four or five hundred scouts. They all book as separate troops, but it usually takes me three or four days to get them all through."

Sam quickly did the math in his head at forty dollars per paddler.

"In the past, without competition, jamboree week was enough to float Woodchuck all season. We'll get troop leaders booking with us from Iowa City to Ann Arbor. If the troop leaders book with us, Woodchuck lives. If they book with Duncan, we'll have to figure out something else."

Sam took off his helmet and let it fall to the floor of the boat. He was thirsty. He thought about the iced Gatorade he didn't have. He thought about Swami, and the kids, and his teaching job in limbo. It was bright out, but Sam felt a sort of fog settling on him, an inability to see a way forward. He imagined Swami hearing what Chip just said, and the fog thickened, had lightning in it.

"I wish," Sam said, very slowly, "you had talked a bit more about the new competition. You know, *before*."

"I didn't know it'd be like this," said Chip. "Last year, Duncan was just some hotshot at the bar. I've seen it before, some kid bragging about his grand plans, no ability to pull it off. He came at this way harder than I thought he would."

Sam stared at the water. He felt rigid. He needed to run away, but he couldn't because he was floating in a raft in Wisconsin with his stoned uncle. He felt his breath grow shallow, and felt himself looking around for something, anything. He snatched the joint from Chip's fingers and took an enormous hit, something he hadn't done in years. He coughed so hard he gagged, handing the joint back.

"Oh-ho, *wow*," said Chip. "Hey, look, buddy, we still got one thing going for us. Sam. Listen. It's the only thing that matters."

Sam looked at the water, blinking.

"Duncan's a class-three guide at best, and all his guides are college poster-board recruits. You, on the other hand, once guided class-five out in West Virginia. You and Swami both. That's as big as it gets. Me and Moon can raft this river until it's up in the trees. We know its moods. Even Randy has a solid four seasons in him. Sam, you hearing me?"

Sam could take a deep breath again. He looked at Chip.

"Hypalon and shiny buses mean nothing if your rafting company can't *raft*. And these guys suck. Trust me. I watched them 'train' two weeks back: horrible, and they trained in on mellow water. When this river gets lower, or higher too, these guys won't cut it." Chip tugged the straps tight on his life vest, looked downstream. "Sam, Woodchuck is better on the water. We really are. So are we gonna bring it to this phony or not?"

"Teach me this river," said Sam, looking his uncle straight in the eyes.

Chip exhaled, smirked like a man about to start a bar fight.

"Get your lid on," he said, tightening the chin strap on his own helmet.

Sam put his helmet on. The rapids were close now. He could hear the rush of water now. Sam's face felt soft; his neck felt loose.

Chip faced forward, wedged his foot under a thwart, then beamed back at Sam. "Sam, you just inspired me." He rustled around in his dry box and came up, smiling, with a bar of soap.

Sam frowned at him.

"You're gonna like this," Chip said. "We are at war."

•••

SAM HAD SEEN BIGGER HILLS, real mountains, and he'd rafted bigger water, but Piers Gorge was truly beautiful, a perfect happenstance of rock bluffs and cedar forests, a reddish carpet of soft pine needles, hardwoods rustling higher up on the hills. Maybe it was the idea that he'd bought into this place now with Woodchuck, or maybe it was the memories he held of the place, but the hills and river valley felt more charged now, more perfect, more profound. Of all the things wrong with Woodchuck Rafting Company, Piers Gorge wasn't one of them.

Chip described the gorge as a section of river with four parts. The first part is Sand Portage, marked by a pine-covered island dividing the flat, dark water. The left channel is runnable but bony. The right channel has better waves, where the glass-smooth river breaks and pours through a small slope of boulders and ledges. Chip let Sam guide it.

"Just a few strokes and you're through," he said. And when they arrived at the big eddy at the bottom, "Easy peasy. You still got it. So, Sand's a good chance to feel out your customers. If Sand scares them, you may as well hike 'em around what's coming downstream. No refunds, though. Once they're in the boat, no refunds."

The second part of the gorge is a class-one rock garden—fun at high water, small waves here and there. The raft caught eddies, spun and skittered like a water bug across the shallow fast water. Sam took a stroke and scraped bottom. The boulders and rocks scrolling underneath the boats were pink and white and golden and black. The banks rose steeply on either side of the rock garden. Chip pointed to an eagle's nest, high in a white pine. Near shore, under the shadow of a cedar tree, a plumed heron studied the water it stood in, head askance, fishing.

After the boulder garden, the river turns right and drops away between two bluffs.

"See that horizon line, with the mist spitting up behind it? That's the top of Mishicot Falls. That's the entrance to the big stuff. Catch that little beach on the left," said Chip. "We'll hike down and scout a few things."

Sam squinted at it, nodded. His face still felt soft from Chip's weed. But the sight of the gorge firmed him up a bit. He'd only seen the gorge from shore as a boy, never from upstream of it in a raft. The river disappeared from sight. A small tornado of river mist rose from behind the drop-off, casting a rainbow between the bluffs.

Sam beached the raft, splashed to shore in the cold water to hold the raft's nose. Chip got out, his body clearly stiff. He spent the next hour limping up and over boulders, pointing at waves and holes in the river, describing it all at different levels, how the river behaves when it's dry or flooded. Chip panted heavily as he climbed hills, and Sam thought for the first time that Chip was older than he seemed. The Uncle Chip Sam knew as a kid was still there—the big voice, the quick laugh, the shiny eyes—but his bones had aged, his movements stiffened. When he caught his breath at the top of the bluff, Chip raised his voice over the roar of the water. Sam could see the falls from its downstream side now. Chip pointed his wooden paddle at things as he spoke.

"So this whole third part is class-four, about a quarter mile long. It's quick. You're in it for a minute or two, *if* it goes good. See how the falls makes that big V shape? That's the tongue. If things go bad, they usually go bad between the tongue and rock. Last year I dropped the tongue of Mishicot, and this old chick wearing a bright red muumuu fell on her back like a turtle, big legs kicking in the air all the way down the wave train." Chip rode his hand down the waves. "And when we swept over Volkswagen Rock—that big hump of water right in the middle—the back of the raft snapped up and out and, boom, out she went with her dress snagged on a valve. She looked like a fiery cannonball, torn dress trailing, right into the drink. She swam the Island Wave, that's the curling one down there, and then she swam the two drops you can sort of see from here, the Twin Sisters. When we finally scooped her back up, she was bare from the waist down. I had to give her my life vest to wear like a big diaper. Gave it a good scrub when I got back to the barn."

Chip beamed at the river, deep love in his red eyes. Story after story, Sam got a sense of the depth of experience this man had: thousands of runs through this gorge. The river and Chip were as familiar to each other as an old married couple. Chip hobbled its shorelines, using pine branches and poplar saplings for support, as if he were being helped up porch steps. Chip loved the river enough he didn't have to say it aloud anymore. It just *was*. They *were*. It made Sam wonder about Aunt Mary, why she'd left, and when.

"Anyways," said Chip. "Run the tongue at Mishicot, over or river left at Volkswagen depending on level, square up with the Island Wave at high water, then hit the Sisters with some left momentum so they won't push you away. Otherwise, bub, it's just read and run. This helpful?"

"Extremely," said Sam.

"Well, I'm rooting for you, buddy. I hope you know that."

And something about those words, spoken by a man old enough to be Sam's father, one who'd shared a childhood with Sam's mother, made Sam feel as if he might almost have to hold back tears. Thankfully, Chip just looked out at the water. They both did.

"It never gets old, you know," Chip said. "Twenty-six seasons and it

never gets old—routine maybe, but never old. Never wished I was anywhere else. The river's not like other things. It's not like people."

Sam thought of his aunt Mary again, and thought maybe this would
be a good time to ask where she went, when the excited chatter of
X-treme's river guests came up the trail behind them.

"All the way up to the top," directed Duncan from the rear of the
line. "We'll get a great look at the river up there!"

Chip made room on the bluff face and smiled at the guests. He
dropped his smile as Duncan's rookie guides filed in.

"Hey, Duncan," Chip said. "If you want to hold your people up top a
minute, me and Sam are about to run it—give 'em a good show?"

Duncan shrugged, looked a bit surprised. "All right," he said, and
then turned to his group to give them his river talk.

Chip hustled down the path to the boats. "Come on." He laughed.
"We have just enough time."

Down at the rafts lining the little sandy beach, Chip rifled through
his dry box and came up with the bar of soap. He broke it against a
sharp rock and flung half to Sam, then scrambled into one of X-treme's
rafts and began scrubbing the side tubes where the guides sat. He put
his whole body into it, as if he were scouring an old rug.

"Damn it, *help me*, Sam!" he cackled, moving on to the next raft.
There were six boats.

Sam looked up the trail again—there was no sign of X-treme. He
felt like a boy holding a raw egg. He grinned and began rubbing the
next raft's tube.

"Don't forget to soap the thwarts," Chip said. "You gotta get the
bottoms, where they wedge their feet!" Chip was delirious, wild with
joy, his face was bright red.

Within a minute, the work was done.

"Let's get the hell out of here," Chip squealed.

Sam pushed off beside Chip, leaping with their raft into the current, and the two dug in hard with their paddles. They made the center
of the river above the falls, and Chip took a few deep breaths, winded
again. He pressed his fist against his chest and winced. Took another
deep breath and shook it off.

Sam heard cheering from high on the bluff. X-treme's guests pointed. Sam could make out Duncan too, looking down with his arms crossed. He was probably telling them all about how he'd run it, how his boats were superior. Sam didn't know how much Duncan knew about the change in Woodchuck's ownership, didn't yet know what their long-term relationship would be, although this morning had certainly marked a trajectory.

"Forward two!" huffed Chip.

They took two strokes in tandem, and the light raft responded, nudging farther right as they approached the falls, only thirty feet away now.

"See that jet of mist?" said Chip. "You want your nose right there— a little left momentum is good, and as you head over the falls you want to pry to the left at the base. You'll feel two thumps of your paddle— wave one, wave two. Then you can let go of the pry and paddle forward again to charge over Volkswagen. Forward two!"

At the lip of the falls, Chip waved up at the watching group like a matador. "Here we go," he said. "Forward two more." Their second stroke sent them over the edge of the falls. It was a beautiful thrill how the river opened up here, a black horizon, then the brink, and then everything was fast and loud. Sam leaned into his pry. Cold waves hit his face and chest. *Thump one, thump two.* The troughs of the waves pressed his paddle blade. He let go of the pry and began paddling forward toward Volkswagen Rock. It was a mound of leaping water about twenty yards ahead. Waves crashed over the bow of the raft.

"Forward!" boomed Chip.

Sam lowered his gravity a bit as the boat charged up and over the top of Volkswagen and then buried its entire bow in the giant standing wave below it. They went down, through, and back up.

"Oh-ho, wowww!" Chip bellowed as they came up from the pit, Chip shaking his water from his face. "*Dead nuts* over the top!"

Sam allowed himself a hoot. Chip gave him a hard high five. A few more strokes and one more big hit, and their raft was floating in the calm of an eddy behind the rock island, midway down the class-four section.

Sam wiped his face with his hand. *"Nice!"* he said. Piers Gorge might be shorter than the New River Gorge, but it was as big as anything he'd rafted in the southeast. Mishicot Falls was an attraction all in itself. No wonder Chip had had the vision long ago to form a business plan anchored by that experience.

"Let's pull up on the island awhile," Chip said. "This is going to be so good."

The falls were hidden from view now. The river, after Volkswagen, takes a right-hand turn. But Sam heard Duncan's rafts coming, the thrilled screams of whitewater customers dropping in. The first raft soon popped into view, sideways and guideless, just above Volkswagen, the customers still paddling, no idea their guide was twenty feet behind them in the water. The raft rode the mound of water smoothly enough, but then instantly flipped in the hole downstream. Eight customers and the black-bottomed raft roiled past Chip and Sam, where they perched on the rock island. The custies swam in a tangle of flailing arms, hair and helmets over eyes, gasping for breath between waves.

"Swim!" yelled Chip, his eyes big with glee. "Swim to your boat! No, the other way!" Finally, the guide swept past. "What do you think you're *doing!*" Chip accused him, just before the terrified young man disappeared beneath the curl of the Island Wave. Chip crouched and watched, his throw bag filled with rescue rope idle in his hands.

"Boy, these guys are a *mess*," he said.

More screams of joy from upstream. A second raft came down without a guide, made it over Volkswagen, and then spun out against the far wall of sloped rock. Chip bawled out the guide as he flailed past, leaving his raft of customers alone upstream, stranded. The panicked boat of guests eventually washed and spun its way across the river toward the island. Chip snatched the nose of their raft.

"You guys okay?" he asked.

"Our *guide* fell out!" yelled a panicked husband.

Chip looked surprised, gave a look toward the back of the raft. "Your *guide* fell out?" he asked, and the man nodded. "Tell you what," Chip told him, "you guys are looking pretty good out here and are past the worst of it. Just head on down and I'm sure your X-treme guide will find you. They're brand-new out here. It's their first season, but I'm sure he'll find you."

"Could you take us down the rest?" the man pleaded as Chip made to push the raft into current again. The man's teenage sons looked around the river with wide eyes. His wife sat rigid.

"You're fine; you're really fine. See those two ledges up ahead? Just square up to them, and then make your way toward river left. Two ledges and then left, nice big calm spot. Okay? Off you go!" said Chip, and the raft spun away toward the sister waves.

"Thank you!" called the husband, ordering his teens to paddle forward with him.

"Raft with Woodchuck next time!" Chip called through cupped hands.

"We're better on the water!" yelled Sam, and Chip clapped him on the back.

Two more rafts came through like the first, guides and customers missing wherever they'd soaped the tubes. A fifth raft came through already overturned. And then came Duncan's boat, devoid of all its customers, Duncan himself clinging onto the back of the raft by a length of webbing. He was trying to pull himself in, and nearly had it when the raft crested Volkswagen and yanked away from him.

"Rope! Rope!" yelled Chip, and launched the throw bag a good twenty feet behind where Duncan drifted and spun. "Bad throw!" said Chip, winding the rope up in a coil. Duncan glared up from the water. Chip smirked at him. Realization and heat dawned on Duncan's face, just as the cold river sucked him under again.

Chip finished coiling his rope and sat down on the warm river rock. He sighed. "I am so happy right now," he said. Downstream, X-treme's entire trip was a colorful flotsam of overturned rafts, customers dragging themselves onto river rocks, boatless guides on both shorelines, blowing whistles, pointing and shouting to customers no longer listening to anything at all. The sky was bright blue. The river roared and sang. The air smelled like water and rocks and pine. Sam took a big breath of it.

"So," said Chip, pulling the neck of his throw bag tight again, "past all that mess is the fourth and final part of the gorge. It's shallow right and left, with one big hole in the middle named Terminal Surfer—too sticky to run at this level, but good to go at really high or really low water."

Sam just smiled at the river.

"You feel trained in?" Chip asked. "Think you can replicate what I taught you today?"

"Think I got it," said Sam.

Chip clapped his big hands together. "Let's hit it, then," he said, and hopped back into the raft, lighter and younger, clipping his rope into a D-ring. For a split second, Sam could see the whole vision again, his family a river family, Sam himself someday an old man with a permanent tan and a beard and the gorge in his voice, expansive and happy and filled.

Later that afternoon, Chip and Moon and Randy and Sam hung up life jackets on their ropes and backed the trailer of rafts into the barn before supper. Randy cooked venison steaks on a grill grate over fire pit coals, stirred a cast-iron skillet filled with butter and onions. The sun set behind the trees beyond the alfalfa fields, and the alfalfa exhaled a deep green scent as the air cooled. They ate quietly on paper plates.

"This is really good, Randy," Sam told him. The steak was perfectly charred, blackened with cracked peppercorns, the onions just barely caramelized.

"You hit him, boss," Randy said. "I just cut him up."

Sam swallowed the bite in his mouth, remembered the wide eye of the leaping deer in his headlights. He set his plate back down in his lap.

"Randy's going to be a chef," Moon said, to which Randy immediately began wagging his head.

Moon whacked him. "You should go to chef school," she said. "It brings you to life. And you're good at it."

Chip nodded his approval while he stuffed another bite in his mouth, butter glistening on his beard.

Randy finally shrugged, then he sighed. "We'll see. Gotta take care of Mom too. Hey, Sam? We wanted to apologize for this morning. Sorry your family had to meet us when we were all jacked up."

Chip nodded his approval again.

Sam's skin felt tight and warm from all the water and sun. "Well," he said. "Next time you guys have a bonfire, I'll let them know. I hope Swami loves it out here. She's a great river guide, you know."

"Swami guided?" Moon asked. "Where?"

"Class-five," Sam said. "She was probably the best out of all of us back in the day. We guided three seasons together on the Lower New."

"Big water," said Chip, wiping his mouth with the back of his hand. "One notch down from the Gauley." He looked at Sam. "We sometimes take off for Gauley Fest together in September once things slow down here. We took the party bus down for a few years before it quit running."

"Gauley Fest," said Randy, slowly, like he was enjoying a good flavor. He folded his paper plate and tucked it into the fire.

Moon lifted her bottle of beer. She was clearly impressed. "I need to get to know Swami better."

"That'd be good," said Sam. He stood and walked to the barn with his plate so he could hide it in the garbage and not have to eat the rest of his roadkill deer. It *was* good, and he was thankful to Randy for feeding him, but he just couldn't stomach it after seeing it rock around in the back of his truck.

In the upstairs of the barn, Sam found an old boys' bike with a banana seat behind a stack of discarded raft paddles with bent shafts or snapped blades. The upstairs of the barn was like a museum. Old life jackets, popped rafts, tangles of rope tucked into all the corners. There were two old refrigerators next to the garbage, plus a bad-smelling brown couch. Sam lifted the bike from the collection and pumped some air into its tires while his guides laughed outside by the fire. The tires held air.

"I can give you a lift, you know," said Moon. "We're living at the same campground. Swami's at site twenty-two. I'm at four."

Randy and Chip laughed at him when Sam came rattling out of the barn on the small bike.

Sam patted the handlebars.

"Thanks," he said. "But I need my own wheels this summer. I'd better get used to it."

Moon settled back into her lawn chair, next to Randy's.

"Big day tomorrow," said Chip. "All hands on deck, early."

"Good," said Sam. "Early. See you, Moon, Chip, Randy."

"Good night, Sam, Sammy, boss," they answered.

It was dusk. Sam aimed the bike for one of the gravel ruts in the driveway and pedaled out onto the road. The bike bounced happily down the gravel shoulder. The moon rose again, and the ditches smelled like the beginning of summer.

At the park, Sam wove down the asphalt lanes between campsites. He was glad to see that Governor's was so clean and new. Swami would like it. He pedaled past campsite four, Moon's place, squinting his eyes in the dark. A small teardrop camper sat behind the fire pit. At the other campsites, families laughed. At one, an old couple sat together in a double lawn chair, each with one bottle of beer.

Site twenty-two was dark and silent, no campfire. Sam's back ached as he stood from the bike and laid it on its side. He was more tired than he'd realized. He quietly opened the screen door on the Brave and stepped inside. There were leftover dishes from supper, wet swimsuits hung above the sink. The camper smelled like sunscreen. Sam smiled, hoped they'd had a good day.

Sam left his clothes in a heap and tried to climb into the bed next to Swami in the camper's rear bunk area. The kids all slept on the other side of her. Everyone was breathing heavily.

Swami stirred as Sam curled in near her back.

"Shhh," she breathed.

"How was it?" Sam whispered.

Half-asleep, grumpy, she elbowed Sam for more space and said, "Shhh."

Sam moved over. Stayed awake in the dark awhile. He could tell her all about the river tomorrow, the way the falls had felt. Sam had a vision for this summer, and today on the river had allowed him to hope. In his vision, he could see his smiling son wiping water from his eyes after a cannonball from the nose of a raft. He envisioned Swami sitting mid-boat with Dell, her legs tanned from weeks in the sun, her short shorts faded from all the river washings. Swami would be rubbing sunscreen into Dell's and DeeDee's arms while the little girls—even more blond now—bounced and laughed on the tube in a raft. Swami would smile at Sam, and Sam would J-stroke the raft from the back, one sandaled foot propped up on a thwart, shoulders bronzed and strong again, on his hundredth raft trip of the summer. And then, toward the end of the day he'd have a cigar in his teeth, and of course there'd be the coffer pressed down and overflowing with easy river money from busloads of guests. And then evenings would come. He and Swami would walk together to some riverside campsite. They'd cook fatty food over crackling coals. The kids would eat and sleep so easily and early. And then, when the whole world was quiet, Swami would wrap her golden legs around Sam and whisper to him how glad she was that he'd brought them all out here, for taking a risk on such a wonderful summer for them and the kids. And they would make love out there in the northern nights, Swami's eyes all lit up in the darkness with campfires and rivers and bright green stars.

Sam heard her breathing heavily, falling back to sleep. Darren snored. Through the camper blinds, he could see the black trunks of trees, beach towels on the table. Frogs sang near the lake and his children breathed in and out and Sam listened to them until he closed his eyes and joined them, the camper mattress carrying them off like a raft drifting above black and pink and golden rocks.

FIVE

THE LAST WEEK OF MAY PASSED WITHOUT INCIDENT. EVERY MORN-ing, Sam woke and pedaled his bike to Woodchuck. Every night, he came home. Swami pretended not to smell the beer on his breath. He asked every morning if Swami wanted to bring the kids out for a camp-fire dinner, or if Swami wanted to go and guide while Sam stayed back for a few days.

"I don't know, Sam," she'd tell him. "We'll stay here for now." The truth was Swami didn't want to feel frightened again the way she had their first morning in. She didn't trust Woodchuck or Sam's uncle. She needed time. The quiet of the campground helped. After the whirlwind of preparation and arrival, it felt good to sleep late with the kids and walk to the beach for a morning swim. She and the kids spent their days exploring the edges of the lake and dirt paths through the woods. Ranger Bonnie let them borrow her own canoe, which Swami kept close to shore in less than two feet of water with DeeDee and Dell aboard. Dell learned the words *lily pad* and *poison ivy*, and how to drink from the red water pump without touching her lips to it. Darren could al-ready tell the difference between a bluegill, a bass, a pike, and two types of turtles. DeeDee liked to kick the water, burbling as she did. There was a ranger station and general store where Swami let the kids buy bottles of juice and look into the live bait tanks, and where Swami could pick up their forwarded mail from the PO boxes. They took naps after lunch, with the fan blowing on them. All of them were already turning a ruddy shade of golden brown, burnished with Swami's zinc sunscreen and clean lake sand.

Moon invited Swami over for lunch on her day off from the river. She'd been stopping by in the evenings to say hello. One time Sam was there, and he seemed a bit too eager to have the younger woman in their campsite, nodding eagerly at everything she said as if to make up for Swami's lack of enthusiasm. Chip stopped out on his motorcycle sometimes too. There was something about Chip that Dell absolutely adored. He was like a big shaggy bear who sat on the ground with her, and he could make her crack up by crossing his eyes. Swami tolerated all of it the way she tolerated paying bills. But now this was Moon's second lunch invitation, so Swami felt she had to go. There aren't too many excuses to be had when you live in a campground, not that Swami was sure she needed them. She liked Moon well enough. The woman was friendly. But her effusive spirit, and crystal waving, just felt like too much static in Swami's quiet woods.

Swami and her kids walked down to Moon's campsite after their swim, about an hour and a half before their nap. Swami had that excuse should she need it.

They came around the bend, and Moon's yellow Jeep came into view behind the wooded hedge.

"She's not going to do that rock thing again, is she?" Darren asked.

"Try to be polite," said Swami, and Darren furrowed his brow.

Behind Moon's Jeep sat her teardrop camper, with its tiny door and bright tin siding, two propane tanks strapped to the hitch. Moon had Christmas lights and colorful flags strung between the trees. On the ground between the camper and the Jeep lay a humongous quilt—brilliant blue with organic smatterings of greens and yellows and reds—next to the burning fire pit with two simmering pots. Something smelled incredibly good. There were glass plates set out on the quilt in a circle, and a big pitcher of ice water with limes in it set on a pine stump along with a basket of bread. The flags and woodsmoke and smell of cooking drifted in the breeze and dappled light. A wooden wind chime knocked and thrummed. The kids gaped at the scene, standing just at the edge of the giant quilt.

"Hey, guys!" called Moon, ducking out from her tiny camper with a huge wooden bowl in her hands. She wore a sundress brighter than her Jeep. "Kick off your shoes! Welcome!" She beamed at them. "Oh, wait, wait."

She hustled over to them and knelt by the edge of the quilt. The bowl she carried had cooked rice in it. "Okay, so I learned this in Bhutan, and it might seem different, but you have to try it. Give me your hands. Darren first."

Darren stiffened. He looked at his mom. She nodded, and the boy held his hands out. Moon pinched a small ball of rice from the bowl and placed it in Darren's hands.

"Now," she said, "roll it up like a snowball."

Darren smiled. "It's warm," he said, rolling the rice between his palms.

"It cleans your hands," she said. "Would you like some?" she asked Dell.

Dell nodded and held her hands out for a warm rice ball. Swami watched the girl grin from ear to ear. "Come have a seat," she said. "You can toss your little snowballs in the fire."

Moon stood. "Thanks so much for coming, Swami," she said. "I love that colorful wrap."

"Thanks," Swami said, patting DeeDee. "And thanks for having us over. Something smells really wonderful."

"Ema datshi," Moon said. "I made a spicy batch for us and a not-spicy one for the kids. Rice?"

"Thank you," Swami said, and rolled a warm sticky rice ball in her hands and slid off her sandals and stepped onto the quilt. It was cool and padded underfoot. Moon set the bowl of rice in the center of the circle of plates.

"This is beautiful," she said. Swami didn't even want to walk on it. On the deep blue quilt, there were bursts of flowers, spirals of teal with gold and silver trim.

"Thanks," said Moon. "It's one of my own." She stopped near the fire and blushed a bit as she dipped a ladle into one of the pots.

"You *made* this," Swami said.

Moon nodded, looking up only quickly, then she sort of shrugged and smiled. "I only bring it out for very important people." She winked at Dell. "Let's eat!"

Darren and Dell were hesitant at first when Moon set two big bowls of thick, orange-colored stew near the rice, and then they giggled when Moon told them how to eat it, but then they tasted it and lifted their eyebrows and grew quiet while they ate scoop after scoop with their hands, packing little snowballs of rice and dunking them in the steaming ema datshi.

"It's mostly cheese and milk and butter, and hot chiles for us."

Moon poured them water and brought the bread over too. Swami tasted her first bite. The rice was sticky, and the sauce rich and creamy and spicy. It was delicious. "The bread's not traditional," said Moon, sitting again, "but I like to dunk it anyway." Dell giggled, packing another rice ball. Moon broke a brown crusty loaf and handed a piece to each of them.

"How do you say it again?" Swami asked.

"Emma. Dot. She," Moon said. "In Bhutan this is like spaghetti and meatballs."

"Where's Bit-ahn?" Darren asked, looking around at the colorful flags overhead, his cheeks stuffed with bread.

"Swallow first, kiddo," Swami said.

He did. "Where's Bhutan?"

"Do you know India?" Moon asked him.

Darren nodded.

"It's connected to India, up in the mountains. Some people say it's the happiest place on earth."

"Is that where you're from?" Dell asked her, wide-eyed. With the pot of delicious food and the colorful quilts and flags and wind chimes, Swami imagined Dell could be easily convinced this woman with star tattoos was from such a place.

"No," Moon said. "But I went there for a time."

"Was it happy?" Dell asked.

Moon thought about this for a moment. Swami noted genuine consideration in Moon's face. "Yes," she said. "I believe they are happy."

"I like the food," Darren said.

"It's really terrific," Swami agreed. She had unbundled DeeDee, who now lay on her back, reaching and kicking at the flags.

Moon smiled. "Thanks for coming," she said, and then dug in herself while the fire crackled and the breeze blew. While they ate, they talked about camp life. All agreed it was pretty good. They talked about whether they had seen any bears. They hadn't. Moon told stories about how she'd gone from North Carolina to Bhutan. She was nineteen. And then how she'd met Chip at a river festival, how she'd started guiding the rivers, made her way north. They took their time with the meal. Moon didn't rush their plates away when it was over. The kids explored the quilt, and then lay back on it, removed from the adults and caught up in their own world, pointing at clouds, while Swami and Moon kept talking. Moon asked Swami about her time in West Virginia, when she was a river guide, and how she'd met Sam. Swami shared a good bit of her story while she fed DeeDee beneath her wrap. The kids' nap time had come, but Swami decided to let it pass. It was quiet enough here at Moon's campsite. Peaceful too. Swami swaddled DeeDee in her wrap and let her sleep on the quilt. Dell was asleep next to her brother now, who looked to be on the edges himself, holding a green leaf up to the light.

"Tired kids," Moon said quietly.

Swami nodded.

"Satisfied," Swami said. "What a great meal. And I think being outdoors has been good for them. They've been sleeping so easily. I've liked spending slower time with them. Do you have siblings?"

"One little sister," she said. "It kind of reminds me of her, seeing DeeDee sleep like that. I was kind of like her mama in a lot of ways."

For the first time, Swami noticed a hint of Appalachian roots coming through in Moon's voice. "I still keep in touch with her. She's a dentist."

Moon rolled her eyes as she said it, and Swami felt invited to laugh a bit.

Moon smiled and shook her head. "She became the dentist. I became the white girl who ran away and went all hippie with Buddhism and tattoos and bare feet." She brushed her hand over the stars on her leg. "I'm proud of her, though, glad for her that at least one of us turned out." Moon blushed a bit as she said it. Looked down at the quilt.

Swami studied her. Moon reminded her in a way of her old guide friend Laura, the dreadlocks and colorfulness. But the difference was

Laura from Boston actually had a huge trust fund waiting for her, a girl just playing the part of a vagabond. Moon, given the little Swami now knew of her story, was none of that. She was actually searching, and living it. What she had now she had made herself, and Swami admired her for it.

"I wouldn't say that," Swami told her. "Not at all. You've got a life many would admire, but frankly aren't brave enough to go live."

Moon looked up at her and smiled.

"Well," she said. She looked at the sleeping DeeDee again, smiled at her. She looked at Swami. "I have had to be brave. That much I will definitely accept."

Swami got the sense there was much more to Moon's story, that it wasn't just adventurousness that had carried the girl so far and wide. Swami also got the sense that now wasn't the right time to ask. She helped change the subject to lighter things.

"This quilt is so amazing," she said again, tracing the swirls of stitch lines with her fingertips. "And the food too. You're an amazing cook. Thank you for sharing that experience with me and the kids. Oh, and that *bread*. Just perfect." It was a chewy, round sourdough, with an indescribable crust. It was the kind of bread that invites you to make a meal of just itself and a stick of butter, and maybe not even the butter.

Moon brightened at the mention of the bread. "The bread wasn't mine," she said. "Randy made it for me, for us."

"*Randy* made that bread? Truck gun Randy?"

Moon smiled and nodded excitedly. "Truck gun Randy. Yes, there's more to him than meets the eye. He is a *cook*. Venison. Grouse. Bread. Homemade sauces. He gets it from his mom. Wait until you try her cooking. It's out of this world. The first time I met Randy he was cooking a meal with five different Dutch ovens in the fire pit behind Woodchuck. That's when I knew he was different from other raft guides I've known. And in the three or four seasons I've known him, he's lived up to that."

Swami waited, then had to ask. "Are the two of you . . ." she prodded.

Moon shook her head. "We're just good friends. His mom sure

wants us to hook up, though. She's just *obvious* about it when we're over there. Randy gets all embarrassed and grumpy."

Swami smiled.

"You know another thing?" Moon said. "Randy is the only male river guide I've known who's never tried to get into my camper at night. Well, Chip too, but Chip is sort of like everyone's bushy grandpa figure. But Randy, he's got this old-fashioned sense of justice, chivalry, that I have come to really admire."

Swami remembered how the men were in West Virginia. How desperate they'd been for the handful of female guides. Swami was glad when she and Sam became an official thing. She could drink beer around the campfire and the other men would stay away. A new girl guide in the camp was like a lightning strike, charging everything all over again. Swami could only imagine what Moon could do to a guide camp. Moon, Swami had to admit, had supermodel legs, with a swirl of blue stars running up into the hem of her rafting shorts. She had a brilliant smile, and a playful, wild-horse sort of quality. Moon would outshine any campfire in any camp.

"The first summer I knew Randy," Moon said, "he and Chip and I caravanned down to Gauley Fest in Summersville. It was my first time. *What* a finale—river guides from the whole country, wrapping up their seasons, tents as far as you can see. Chip did warn me, but I went overboard, ran off. There was whatever you wanted there. And I don't even remember how I got back to my little camper. I remember I could barely walk at one point. And there were these guides from the Pigeon who tried to get me back to their campsite. I got sick too. And I would have gone with those guys if Randy hadn't found me. Anyway, long story short. I wake up the next morning in my camper, blisteringly hungover. I'm dressed, zipped into my sleeping bag, and there's a full bottle of water next to my bunk. When I stumbled outside, guess who I nearly tripped over."

"Randy?"

Moon nodded. "He carried me back to my camper, and then slept the rest of the night in his sleeping bag on the ground in front of my camper door. That's when he became one of my best friends, this guy with a truck gun who liked to hunt and cook and was as noble as I've ever seen anyone be."

"There's a lot to be said for that," said Swami. "There really is."

Moon nodded. "He brings us all fresh bread every Saturday."

Swami smiled. "There's a lot to be said for that too." She looked up at the sky. It was pale blue now, well into the afternoon. She should probably get the kids back soon. She didn't want to overstay her welcome.

"Do you think you'll come around Woodchuck a bit more this summer?" Moon asked. "It'd be cool to have another girl guide around."

Swami thought about it. For some reason, she still couldn't imagine herself actually rafting again. If she was honest, getting in a boat would feel like too big of a *yes*. And she still felt a bit frightened of it all. Not the guides as much as what it all meant. The whimsy of it all. The very real financial commitment. Sam guiding again, even if he did have summers off from a full-time job. She just didn't know if she could go all in.

"Maybe," she said. "I think so, once we get our camping legs under us. That property could use some work. I like painting. The kids could use some chores too this summer."

"Well, if you want to paint that old barn, I'm in. Oh, and I wanted to say that you can use my Jeep whenever you want. Randy said Smitty's a good mechanic, but he's getting into his busy season and apparently only works at his own speed. Like really, just ask and the keys are yours whenever."

"Thanks, Moon," Swami said, and she meant it for the kind offer, and the vision of a painted barn, and for the really great lunch. And as she thanked her, Swami reached toward Moon and squeezed both of Moon's hands in her own, in a way that felt both surprising and completely effortless.

Moon squeezed Swami's hands back and beamed at her like a little sister.

"You're welcome," Moon said, and then Swami helped her pack up the lunch, and stirred the kids, and Darren and Dell said thank you to

Moon before they said goodbye and walked slowly home to campsite twenty-two.

•••

SHE COULD DO THIS. SWAMI wobbled the big stick shift in her hand. The day after her lunch with Moon, Swami asked to borrow the Jeep. What she hadn't considered, and what Moon hadn't asked, was whether Swami knew how to drive a stick. "It's a three-speed, big V8" is all the coaching Moon gave her when she handed over the keys. Swami had driven a manual once with her dad when she was seventeen. She remembered his eyes watering from holding back laughter as she bunny-hopped his little Toyota pickup through an empty parking lot. She was furious with him, which made her hop the car even more.

"Everybody ready?" she asked. Swami was thankful she had no audience other than her kids. Randy picked up Moon for work, and Sam left on his pedal bike in the early dawn. She was also thankful for the new car seats they'd purchased for the trip. They made her feel a bit better about the open top. DeeDee and Dell both snugged into their harnesses, the big teal roll bar caging them in. Darren had to sit in the front, which worried her with the lack of doors. But Swami buckled him in tight and would take the back roads to Crivitz, the "big town" a half hour south, with the real grocery and hardware store. She reached back and brushed cheesy crumbs from Dell's cheeks. It was beyond time to go get groceries. Dell smiled at her. DeeDee kicked her legs the way she kicked at water.

Darren nodded excitedly. He pulled the green compass out of his shirt on its lanyard and held it in both hands.

Swami wobbled the stick again and made sure it was in neutral, pressed the clutch, and turned the key. The big motor rumbled to life. Swami found reverse, revved the big motor, and the Jeep yanked back too fast through her turn, its tires spinning the gravel in the campsite. Swami mashed the brake before revving it into the bushes, stalling the motor.

"Mom," said Darren. "Can you drive this?"

Swami brought the motor to life again, shifted into first.

"Mommy can do lots of things," she said, and then very gently this time let out the clutch and crawled onto the path toward the campground gate. It was a big motor. Swami barely had to give the Jeep gas at all to get moving. Darren's grip on his seat relaxed by the time they reached the general store, where Swami asked him to run in to get their mail. She left the Jeep running.

When Darren bounded back he handed her the small stack of letters and buckled back in.

"We got a letter from Grandma," he said. "Can we open it?" There was a fat letter from her parents for the kids, three utility bills—two from home and one for Woodchuck—plus a letter for Sam from his school. And beneath it all was a bright green advertisement for X-treme Outdoor Adventures Rafting and Zip Lines. It had a picture of smiling customers in fresh rafting gear, with bright helmets and smiles and a guide that looked like he smelled good. Swami tucked the letters into her bag. *She could do this too*, she thought to herself. She was starting today. Woodchuck was starting today.

Swami tucked the letters into her bag. "Let's open them later," she said. "We've got shopping to do." Swami revved the Jeep back onto the road and out the gate, and gently brought it up to third gear without much drama. The back roads were empty, and Swami took her time.

"We're going south now, Mom," Darren said, compass in his lap.

"Good," said Swami, and she smiled at him. The Jeep droned along happily at forty miles per hour on its knobby tires, tall pines sailing past it on both sides of the empty road. Here and there, the river sparkled through gaps in the trees. The sun was high and warm. Swami could smell the forest too. Her kids watched the forest and sky, smiling, curious, their hair blowing in the piney wind.

"I see something . . . *green!*" Dell announced.

"The trees," answered Darren, in a bored voice.

"Yes!" she said, beaming and wiping the blowing hair from her eyes.

Swami had already compiled a list of what had to be done. Paint first, then new gear, maybe even some new guides if Woodchuck could advertise and grow. She and Sam owed thirty-two thousand dollars on

Woodchuck, and had just over three thousand in savings. Their mortgage payments for the outfitter and their home in Chicago amounted
to nearly two thousand a month. Swami flexed her grocery spending in
her mind. She could also have the mechanic—Smitty—fix only the RV's
motor and leave the bodywork until later. With Sam's summer teacher's
salary plus projected earnings from Woodchuck, they'd be above water
through August. At that point, there was the safety net of selling out. It
was Sam's biggest promise in all of this when they closed on the deal.
He'd put Woodchuck in Swami's name, the same as he did with their
house in Chicago. He'd told her if at any time the Woodchuck adventure wasn't working out, Swami could put it back on the market, sell
the camper, pack it all up, and head home. It would be her decision.
Today, she decided on paint. Swami's mom was a Realtor. She never
sold a property without a quick coat of fresh paint. *Fresh paint greases
the rails of realty*, she was fond of saying. But it wasn't even June yet.
Swami wanted to give Woodchuck a fair shake. She could help steer it.
It needed steering.

Around the next bend, a bright green billboard with hot pink let-
tering outshined all the pines. Swami let off the accelerator, and the
heavy motor churned down. She pushed the clutch in and coasted.

You've arrived at your X-treme Vacation! Turn now!

Swami turned, and then sat parked by the entrance. On either side
of the freshly groomed gravel drive sat a house-sized arrangement of
stacked landscaping boulders, with smaller river stones and neatly
mulched grasses arranged to look like a cascading river, complete with
riverbanks and miniature baby pine trees on shore. Beyond the dra-
matic entrance, freshly trimmed cedars lined the road until it ducked
into a deep emerald forest. Swami felt a sinking feeling as she rolled
in atop the crunching gravel. The forest opened up to a large meadow,
the river sparkling at its shoreline. Zip lines and an adventure climbing
tower—peppered with guests in orange helmets—weaved in and out of
the forest. Swami had to lean into the windshield and squint in the
sunlight to see the top of the nearest tower. It was a nest of fresh lumber
built atop power poles, with green flags at its top. A smiling couple rode
in front of her stopped Jeep on matching green mountain bikes. Swami

followed them with her eyes as they circumnavigated the big gravel loop near the water, dotted with signs for campsites, yurts, firewood, a climbing wall, and even a riverside sauna. Swami spotted a boathouse by the river built from freshly varnished logs, and then—her eyes had been avoiding it—she looked at the center of things: the X-treme Outdoor Adventures welcome center. It was a two-story vaulted log structure with a high glass face. Even from where she sat, Swami could see the inside of it, the bright paint, the big-screen TV showing video of outdoor adventures, the minimalist and modern reception desk spanning an entire wall. In front of the center was a massive covered patio with about ten tables with padded chairs. Two families ate lunch there, some smaller children running circles in swimsuits. In front of the patio, in the center of the driveway loop, another river-rock landscape framed in a fire pit the size of a hot tub was surrounded by varnished log Adirondack chairs.

Swami flinched when a shrieking adventure guest zoomed overhead, harnessed and zipping through the sun with her arms outstretched. She landed in the nest. Another woman zipped down after her.

Who on earth, thought Swami, *would buy Woodchuck with this level of competition now in town?* No one. Except for a middle school art teacher and his wife from Chicago with a brand-new baby. That's who. The amount of money backing X-treme must be immense.

"Did you see that?! Mom, Dell, did you see that?!" Darren gushed.

"What *is* that?" Dell yelled.

Swami pulled slowly through the big loop. "Shhhh," she said, the way she did automatically when her thoughts were so fully elsewhere.

"Is this part of Woodchuck?" Darren asked.

"No," Swami said.

Swami pulled near the glass outpost now. She slowed down even further to looked inside, leaned over Darren a bit. There were clothing racks, sunglasses, outdoor gear, drinks. A young man working behind the counter smiled as he spoke to an arriving family, handing them pens and rental agreements next to the credit card machine.

This is what Woodchuck could have been, she thought, slowing the Jeep to a crawl. Just then another employee inside spotted her. It was a young woman with a bright green T-shirt and spandex pants. She looked like she'd just been rock climbing, or modeling backpacks, and was carrying an armful of hats toward a rack when she saw Swami. The young woman changed course when she saw Swami, pushing through the glass door, already lifting her hand in a greeting.

Swami floored it. She spun gravel. Darren gripped his seat. As she revved the motor into second gear beneath the zip lines—she was getting the hang of this now—she saw the woman standing on the patio with her green hats, her head tipped in question.

"Yeehaw!" yelled Darren as they cruised around the gravel corner. Swami quickly remembered herself and slowed.

"Ah, keep going," he begged.

"Mom! What, Mom, what?" said Dell.

Swami took a breath.

"Mommy just needed to speed up for a moment," she said.

At the exit, Swami waited while an X-treme bus pulled into the drive. It was shining and green and brimming with customers. A guide with long blond hair stood in the front of the bus, speaking loudly, something about wet suits that must have been a joke. All the guests laughed as the bus roared in.

The driver's window was down. He was a big man with gray hair.

"Cool Jeep!" he called to her, and gave her a quick thumbs-up as he muscled the big wheel. Swami nodded and smiled at him, and the guide with the long hair who had just told a joke looked down at the Jeep too, made eye contact with Swami as the gleaming bus scrolled past, towing a trailer full of new rafts.

"Let's go get some paint," Swami said. "Lots of paint." Swami got the Jeep rolling and pointed her way to Crivitz. Swami thought about colors as she drove. Her mind raced through visions for Woodchuck. How could a sagging barn in a hayfield compete with X-treme?

"Mom, what are these signs? 'Stop Whining, Start the Mining.'"

"I think they mean people need to make money," she said.

"What, Mom?" Dell shouted.

Swami shook her head in the rearview mirror.

Dell moved on. "I see something . . . *blue*," she shouted.

"The sky," moaned Darren.

"*Yes!*" said Dell.

Blue. Swami thought about Moon's blue quilt, her retro teardrop camper, the unexpected meal. Moon's campsite was such a unique presence in the middle of a campground where all of the tents and pop-ups and oversized campers looked more or less as expected. Moon stood out not because she'd competed and won, but because she just did her own thing, stepped outside the competition. Maybe Woodchuck could be like that. Words like *boutique*, and *niche*, circled Swami's mind as they neared town. She thought of an old single-story motel she once saw, bright purple and yellow, that embraced its 1950s quirkiness instead of trying and failing to compete with modern chains. *Vibrating Beds! 25 Cents!* bragged the motel sign. People pulled in for nostalgia, charm. Swami imagined a new sign for Woodchuck, laughed at herself. *Scary, hungover river guides!* She shook her head. Woodchuck could do much better. It had to.

The hardware store was on the north end of town. It was also connected to the grocery store, which Swami counted as a win as she unbuckled her kids and walked inside. There was a big outdoor greenhouse on one end, and a car wash and gas pumps on the other. It struck Swami as a family business that kept growing, adding on, growing the parking lot and building as the next generation found another need to fill. A line of mowers and wheelbarrows sat along the building, signs pointing out back that read: *Fencing, Mulch, Feed, Lumber.*

"You want blue?" asked the man inside. "Boy, do we have *blue*. You're in luck." He stood behind the counter, an old plaid shirt tucked into jeans. He had a work apron. He clapped his hands together and waved her to follow him down an aisle.

"It's a heck of blue, though," he said. "I'll show it to ya."

Swami followed with DeeDee in her arms, her daughter's back still warm from the car seat. Dell stared into the front of the glass counter filled with boxes of beef jerky, a dusty display of Case pocketknives, and an assortment of green and yellow and white ammunition boxes. Walnut-stocked shotguns sat in a rack behind the counter. A stuffed bear stood behind it all, baring its teeth and long yellowed claws. Darren turned back and took Dell's hand to help her catch up. She absolutely glared at the bear.

The walls of the hardware portion of the store were covered to ladder height with hammers, work gloves, orange hunting caps, drawers of bolts and washers, coiled plumbing snakes, and grills.

The owner waddled through a tight aisle of American flags and grilling accessories. "Had to store this big order in back here. Didn't know what to do with it. A couple ordered this all for their *cottage*—three thousand square foot—but the wife didn't like it. Can't refund on mixed paint, but if you like it you can have it half price plus the cost of delivery. It's *blue*."

The man arrived at a stack of fifteen five-gallon buckets of paint. "It's oil-based," he said, unscrewing a small cap from one of the plastic lids. "Would be good on an old barn, as you say—soak up nice." He grabbed a stirring stick from a shelf, dipped it in, and then held it up on a paper towel for Swami to see. The gesture reminded Swami of a mechanic holding a dipstick and recommending an oil change. Except this oil wasn't black. It was electric blue, like a sky and a tropical ocean, stirred together with a shot of lightning.

"Whoa," said Darren.

Swami felt the same way.

"We'll take it," she said. She felt a charge of lightning through her body, as bright as that paint. "And I'll need five of these in a nice bright silver for the roof, and rollers, lots of rollers."

The owner wiped the stick off, clearly happy.

"Where you folks from?" he asked. He smiled at Dell. "Beautiful kiddos. I have fourteen grandchildren and two great-grandchildren myself. Love every one of 'em. They call me Grandpa Birdy."

Dell smiled at him.

Swami knew by now that telling people they were from Chicago always drew a bit of a forced smile.

"A bit south," she said. "My husband and I just bought Woodchuck Rafting Company."

"Oh, the heck?" he said. "Yeah, I been by there. Say, you should join the Marigamie County League of Business Owners. We meet at Rita's

Lanes and Lounge once a month just to keep in touch. Mostly we go bowling. Lot of new business coming up here, and what's good for the area is good for all of us, that's for sure. You kiddos like bowling?"

Swami followed him back to the front counter. Darren didn't answer him.

"They haven't been bowling," Swami said.

"The hell! Never been bowling!" exclaimed the man. He stopped walking and eyeballed them as if he'd been struck. "Well," he said, "I'm gonna give you my business card up here, and tell you what. You and your husband come bowling sometime with Grandpa Birdy, and the bill's on me. Rita's got some good pizza and root beers too." Birdy handed her his card and lifted a handful of suckers from the drawer.

"Okay, Mom?" he asked.

Swami smiled and nodded, and Birdy beamed and handed out the suckers.

"That's quite the bear," Swami said.

Grandpa Birdy slowly turned to look behind him, and then pretended to be scared when he saw the bear, which made the kids laugh. He put a hand flat on the counter and leaned on it, tossed his other thumb back at the bear.

"I popped that fella the year Nixon took office. It was just me and Bell up here then—she's passed now—with a tiny hardware store and an even tinier house. This guy kept sniffin' around and we let him be even though he was wrecking Bell's bird feeder. But then one night we heard him mashin' on the front door. Whole house was shaking."

Swami could tell all fourteen of Birdy's grandchildren and two great-grandchildren had heard this story too. He knew how to tell it. Darren stopped unwrapping his sucker.

Birdy raised his hands in the air. "'There's an *earthquake,*' I yelled, and my wife says, 'That ain't no earthquake, it's a *bear*!' So I jumped outta bed in my stockings and grabbed my pump gun—had these kinda slugs in it right here." Birdy reached under the counter and grabbed a white box of Winchesters. He dug out a bullet as fat as a cigar. And then, as Swami winced a bit but kept smiling, he grabbed one of the shotguns off the rack behind him to complete the reenactment. "And there's that bear, banging the door, and I rack my pump gun just like this one." He racked it. "And when the door burst right off its hinges, I seen this bear standing there just like he is now, growling, the bright moon glowing behind him. And my wife, Bell, yells out, 'Give him hell, Birdy!' And I fire—Blam! Right through his breadbasket. Tipped him over right there in our mudroom. Had to take off the porch railing and drag him back out the door with my truck and tow strap."

He chuckled and put the shotgun back on his rack.

"Oh-ho my," said Swami, patting DeeDee's rump. Her eyes were as wide as her kids'.

"Anyhow," Birdy said, "everything works out in the end. Got that bear back when me and Bell didn't know if it was the best thing to try to keep the hardware store going. But look at the place now. We did good. This bear's stood here as a reminder. Life will turn out. Especially if you keep a pump gun handy. Couldn't interest you in a pump gun along with that paint, could I?"

"Mom, get a pump gun!" said Darren.

"Just the paint today," Swami answered, reaching for the checkbook in her back pocket. "How much was delivery?"

Grandpa Birdy looked at her, then at the kids.

"No charge," he said. "I got a driver headed through Thunderwater next week anyhow, and I'll have him drop it off then."

"Really?" Swami asked.

He nodded. "I like seeing young families coming up here, up north. It's good."

"Thank you, Mr. Birdy," Swami said, and smiled at him. As she wrote the check, she asked if she might take two or three pails of the paint with her today, and some brushes, to get started on the barn.

"I'll have someone bring 'em out to your car," Birdy said.

Swami tore the check from the checkbook. She could almost see it now: a better Woodchuck. A few fresh cedar trees planted. Landscaping boulders. Perennials and a mown lawn. She pictured a family eating Randy's bread on one of Moon's quilts, teenagers playing Frisbee. As she shopped for groceries in the adjoining store, Swami promised herself Woodchuck would become a business, with a plan, that could at the very least be sold.

"Can I open the mail now, Mom?" asked Darren as Swami packed bags of groceries into the back with the girls. The paint and rollers took all of the space behind the rear seat.

"Yes," Swami said, checking the time. "You can open the mail now."

SIX

LATE THAT AFTERNOON, SAM COULDN'T STOP LAUGHING AT CHIP'S story while they smoked more of Chip's weed at the gravel boat landing. They'd already loaded the day's boats onto the trailer. Ratcheted the straps. Randy and Moon bused the customers back to the barn. Once alone, Chip had a ritual of smoking a joint along with a few sips of whiskey he kept in the glove box of the rafting van. Sam sat with him on the back of the raft trailer, his feet in the river, passing the weed and the whiskey back and forth, the surface of the black river lit up bright orange. Sam's guiding was becoming smoother each day, the paddling and sunlight loosening and browning his shoulders. Chip's homegrown dope, as he called it, helped Sam melt even further into that warmth. He'd been feeling stronger, happier, out here in nature with the pines and boulders and flow of things. Bass and panfish began to rise and feed now, rippling the surface of the river.

Sam wiped his eyes. "You named it Woodchuck . . . because you saw a woodchuck?"

"Like I said"—Chip shrugged—"I was sitting there with the bank papers and couldn't think of a name, and then, whoop, there's a woodchuck coming across the road. So I wrote down, *Woodchuck*. It's as good as anything."

Sam shook his head and exhaled.

"'Woodchuck' had a ring to it," said Chip. "And it fit. People don't think woodchucks can swim, but they're actually good on the water. People told me the same thing about rafting back in the seventies. 'That won't fly,' they said. 'People won't pay for that.' But it's big business now. Rafting outfits from Costa Rica to New Zealand." Chip blew smoke out over the water. "Was lucky I seen a woodchuck," he said. "Could have been a cat. 'Cat Rafting.'"

Sam dribbled whiskey down his chin. Chip took the bottle back from him, capped it. "You really are a lightweight, aren't you," he said.

He slid off the trailer into the shallow water. "Well, Randy's doing venison gyros tonight. Let's head 'er."

Yes, thought Sam. *Randy's gyros.* He was famished. Sometimes the best part about rafting was eating afterward. Food tasted so good after a day of paddling. And dry clothes felt like heaven. Sam splashed down from the back of the trailer and got in the rafting van. He felt positively happy during their slow drive back to the raft barn, out through the pines to the highway, up the long hill with the green hardwoods and hayfields. Sam dried his feet out the window. He was buzzy, glad. Every day for about two weeks now, he'd woken early, rafted—or worked around the barn when there wasn't a trip—eaten Randy's campfire cooking, and then pedaled his bike back to the campground, where the kids would tell him all about their day, what they'd caught in the lake, the painter turtles they'd seen, the grass snakes, a beaver, a loon. His relationship with Swami had been quiet. But it had been quiet for years. He kept inviting her to raft, offering to watch the kids. Maybe it would just take more time. She at least seemed happy enough when Sam told her about the money he made each day. The coffers were filling. It wasn't enough quite yet, but money *was* being made. Part of him hoped, really dreamed, of never having to go back and teach art classes and monitor cafeterias again. If only he could make enough, and if Swami could see what he'd been seeing up here in the north. It was a better life. It was, plain and simple, a better life.

"What's this now?" said Chip. He slowed as the raft barn came into sight, and wrestled the old van from the highway onto Woodchuck's gravel drive.

Sam pulled his feet in from the window and sat up. The last of the customers were leaving in their cars. The bus was pulled around back. Then Sam saw her and became suddenly very self-conscious of how numb his face felt from the weed and whiskey.

"Oh no," said Sam. "What's she doing?" He wanted Swami involved, but not right at this particular moment. She'd always frowned on the river guides who smoked and drank every day, even back in West Virginia.

Swami stood on a chair facing the wall of the barn. Darren and

Dell were planted in a row along the stone foundation. All of them were *waving*? Randy was up on a ladder, waving too. Swami turned and looked at them with a paintbrush in her hand while Chip bounced the rig out of sight around the barn. Swami glared at the van. Sam shrank in the seat.

"What am I gonna do? Why is everybody painting?" asked Sam.

"Stay cool, buddy," said Chip.

"Are my eyes all red?" Sam asked.

Chip looked at him. He didn't say anything. He just handed Sam the sunglasses from his head. Sam pressed the big glasses onto his face, gave his hair a quick rub in the side-view mirror. He stepped out from the truck, took a breath, and then tried to walk nonchalantly down to the front of the barn.

"Daddy!" yelled Dell, dropping her entire paintbrush into the bucket of paint she and Darren shared. Dell ran to Sam, a bright smear of blue in her blond hair. Sam scooped her up. Darren remained immersed in his work. Swami stooped over the paint bucket, hurriedly wiping off Dell's brush with a rag.

"We're painting the barn *blue*, Daddy!" exclaimed Dell. She and Darren had covered a ten-foot swath of the barn's foundation with the brightest blue Sam had ever seen. It wasn't bad, exactly, just unexpectedly bright. Sam almost took off Chip's sunglasses to see it better.

"I see," Sam said, looking at Swami now.

Dell squeezed Sam's neck and planted a huge kiss on his cheek. Then she whispered to him, "When are we going to see Chip's deers, Daddy?"

Sam was at a loss. Swami had given no indication that she'd be stopping out at Woodchuck today, and hadn't spoken a word about painting. Randy paused from painting up on his ladder and looked at Swami and then at Sam. He was clearly unimpressed to be up on a ladder at the end of a day on the water.

"Wow," said Chip, jingling his keys into his shorts pocket. "A barn painting!"

Swami wrapped Dell's brush in a rag, and then stood and looked at Sam.

"I need to talk with you right now," she said.

"Sure," said Sam. "Honey," Sam said to Dell, setting her down. "Why don't you ask Uncle Chip about the deer for a minute. Daddy's going to talk with Mom."

"Chip, where's your deers?!" yelled Dell, laughing. Chip knelt down in the grass, pulled his shorts pockets inside out, and dropped his jaw at Dell in mock surprise as if he'd lost the deer. Dell gave his meaty shoulder a big shove, and Chip made a show of falling over, making Dell laugh.

"Show me your painting," said Chip, and Dell yanked him up and dragged him over to the blue foundation. He gave Sam a wary glance as Sam turned to follow Swami out back. Sam now realized the whole property had been weed-whacked, shorn. Even the old bush with the sneakers in it had been torn from the ground.

"Sam," called Randy from his ladder, "make sure Pete isn't killing my meat."

Sam nodded, jogged after Swami.

Out back, smoke poured from the grill manned by Pete, his black braids sticking out the back of his tattered ball cap. The massive Siberian husky sat by his side, licking its lips in the woodsmoke. A big grease flame rose up. Pete jumped back and then hurriedly dumped some of his beer into the grill. He waved the smoke from his face and then lifted what was left of his beer in greeting. Swami stalked past the grill and toward the party bus. The bush with the sneakers was piled onto the fire pit. Sam tried to walk fast without seeming to walk fast. The buzz in his body had stiffened into rigid self-consciousness. He felt like he was stomping while he walked, and wondered if anyone noticed. Pete raised his eyebrows at Sam as he went by, gave a glance at Swami.

Inside the party bus, Moon was busy mincing something on a wooden cutting board. DeeDee kicked happily in her bucket seat on the counter. Swami scooped her up.

"How was she?" Swami asked.

Moon wrinkled her face in a smile at DeeDee. "Happy," Moon said.

"Hey, can I talk to Sam alone for a second?" Swami said, handing the baby to Moon. Moon wiped her hands on a towel. "C'mere, peanut," she said. Sam was very confused by this new dynamic between Swami and Moon, like they were sisters and had been for a very long time.

"Randy said the onions need to go in that bowl with the cucumber and sour cream, but he said he'd come and season it." Moon bounced DeeDee on her hip, made her little hand wave while she slipped past Sam. "Hi, Papa," she said, then "Hey, Sam," with a troubled look in her eyes.

Swami smiled as Moon left the bus, and then her smile left her face. Moon strode toward the grill. Randy came rushing up the hill with a paintbrush in his hand. "No, Pete!" he cried. "*Low*, low heat." Pete gave a huge shrug, gestured back at the bus where Swami and Sam had gone.

Alone, confused, Sam managed to get some words out. "What is going on?" he asked Swami.

"*Don't* . . . talk," said Swami. She set the purple onion on the wooden cutting board and clipped it in half. Sam looked around the bus for something to drink. He was so thirsty. He could hardly stand these moments when Swami was clearly upset but she made him wait to hear it. It made him feel like a stupid child. He found a beer in the cooler. He cracked it open and tried to drink it nonchalantly, as if he didn't know he was in such hot water. The beer was cold. Sam felt like he could take a breath again. He tried to lean confidently against one of the bus's remaining bench seats. The bus was up on blocks, its wheels and brakes cannibalized for parts, but it was still a semi-operational camper. A small cooler, some fold-down beds, a propane stovetop, and a restaurant-style booth made out of two bus seats and a Formica tabletop.

Swami glared at the beer in his hand and then at him. She turned one of the onion halves on its side and sliced it in two, then again, and again.

"I'm taking over here," Swami said, the smallest tremble in her voice. "You're not in charge of Woodchuck anymore, Sam. *I am.*"

This was all too much, the mystery and suspense of it. He wished Swami would just let it rip and let him know what was behind all this. Sam looked out the window at the alfalfa field, then out at Pete and Moon hovering over the smoking grill while Randy tried to salvage his ruined meal, still holding his paintbrush. Everything was off-kilter. Frustration overtook Sam.

"You know what?" he blurted out.

Swami stopped him by bringing the knife down, hard, on the cutting board.

"Do you know what?" she hissed through gritted teeth. "Your guides are a mess, this place is a mess, and you . . ." She pursed her lips then, holding back. Instead of letting it out and saying what she had to say, she just put on a calm face and studied him. It said, *I am the bigger person on the playground, and you are not even worth insulting.* Swami always managed to do this right as Sam began to boil over. It was always a punch to the gut.

"Are you *high*?" she said, venom in her voice.

"I—" Sam managed.

"Unbelievable," she said. She couldn't even look at him anymore. Sam wilted. Swami turned back to her onion.

"We are painting the barn," Swami said, chopping the onion and talking as she did. "We are getting the guides into shape. We are going to start calling our clients *guests*, not *custies*. I'll be leading check-in from now on. We're ordering new gear because the life jackets are disgusting. And we are having gravel and landscaping stone brought in. Please take off those ridiculous sunglasses."

Sam straightened, almost said no, but then he took them off. "Swami, we don't have money for all of that. We don't—"

Swami slammed the knife down so hard on the cutting board now that onions splattered all over the bus. She left the knife there and turned on Sam with a fiery hiss that scared him.

"I know how much money we don't have. And I know all of it. I have worked all day, and I will continue to work all day to rescue myself and the children from this *disaster*." She looked at his eyes, shook her head in disgust. "I am not an idiot, Sam, and I won't play one."

Swami's face was red, her hair pulled tightly back into a ponytail. Her chest was heaving. "Woodchuck is for sale," she said, and then she reached into the back pocket of her jean shorts and pressed a folded piece of mail into Sam's chest. It was from Sam's school. Everything suddenly made perfect sense. Everything left in him sank. Swami looked sadly into his bright red eyes. There was a sad question in them. A genuine question. "And you are going to get serious and do *everything* you can to help get us out of this," she said. "I would leave right now if I could."

"I will," said Sam, very quietly.

"You'd better," she said.

She left the letter in Sam's hands, and then left the bus, walking not toward the barn but in a straight line away from it, alone into the alfalfa fields. Sam watched her go, saw her wipe her face with both hands. He opened the letter, and the first line confirmed it. He didn't need to read the whole thing. *Regret to inform . . . as discussed earlier this spring . . . the board has decided . . .* Sam exhaled a rattling breath. Swami didn't know that arts funding had been under review. She didn't know that he'd been too afraid to tell her. But Sam knew that going out there and trying to explain that wouldn't make any difference at all anymore. He hadn't told her. That's all that mattered.

By the fire pit, Sam heard Dell giggling. She'd walked up with Chip and Darren, and the three of them now sat on a log bench next to the fire pit. Chip made Dell laugh again, and then gave a wary look toward the bus. Moon looked too. Pete watched Randy finesse the grill. On the other side of the bus, Sam watched Swami walk slower across the field now. She stopped and stood in the middle of it. The long shadows of the distant wood line stretched toward her, and toward Sam.

• • •

EVENTUALLY, FIRELIGHT FLICKERED AGAINST THE broad face of the barn. Dusk deepened and bats flew in and out of the loft, circling for a few early mosquitoes in the stars. The fire crackled, and the horizon was now a dim purple glow behind the pines near the highway. Randy's blue truck sat parked nearby with its windows down, the radio playing a classic country station. Randy's meal seemed to give everyone something to agree on. The heat and stress of late afternoon faded a bit in the light of a fire and Randy's comfort food. He sliced homemade focaccia breads in two, and then split them down the middle like big buns, one on each plate. Then he stuffed the breads with seasoned venison and fresh onions and topped them off with his own spin on cucumber sauce. Even Swami, who had been very quiet after her argument in the bus, agreed that it was good. Darren asked for seconds, and Randy happily obliged.

Now the paper plates from dinner had long been turned to ash, and people talked quietly about the day in short sentences that didn't go very far. Everyone seemed to be waiting for Swami. Sam certainly was. He looked across the fire at her. She didn't look back. Darren tended the fire, poking logs with a stick, and running to and from the woodpile behind the bus, building a small pile of split pine next to the fire pit, dropping logs on and poking them into place. Dell knelt next to Pete's huge dog, petting its fur, while the giant dog lay on its side with its paws in the air.

"I've been to X-treme," Swami finally said, to no one in particular. Everyone looked at her. Darren dumped another armful of logs near the fire and bolted off again.

"What's it like?" asked Chip. "I drove out there once when they started building."

"It's everything Woodchuck is not," Swami said. "If you all want Woodchuck to even exist next season, this place needs to change, tomorrow. I'm being perfectly serious."

"We are too," said Sam. Swami looked at him, and then nodded.

The guides sat awkwardly around their own fire, while Swami described a laundry list of action items to be started tomorrow. That's what she called them, *action items*, and Sam winced on behalf of the guides. Swami did that in the kitchen back home sometimes, striding in with her lists just as Sam sat down somewhere, or was already folding a pile of clothes. Randy and Sam were tasked with painting, the face of the barn first, on the road side. Chip was tasked with cleaning the guide loft, and everything had to go. She wanted the barn empty, nothing left in it but rafts, paddles, and hard-swept wood. Moon and Swami would be on customer service. Sam would shuttle rafts and then watch the children until the trip left, and then he would guide and Swami would stay back and work on the books during naps.

Sam watched the guides absorb this new order. Randy looked at Moon, and Moon looked at Chip. Chip looked at Sam. Sam knew they'd never seen this sort of thing under Chip's watch—Woodchuck treated as a workplace, with roles, assignments. They didn't look so much resistant as bewildered. They weren't used to being around children either. At one point during Swami's speech, Chip pulled his papers and baggie out of his parka pocket. Sam quickly shook his head with wide eyes. Chip tucked it back in.

"Well," said Chip. "That sounds like a good plan, Swami."

"It's not all of it, but it's a start. This place needs to become something else entirely—the way the trips are run, the spirit of the place, everything. We can't just run river trips and expect to compete with X-treme. Woodchuck has to offer what a bigger outfit can't."

Pete piped up. "They bought more riverbank this week," he said. "Between them and the mine, there ain't gonna be any riverbank left."

"Is the mine really coming?" Moon asked.

Pete shrugged. "They just offered to buy the power dam from the village. If that happens, I'll be a NorthSky employee. They'd own the dam and the whole bluff, straight down to the rapids."

"What'd the village say?" Moon said, sitting upright in her lawn chair.

"Don't know yet," said Pete. "There's a big town hall scheduled. Thing with mining is they won't dig without local support. If people don't buy in, it's too much of a hassle, legal and otherwise. That's why they've been scouting, seeing how big of salaries they can promise."

"I'm going to bring some *hassle*," Moon said. Randy smiled at her.

Pete shrugged. "People are pretty broke. Money's good."

"Clean, sustainable water is good too," said Moon.

"Yep," said Pete. "It is."

"Stop whining!" Dell pitched in. "Start the mining!" She pumped her little fists in the firelight. Pete's husky lifted its head, then settled back down.

"No, no, honey," said Swami. "Wrong team."

"Love that fighting spirit, though," said Moon, which made Swami smile.

"Thunderwater wasn't exactly founded on clean, sustainable principles," said Chip. "People here are the great-grandchildren of those who came here to clear-cut, dam, and blast."

"Not me," said Pete.

"True," said Chip.

"And that's the thing," Pete went on. "You ask people to suffer now or suffer later, nine out of ten are going to *choose* later. Who wouldn't? You offer me a mining salary, I'm taking it."

"Well, maybe this town could choose a different path this time," said Sam. "I was saying that to Chip a while back. Thunderwater could become one of those new, hippie, artisan eco-towns. It'd take time to build it up, but it could be done."

"Yes!" gushed Moon.

Pete raised his eyebrows at them.

"I'm with Moon," Randy said, nodding his head. "I'm for no mine."

"Thank you, Randy," Moon said.

Randy blushed in the firelight. Pete smirked at his friend. Sam knew what Pete was thinking. Randy wasn't for anything except the star tattoos on the thigh of the woman next to him. But Pete didn't say anything, and everyone watched the fire awhile. Darren went away for more wood.

"I'm selling Woodchuck," said Swami.

Everyone looked at her. Even the dog looked at her. A log popped and sparks rose up in front of her.

"It's only fair you all know that. No matter what Thunderwater decides, or the river, or the mine, I want you all to know I'm selling this place the moment I find a buyer. I'm building it up to sell it. I don't believe in secrets, or lying to you. You at least deserve to know."

Sam looked down at the coals and ashes.

"Maybe you could give it a chance, Swami," Chip offered quietly.

"I am," said Swami.

Chip wagged his beard a bit. "I know I've let things slip around here, but that's why I sold it, for what I did, to people I trusted. With you two steering, Woodchuck could be more than it's ever been, something you'd never want to sell."

"Well, you've got one season to help make that happen," she said. "But for reasons I am not going to discuss at this moment, you need to know I will sell tomorrow if I can, and I've already made a few phone calls, put the word out."

"*What?*" blurted Sam, without thinking, and Swami looked right at him.

Chip bit his tongue, sat back.

Randy frowned at Swami, as if trying to figure out if she was joking or not. Sam knew she wasn't. Pete just nodded at the fire, nearly imperceptibly, a look on his face that said I *told you so.*

Chip sat forward again, about to speak, but was cut short by the roar of a big diesel motor coming up alongside the barn. Everyone turned to see a big green bus rock to a stop, dust roiling in the glare of its headlights pointed right at the group.

Sam shielded his eyes from the glare.

"The hell is this?" said Chip.

The door slapped open, and an angry voice immediately emerged from the bus. "Which one of you dirtbags keeps soaping my rafts?" Duncan stood in clear silhouette now, a handful of his guides next to him.

"Turn your lights off," spat Chip, holding his hand up.

"I'm going to ask again. Which one of you dirtbags keeps messing with my trips?"

Chip shook his head and mumbled something.

"What's that?" Duncan said.

Chip stood from his chair. "I said I soaped your boats. Now you and your high school friends can just bump it down the road."

Duncan got up in Chip's face then, which was incongruous, like a child puffing his chest out at a bull. Randy stood up. Pete watched them with steely eyes. Moon shuffled Darren and Dell toward their mom.

"Calm down, Duncan," said Chip. "Soaping boats is all part of it. Soap *my* boats. I know you haven't been a river guide very long."

Sam glanced at Swami. She narrowed her eyes at him. *Soaping rafts?* they seemed to say. *Really, Sam?*

Duncan got a gleam in his eye, looked beyond Chip into the shadows. "So, which one of you is Swami?" he asked.

Sam stiffened. His hackles went up.

"I am," she said, glancing quickly at Sam and Chip and the other guides. Sam studied her for a long moment. She held DeeDee tight to her chest and wouldn't meet Sam's eyes.

"I got your phone message," Duncan said. And then he looked around at the grounds and the barn with a sneer. "I gotta talk with my uncle, but we'll talk soon," he said.

"Talk about what?" Chip asked.

Duncan slowly backed away, spread his arms wide. He had the upper hand now and knew it. "Don't tell me about guiding, Chip. I'm about to be the only guide in town." He gave a low five to one of his guides then, and turned to walk back to his bus. As he did, one of his guides actually made an *X* in the air with his forearms.

"Oh, come *on*," grumbled Randy.

"Don't walk away from me, Duncan, I asked you a question," said Chip, angry now. Duncan didn't turn around, so Chip stepped after him and put his hand on Duncan's shoulder.

Duncan spun and struck, shoving Chip with both hands, stepping into it. It barely moved the giant man, but it moved his friends.

"Nope," said Randy, as he shot in from a few feet away, his fist a whip in the firelight.

Pop!

The punch landed on Duncan's eye, crumpling him into the dust. Everything erupted at once. Two of Duncan's guides leapt at Randy. Hesitantly at first, until Randy swung on them too. Chip lunged for them and soon had another of Duncan's guides on his back. Pete was out of his seat and rounding the fire. Moon yelled for everyone to stop, but when she got pushed aside by the man who came at Pete, she squared up and kicked the guy in the back with the sole of her river sandal, dropping him on the grass. Chip bellowed in the midst of it all, swinging his cedar tree arms while Duncan's guide rode him in a choke hold.

Sam looked for his kids and wife, and saw Swami already shutting them inside Randy's truck. He got punched in the jaw then, swung back and knocked someone down, and then leapt in to pull one of the two guys off of Randy. As he did, he caught an elbow in his nose and went down hard next to the fire. Bright white pain shot through his vision. His nose gushed blood, and he caught in his hand a black, shimmering pool of it. He looked up and blinked just in time to see Pete, wearing a big leather glove, grab a firebrand from the fire and begin swinging it.

Pete yelled and cackled, not connecting with anyone, just yelling and threatening. He held the firebrand toward a guide who had fallen, wagged it right in his face. Duncan finally stood up. Chip dropped him again.

Sam watched the guide on Chip's back bring a beer bottle high overhead, about to smash it down, when a gunshot rang out in the air.

Everyone froze, spinning to their hips in the dusty grass. Pete dropped the firebrand and held his hands up.

"Stop!" bellowed Swami, her voice as loud and big as the gunshot. She was holding a lever-action deer rifle in her hands. Its brass receiver smoldered in the firelight. She looked as scared as everyone else that she was wielding a gun and that it had just gone off.

No one spoke. They were all sucking wind. Everyone had been punched in the face at least once, which in a real fight was usually as far as it went. Anything after that was just halfhearted wrestling and cussing. The fight was over.

Swami cut a tall figure between the fire and the headlights, childless now, panting, glowing, lowering the glimmering gun in the firelight. Sam saw Darren and Dell peering through the back window of Randy's truck. Darren held his baby sister.

"Where'd you get that?" Sam asked, still catching blood in his hand.

"From my truck," Randy said, unimpressed. He touched his finger to his bleeding mouth, then his eyebrow. Swami seemed bigger than Chip at the moment. She stared at them, and they stared at her, and no one knew what would happen for the space of several of Swami's breaths. And then she set Randy's rifle down on the log bench by the fire.

"Everyone leave right now," she said.

Duncan and his guides picked themselves up. They had to help Duncan stagger to the bus. He'd been punched in both eyes, by Randy and by Chip.

The door to the bus closed, and Swami waited for it to back down the hill. Randy picked up his rifle and unloaded it.

"Moon, I need a ride to camp," said Swami. "I'd have left in Randy's truck if I'd had the keys."

Moon nodded, and walked toward her Jeep. She touched Randy's shoulder on her way past.

"You okay?" she said.

Randy nodded, walked with her. Pete had already left in his truck. Only Sam and Chip remained.

"Sam, you are going to stay at Chip's house from now on, or the barn. I don't care where. But you are not coming to the campsite." Her voice was just barely calm enough to speak.

Sam didn't argue. He just held his T-shirt against his nose. There was a nakedness to the moment. Everything so thoroughly shamed, broken. His son and daughter gaping at them all from Randy's truck. He didn't speak.

"Swami," said Chip in a low voice. "What did Duncan mean he got your message?"

Swami ignited a bit again. She took one step toward Chip and her bleeding husband. "Don't even *ask* me questions. Do you understand?" She spoke through clenched teeth. There were tears in her eyes. She looked around at the tipped-over camp chairs, the scattered coals smoking in the grass.

Chip didn't answer.

"We have guests arriving in seven hours," she said. "Have everybody awake and ready by six. Or none of this will exist. Do you *hear* me?"

Sam knew, from this moment forward, Woodchuck really was hers now. The guides were hers. The barn and rafts were hers. The stars and the pines were hers too. If anyone questioned whether Swami was serious about the changes to Woodchuck, or her willingness to sell it, they wouldn't doubt her anymore. Sam nodded, swallowed blood down the back of his throat.

Swami gathered the kids, and in another moment, the headlights of Moon's Jeep carefully carried them away onto the highway toward Governor's. Randy followed them out the driveway and turned toward his mom's place.

Chip limped over to two collapsed lawn chairs, picked them up and shook them open, and set them near the fire.

He sat in one. Sam sat in the other.

"You all right?" Chip asked.

Sam's nose had stopped bleeding. "No," he said.

Chip looked at him with worry in his eyes, was about to speak but then didn't. He let out a long breath and looked at the fire, crossed his feet before the warmth, tucked his hands into his poncho. The coals clinked, glassy and hot. Sam and Chip sat that way for a very long time, uncle and nephew, staring silently into the fire or up at the cold and starlit northern sky.

JUNE

SEVEN

IT WAS DRIZZLING RAIN, AS IT HAD BEEN FOR DAYS. SWAMI INHALED, bare feet planted on the riverbank, then lifted her hands in a wide circle toward the pines. She reached, her limbs like the tree limbs, her breath heavy and full as the fog on the river. Swami exhaled and reached down toward the ground, pressed her whole palms onto the soft mat of white pine needles. The wet pine needles stuck to her hands, a rusted orange latticework. She smiled at DeeDee, who was chewing on a stuffed giraffe beneath her car seat's rain umbrella. *Inhale*, halfway up. *Then exhale*, and fold deep down. Swami sank into this new morning routine with her guests. It was the one real time in her day to relax.

"Okay," said Moon. "Now exhale heavily—*Huh!*—like a bear huff. Get it out, and then rise up to our last tree pose."

Swami let her eyes close and did a bear huff, and heard fifteen other bear huffs around her. Some were halfhearted. Chip's was full and deep and windy. As Swami rose to the trees, she opened her eyes to see Chip rise as steady as a totem pole, palms at sternum, and tuck one massive leg like a wing, the sole of his foot planted inside his other leg. On either side of Chip, the day's guests wobbled for balance, some more than others.

"Inhale pine. Exhale pine. Be pine," said Moon.

Two teenage sisters giggled at each other. Their dad smirked with his eyes closed. Their mom opened one eye and trained it on Moon, breaking form to swat at a mosquito. Randy stood next in line, grumpy, dropping his foot to maintain balance.

This pre-trip routine wasn't for everyone, Swami knew. But it was better. Woodchuck now began each day with guests in the stand of pines below the last rapid. After yoga led by Moon, half of the guides would hike with the guests the two riverside miles to the top of the rapids while the rest of the guides floated a string of rafts down through the flats near the bluffs to meet them at Sand Portage. The guests would breathe, walk, swim the channel, float in some current, enjoy the riverbanks upstream and down. Moon encouraged them to *bathe* in the forest while they hiked, touching the bark of stumps, holding fist-fuls of dirt, pausing to hold a leaf of wild mint on their tongues.

"Swami," complained Chip, the first time she described the new plan. "We don't run trips like that. No one runs trips like that."

"Exactly," she said.

Chip frowned. "People come here to camp and drink and raft, not to *find their center*, as Moon calls it. No offense, Moon."

Swami stopped him. "Most people don't know what they came up here for. The rafting, yes, but there is more to offer here. As it is, Wood-chuck offers moldy life jackets and a frightening bus ride. It's chaos. No more chaos, Chip."

They'd already felt the power of Swami's lack of chaos, her daily regimented order, the way she strode through the recently hard-swept barn with her clipboard filled with action items—paint, clean, mow, weed, spray, disinfect, sleep, rise, eat. Although as the weather warmed it was harder to schedule these. Woodchuck had trips nearly every day of the week now. Most were small, but Chip had established quite a cus-tomer base as the only outfitter in the state for so many years. The barn's face was only about one-third blue, and the old peeling sign bolted to it with the rafting rodent was still hanging.

"If you don't like this," she told Chip, "you can go work for Duncan."

Chip exhaled, looked at her, and then looked around at the much cleaner Woodchuck. He nodded. "Okay, Swami," he said. "Okay."

Swami was impressed by how he didn't offer his complaints again. She was relieved. She needed her guides on board, especially Chip. Duncan had come out to Governor's a few nights back to discuss Swa-mi's offer. He'd revved his bright green Mustang into her campsite and interrupted supper. Swami had steeled herself, invited him into the camper, and proposed the sale of Woodchuck. There was a pot of Moon's ema datshi simmering on the stovetop. Duncan listened, then shook his head, pushed his hand through his hair. He still had two pur-plish rings around both eyes. "I just came out here to tell you my uncle and I aren't interested," he said. "No offense, Swami, but why would we buy a competitor who will most likely disappear? Would you buy it?" Swami didn't answer him. Duncan left in his Mustang, and Swami let the metal blinds in her camper slap shut.

After her talk with Duncan, she raised the pay of all her guides by five dollars a day on the condition they stopped whining during yoga. The extra pay was too much, but ultimately, the expense didn't matter. Duncan was right. It was all or nothing this season. Swami had a long talk with Chip, went over all the books. Swami either cleaned up their act enough to keep Boy Scout jamboree business out of Duncan's hands—and Swami was making call after call to troop leaders based on Chip's old hand-scribbled notepads—or they lost the jamboree work to Duncan, and that would be the end.

Moon was overzealous about the new Woodchuck. Swami had to ask her, gently but firmly, to not press her crystal against the foreheads of the guests. Swami once opened her eyes between sun salutations to see Moon standing awkwardly close to a couple from Waukesha wearing jean shorts, Moon's pink crystal carving a circle shape in the air between them. The man's wife glared at Moon for the rest of the trip. Her husband watched Moon too as she walked up the trail ahead of him, her fluid strides and long, tattooed legs, his eyes always pulled back to this new kind of woman he'd never before encountered.

"But can I *ask* the guests if they want the crystal?" Moon asked.

"No," said Swami. "You may not."

"What about the mining? Can I invite them to my River Keepers party?"

Swami relented. Moon's upcoming event at least projected organization, environmentalism. "That would be okay," she said.

Chip was the biggest surprise. After awkwardly bear-huffing through his first week of yoga—with Dell giggling at his side the few mornings a week she accompanied Swami—Chip began to enjoy "the morning stretch." Chip would huff and bend, and Dell would huff and bend with him, a big bear and a tiny bear, and each day Chip became smoother. Within the space of a few weeks, he could move his big body like river water, heavy feet planted like stones in his sandals. And then he'd hike the guests up the river with Moon, pointing at rapids, explaining the flows with his whole arms, telling stories, making people laugh. Swami was thankful for Chip's willingness, even though he still had his rough edges. One day after a trip, Swami found Chip holding a warrior pose behind the barn with a big, soupy joint between his lips. Some things were nonnegotiable, and Chip's weed was one of them. The man had more or less stayed stoned from dawn to dusk for forty years. Taking it from him would be like taking Valium from a zoo bear.

"It's organic," he said. "Like them fancy crackers you eat. I grow it myself." Smoke dribbled from his big red beard. He spoke while holding the smoke in. "You should have a puff, Swami. It'd be good for you." And then he exhaled the whole lungful of the skunky blue smoke.

"Please go smoke that behind the bus," she said. "Customers are pulling in." And then she tried to walk away without letting Chip see her smile as she shook her head.

"I like Uncle Chips," Dell said as she walked with her mom to yoga this morning. "He's big and funny," she added, skipping down the damp tire track worn in the thick grass.

Swami smiled at her. "He is funny," she said.

"Is Daddy on rafts again today?" Dell asked.

Swami nodded. Throughout all of this, she'd scheduled Sam wherever she wasn't. If she was doing yoga with Dell, Sam was blowing boats upriver. If it was Swami's turn to hike with guests, Sam was watching the kids back at the barn. Sam was spending his nights out at Chip's, and Swami didn't really miss him if she was being perfectly honest with herself. It felt good, in the midst of so much tension, to step away from it. Every marriage counselor they'd ever seen had encouraged them to meet their problems head-on. *Work through it now, or work through it later,* their counselor had said. *But waiting will make it worse.* He used a metaphor about weeding a garden. But it felt good to just step away for a time, ignore the weeds. Their only real contact was when Swami would stand up on the cliff above the gorge to watch the rafts come through. She didn't raft herself. She managed the rafts. She'd count them as they came through, count the money they offered, subtract the debt she owed. Swami would fold her arms atop the bluff, feeling the cold breeze push up from the river water. Sometimes Sam looked up at her as he bobbed past the bend. Other times he didn't. And as soon as Sam rounded the bend, just like that, Swami felt better again.

"And now," said Moon, "final move—press those palms up, up overhead. Up. Up, you beautiful powerful trees! Yes!"

The teenage sisters tried not to laugh. Their dad opened his eyes and looked at Moon. The extended tree pose lifted the whole front of Moon's body, her T-shirt damp from the rain and clinging to her.

"Up," said Moon, panting with exuberance. "Hold, and now slowly release," she said. "Shake it out. Great job, everyone!" She clapped her hands and smiled. Chip and Dell clapped. Randy, done with his duty, smiled at Moon and then stalked off to get the paddles out of the rafting van. The guests smiled and blinked as they stood, a bit bewildered, in their shorts and swim tops, surprised that morning yoga in a wet pine grove in Wisconsin could be this enjoyable.

Swami's new cell phone beeped in her bag as she walked back to the van with Dell. Swami couldn't take a call down here by the river. The signal only reached the hilltops, but Swami had ordered the phone from the nearest store in Green Bay so that she could answer as many booking calls as possible. She didn't want any potential customer to call X-treme while they waited. She saw her mom's number on the screen now, and there was also a missed call from Birdy's in Crivitz. Her mulch was arriving today. Swami stuffed the phone back in her bag and strode toward the shuttle van. Dell trotted behind her. The barn painting had been put on hold because of the wet weather, so Swami turned her efforts elsewhere. Randy helped build a new retaining wall where the overgrown bushes had been. Swami planted hardy perennial grasses and coneflowers along the front of the barn, and a hedge of Proven Winners arborvitaes to guide the flow of foot traffic from the parking area to the check-in. A sitting area with tables and umbrellas was next on her list.

Swami buckled DeeDee's car seat into the rafting van. Dell buckled herself in beside her little sister. The wet weather made the van stink, and Swami made a mental note to add *van scrubbing—Randy or Sam* to her clipboard. This morning, she and the kids would level the black oak mulch over the coneflower beds. Then there would be time for a nap for the girls. Swami could call her mom back as she reached the highway on her way to pick up Darren, who was sorting life jackets and helmets. Then she'd take all three kids back to the river, to her perch, and watch the rafts come through. There'd be time for a bath in the lake before dinner. Swami buckled herself into the driver's seat and waited for Randy to come back after handing out helmets and paddles.

She looked in the rearview mirror at her kids, at the small group of customers getting their paddles, trying on rafting helmets. Sam was the furthest thing from her mind. She wouldn't think about him at all. The day was planned.

•••

"THEM TREES SHE PLANTED LOOK good," said Chip, calling back to his passenger as he motored his dirt bike out onto the highway. Sam had been ditching the pedal bike and began riding out each night on the back of Chip's dirt bike, bear-hugging his thick, fragrant uncle. Tonight he smelled like lemon dish soap. They both did, having spent the last two hours of their day shampooing the inside of the rafting van. The van's faded carpet was like some kind of stiff animal hide, a compost of chips and pretzels and cigarette butts and spills. Behind the passenger seat was a bright orange patch with fuzz growing on it. Sam winced. They took brushes to it. Soapy buckets. Then they Shop-Vacced out the brown, lemony slurry and tossed the water in the bushes. Then they parked it in the basement of the barn with the doors open and the big metal fan blowing through it. Swami had already taken the kids back to the campground. She didn't say goodbye to Sam when she left. She'd just left, kids packed into the cab of Randy's truck to stay dry in the drizzle.

"Yeah," said Sam, turning to look back at the barn, with its new retaining wall and the black mulch and the small row of adolescent cedar trees. "They look expensive."

Chip tilted his head back to speak again, paused, then spoke. "I got a big question I need to ask you," Chip hollered back.

"What is it?"

"I'll tell you out at the farm. I gotta show you something." Chip wrung the throttle on the little bike, and they raced down the edge of the highway.

The ride to Chip's house lasted twenty minutes—the droning putter of the underpowered bike, the smell of cedar in the mist, the narrow curved roads, the sky gray and rippled above the dark pines. Sam wondered about his wife and kids while the bike glided across the pavement, the same way he did when he drifted the rafts downriver, the gravelly sandbars passing beneath the boat. How were the kids sleeping? What did they talk about during breakfast? What did Swami say about Sam? Sam didn't know what else to do but wait for life to turn somehow. He'd think and think until it exhausted him. Swami held every card.

Chip lived in a brown cabin parked on a twenty-five-acre river peninsula with a red cattle gate where the gravel drive met the backroad. He'd inherited the land, an old flood-prone farming plot that went back before his great-grandfather. Two bone-dry cedar posts still stood by the road, nail holes where the sign used to hang that Sam remembered as a kid when he visited with his mom. The sign had been bright white, with green deer antlers and black letters: *Chip and Mary's Deer Farm. Come Meet Old Mossy.* The peninsula itself was composed of a meadow and hardwoods and a boggy strip of land near the drive where the river burrowed a seasonal creek through the neck of the peninsula's oxbow. The cattle gate had a little side trail between its anchor pole and a boulder, wide as a footpath, where Chip would burp his little dirt bike through the weeds without needing to get off and unlock the gate. The guides, and a very few others, were the only ones who knew the combination. Across the culvert and around a slight bend, his cabin and a three-stall machine shed sat in the five-acre clearing. The brown cabin had a sagging screen porch built onto it, as large as the house. The porch overlooked the deer pasture surrounded by a ten-foot-tall fence, a marshy pond at its center. Chip's whitetails grazed and dozed. This early in June, some of the bucks had round-tipped antlers in velvet, which for some reason made Sam think of reindeer more than whitetails. And then he'd think of Christmas, and his wife and kids. Sam liked to watch the oldest buck sleep in the sun. His name was Old Mossy II. His massive antler beams would sometimes nod as he dozed, the pond water shimmering behind him.

Chip pulled his dirt bike into one of three open stalls in a tin-covered machine shed. He turned off the bike and sighed. Wiped his face and beard with his hands.

"I'm all wet," he said.

Sam had taken shelter behind his uncle for most of the ride, and didn't get the worst of it.

"Well, I hate to ask you, bud," said Chip, "but do you have another hour of work left in you? I want to get those fish in the ground in case it rains like they say it will."

Sam stood in the gravel beside the bike, wiped his face with his T-shirt. It still smelled like soap and whatever else had been in the floor of that van.

"No problem," he said.

"Thanks," Chip said, walking toward the row of chest freezers humming in the back of the barn. "Figure there's just two or three bins' worth." Chip pointed to the big storage totes next to the freezers, and then opened a door cut in the shed's back wall that opened into his warm hoop house. Attached to the machine shed, the plastic-covered hoop house was where Chip grew his own food, and more. The first time he showed it to Sam, it was a warm day, and stepping inside was like stepping into a secret garden. The garden was incredibly well-kept, unlike everything else on Chip's property. The sun shone through the opaque plastic tarp. The pea-gravel floor was raked smooth into paths between the raised beds. Chip had seven hoses tied into a sand well that he could turn on with one spigot to water all twenty beds. Chip grew lettuce, tomatoes, squash, green peas on trellises, bushy rows of beans, sweet corn that he pollinated by hand, and his prized plot of marijuana. Sam smelled it the moment he walked in.

"I can get two full growing seasons with the hoop house," Chip had said when he first showed Sam around. "Between each bed, I got these rotating compost piles. They act as heaters. On cold days the compost will actually steam. Pretty neat. New Year's through March is basi-cally the only time all the beds are fallow." Chip was proud of his hoop house, and the system he'd developed over the years to keep himself in canned vegetables and weed.

Chip opened the first freezer now, the one he called the fish freezer because it was filled with dead fish. He grabbed one of the totes and began loading frozen carp into it. If a carp was frozen fast to another, Chip used a big screwdriver he left tied to the freezer to pry them apart. Chip already told him that once or twice a year after a big rain, the scaly fish got trapped in a shallow pool near the culvert creek. They'd swim out over the long grass and then end up lying in the sun once the water receded. For as long as he could remember, his family had made use of the fish, like the Egyptians with the banks of the Nile, he said. He read about it in one of his books. They used the river's fish as food and fertilizer. Whenever the rains and carp came, Chip would wade into the pool to spear a few fresh ones. These he'd chop into thick steaks for his smoker, bringing a few out to Randy's mom in exchange for applesauce and a couple of her frozen venison pasties. Any dead carp went in the garden beds, or into the fish freezer once he'd buried enough.

Chip filled his tub and then Sam's too, and they carried them into the fragrant hoop house. The air was warm and humid inside, which felt good after a rainy day on the water. Sam knelt by one of the empty beds and pressed his hands into the loose, warm soil. He'd helped Chip with this already, and the two worked in silence now, raking a small trench into the dirt with their hands, burying a frozen carp, moving onto the next. Sam lifted a stiff fish into its grave. Its glassy eye was frosted over. Down the row, Chip grunted and dug and pressed the soil down.

Sam was thinking about his kids again. He thought about Swami too. But as he dug another trench he realized that he missed the kids but didn't really miss his wife. The thought stung him with guilt. He knew he was supposed to miss her. But he just couldn't. Their life had grown so fraught and tense, her looks of disappointment so severe and frequent, that Sam felt relief layered on top of the guilt. It felt like setting down a very heavy pack. Sam knew he'd have to lift it again, somehow. But for now his shoulders didn't miss the nearly constant weight of his wife's displeasure.

"Chip," said Sam.

Chip grunted in response.

"What happened with you and Aunt Mary?"

Chip froze. Then he started digging again, pulled a frozen carp over the lip of the tub, and flopped it down in the dirt. "She's gone," he said. "Didn't want me anymore. Didn't want *this*." He gestured at the hoop house, and the cabin beyond it, and the river beyond that.

"But she did once."

Chip sighed, sat back from his work. "She did." He eyeballed Sam. "It doesn't have to be that way for you and Swami, if that's what you're thinking of. Is it the money?"

Sam nodded. He'd told Chip about the loss of his teaching job. "But it's not just money," Sam said. "Things just don't work, lots of things."

"Is it your weiner?" Chip asked quietly.

Sam laughed. "No. She's just mad. She's been mad for a long time."

Chip nodded. "With me and Mary the problem was we couldn't have kids, and then it was money too, and then it was everything. I was happy to raft and live out here, and she was too for a long time. But then she wanted kids. We couldn't have kids. Then she started complaining we were too broke to raise kids anyway." Chip sat back from the garden bed for a moment, brushed his hands off and looked at them. "I started the deer farm after that. Families came out to see them. A little extra income. But it still wasn't enough. I wasn't. The river wasn't. Nothing was."

Chip shook his head. There was more there to tell. Sam could see it in the way his uncle looked out across the soil, wincing at some memory.

"Sorry to bring it all up," Sam said. "I just wanted to ask if you had advice."

Chip wagged his head, took a deep breath, and puffed his cheeks out.

"I'll tell you if I can think of any," he said. "I'm not really a model for married life." He huffed through his nose and smirked. "Just bring your wife out here to bury dead fish, show her the cabin's screen porch. I'm sure she'll melt into your arms once she sees all she's been missing."

Sam allowed himself a smile. "Well, I think it's nice out here," he said.

"I like it too," agreed Chip.

They dug in silence again, went out to grab one more tub full of fish. When they finished up, Chip washed his hands with a hose and then walked over to his prized plants. He rubbed a few swelling buds between his fingers, smiled at them. The riper buds seemed more animal than plant, furry clumps and knuckles frosted with silvery feathers and orange hair. Chip talked to the plants—*There's a good one*; *Keep at it*; *Oh, wow*—as he rustled his hands through their leaves. The plants released their sharp fragrance in return.

Sam washed his hands and sat on an overturned bucket in the gravel. Chip continued inspecting his plants, picking a leaf now and then, squeezing the buds, poking his fingers down in the rich soil near their roots. Sam felt the guilt again, sitting here in the warm greenhouse instead of the camper with his family. He felt tired and dirty, but he also felt at rest out here, and the rest felt very good. For as long as he could remember, he'd just wanted to stop. Sam was, used to be, a good teacher. He'd worked hard in his classes, trying to get the kids interested in ceramics when all they were interested in was one another. And now the school wasn't interested in ceramics either. Sam had never been after money. He'd been after rest. He'd chosen art because it calmed him. He'd chosen teaching because of the summers off. He'd chosen Swami because she once felt that same way. Swami felt like good shade. Sam once read a Tammy Tells article in a paper left open in the teachers' lounge in which a man wrote in to describe how his wife's presence literally lowered his blood pressure. They verified it with a nurse. Reading that made Sam feel punched in the gut. Swami had become spiky by then. The thought of finding rest in her presence was so foreign now. Sam didn't know what to do.

"Sam, I got that thing to tell you."

Sam didn't respond right away. He was nearly falling asleep. It was dark outside now. He'd forgotten about Chip's big question.

"It's about money," he said. "More than you or me or Aunt Mary or Swami ever seen."

Sam sat up.

Chip turned to him, worry on his face. "It's about more than money too. Come on, I gotta show you something."

Back in the machine shed, Chip grabbed a big flashlight and handed Sam his rain jacket. Chip started walking toward the meadow along the deer fence, out toward the far wood line. Sam followed. The grass was tall and wet. Chip swiped his flashlight into the pasture, and the eyes of many grazing deer lit up like diamonds. Chip put the light on the ground again and kept marching beyond the fences.

"What's this about?" Sam asked.

"I got a letter in the mail. And then two phone messages this week. I didn't answer them yet. It's that new mine, NorthSky. They want to buy this whole peninsula from me."

"You serious?"

Chip gave a big nod.

"What are you going to do?" Sam asked.

"I don't know, bud. Thing is, this land doesn't just belong to me, and NorthSky isn't the only one who offered to buy it. You'll see." He pushed through the wet bushes at the forest's edge. He stepped over a dead, dry tree, and then held back some low-hanging branches. "Watch your step," he said.

Sam stepped and held back the wet pine branch. He hadn't been back here in Chip's woods yet. The driveway was at the neck of the peninsula, the cabin and deer fence in the middle where it broadened. Back here, the ground rose up toward the peninsula's main bulb. The forest opened up between massive oaks. Chip walked another hundred yards in and then stopped and pointed the beam of his flashlight between the massive trunks. The ground was a wet mat of leaves, a few ferns and leggy oaks trying to grow up among the giants. A few rock outcroppings pushed the forest floor up in places. The ground was higher here. Eventually, it would become an island.

Chip panted from the hike. Sam waited.

"Indian mounds," breathed Chip.

Sam looked closer at the rock outcroppings. They weren't out-croppings at all. They were burial mounds. Chip pointed his light from one to another. Sam counted three of them.

"There's two more over the rise where the river slopes down," said Chip. He spoke quietly. "They're Menominee. Pete came back here with me and one of his elders once. It's when I met him, really. He was just a local teenager, back when Mary was still here. The old guy said his tribe would have sold this land, along with most of northeastern Wiscon-sin, to the U.S. government back in the 1850s, which then tried to push the tribe further west, to Minnesota. The Iroquois had already been pushed here from out east. My great-grandfather, your great-great, bought this parcel when Thunderwater was established a few decades later. The settlers didn't know that the Indian word for *thundering waters* wasn't even a Menominee word. It was Iroquois."

Sam didn't know what to say. He looked at the dark, silent mounds, the very old trees. He felt like he should talk quietly, so he did.

"What are you going to do?" Sam asked.

Chip wiped mist from his beard, shook his head. "The Menomi-nee tribe never went to Minnesota. And the *treaties* they made have been argued in courts for the last two hundred years, still are today. The tribe offered to buy this peninsula from me too. Mary said not a chance. They offered thirty-two thousand dollars. This was maybe fifteen years ago."

"So you didn't sell."

"To be honest, I'm glad they didn't offer more. This little piece of land is the only home I've ever known too. It's my sacred place too. I used to sit out here when I was a kid. Kissed my first girlfriend back here too. Right there, actually." Chip shined his light at the base of a big oak. "Jenny Welston."

"What about NorthSky? What are they offering?"

"In their letter they said five hundred and eighty thousand."

Sam choked, started coughing in the forest.

Chip waited. "And maybe more, pending all of the tests they'd do." He shook his big head. "There must be some real valuable vein of dirt beneath us, beneath these mounds. Who knew?"

"Have you told anyone else?"

"Just you. Don't tell Moon about it either. She's been working hard on her River Keepers party, out at Randy's ma's. In fact it'd be better if you didn't tell anybody about it. I just don't know what to do. It's an awful lot of money they're offering."

Chip looked at his nephew, and then out at the forest again. Sam and his uncle just stared into the dark forest together. He imagined all the different people who'd walked here, who'd called it home. The warmth from the hike had left Sam's raincoat. He felt cold.

"I just remembered a piece of advice my grandpa gave me when me and Mary were thinking of getting married. He still lived out here then. He said, all you have to do is love her. That's all you have to do."

"All you have to do is love her," repeated Sam.

Chip nodded.

"But how do you love her when she's *so damn mad*?" Sam asked.

"That's the trick," said Chip. "You gotta love her even when she stops loving you back. I didn't know how. Grandpa never told me that part."

Sam nodded, looked off into the woods.

A massive owl swept silently down through the trees, glided off into the shadows beyond the reach of Chip's light.

"Well," said Chip, a few breaths after the owl had gone. Without saying more, he turned around and started for the cabin. Sam followed close behind, arms bundled around himself until the walking might warm him again.

EIGHT

THE FRESH GRAVEL ARRIVED EARLY, ON A RARE DAY OF SUNSHINE and no river trip. Grandpa Birdy was still out on Woodchuck's driveway, showing his two teenaged workers how to grade the gravel. Swami loved the sound of the small, beeping dump truck, and the ringing of metal rakes smoothing the stones. Work was being accomplished. Swami waved at Birdy in his truck as she stepped hurriedly into the barn. DeeDee squirmed with a dirty diaper now seeping through her yellow-striped onesie. Swami also needed to catch a call from the Boy Scouts. And Moon would be here soon. Today was Moon's River Keepers party, and Swami had told her she'd head out early to help set up.

DeeDee squirmed again as Swami unbuttoned the bottom of her onesie while she ducked in from the humid heat, into the cool darkness of the barn. Inside, Darren and Dell were sorting bins of helmets, or were at least supposed to be. At present, the two were laughing and butting heads, holding the oversized yellow helmets over their ears, circling each other like young rams.

"Darren and Dell, I need those bins done before Moon arrives. We're leaving soon."

Darren didn't hear, or pretended not to. He scuffed his foot on the sandy concrete, and charged his little sister. Their heads met. Dell fell on her butt and cried. DeeDee pushed against Swami now, tried to climb out of her arms, and yellow poop seeped out of the back of her diaper and onto Swami's arm.

"Darren!" Swami snapped. "Help her up! Apologize!"

Darren looked at his mom as if noticing her for the first time. His shoulders slumped. "Fine," he said.

Dell wailed.

"Now!" Swami said.

DeeDee cried too. Swami put her on a beach towel on the table next to the rafting waivers and undressed her. The box of diapers Swami kept beneath the table was empty, but she already had DeeDee naked and kicking. The tiny girl had little patience for diaper changes. It was so far one of her most developed personality traits.

"Darren, please get me a diaper from the cabinet."

He was still lifting Dell from the floor, and so he let her drop back down and ran to the cabinet, relieved of his little sister. Dell bellowed in rage.

"Here, Mom," Darren said, so sweetly.

"Darren," whispered Swami, wiping the baby. DeeDee kicked at her mother's hands. "Please go and help up Dell, immediately."

"You told me to help you," he complained.

Swami couldn't whisper anymore. "Darren!" she said, with enough heat that her son's face began to redden and pinch. He stomped over and hoisted his crying sister to her feet.

The phone rang. Swami hurriedly sandwiched DeeDee into the fresh diaper. Swami balled up the soiled outfit and tossed it onto the wooden steps in the corner, wiped her arm off with a baby wipe. She needed this call to go well. She needed to write Birdy his check. She needed Darren to help his sister sort the helmets, and for DeeDee to take her nap. Swami lifted the diaper-clad girl to her shoulder.

"Darren, Dell?" she said. "I'm sorry for yelling. Mommy needs to take this call, and it is very important, and could you please turn on the fan? It's so damp in here. Thank you." She patted DeeDee's back. "All better," she said, as she let the phone ring once more and took a breath.

All better. Oh, how Swami wanted to believe that. As Swami grasped the clunky old beige phone with its beige cord, a memory came back to her she hadn't thought of in a long time. She was nine or ten, the family back from California, and she woke to the sounds of an argument her parents were having about Dad needing to use the car—the rusted Buick with one mismatched wheel—last minute on a grocery day. He was covering a high school hockey game for the local newspaper. When her dad took the car, the apartment went quiet, and Swami slipped barefoot into the kitchen to find her mom silently sobbing with her back turned to Swami, pressing her fists against the counter, wearing one of her nice robes—one of the old ones—with the belt now frayed. Swami's mom beat her fist against the counter, and the beige phone dropped from its wobbly receiver and dangled by its cord from the cabinet. It was the first time in her life Swami felt the pressure to provide stability. And it was the first day in her life she learned how effective she could be. She cleaned her room that day without being asked, and then cleaned the living room, and when she asked her mom if she would like the dishes done, she saw something visibly relax in her mom's body. It felt good to see that, to feel that sort of agency. So Swami developed it, refined it, owned it. It was that same year her mom got into real estate.

"Woodchuck Rafting Company." Swami smiled into the phone. "Yes! Oh, so glad to hear from you. Thanks for returning my call. I just wanted to discuss this year's Labor Day scout jamboree—what's that?" She paused. "That's correct."

Darren and Dell began to argue about the helmets. Darren was in no mood to be nice, and Dell wasn't taking it. Swami snapped an angry finger at them. "Wait, I'm sorry, could you repeat that? But as I understand you've booked with us every year during the jamboree." Ice crept through Swami's body. Not another one. The troop leaders had been calling one by one—or Swami had been calling them—to say they were going to "try out the new competition, just this once." They were nice about it, but there weren't too many left. Swami had convinced a newly organized troop from Green Bay to come out in mid-July for an early courtesy trip. It would be just the leaders, and it was critical it went well. Swami forced a smile into the phone, bounced up and down with her daughter.

"Well, may I ask what kind of price they offered you? I'm sure we can offer a better one. Also, we've offered free courtesy trips for just the troop leaders to scout us out." She leaned into her pun and smiled far too broadly into the phone now. "We're better on the water here at Woodchuck. Say again?"

Swami looked out at the square of light. Birdy and his crew were touching up the edges of the fresh gravel. It seemed so futile now, so pathetic. They'd lost another big booking. Swami talked quietly into the phone now. "No, we do not have zip lines," she said. "Yes. Thank you for calling. I hope to see you next season as well."

Swami gently placed the receiver back on the hook, the way her mom had done so many years ago. She leaned her forehead against the wooden pole for a moment with her eyes closed. With this last booking with Duncan, there wasn't much jamboree pie left to be had. Even if Swami could impress the leaders of the Green Bay troop, that booking would be barely enough to keep them afloat. Duncan was right. Woodchuck was going to simply disappear. The thrumming metal fan oscillated behind the wet life jackets, lifting a musty scent from the floor. Darren and Dell argued, and Swami just let them. DeeDee grabbed her mom's nose. Swami hoisted the girl in front of her and looked right into the baby's blue eyes, the whole cosmos kept there. DeeDee gurgled. "It's okay, sweet baby," she whispered, just focusing on those beautiful eyes. "It's all going to be okay."

"All righty!" said Birdy. "Gravel's in!" He stepped into the barn from the bright light and wiped his forehead with a handkerchief, the two teenagers horsing around outside by the red truck. Moon's Jeep pulled in from the road, and the two boys stopped to watch her drive past.

"Boy, them arborvitaes and mulch look sharp. You did a nice job, Swami. Hey, kiddos!"

"Birdy!" said Dell. She remembered the suckers he always had.

"That's *Grandpa* Birdy to you, tater tot." He smiled at her, folded his handkerchief into his back pocket, and then delivered two small suckers from his overalls pocket.

He turned his attention back to Swami. She must have looked the way she felt, because Birdy's brow furrowed a bit when he saw her.

"So, how you holding up?" he said.

"We're holding," she said.

He gave a kind and commiserating nod. "First year in business is rough," he said. "Livin' on a prayer, like Bon Jovi says. Gotta hold on to what you got." He looked at the kids, who were now sorting the helmets more happily with suckers in their mouths.

Swami laughed. "What do you know about Bon Jovi?" She got the checkbook and a pen out of the money box.

"Fourteen grandkids and two great-grandkids," he said. "There's two of 'em out there. They're good boys. I let them do their radio stations when we're out working. Bon Jovi ain't bad, but I much prefer Dwight Yoakam if we're talking new stuff. Now, *that's* a young man who can sing."

Swami smiled. She held the checkbook open with one free hand. "It was three seventy-five, correct?"

"Make it an even three fifty," he said. "This job went pretty quick. Sun's shining."

"Thank you, Birdy," she said.

Moon bounced in. "This place is looking *great*," she gushed, and then to Birdy, "Hello, I'm Moon."

Birdy looked a bit confused by Moon's name, and probably her braids and tattoos too. But then he shrugged. "Birdy," he said, and smiled and shook his head. He was a man who could let things wash over him, Swami thought. He'd clearly seen enough in life to not be baffled by it anymore, or just to not sweat being baffled. Dell and Darren were done with helmets. Moon took DeeDee into her arms while Swami finished writing the check.

"You know," said Birdy, stuffing his hands in his pockets, "I seen this rodeo clown once at the county fairgrounds. He was dressed up like one of them Spaniard bullfighters. And when them bulls came at him, he just stepped out of the way and yelled, *Olay!*"

Birdy accepted the check from Swami and did a stiff hop-skip in his baggy overalls, waved the check in the air like a matador.

"That's what you gotta do in life," he said. "*Olay!* That and keep your pump gun handy."

Dell laughed at him.

"That's good advice," Swami said. "Thanks again, Birdy."

"Here's some more," he said. "Two things. First, if you want some scaffolding for your paint project, I got some and you can use it. I can have the boys set it up. They need some chores this week. It'd be quicker than ladders, yeah?"

"Okay," said Swami, "but I'd like to pay you for it."

He swatted the air. "It's been collecting dust for ten years," he said.

"Next time we get out this way we'll bring it along. *Second thing*. You still gotta come bowling. The whole family comes, all the grandkids. These kiddos would have fun. You'd have fun. Moon, you come too. We go every Saturday at Rita's." And then he nodded as if that settled it.

"Sounds fun," said Moon. "Hey, do you want to come to my River Keepers party tonight?" She pulled an invitation card from her back pocket. It had the address to Randy's house on it. She'd been handing them out for two weeks.

"A what party?" he said. He lifted the card close to his eyes, squinting at it just right. "Say, I know this address."

"River Keepers. I'm raising awareness about the environmental hazards of the prospective mining operation. There's a town hall next week, and I want people to be informed of the realities of the proposal."

"This is Debbie's place, no?"

Moon nodded.

"Boy, she's a good cook. Gave me pasties when I brought her a load of brick. Buys a lot of ammunition from me too."

"She's making pasties tonight."

"I'd love to, but I can't. Already got supper plans out at my daughter's. But thank you for the invite, though." He handed the card back to her. "Nice to meet you, Moon. Swami. Kiddos."

"Bye, Birdy," said Dell, her sucker wedged in her cheek. Darren echoed her.

He waved as he waddled back out into the sunlight.

Moon took a big breath. Exhaled.

"You ready for your big day?" Swami asked. Moon had been distracted with stacks of papers from the county surveyor's office, weekly runs to the county library for printing.

Moon smiled. "I'm nervous," she said. DeeDee batted Moon's cheek. "Yes, I am," Moon said to the baby. "I'm nervous."

"Don't be nervous," said Swami. "We all support you. And Randy is utterly in love with you."

Moon looked at her, tried not to smile. "Well," she said.

Swami squeezed her arm, took DeeDee back. "Let's go," she said.

•••

THEY LOCKED UP THE BARN and drove out together in the rafting van so they could all fit. Swami didn't mind transporting her kids in it as much since it'd been cleaned. Nevertheless, with the afternoon sunshine, they rode with the windows down. Dell and DeeDee fell asleep almost immediately, their heads slumped in their car seats. Darren was hungry, but he was worried about eating a pasty.

"What is it, anyway?" he said.

"You'll love it," said Moon, turning backward in her seat. "You ever eat a calzone?"

Darren nodded.

"It's like a Northwoods calzone. Meat, potatoes, all wrapped up in a handheld pie crust. You dunk it in gravy or ketchup. It's what the copper miners used to take down in the mines for lunch. And Debbie's are the best in a hundred-mile radius."

"Remember how good Moon's ema datshi was when you tried that?" Swami said.

"I guess," said Darren, burying his nose in a comic book. "It sounds good with the ketchup."

They drove about fifteen miles in silence, out onto a narrow, winding back road.

"So, about Debbie," said Moon, a bit quieter so that only Swami might hear.

Swami nodded. Moon paused.

"What about Debbie?"

"I'm really impressed that she allowed me to host the party out at her place. She can be a bit squirrelly around strangers."

"What do you mean, *squirrelly*?"

Moon shook her head. "I probably shouldn't even say anything. Debbie's the coolest woman I've ever met. Totally self-reliant, loyal and kind like Randy. Really good. Salt of the earth. She just has this really strong sense of her people, maybe, that can make others nervous around her. She's protective."

Swami waited for more. "What I should say is she's the kindest person I've ever met, but really strong if she feels threatened. Don't mess with her family, you know? I guess that's not much different from anyone else, especially around here. *Don't* mess with the family. It's just her and Randy out there, but Randy has told me some stories about her from when he was back in high school. This is the turn, up here."

Swami tried to absorb all of that in a positive light as she turned onto a gravel road. It was a beautiful road with some old cow pastures on one side and green, open hardwoods on the other. The gravel road rolled gently up and down. Bright-stemmed tiger lilies grew thick along the ditch, pushing up stiff clumps of unopened bulbs.

"Oh, look, she made a sign," said Moon.

A gravel drive was attached to the gravel road, and at its entrance a homemade sign leaned against a maple. *MOON'S RIVER PARTY*, it read.

"That's so nice," Swami said, glad to see support for her nervous friend, and also proof of Debbie's warmth.

Swami turned onto the driveway. A black cow gate with a *NO TRESPASSING* sign was chained open. Unlike the rest of the forest, a thick stand of pines had been planted here to block any view from the road. Swami drove slowly into the pine thicket. There were signs nailed to the trees, hand-painted on boards. *TURN AROUND. BEWARE OF DOGS. BEWARE OF OWNER.*

Moon gave a nervous laugh. "Keeps the teenagers away," she said.

The driveway took a hard right-hand bend, deeper into the pine thicket. Swami nearly yelped out loud. There was a scarecrow with a pig mask hanging in a tree. Swami hit the brakes. The scarecrow held a square sheet of board in front of its chest with a target painted on it, peppered with a shotgun blast.

"What is *that*, Mom?"

"Oh no, I asked Randy to take that down for the day," murmured Moon.

"What *is* that?" Darren asked again.

Swami looked up quickly to see Darren gaping wide-eyed. Dell was still sleeping, thankfully. Swami accelerated quickly past the terrifying scarecrow. There wasn't room in the driveway to turn around. She had to go forward if she wanted to leave. And she did. Why on earth would Moon choose to host a gathering out here? Woodchuck would have been worlds more welcoming. Swami had never thought she'd be able to say that.

Around the next bend the pines opened up again, and a bright meadow was beyond it. In the center of the meadow was a bright mint-green trailer house, neat as a pin, with a small and freshly painted barn behind it with a green single-cab truck with a wooden flatbed parked inside. The grass was level and mown. There were flower beds near a square wooden deck, a huge garden with a fence on fresh poles and neat rows of baby vegetables. There was a massive shade tree with a child's swing hanging in it, and a couple of rows of hay bales arranged in a circle. The smell of wonderful cooking drifted toward them. Randy stepped out on the porch and waved to them, and then bounded down the weedless driveway with tin snips in his hand.

"Hey, guys!" he said, leaning into Moon's window. He must have seen the look on Swami's face. He lifted the tin snips and smiled. "I'm going to take down some of Ma's decorations."

"Has anyone else arrived yet?" Moon asked.

Randy tilted his head. "Well, you're two hours early, right? But not yet. It's gonna be great, Moon. This is the first step. You guys can head in. I'll be right back."

Randy trotted off. It calmed Swami a bit to see the flower beds, the trim house, and even Randy too. She eased the van forward again, parked it, careful to keep her tires on the gravel. She didn't want to step on any toes here. No toes. No grass. No family.

The door to the trailer opened. And a short, thick woman wearing an apron stepped out of it. She was beaming and waving them in with a spatula before they even stepped from the vehicle.

"Hey, Moony!" she said. Her voice was raspy but warm. Her apron had apples on it. She had long brown, graying hair tied back in a pony-tail. She wore a big, light-colored, flowing sundress, and colorful neck-laces of polished beads. She stepped all the way out on the porch now and put her hands on her powerful hips.

Moon walked toward her while Swami unbuckled the waking Dell.

"Hey, Debbie," said Moon.

Debbie gave Moon a hug.

"Moon, I drank half a beer because I'm nervous, but the pasties are nearly done, buncha cookies too. I had Randy put the hay bales out by the tree for seats, but he can rearrange 'em if you want."

"No, it's all so wonderful. Thank you so much again. I don't know how to thank you."

"Take that son of mine off my hands," she said, giving Moon a pat on the arm. "The two of you have much in common."

Swami arrived next to them with a sleepy Dell and curious Darren standing beside her, DeeDee sleeping and wrapped on her chest. Darren was looking out at the barn, where there were two cows and a handful of pigs taking turns at a water trough. Beyond the barn sat a small red tractor in front of a small field of what looked to be baby cabbages, green puffs of leaves dotting the slope in rows.

"And you must be Swami, hey?" the woman asked.

Swami smiled and nodded.

"Well, it's nice to meet you. Call me Debbie. Chip's family's my family, the way I see it." And she gave Swami a side hug so as not to squeeze the baby.

"Thanks so much for having us out," Swami said.

"Oh my goodness, look at this," Debbie said, stopped by the sight of DeeDee sleeping with her mouth open. "What a beauty she is."

Swami smiled and angled herself so Debbie could get a better look at DeeDee.

"And who are these guys? Youse guys like pasties?"

"This is Darren and his little sister Dell."

"I'm three," said Dell.

"Well, that means you get at least three cookies, then," Debbie said. Then she shook Darren's hand and pumped his tiny arm with her big one. She had the arms of a farmer. "Good to meet you, young man," she said.

Darren smiled. "I never had a pasty before," he said.

Debbie stood up straight.

"Prepare to be dazzled, young man," she said with complete sincerity. "Come on in, everybody. I got coffee brewing. Juice for the kids. Just kick your boots off at the door." She turned and hiked back toward the house. Her whole body rocked side to side with each step. She walked with a limp she didn't seem to notice.

Inside, the home was pristine. And nothing looked like a trailer home. Swami remembered the cheap apartments of her youth, carpet lifting at the edges, cheap cabinets, the sound of hollow walls and floors. Nothing in this place was like that. There was a long kitchen with what appeared to be handmade cupboards, a range oven with six burners, thick chopping block countertops, iron racks with cast-iron pots and pans of all sizes hanging from them. Adjacent the kitchen was a small living room with a wooden box TV, two aged recliners with quilts folded over the backs, a leather couch with some cactuses growing on the windowsill behind it. And the smell was mouthwatering. Heaps of golden-brown pasties filled green glass trays. Debbie stooped and pulled two sheet pans of cookies from the oven. She put Moon to work chopping purple and green cabbage for her coleslaw. She put Swami in charge of ice cube trays and drinking glasses. The kids sat in wooden chairs at a small round table, and Debbie set them up with some juice.

"That's Mike," said Debbie, noticing Swami looking at a picture of a man in uniform next to a cased and folded American flag. "Randy's dad. My man." There was a wedding picture there too. A laughing man with hippie hair and a tan suit holding a beautiful young woman wearing a white dress in his arms. In the picture, the young Debbie threw her head back and laughed, holding a wreath of flowers on her head with one hand, her long brown hair trailing down. In the military photo, Randy's father's flowing hair had been clipped short, but he was still smiling. Then there was the folded flag in its glass-covered box. After that the wall only had a few pictures of a lone woman, alone with a baby, a toddler, a teen, Randy.

Debbie doled out steaming chocolate cookies onto a plate in front of the kids. "They're too hot to eat," she said to Dell. "But in a few minutes you can help yourselves." She didn't ask Swami's permission, but Swami didn't feel offended at all. This was Debbie's house, land, kitchen. It was welcoming, but Swami got the sense she was just along for the ride this evening.

The kids each ate a cookie when they cooled. Debbie prepared her coleslaw in big tin bowls, told them about the house and land, julienned a carrot. The land was her father's. She and Mike had put the trailer on it before Vietnam with plans to build a home. She and Randy had ended up just rebuilding the trailer over the years, walls, wiring, basement, everything. "Six-inch studs in these walls," she said. "Strong as a log cabin. The tax people still think it's just an unimproved trailer property. And I never let the government step one foot inside here, that's for sure. They can try it, but they don't." She huffed through her nose and set down her chef knife and placed big fistfuls of cabbage into her bowl, a handful of carrots, and one of onion. She shook in sugar and salt straight from their bags, two kinds of vinegar and oil, and then after tossing it with her hands licked a finger and nodded. She rinsed her hands in the sink and then wiped them on her apple apron.

"Looks like Chip's here with your man, Swami." She nodded out the window, laughed. "Chipper and his dirt bike. You know I seen him drive that thing in a snowstorm once? Pure blizzard, and here he come, up the driveway in a foot of snow, beard pure ice. He needed sauerkraut. Drove out in a blizzard for a jar of my kraut." The kids laughed at this.

Swami looked out the window and saw Randy talking with Chip and Sam. Chip parked his bike around the side of the house, near the barn. Swami saw Sam laugh and felt her jaw get a bit tense. Tonight would require them to be in the same area, to be married in front of strangers for an extended period. She took a deep breath.

"Oh no, you *don't*. Not again, you buzzards!" Debbie yelled, peering out at the window. She ripped off her apron and balled it up, threw it on the counter.

Swami and the kids startled. Moon stood.

"What is it?" Moon asked. "What's wrong?"

Debbie opened a small broom closet. She came out holding a scoped rifle, and slung it over her head on its leather sling. The sling had cartridges in it, like a bandolier some cowboy might wear. The brass cartridges looked to Swami to be the size of small carrots. Swami slid her chair back. She feared for Sam now, as Debbie made her way across the kitchen.

"Turkeys!" Debbie answered. "They been plucking my cabbages. Excuse me," she said, yanking open the door. "Didn't mean to startle anyone."

Swami stood by her kids as they stood on their chairs and watched Debbie storm across her yard toward the barn and pigs. She moved fast. Randy and Chip and Sam watched her go. Sam looked as startled as Swami felt.

By the corner of the barn, Debbie crouched and huffed out to her little red tractor. She peeked around its tall rear wheel. Swami could see four redheaded turkeys strutting into the cabbage field from the wood line. The turkey in front reached down and pecked at a baby cabbage, pulled it up from the dirt and shook it and dropped it.

Debbie wrapped the leather sling around her forearm and worked the bolt action in one smooth movement, braced her rifle on the knob of the tractor tire and peered through the scope.

BOOM!

A big flash erupted from the muzzle and echoed through the field. Pigeons flew out of the barn above her. The lead turkey slammed over in a puff of feathers near the cabbage he'd pulled. The other three turkeys started running.

"Whoa!" said Darren.

Dell covered her ears. Swami scooped her up from the chair and hoisted her onto her hip, let her hide her face in her mother's hair.

Debbie worked the bolt action again.

BOOM!

Swami jumped. She could feel the report in her chest. Debbie nailed another turkey, dumping it between cabbage rows. At this point the remaining two turkeys had enough running speed to lift off. They cackled madly, taking off in a beeline for the far woods. Debbie rose with them, chambering another round into her incredibly loud rifle.

She moved to the front of the tractor and rested her rifle across the metal arms of its loader bucket. The turkeys flew in a slow arc. Debbie's rifle followed them.

BOOM!

The turkey flying in front dropped from the sky and fell in the damp cabbage field, black feathers drifting down like chaff above it. The last turkey swerved and then flapped wildly, bursting into the tree line and snapping branches as it flew.

Debbie stood to her full height, looking out over the fields.

Everyone stared. Randy gave a shy glance back at the trailer. Debbie ejected an empty round from her rifle, nodded, and started walking back toward the trailer. She spoke to Randy as she passed.

The door to the trailer opened again. Darren scurried down from his chair. Swami realized she'd been holding her breath. Debbie put the rifle back in the closet next to the broom.

"Turkeys!" She smiled at them all. "I asked Randy and the boys to go grab 'em." She winked at Darren. "They eat our cabbage, we eat them."

Debbie appeared to notice the looks of surprise in the kitchen, but also seemed to shrug them off. Swami was somehow both oddly enamored and afraid of her.

"How's them cookies, sweetheart?" Debbie smiled at Dell, who nodded politely in Swami's arms.

In another hour, all was set. The afternoon sun was behind the trees, and the shadows grew long. The pasties sat warm beneath tinfoil on a picnic table under the big tree, alongside condiments and coleslaw and four sweating plastic pitchers of iced lemonade. Moon's River Keepers talk was at five. It was now five fifteen and the hay bale seats were nearly empty, except for Woodchuck employees and three others who'd driven in very slowly around quarter to. Swami made the extra effort to go out and greet visitors with her baby in her arms after that driveway experience. They seemed relieved to see her.

Moon bit her lip in the kitchen. She had tears in her eyes. "I'm embarrassed," she said. "All this work, you know, all this food. You did so much and hardly anyone came. I don't understand."

"We came," Swami said, and gave Moon's arm a squeeze. "And so did that young guide from X-treme and that retired couple." Swami looked out the window at them. The young guide's name was Sally, and she was a fierce-looking brunette college student who'd driven herself out in a Ford Fiesta. She was the one Swami first saw at X-treme. The retired couple were both professors emeritus who had moved up to the river after careers with the University of Wisconsin. They sat on hay bales eating pasties, listening as the young guide, Sally, gave some speech with her arms. "They're having a good time out there," Swami said. "This is a great start."

Debbie gave Moon a paper towel. Moon crumpled it and wiped her eyes.

"Honey," Debbie said. When Moon wouldn't look her in the eye, Debbie gently took Moon's hand in her own. Moon looked at her.

"Sweetheart. Don't worry about the pasties. They freeze good, and I like cooking. Moon?"

Moon looked right at her. She took a deep breath and gathered herself.

"Moon, you just give us the talk you came to give." She stood up taller when she said it, and Moon stood up a bit taller too. "You give your talk."

Moon nodded. Debbie and Swami went out and fixed plates and sat under the tree. Swami sat two hay bales away from Sam, nodded at him. She was thankful the kids sat between them. On the other side of Sam sat Chip and Randy. Pete came out to listen, and his big husky sat with him, panting happily for bits of pasty Pete dropped in the grass.

"Bear got herself pregnant." Pete beamed. "She's been extra hungry."

Next to the dog sat the retired couple and the college student. She was still describing her winter break trip, something about her and a friend protesting a logging claim in Northern California. Moon had her allies, even if it was a small bunch.

Darren was engrossed in his plate of food. Dell wiped her blond hair from her eyes and took a big gulp from her iced lemonade. Swami took one bite and then another, larger one. She smiled. The pasty was excellent, a pocket of buttery pie crust filled with spices and steaming potatoes and venison.

"Swami," said Sam. "I wanted to mention that Smitty, the mechanic in town, finally has the parts in for the camper. He said he could come out next week to get a start on it."

"Good," Swami said. Her tone was so flat, cold. She couldn't help it. Sam felt right now like one of the other strangers sitting in the circle.

"I can come out with Smitty, if you want," Sam said. "Make sure it gets done right. I was thinking too that maybe once the Brave is running, I could take the kids on a test drive out to Chip's place. Show Dell the D—E—E—R."

"Deer," said Darren, chewing his food.

"Where, Darren, where?" said Dell.

Swami shook her head. "Sam, I don't want the kids out there." Swami said it quietly enough that Chip couldn't overhear her. Sam winced, paused, opened his mouth to speak again, but Moon had come out now and made her way to the center of the bales. She carried an easel and an armful of poster boards covered in a sheet. Randy leapt to his feet to help Moon situate the easel legs in the grass.

Debbie made everyone shush when Moon was ready. Swami was thankful to pay attention to the presentation, to have a reason she and Sam couldn't talk anymore.

"Thank you for coming," Moon said. She'd removed the sheet from her easel, and the first poster said *River Keepers* in a bright blue script above a photograph of Piers Gorge, and then in subtext, *A Body for Water.*

She pushed her hair behind her ears in a way that reminded Swami of Dell, both shy and incredibly brave at the same moment.

"To be honest, as Debbie's wonderful feast attests," Moon began, and people applauded Debbie's cooking, "I was hoping we'd have a group of at least fifty people. We are going to need a hundred. But tonight's talk is about doing what's right, and what's right is worth doing, and one or two people can start a movement toward what's right, if they choose. And I'm thankful to each of you for choosing to be here."

"Damn right," blurted the college girl. Debbie frowned at her.

Swami frowned at Sam. What was the right thing to do about him? Here were her beautiful kids sitting on hay bales. And here were their two parents, failing at being married, failing at making money. Swami felt loneliness again, and frustration too. To her mind, they were crumbling, and Sam was still buzzing on about deer farms, asking for more, irritating her. Sam the mosquito.

"Tonight is a first step," said Moon. "Next week, NorthSky is hosting the first of two town halls in Thunderwater. They've also set up a prospecting headquarters near the river just outside of town, two construction trailers and a tall chain-link fence."

Moon removed the first poster to reveal another, a topographical map of Thunderwater and the surrounding land. She described NorthSky's bid with the state to begin underground mining near the river, pointing out the property they'd already purchased based on Moon's interviews. It was a section of riverbank, shaded orange, that stretched from Thunderwater, downstream through the gorge, and butted right up to Chip's peninsula. Chip, next to Sam, set his plate down in the grass and leaned forward. Moon described the history of sulfide mining, the short-term jobs it would bring to the area along with the long-term cost.

"Pay now or pay later," Pete said, his mouth full of coleslaw. "That's what I've been saying. Human nature. White man nature."

"Next person interrupts Moon gets a boot in his ass," said Debbie. "Raise your hand if you want to say something."

"Sorry, Deb," said Pete.

Debbie nodded at Moon to continue.

Moon's next poster showed a picture of what looked to be a giant gravel pile. "This is called a tailings dam. They mine underground, bringing up everything. They crush it and separate out the metals they want—copper, zinc, silver. What's left over is tailings, these ground-up gravel mounds, and these are the main hazard. The crushed tailings acidify once exposed to the surface. They leach heavy metals and sulfuric acid. A mine might bring jobs for a decade and then move on. The tailing dams stay behind in whatever community they were mined in, and remain hazardous for hundreds of years."

Sam shifted on his hay bale as Dell crawled into his lap. Swami couldn't help but think about their marriage as a sulfide mine. There'd been great promise. And then they'd begun to dig. And then dormant soils were brought to the surface and acidified.

Moon showed another picture of a bright orange river, white-bellied fish floating dead in a marsh of bleached and wilting wild rice. "NorthSky will claim they can store the tailings safely, but they leak, and one major rain event can burst the dams, as has happened elsewhere on nearly every continent." She showed aerial photographs of five collapsed dams around the globe, paging through the posters slowly—bright orange rivers, abandoned fishing boats, bone-dead trees, a puffy white crocodile, rusted mine equipment. Everyone in the circle stopped eating while Moon showed these pictures. Swami imagined the Piers Gorge rapids, milky orange and charging down toward Lake Michigan. She could tell the others were imagining it too.

"And in Thunderwater, there's more than just a river to protect. The riverbanks where they propose to dig represent several sites sacred to the Menominee Indian Tribe—mounds, burial sites, deep heritage that will be lost forever."

Pete didn't speak out of turn this time, but he nodded deeply. He looked at Chip, and then back at Moon.

"NorthSky will try to come in here to these town halls and act all wholesome and local, just a small company wanting to start a quarry. They'll talk about respecting indigenous and historical sites. But I've read up on them. NorthSky is a multinational company with global investors. Their revenue last year was two billion dollars, and their track record is dirty. For forty years they've leapfrogged their way around the globe, their land managers leasing and buying, leaving pits once the ore is gone."

The mention of that much money made a few people sit up straighter. Moon had Swami's full attention now too. She had to admit she hadn't given Moon's mine opposition much thought. Moon was just the type to find a cause and protest it, handing out her library-printed flyers in parking lots, much like this college girl who now sat with her jaw clenched tight. And Moon was as natural as the river itself. If the river was in any danger, of course Moon would stand up to protect it. But this was bigger, what NorthSky was proposing. Swami could tell from the looks on the faces of those sitting around her that they were thinking the same thing. Moon was taking on a giant with a handful of posters, a corporation with a bigger budget than some of the countries it mined in. Debbie shifted uncomfortably on her hay bale. Her face looked a bit pale.

"There's one thing that can stop mines like NorthSky, and that's local opposition. I found at least two instances, one in Minnesota and another in New Mexico, where *people* stopped these mines. These mining bids are highly complex. They need politicians at the state and county level, private landowners, federal and local agencies, investors. If any of these feel enough opposition from locals, these bids fail. Someone just has to stop the momentum."

Moon placed the *River Keepers* poster back on display. She took a deep breath.

"This April, in his Earth Day address, Vice President Al Gore said this country needs change. He said we have to 'put behind us the false choice between the economy and the environment.' I know Thunderwater needs jobs. But it doesn't need NorthSky jobs."

Debbie exhaled a big breath at the mention of Al Gore, shook her head a bit. She rubbed the palms of her hands on her dress.

A bank of clouds had moved over the setting sun. Moon's eyes became wet.

"I have been looking for a place to call home for a very long time," said Moon, her voice trembling a bit. "Thunderwater is the closest I've come. This is a special place. The bluffs, the forests, the river. It's *home.* And its people are family. And I plan to run NorthSky right out of here."

Moon smiled and wiped her eyes.

"I'm starting protests next week, on the day of the town hall. I'm going to stand outside their big new fence. I'm calling news stations. And I'll stand there alone if I have to, but I hope all of Thunderwater joins me. Thank you for coming and listening tonight. And thank you, Debbie, for the wonderful meal."

Everyone clapped. The professor put his fingers in his mouth and whistled support. Moon smiled and bowed and beamed. Debbie sat quite still. The college girl raised her hand, and Moon invited her to speak.

"I just want to say yes!" she said. "I'll be with you at those protests."

"Me too, Moon," said Randy, and Pete smirked at him. Randy ignored his friend. "Whatever you decide to do, I've got your back," he said. "All the way."

People nodded and clapped again. Moon thanked them all and smiled, gathered her things while others picked up their paper plates from the grass, repeating things they had just seen and heard. Dell asked for another cookie. Debbie sat very still. She hadn't moved.

"Honey?" said Debbie, and everyone stopped chatting.

"Yes?" said Moon.

Debbie looked at the grass, and around her property, then at Moon.

"Billions of dollars is lots of money," Debbie said quietly.

Moon agreed.

"Where there's that kind of money, there's a lot of power too. And it's one thing for Gore to talk. He's got power. But for people like us, Thunderwater people, it ain't the same."

The sky had become nearly entirely clouded over now. A breeze moved in from the pines.

"I'm not telling you not to fight your fight, Moon. I've fought too. I'm proud of you. But I'm saying be careful. Power like that is going to do what power's going to do. People like us tend to pay."

Swami thought of the photos hanging in Debbie's kitchen, and the woman's life spent alone with her son on this farm, quietly rebuilding, preparing, planting her wall of pines.

"Fight your fight, honey," she said. "But please be careful. All of you." Debbie stood, stiff from her hay bale. "Well," she said, limping toward the table. "I'm gonna go wrap up pasties for you all to take with you. You don't need to leave, but don't leave without pasties."

That night, on the drive home to the campground, Moon was energized, chatty, motivated. Swami drove slowly around the piney curves, the headlights sweeping the landscape. In the rearview mirror, she could see Darren's face watching the blue darkness, his eyes gentle and glimmering. Swami listened to Moon, and saw her son listening to

Moon. She thought about the things Debbie said about power, and what Moon said about Indian mounds lying along riverbanks. She thought about Sam promising to fix the camper, and her own coolness toward him, the way the air was cool drifting in through the old vents of the Woodchuck Rafting van. She thought about Birdy, saying "Olay" in the barn.

As Swami dropped Moon off at her campsite, it started to rain. She couldn't quite name her discomfort as she watched Moon jog toward her tiny camper, but it felt something like dread and something like re-luctance. She felt too close to things, too involved with people and dan-gers she wasn't sure were supposed to be her own. She got her kids into bed and snuggled very close. It felt good to close the camper door and pull up the thick blankets and watch it rain outside, listen to it drum the camper roof. *Outside*, Swami thought, falling closer and closer to sleep. *Keep the rain outside. Olay.*

NINE

"WAKEY WAKEY, EGGS AND BAKEY," CHIP CALLED OUT. SAM OPENED one eye, still lying on his cot on the screen porch. The light was gray. It had rained all night, even thundered a little. Sam was cold, and the air was damp, so he pulled his sleeping bag up under his chin and clamped his eyes shut.

"Breakfast!" called his uncle.

Sam exhaled a shiver and forced his eyes open. Through the porch door, Sam could see into the kitchen. His uncle was standing in front of the hot stove in his tight wet-suit pants and his flannel poncho and flip-flops. He shuffled something from the pan to a plate. It smelled good. Chip made good breakfasts whenever it was his turn. He dropped what looked to be a sausage on the floor, and stooped down with his hot pan and tongs to chase it under the sink. He found it, rinsed it off under the faucet, and popped it in his mouth.

"Oh, hoo, hot!" he mumbled.

"Let's cancel the trips," said Sam, sitting up, still zipped in his bag. It was gray outside, foggy. Sam winced at the field. He couldn't make out the deer pasture, the mist was so thick.

"No can do, buddy," sang Chip. "Swami's yoga class in one hour, and a big cold river after that. Need some big calories this morning."

Sam sighed and unzipped his feet and waddled to the table. Chip waddled over in his wet-suit pants and put a plate of eggs and sausage and two fresh biscuits in front of Sam. There were already two big mugs of coffee poured and two plastic cups and a jug of IGA orange juice.

"Thanks, man," Sam said.

Chip grunted his acknowledgment, shoveled eggs into his beard. Yesterday was Sam's turn to cook. He'd made frozen waffles and bacon.

"I been thinking," said Chip, pouring himself some orange juice and drinking it.

Sam cradled his coffee and took a sip.

"About you and Swami," Chip said.

"What about us?"

"You need a grand gesture."

"A what?"

"You need a grand gesture," said Chip. "To win her back. That's what they do in all those Hallmark movies." Chip was being perfectly serious.

Sam laughed. "Hallmark movies," he repeated.

"I pick up a couple on VHS every Christmas," Chip said. "Them ones with the red-and-green sweaters on the cover. Every one of them is the same story. Some guy comes back to town, a veteran or something. And then there's some girl who doesn't have a boyfriend 'cause she's too old and jaded. And then they start to like each other but something bad happens and the girl feels betrayed, so the guy does some grand gesture and they kiss in front of the girl's old parents. There's usually a dog, or something brave said in front of the whole town."

Sam grinned and set his coffee down. "You watch Hallmark movies," he said, just to clarify.

Chip looked only mildly offended. He stabbed a sausage. "They're very heartwarming," he said while he chewed.

Sam nodded. A puppy wouldn't do it for Swami. A heap of money might. Or a do-over of the last ten or so years. Sam called the bank last week. He and Swami had about eleven hundred dollars left, total. What came in from rafting trips went out in insurance payments and guide salaries, and then some. After his last teaching paycheck, what small cushion they'd had just shrank away like a small weathered hill. Sam had already called his superintendent, pleaded, argued. The super was nice about it, but there was nothing to give. He told Sam he'd be first on the list for subbing. And if he had a commercial driver license, the district might need a part-time bus driver. Sam thanked him and lowered the phone.

"Well," Sam said. "I'm heading out to Governor's with Smitty this afternoon to start on the camper. He's got most of the parts in."

Chip nodded, bit into a biscuit. "That's a good step," he said, pointing his fork at his nephew. "You just gotta keep thinking big. Grand gesture. Unexpected. Flashy."

"Thanks," Sam said, and meant it. The coffee and food were warming him up. "And what about you?"

"What about me."

"Did you decide on NorthSky's offer yet?"

"Their guy keeps calling. I don't answer. I got another letter. I haven't called back yet. I guess I been waiting on the town hall. If this thing is going to happen with or without me anyway, I'm thinking I might sell. But I'm going to speak up against it too. I don't really know."

Sam nodded, let it rest. To be honest, as ugly as the orange rivers were, he didn't know what he'd do right now if someone offered to buy Woodchuck for half a million. It was a lot of money. They'd be set for life just living off the interest. And the jobs for Thunderwater were real too, the crumbling porches and neglected roofs. And then there was the river sparkling through the middle of it all, that beautiful, humming, sacred gorge. Sam shrugged off the question. He had enough of his own predicaments.

The last few weeks had been cold weeks on the river. Drizzly. Overcast. Wet gear and cold water. Even in a wet suit, Sam just felt chilled. He'd see Swami in the morning on her way to yoga, and that was basically it. Sometimes he'd see her up on the rock bluff, supervising the rafts as they went through the gorge. Sam was careful not to wave at her or look up if he could help it. He wanted Swami to see him paddling hard, throwing a solid draw stroke just before nailing the run over Volkswagen Rock. He wanted her to see him working hard, focused on the work. He wanted her to see him trying.

Sam had to sit in the back of the boat for hours every day, chatting up groups of happy or complaining customers. He'd hand out snacks from his dry bag to the preteens. He'd hand out Advil to the hungover aunts and uncles. The newlyweds were the worst. These young couples with hope and adoration in their eyes, always touching each other, making sure the other was warm enough, offering encouraging words when the paddling got confusing. One day last week, this young couple sat up front, both of them tanned and well-muscled, traveling around in a van. They were honeymooning, they told the boat, and they were taking the whole summer to do it. They gave a speech about it in the raft, during the flat water, when different groups of people in the boat begin chatting and introducing themselves. They said they were taking a whole summer to establish their connection, adventure and travel and hike together.

"We're in this for life," said the husband. "So we want to start with as much life experience together as we can get." The wife smiled at him, and at the rest of the raft.

Sam forced a smile. Even though it was raining, he put on his sunglasses so they couldn't see him closing his eyes in despair. There was an older couple in the boat that cooed at this, ate it up. And they seemed happy together too. They'd helped each other into the raft, patted each other's wet-suited legs.

As Sam's life savings and marriage were dwindling away, the river rose. It was getting harder and harder to guide boatloads of inexperienced paddlers. A typical water level this time of year was about two thousand cubic feet per second out of the dam. For two weeks now it had been above four thousand. The cutoff for commercial rafting was six thousand. At four grand, the gorge ran flush and booming. It wasn't enough water to completely change the river, but it was enough to make the holes deeper and the wave trains rowdy. All of the rocks were completely covered, so hazards like wrapping a raft on Volkswagen Rock were absent, but flips were much easier. The rafting reminded Sam of the New River in West Virginia. It was no longer tight and technical. It was broad and big. It was all about momentum and energy, and most of all holding your angle, squaring up perpendicular to each wave so the boat didn't flip. The big hole behind Volkswagen was massive. And Sam would punch the nose of the raft into it and under it, feel it stall. He'd hold the hard water with his paddle blade and ride it back up, the customers coming up gasping and cheering. It was the one time of day Sam truly smiled, felt like something was going right. The river was one place he felt confident. It was a different story for the rookie X-treme guides. Even Duncan struggled in the bigger water. His outdoor management degree hadn't prepared him for a swelling river. Raft after raft, they flipped as often as they made it. On an almost daily basis, Sam had to coach stranded and terrified X-treme customers which trail to walk back on to meet up with the rafts. Chip had refrained from soaping their boats since the firelight fistfight. That had been a direct order from Swami. But there was no need to anymore.

On the day the young husband gave his speech about life, Sam felt particularly cold. He sat hunched over and quiet, paddling as quickly as he could through the flat water while the guests chatted. As the old couple shared their story too, which was all roses, which didn't seem right, didn't seem honest, Sam began to roll his eyes behind his sunglasses. But the detail with which they described their life together began to make Sam believe they were actually telling the truth. He made her coffee every morning. They read together. The husband liked foot rubs and naps, and the wife gave him both. The wife liked their special vacations, Hawaii, the Grand Canyon, Fiji. They were both originally from the Upper Peninsula, so they made a biannual trek up here to their cabin. Sam imagined the husband napping his way around the globe on king-sized resort mattresses with puffy comforters and ceiling fans, his happy wife checking out the pool before some dinner and dancing together. "We keep the romance alive," said the older woman, and she blushed a bit while the newlyweds gobbled it up. The old husband nodded and smiled a genuine smile at her. "We always have," he said. "But you'll have your arguments too," he coached the young couple. "Your hard times."

Here we go, thought Sam. *That's right. Tell it like it is. Tell the worst.*

The wife agreed, winced. "Like that time we argued about where Claire wanted to go to college," she said, and her husband nodded solemnly. "She's a nurse practitioner now," she informed everybody.

Sam deflated, felt a small growl in his throat.

The husband kept nodding as if that argument was his biggest regret in his life. "We didn't talk for, what was it, nearly a whole weekend. We lost a lot of trust. I slept on the couch. Two whole nights!"

His wife looked a little embarrassed now, as if they might be sharing too much. But her husband reached across the raft and put his hand on her leg. They smiled at each other. They kissed.

The newlywed wife nearly melted, beamed at her husband. There was a long enough pause in the conversation then that Sam knew from experience the questions would start to be directed at him. It was get-to-know-your-guide time. He quickly filled the silence himself with talk of the upcoming rapids, rescue techniques, where he'd seen a beaver, an otter, and an eagle's nest. Sam didn't wear his wedding ring on the river. The cold water made it slip off, so he tied it to a piece of cord inside his life jacket. He could feel the hard metal against his skin now as he coached the guests toward the falls and gorge, chatted them up about anything else except marriage and family.

On their first run through the gorge, just before they dropped over the falls, the newlyweds took out a disposable Kodak waterproof camera and snapped two pictures of themselves with the gorge behind them. Way up in the distance, on the bluff above the river, Swami's figure stood still in the trees in a blue rain jacket.

Sam bellowed a "Forward paddle" command. He had to bellow something. It was hard enough to feel so isolated in a group of happy married couples. It was intolerable to feel it when he was about to drop into the one quarter mile of solace he still had in his life. That solace was what he loved most about rafting the river. In the middle of a wave or a drop, in all that swoop and boom and spray, it was impossible to think about anything else.

The young husband hurriedly tucked the camera back in his vest. The guests paddled forward. They dropped the falls. The wave train rotated the nose of the boat over a peak. The next wave rotated it some more. And for some reason Sam didn't correct it, even though he knew how, and could. He wanted more boom and spray, more solace. So he just let the raft charge dead sideways toward a mound of water coursing over Volkswagen. The clueless guests shrieked with excitement. Sam stared at the mound. In his peripheral vision, Sam was aware of the blue dot of his wife on the bluff. He was aware of Chip, downstream, already blowing his whistle. The raft went up. The raft went down into the hole. And Sam just let the river eat them. He let go of his paddle as the raft flipped. All the paddlers went in, and Sam did too, down deep, where it was cold and loud and no one could speak to anyone else anymore. Swami would be angry. But Swami was always angry, so at least for now, for a few moments, Sam could hide under the thick white blanket of this raging current.

What a silly mistake, he'd tell them all. *Happens to the best of us. That's the river for you.*

After breakfast, and boat loading, and the morning's uneventful river trip, Sam had Chip drop him off at Smitty's Shop in Thunderwater. It was an old shop built at the base of a hill of pines. It had two auto bays, a single gas pump, and a tow truck parked outside with a rusty boom. *Smitty's Speed Stop,* read the red-and-blue-painted sign. But there was nothing speedy about it. As frustrating as it was to wait this long for parts for the Winnebago, Sam also appreciated the low-speed way Smitty did business. The gas pump was full service, which Sam hadn't experienced since he was a kid. You pulled in next to the pump, beeped your horn, and a teenage employee wearing a pair of striped Dickies coveralls with a *Speed Stop* patch sewn on the chest would come out and fill your tank, clean your windshield, and check your oil. And if you wanted a candy bar or a cold pop, they'd bring it out to you along with your change. Sam loved gassing up the rafting van there. He even loved the way Smitty—also in coveralls—took too long to look through parts catalogues, his huge dirty glasses slipping down his nose. "Chevy chassis is easy enough. But the Winnebago parts is *proprietary*, and I don't usually work on 'em. Had to order the parts catalogue before I could order the parts, see." He licked his stained fingertip and flipped another page, peered down his nose. "What's this now? Nope. That's not it." As much as Sam loved the shop, there was a sweet sadness that hung beneath his visits too. The old-school space reminded him of his dad—the smell of the motor oil, the cans of Coke, the feel of a sun-warmed bench seat in a simple Ford truck. Smitty's shop reminded Sam of loss.

Smitty left his shop in the hands of his employee and gave Sam a ride out to Governor's State Park in the tow truck, loaded down with the long-awaited parts strapped to the flatbed—a headlight, a radiator, and in a massive box the tall plastic body panel that fit over the front bumper. Smitty drove twenty miles an hour through town, and thirty-five miles per hour on the country highway.

"Rafting, you say?" he said for the second time, not looking at Sam as he spoke but peering through the windshield. His glasses were so smudged, Sam wanted to offer to clean them on his T-shirt.

"That's right," said Sam for the second time.

"Well, like I said," said Smitty. "I heard of it—we see the rafts coming through town—but I never done it. You won't see me out there, doing that rafting."

Sam tried to picture himself in a Hallmark movie, riding shotgun in the antique tow truck, showing up with the parts and mechanic to heal the camper. He knew better than to hope for an easy reunion. But like Chip had said, it was a step. He was offering something.

Swami and the kids weren't home when Smitty pulled in. Sam called around, opened the camper door, and then remembered Darren saying something about an owl and hawk rehabilitation center that Ranger Bonnie might show them around. Sam closed the camper door. The movie had to change in his mind. Now he'd fix it without her knowing, let it surprise her, just sneak away and wait. Maybe he'd come striding in, apologetic but hopeful as he hands Swami the keys, watches her start the motor and try out the headlights while the kids cheer. Sam unloaded the parts for Smitty, cut open the boxes, and fetched bolts and wrenches to help the old mechanic along. They removed the cracked body panel first. Then they replaced the headlamp. Flicked it on and off. The cracked radiator came out next. But when Smitty creaked down onto his back while Sam held the new radiator in place, Smitty's capable, stained hands stopped all labor.

"This ain't it."

"What's not it?" asked Sam.

Smitty grunted and shimmied himself out from beneath the front end. He stood up and wiped his hands on a rag, then blew his nose into it.

"Wrong part. Headlamp is Chevy, the body panel is Winnebago, but I guess I don't know what that *radiator* is. The in and out's all flipped."

"The in and out is flipped," said Sam.

Smitty nodded, stuffed his rag back in his pocket. "Like I said, these parts is all proprietary. I'm gonna have to go back to the shop and figure out what's what with that radiator, order one where the in and out ain't flipped. Shouldn't be two or three weeks at most, unless I have to order another part catalogue before ordering the parts. That happens sometimes."

Sam sighed, looked around at the campsite strewn with cut boxes and packing foam. He'd clean it up. But now the camper didn't just have a cracked front end, but a naked one—a motor without a radiator, just pulleys and wires and belts and two headlights bulging out above it like surprised, embarrassed bug eyes. At least the headlights worked. They could leave the new body panel leaning against the front driver's side until they could get back to work. Maybe Sam could come out here alone and tack it on temporarily to at least give it the *look* of being fixed. Sam sighed again, very deeply.

"All right," he said. "Back to the shop."

•••

THAT EVENING, THE DRIZZLE TURNED to rain, and then a downpour. Chip and Sam rode into town with Randy and Moon, all four of them wedged onto the bench seat. The truck's musty heater dried their feet from the short jog from Chip's house to the end of his driveway. Sam felt stuffy in his raincoat. The old wipers could barely keep up with the deluge. It took Chip a long time to catch his breath.

"*Man,*" said Randy for the second time, leaning forward to peer through the windshield. "*Look* at this. This is gonna blow out the river." He had to talk loud, nearly yelling because of how much rain was drumming the cab.

Chip had stopped puffing. He nodded in agreement. "Pete says they're gonna open another gate on the dam, keep the reservoir from tearing off people's docks." Chip paused for a breath. "We'll probably see five grand on the river this week."

Randy whistled, slowed down his driving even more. "*Look* at it," Randy said. "No wind either, just straight dumping."

"Five grand's gonna smoke me in that gorge," said Sam.

"Gonna smoke me too." Randy laughed.

"You'll be all right," said Chip. "Duncan's people won't."

"Well, I hope people come out tonight," Moon said. "You think they'll come?"

They passed the big musky sign welcoming drivers into Thunderwater. The few streetlights helped make the road visible again. Small rivers already ran down the sides of the streets. There were no other cars in sight.

"They'll come," said Randy, looking out at the little houses. "Everyone I've talked to has been talking about it. Rita even said she was closing her bar for two hours tonight. Rita never closes that bar."

Nearly every one of the small front yards had a sign in it at this point. Earlier, on his drive back to the shop with Smitty, Sam quietly counted twenty-six *Start Mining* signs, but only two *River Keepers*. He didn't mention it to Moon. She sat proudly in the cab next to Randy now. Sam knew she must have seen them by now, but Sam was glad the rain obscured the signs tonight.

Randy splashed his truck through a river onto a side street. He grinned. "See, Moon? They came." Moon clapped her hands, and looked nervous too.

The side street was packed with cars and pickups, lined down both sides and angled up into the grass too. Duncan's bright green Mustang was there. So was Pete's big red truck. A person jogged toward the grange hall under an umbrella, splashing through a puddle in big green boots. Randy put his truck in park right in front of the hall's front steps. His tires sent small waves onto the cracked sidewalk.

The old converted barn had a broad porch built onto it. The double entrance doors were propped open, and the warm light inside revealed the place was packed. Sam and Randy carefully wrestled Moon's easels from behind the seat—she had five of them now—and ran them all up to the wooden porch. He was thankful for his river sandals. They had to wade a bit. Chip and Moon carried the poster boards wrapped in black garbage bags.

"Be right back," Randy said, and slammed the door of his truck and roared off through the puddles. The rain fell down from the porch roof like a bright white curtain. Chip leaned his bag of posters against the dry wall beneath the grange hall sign. A myriad of voices came through the double doors. Someone laughed inside. It smelled like coffee.

"Moon, I gotta take a leak," he said. "I'll see you guys in there."

Moon thanked him, and Chip shook off his rain jacket and went inside. Sam read the grange hall sign. It was hand-painted, a golden shield with a blue ribbon tying a bundle of wheat alongside the big blue letters *P* and *H*. Sam read the brass plaque below it: "'The National Grange of the Order of Patrons of Husbandry in the United States.' What is this place, anyway?"

"It's an old farmers' union. They took on the railroads once. It's where people come to vote on election days," said Moon, still holding her posters.

"Well," said Sam, hoisting two easels. "Let's go help the people vote."

Moon smiled, lifted her head high, and walked inside.

The place was packed and loud, with at least one hundred people, and the open room was warm with bodies and humid with wet jackets. At least half of Thunderwater was present. The rows of folding chairs were all filled, so people stood behind the chairs by the coffee and cookies, and in the hardwood side aisles. Neighbors chatted and laughed. A few sullen teens stood near the wall. In front on a small bandstand sat a folding table with a plastic tablecloth and three men and a woman seated behind it. The woman sat with her hands folded, looking uncomfortable in her thick khaki shirt with epaulets and patches on the sleeves. The big man sitting next to her looked blank as a bull. The one next to him wore a baggy suit and wiped his fogging glasses and sweating forehead. The last man at the table wore a denim shirt and a broad, constant smile. Sam couldn't find Chip in the crowd.

Randy bounded through the door, wiping rain from his face.

He spotted where Sam and Moon were setting up the easels by the coffee table, but was intercepted by locals. Men, and old women too, shook his hand and clapped his shoulder. Randy wiped his face again while they started telling stories, catching up. Sam noticed this happened wherever Randy went in Thunderwater. He was one of the town's few children who hadn't moved away or become an obvious disappointment.

They loved him for it. When the crowd shifted for Randy, Sam noticed another cluster of townspeople gathered around a sitting family—a woman bouncing a baby on her lap, two little heads sticking up from the chairs beside her. Swami was here, and the older women and a handful of men who stood talked with her and the kids and smiled. *Good*, thought Sam. He'd hoped she'd be here. Fixing the camper hadn't panned out, but Sam had another plan. The whole town was gathered. Sam remembered how Swami and Moon talked about the Earth Day speech of Vice President Al Gore. They'd called him a leader. At least Al Gore was *trying*, Swami had said. Well, Sam would try too. Sam would lead. He was an educator, after all, and a business owner, and a class-five river guide.

"If I could have your attention," said a small voice. "Attention, please. Hello? Hello?"

The woman onstage spoke into the microphone. Her face was bright red. She wore a black brimmed hat low on her face, her short hair tucked behind her ears.

The man with the broad smile thumped his mic a few times, and the bass quieted the crowd. He smiled again, raised his hands in apology. People sat, ended their conversations. The woman nodded her thanks at him. When it got quiet, the heavy rain could be heard drumming the roof. Someone had closed the hall's double doors to the porch to quiet the downpour outside. The air became muggy inside.

"Okay," she said. "Welcome." She looked at her notebook and read into the mic. "Welcome to the end of June Thunderwater community forum. My name is Ranger Bonnie. I am a state forest park ranger and interim Marigamie Sheriff's Department deputy. I'd like to thank the friends of the grange hall for providing the real good cookies and coffee—and a roof that don't leak." The people laughed as the rain roared outside. Ranger Bonnie looked incredibly pleased with her off-script joke. She seemed to loosen a bit. "It's a wet one for sure," she said.

Now that people were mostly sitting down, Sam noticed the man with the broad smile stop smiling for a moment as he studied Moon's poster boards in the back of the room. He leaned and whispered something to the man in the suit, who peered toward Sam and Moon over the top of his glasses and then scribbled something on his notepad.

"Tonight is an open information night," said Ranger Bonnie, "with time for questions at the end. We have three guests, and I'll let each of them introduce themselves."

Bonnie slid the mic down the table.

The big bull man leaned in. "I'm—hi there—Bruce Tapper," he said. "Second mine foreman with NorthSky Enterprise." He pushed the mic and leaned back.

The suited man cleared his throat, and spoke in a high-pitched voice. "So nice to meet you all, and thank you for the opportunity to share tonight. My name is Daniel Abrams, and I am pleased to share this wonderful economic opportunity with the town of Thunderwater."

The man with the smile introduced himself as "Mr. Blakely, local property owner and co-owner of X-treme Outdoor Adventures—which has just this year opened business in the beautiful town of Thunder-water. I'm here tonight to represent landowner concerns on the impact the mine may have. As some of you know, I grew up in these parts. It's good to be back. I'd like to retire here. Like all of you, I want what's best for the area."

Sam frowned at Moon, and Moon frowned back.

Someone hooted support from the front row. It was Duncan. The man smiled at him.

Chip stood from a few rows in, offered a lady his chair.

"Now, who the heck is *that* guy?" he whispered as he arrived by Moon and Sam.

Sam frowned and shrugged. The man watched the three of them now. Swami looked back at Sam now too. Sam smiled at her. She nodded back.

"Is that Duncan's uncle?" Moon whispered.

"Must be," said Sam. "You've never seen him?"

Chip turned toward the table and grabbed a big cookie, bit it, swiped crumbs from his beard. "His voice reminds me of someone, but I don't know who. Never seen him before, but I like him less than Duncan," he said. "I know that. Guy looks like he sells crap cars."

After introductions, Ranger Bonnie haltingly moderated very scripted conversations among the three men. Suited Daniel went first, wiping his head and giving an overview of the scope of the prospective mine, and NorthSky's historic community funding. He talked about the skateboard park they built on a reservation in southern Ontario. When he talked about salaries, people in the crowd whispered to one another. Even the sullen teenagers near the wall perked up. Thunderwater municipal residents would be given first opportunities. The lowest starting pay would be upward of fifty-five thousand a year.

After Daniel, Bruce the bull described the actual mining practices. He was real short about it, used his big hands a lot.

"We dig down," he said. "Bring up the dirt, shake out the good stuff, and then mostly backfill. The only real byproduct is a kind of gravel. Now, some of this gravel can rust—it *oxidizes*, so we keep it in one spot behind a dry dam in the woods."

"It doesn't just rust!" yelled the college girl who had come to Moon's party, Duncan's guide.

This outburst caused a general stir. The girl had stood when she yelled it, finger pointed. "Tell the rest of it," she said. "Tell the rest!"

"And there's Indian mounds in them woods," shouted an old man.

Sam saw Duncan's blond head nodding heartily in agreement. The college girl must have filled others in. Moon's River Keepers message had been spreading.

Moon smiled a tight-lipped smile. "We've got photos right back here!" she said. Heads turned.

At this point Ranger Bonnie's face grew red. She started waving her hands apologetically. "Everyone will have a chance to speak tonight," she said. "The grange hall is a nonpartisan organization. It's nonpartisan." But she didn't have her mic in front of her and got drowned out in the murmur and the noise of the downpour.

"How about we go dig up your great-grandma and make a gravel pit!" yelled the old man.

Sam had been watching Mr. Blakely. The man kept that smile plastered on, except for when his nephew started nodding along, clapping. Blakely clearly liked to do the talking for the business. He took the mic.

"Folks," he said, beaming that smile, standing from behind the table. "Folks?"

People quieted down. The man in the suit wiped his head. The bull man next to him just looked bored.

"I share your concerns," said Blakely. "I really do, and my main question for the panel tonight, which I was just going to ask, had to do with environmental concerns. I wanted to ask about that too. Here, I'll read my question. I have a little speech. We ready?"

People nodded. Just then the roof started leaking in front of the stage, a steady stream of water thick as a pencil spattering on the floor.

Blakely chuckled. "No problem," he said. "Got our own little waterfall here." With mic in hand he grabbed a garbage can and moved it under the flow, looked up at the wall. "If it's all right with the parents in the room, I'd like to ask some of these fine young people to keep these bins emptied as we talk tonight." Parents nodded. The teens looked startled to be mentioned in public, then marched off to gather the other trash cans.

"Again, my name is Mr. Blakely, friends call me Greg. And I consider everyone here as my friend. I'm a builder. My nephew and I, as many of you know, have begun to operate an outdoor recreation company in the area. He's a great business partner, by the way, even if he could use a haircut."

People laughed. Duncan laughed. The teens stood ready with emptied trash cans. Sam looked at Moon. Moon looked at Sam. This guy was good.

"There's two facts we have to balance if we're building a new house, a new business, a new anything. One, jobs are good. Two, a clean and protected environment is good, which is particularly apparent in a place as beautiful and rich in history as Thunderwater." He studied the crowd. "I believe God gave us this earth to tend to it, which means building and protecting."

"Amen!" said a mother holding a toddler in her lap, and then she chuckled with her husband at her outburst. The teens replaced the trash can and dragged the full one to a side door and dumped it.

Blakely beamed. "As I see it, the economic benefits of this mine are clear. Friends, if you get this mine in Thunderwater." Blakely whistled. "Those porches get painted, and you get new trucks, and that vacation too. Clearly, it's a boon. It could bring Thunderwater right back to its paper-making days. People building again, families multiplying, grown children *staying*. I'm not gonna lie, more money in this area will help the business I'm starting with my nephew, but I think it will help all of you too."

There were positive murmurs now. Duncan didn't take part. He tilted his head at his uncle. He looked a bit surprised.

"We don't even have our own school anymore," said an old man in a blaze orange cap. "When I was growing up we had our own school. And a ball field. We have to drive all the way to Crivitz for Little League, can't even afford to have our own team for the grandkids."

Daniel spoke to Blakely from his seat. Blakely looked surprised by what he said.

"Now, this man here," he said, "just told me that baseball fields, nice ones, with lights, are exactly the kind of community projects that NorthSky will commit to take part in."

A younger man stood up now. It was the husband of the *Amen* woman. "You sign me up for a new Dodge and a ball field."

Chip spoke out. "We don't need to sell off our land to a big mine to make a living up here."

"No offense, Chip," said the younger man, "but you don't got a family to support. You don't speak for me."

"And you don't speak for me," said Chip. "I've made a living up here for years, just rafting."

"Yeah, and you're all washed up is what you are. Driving around on a crap dirt bike. No thanks."

The old man in the orange hat let out a cackle, then stifled it with a cough. Sam heard Chip's chest rumble as he shifted his weight.

Blakely spoke quickly into the mic again, and his voice overpowered the rest. "To be honest," he said, "I came here tonight to pump the brakes just a bit. As an outdoor business owner, just like Chip there, we know there's no business if the river comes out looking like the ones that young woman has posters of back there. What's your name, miss?"

"Moon," she said.

The young man who wanted the truck snorted. Randy stood up, jaw tight.

"Moon," said Blakely, oozing a smile. "I like that name. Now, I don't know mining, but I know building, and my guess—my hope—is that mining is like building homes. We used to use lead paint, and *asbestos siding* for insulation."

"Good and warm!" blurted the old man in the orange cap. Sam wondered now if the man had come from the tavern. People shushed him.

"True," said Blakely, "but practices have changed. Maybe mining is like that? Safer now than it used to be? I don't know, Moon. But I'll yield the floor back to these men from NorthSky for a moment and ask them what I came to ask for me and you and Chip." He turned toward the two men from NorthSky. "I want you to answer directly and plainly," he warned them. "Will this mine disturb Native American heritage sites? And will it do to the river what those pictures show?"

Blakely sat down and slid the mic back to Daniel and Bruce.

Bruce leaned in. So did the crowd of people. "No," Bruce said. "It will not."

Positive murmur started again. Bruce went on to describe in detail the concerns of sulfide mining's history, and the new methods that prevent failures of the tailing dams. Daniel took a turn, naming federal and state statutes that now govern the operation. Moon spoke. Went back and forth with the man. He had a calm rebuttal for everything. Moon became flustered. The teenagers dumped another trash can of water out the door. The leak in the ceiling had multiplied, more streams springing along the line of the old tongue-and-groove. Ranger Bonnie looked very pleased to get the mic back and open the floor to questions. The formal part of her panel session was accomplished. It was up to the people now.

A few people stood and moved away from the front row of seats by the roof leak. Others collected umbrellas and rain jackets from the floor and the backs of chairs.

Sam looked at his wife. And his kids. Something about Blakely's oily talk, and the young father standing up for Little League, and Moon's frustration when people asked more questions about ball fields and job applications, made Sam feel like retreating into his own tribe. Swami's ponytail fell over her neck as she leaned over to gather some things into her bag. Dell's small hand came up from the seat and rubbed her mother's back. Darren's messy hair turned this way and that, curious about it all, listening to everything, eyeing the roof leaks. The innocence there reminded Sam of his own time with his own father, sweet times, when the world still worked the way it should. Sam wished he could just bottle that up, protect what little of it still existed, gather his family and sleep in a warm clump with his wife and three kids in the refuge of their camper. Sam felt nervous, longing tears in his eyes. He stepped forward and raised his hand. He wanted Swami to see him being serious. He wanted her to see it in front of the whole town.

"We have a question," said Bonnie, calling on Sam.

Swami looked at Sam. Moon looked at Sam. Everyone looked at Sam.

He spoke the line he'd memorized very slowly. "We have to put behind us the false choice between the economy and the environment." He paused. Everyone waited. "I'm Sam. I am a business owner too, me and my wife."

Swami's face reddened a bit when people looked at her. She flashed a quick smile and then watched Sam warily. Sam stammered his next line. Why was he crying? He couldn't cry right now.

"My kids are here. I'm a teacher. I *was* a teacher." Everyone stared at him. Sam paused and took a breath. He could do this. He practiced this. He unfolded the damp note he had in his pocket, bullet points he might address, but the ink had all bled. Swami frowned at him. People looked at her now too. There was a deep regret or embarrassment or pain in her eyes.

"I'm saying," said Sam, "there's a way for this place, for everything, to still be different. Thunderwater could be better than it's ever been. They're calling it *eco-tourism*. Rock climbing. Rafting. Bed-and-breakfasts. Guided fishing. I've seen towns do it. We can do it."

Moon was nodding encouragingly by Sam's side. Sam looked right at Swami. She was looking at the floor. Sam pressed on, imagining again a younger Swami, who once looked at him on a riverbank in West Virginia and said, "Good."

"We could still thrive, you know," Sam said. "We could work together. Preserve the river. Build ballparks." Sam looked at his kids.

Darren was staring at him. "We could make it good. I don't know how, exactly. I can't do it alone. Maybe I can't do it at all. But it's up to us. If we both try."

Anger and tears flashed in Swami's eyes now. She shook her head so imperceptibly only Sam could see it. Rainwater spattered on the floor. People waited to make sure Sam was finished, confusion in their faces.

Swami stood abruptly, waved the kids quickly toward her as she stepped into the aisle. She wrapped her raincoat over DeeDee. Swami didn't look at Sam even once as she hurried down the center of the room and toward the double doors. She had fierce red eyes. The porch doors opened, and there was the sound of rain. Darren looked back once as Swami took his hand and led him out with Dell. And then the doors rocked closed again and Sam's family and the sound of the rain were gone.

Sam looked at the center aisle wood floor where his family had been, middle distance, until the whole town of Thunderwater turned slowly back to the stage.

More questions were asked. Sam didn't hear them. After questions, people stood and chatted and put on coats. The door opened and shut again and again as they trickled out. Randy spoke with his whole body somewhere nearby. People shook hands. Clapped shoulders. Sam just fixed his eyes on the old floorboards of the grange hall, the yellowed finish, the black scratches, rain boots walking across it. The sound of rain going on and off like static. And then Sam remembered something, or felt something he hadn't felt in a long time. He remembered the night his dad's bench-seat Ford slid on the wet road. Sam was buckled in, and his dad was not. Just him and Dad and two cans of Coke on a rainy night. And then the truck skidded and there was gravel and grass and the impact, and then rain drumming on the bottom of the stone-still truck, one headlight shining on a wet tree through the shattered windshield, the cab dark and empty except for Sam, alone.

TEN

IT WAS THE THIRD STRAIGHT DAY OF RAIN, AND SWAMI STOOD ALONE with DeeDee wrapped against her chest on the rock bluff overlooking the gorge. DeeDee was warm in her wrap beneath Swami's chest. She could really hold her head up now, turn it to look at things. DeeDee's eyes were wide open, taking in the green canopy of trees, the gray sky over the gorge, and, if Swami turned sideways, the rushing brown river. The gorge was milky brown. The river was at six grand now. High enough to scare away customers, and guides. A small trip had canceled today, and Swami was considering canceling another. Even Chip winced and nodded at the idea. "Six grand is no joke," he said. "It's not the swim that will kill you, but the exhaustion." Swami remembered the guides in West Virginia describing a flush drowning. There was so much pressure against the shorelines at high water that the river would lap back, push a swimmer back to the middle when they'd almost made it. And the strainers too. Once the river rose high enough to flow through trees and bushes, the entire shore became a strainer hazard. Swami needed money, but she needed dead customers even less.

She turned DeeDee so she could see the river. They watched from under the umbrella together.

"What do you think, beautiful girl?" Swami said. "What should we do about the trips?"

DeeDee bobbed her head, mouth and eyes open. Rain spattered down from the trees into the muddy trail. The air smelled like pine and rain. DeeDee looked surprised by it all. And then she looked bothered by it all. She squawked.

"Yeah, I feel the same way," said Swami, stepping back from the bluff to a rock beneath a thick pine tree. "You hungry? Well, at least you'll eat if we're broke."

Swami propped her umbrella in two branches overhead and sat cross-legged on the cold, wet rock. She unwrapped DeeDee and let the girl nurse. Swami leaned back against the pine tree and closed her eyes, the baby girl drinking noisily along with the rain drops. Breastfeeding was the one thing in Swami's life that wasn't a horrible inconvenience. The baby got hungry, and Swami had food. They were a problem and solution all in one, a perfect pair.

Swami shifted from the cold rock onto the ground. The ground was wet, but at least it was soft, and warmer. Swami sighed. She shook her head.

She'd seen what Sam had done from that bluff. She'd seen him not straighten that raft. And then he'd had the audacity to give some speech about cooperation and hope and not doing it all alone. What *was* that? The anger she felt, the embarrassment, swirled in her mind for the last two days it'd been raining. *If we both try,* he'd said. Inconceivable! The rising river had become a problem for all the guides, Duncan's especially, a fact that Swami had been particularly enjoying. Woodchuck really was better on the water. But then comes Sam, purposefully sabotaging his own run? Moon and Chip made it through, up and over Volkswagen Rock, or to the left of it, squared up as they should be. And then there was Sam, letting the boat over-rotate. He did nothing. Swami saw it. Sam did nothing in the back of that raft. Sam did nothing anywhere. He didn't finish the barn paint. He'd lost his teaching job. He didn't manage the rafts or the money. He'd come out to the campsite and disassembled the van into even worse shape. And then he'd dumped customers and later tried to give a speech about trying? Sam couldn't square up to anything at all.

Swami let DeeDee switch sides. "And he doesn't seem to love me either," she said. And that's what hurt most. He wouldn't move toward her. How many times had Swami stood on this bluff and watched the rafts come through? How many times had Sam not even looked up at her? That's the thing that stung Swami most. He'd talked about these visions of family in the north, and now he couldn't even look up from the river and wave, try to smile, lift his paddle blade in a greeting. Swami kept thinking of the time Sam sat with a snake in his lap so long ago, the way his body trembled and neither of them knew what to do, the way they just waited and held steady until the sun rose and the snake was gone. Swami couldn't get the memory out of her head all day and couldn't fathom why. She stacked yellow paddles in a wire bin, remembering a time when Sam retold the story at a barbecue—Sam with his arms held high, his eyes so wide, the snake so much larger than it was, friends laughing. They all drank too much wine that night and Swami and Sam ended up doing naked cannonballs together, into a pond in a park, long after midnight. Now she was the one with a snake in her lap, waiting for some sort of sun to rise. And who was holding up her arms?

After their last river trip before the river rose and they had to consider canceling the next trip, Swami stretched her sore back in the bottom of the barn. The gear was put up for the day, PFDs sprayed and hung to dry. Moon and Chip had the rafts stacked and the yard cleaned up. Chip appeared at the door.

"Need anything else, Swami?" he asked.

A refund, she thought. And when she thought it, she lumped her marriage and most of her adult life in with the bargain. All but her kids. She never regretted her kids. And she couldn't be as mad at Chip as she could at Sam. Chip was a nearly entirely dysfunctional adult, but at least he was a dependable sort of dysfunctional, like a faucet that only gave so much water. Swami knew what to expect from Chip. And she also knew how upside down he was with the bank before selling Woodchuck, and how frank he was about the numbers with Sam, and how naively hopeful Chip had been that they might breathe new life into the place. Chip had grown quieter around Swami, gentler, like a wounded, stoned zoo bear. Dell brought him flowers she picked, made him paper bracelets that he and her dad could wear for luck on the river. It all just made Swami so tired, the tension of what could have been and what now was. She felt as if she were all out of outrage, or at least unwilling to spend her reserve should she need it.

"I need the Green Bay trip," she said, stepping to the threshold of the barn to stand by him and watch the rain.

"Troop leaders still coming to try us out, right?"

"Right after the Fourth," Swami said.

Chip smiled. "We'll impress them."

Swami gave a weak smile, looked up at the face of the barn.

The scaffolding had been set up weeks ago by Birdy's grandsons, but the paint still needed finishing. It had been too rainy, and the bright blue boards and foundation still held up a weathered gray peak. The gravel lot was graded and smooth. At least the rain was watering her cedars and flowers. The cedars and flowers would do well. She looked at the paint again. Each morning she noticed more work had been accomplished.

"Keep going, Swami, okay? Things are looking good around here. We'll get it sold."

Swami had to go. Moon was up top with the kids.

"Have a good night, Chip," she said.

"You too," he said, and lumbered out to his bike, while Swami took one last look around. Swami jogged down the gravel driveway to the mailbox out by the road. The ditch grass, wet and bowed over, released its sweet fragrance.

Swami pulled up the hood of her damp sweatshirt and opened the mailbox to a stack of bills, forwarded from home, bills she no longer had enough money to pay. There were two mortgage payments, their home, and Woodchuck. Plus a half year's insurance due. Chip burped his bike past her and waved and buzzed away onto the wet highway. She waved too, and then stood staring at the envelopes in her hands. She held them as if they might bite her. They would. She didn't know which to drop first. She had never been in this position in her life. Her parents had, but she had not. She could not see a way through. The money simply and purely wasn't there. Swami had thought about these coming bills for days now, sorted them in her mind. Her priorities kept falling to her home payment and family groceries, then Woodchuck, then everything else. The property insurance for Woodchuck fell into the "everything else" category. She could cancel the property insurance first, keeping the liability for her guides and vehicles going as long as she could.

Swami stared at the swollen river now. DeeDee finished nursing, and Swami patted her back awhile. Then she stood and looked at the river. There was no chance it would drop by tomorrow. All the puddles and mud in these hills would seep and seep. The river would only rise now.

"Come on, beautiful girl," Swami said, tucking DeeDee back into her warm wrap. "Let's go cancel some trips."

Swami walked away from the river and down the trail into the forest. The gray sky made the woods feel extra green, but empty too. The yellow Jeep was the only car in the parking lot, and she and DeeDee were definitely the only hikers today. Swami thought about Randy's mom, Debbie, the way she took those turkeys out of the sky with a rifle and built herself and her baby boy a small fortress behind those pines. Swami could never see herself owning a gun—the time she fired Randy's into the air, she was terrified and hardly knew what to do about it—but she could understand why Debbie did what she did, living alone in the woods with her baby. DeeDee was asleep with her mouth open against Swami's chest, wrapped in the rain jacket. Swami kissed her forehead. The little girl was so small and helpless, but she was also a galaxy.

Swami picked her way carefully down some wet rocks and across the bridges spanning the two small tributary creeks. Moon's bright yellow Jeep sat alone in the muddy gravel lot, its leaky canvas roof snugged over the roll bar. Down the lone road, headlights appeared in the rain. Swami moved to the Jeep and had the driver's door unlocked when the truck wheeled through the lot and pulled to a stop right next to her. The truck was big and new with tinted windows. Swami didn't want to jump into the driver's seat of the Jeep with DeeDee still wrapped on her chest, but she certainly would.

The black window rolled down and a lone man sat inside. Swami recognized him and exhaled a bit, even though it wasn't anyone she'd choose to chat with while standing in the rain. It was Greg Blakely, Duncan's rich uncle. Swami nearly laughed to herself. Why couldn't Sam have had a rich uncle, like this guy? Duncan had a seemingly bottomless bankroll. Swami had Chip. The last she'd heard of happenings out at Chip's deer farm, he was burying dead carp in his garden.

"Mornin'," said Blakely, smiling down from his truck.

"Afternoon," said Swami.

Blakely looked at his big gold watch, and nodded in his fresh leather seat. "How's business?" he said, sort of rolling his eyes at the river through the trees to commiserate. Swami hadn't talked to this man in person. She waited. She just wanted him to move his truck. "You're Swami, right? You own Woodchuck?"

"That's right," she said.

"I just stopped out there. That young lady, Moon, said you weren't in. Your son said you might be down at the river."

"How can I help you?" Swami said. This was the man who, as the investor behind X-treme, threatened Swami's financial livelihood, and who, with his buoyant view on the mine, had thrown Moon into a genuine mood the last half week.

"Down to business," he said. "That's why I'm here. Listen, I know you're looking to sell Woodchuck. And I'm looking to buy. You interested?"

Swami looked at the man. "Immediately," she said. She'd sell it at cost, or below.

Blakely laughed. "You're not much of a negotiator," he said. "But here's my deal. I don't know if you know this, but that mine, NorthSky? Word on the street is they made a heck of an offer to buy that peninsula your uncle lives on. The deer farm."

"*Sam's* uncle," Swami corrected him. "But what's this about the offer?"

Blakely gave a slow shrug. "I've been developing and building for a lot of years. I grew up here, but I've been all over. And I know money is money, no matter how it comes to an area. So I've been in contact with NorthSky. Chip's land is sort of central to their hopes. They've offered him over a half million dollars."

"*What?*" Swami blurted, and DeeDee startled and Swami quickly patted and bounced her back to sleep.

Blakely smiled at the baby girl. "Got your hands full there," he said.

"A half million dollars," Swami hissed.

Blakely gave a big nod. "And so far he won't sell."

Swami didn't know whether to feel disbelief or anger. Her mind was swirling. "But what's this have to do with Woodchuck?" she said.

"Here's my proposition, Swami. If you and Sam can encourage Chip to sell his peninsula—you're family; you have to have some kind of influence—I will purchase Woodchuck from you for your full asking price."

"Why?" Swami said. "I'm not putting this together. I mean, yes, of course, I'll try. But what's in this for you?"

"What's in it for me is that a billion-dollar company wants to flood these woods with money, and I want to encourage that and make sure they get the land they need. And if I could help that along and simultaneously buy up Woodchuck, the only competition in the area, all the better. No offense, but just to be straight with you, I'd bulldoze Woodchuck and start building some homes the moment it was mine."

"None taken," said Swami, dazzled by this opportunity. "I'll do what I can," she said.

Blakely put his truck in gear, smiled, and nodded. "Keep in touch?" he said.

Swami nodded.

Blakely drove the truck away, and Swami watched its taillights disappear around the distant curve in the gravel road. She imagined Blakely watched her in his rearview mirror, this startled young woman standing in a puddle. Swami rubbed DeeDee's back, looked out at the trees and the flooded river. She didn't care if she looked foolish, or if she was a bad negotiator. Her mind raced through the possibilities, deleting bills and obligations and problems in one fell swoop. She thought about Chip, sitting somewhere and lighting his joint, doing nothing. Well, he was about to.

•••

THE FIRST BIG RAIN OF the summer finally moved on, but the air was still thick with it. The stars were still blocked by a bank of clouds as Sam and Chip rode the dirt bike past the musky sign into the town of Thunderwater, past the small-porched river houses and the few remaining redbrick storefronts. The dirt bike's old motor rattled contentedly, leaving a trail of blue smoke in the still evening air as its knobby tires zipped across the wet asphalt of Main Street. The rafts were put away. The barn was swept. It was too wet to paint. It was Saturday night, and after a rain like that there was only one place to go to talk about it.

Chip downshifted. The gravel parking lot of Rita's Lanes and Lounge was nearly full—a couple of big pickups, Pete's red Dodge among them, a handful of Harleys, an old station wagon or two. There were also three big white trucks, new, white leases with out-of-state plates and NorthSky decals. Duncan's green Mustang was in the lot too.

"This should be interesting," said Chip as he pulled the keys from his bike.

Rita's was one-third diner, one-third bar, and one-third bowling alley. It had a handful of tables and booths and a rollaway Sunday brunch buffet, a marker board with a hand-drawn piece of pie near the serving station with its ketchup bottles and ashtrays, and then the bar, with its long oak rail and weathered stools and a deer head mounted over the bottles. The bowling alley had two lanes, just enough to accommodate the women's league, who were noisily high-fiving and drinking highball rum and Cokes through oversized straws.

Sam pulled on his flannel as he walked into the air-conditioning. The first-shift happy hour was still at it, a crew of mechanics and pipe fitters in their Carhartt pants and polka-dot welding hats. They leaned over packs of Camels and Newports, cans of Miller and Coors, empty shot glasses Rita hadn't yet collected. Bruce from the town hall towered among them, leaning at the bar with a crew of locals gathered around. He was buying drinks. A crew of younger men, already very drunk, fired darts at the dartboard and laughed.

Chip clapped a few men on the shoulder and they nodded and smiled as he passed. He lifted his chin at Duncan. Duncan lifted his chin back. He was hunched over an empty beer, looking sullen. Pete sat with Randy near the end of the bar and watched the weatherman on TV, offering up the weather forecast in his tan jacket. *Rain, rain, and maybe even more on the way*, he said.

"Well," said Chip, sidling in next to Pete. "Let's get tuned up, then. How's Bear?"

Pete lifted his can of beer in agreement. "Bear's good. Fat and happy. No puppies yet." He nodded down the bar. "Been listening to Bruce over there," said Pete. "He keeps buying drinks and telling everyone how great his company truck is. Thinking once I get enough beer in me I might hook up to its bumper and drag it out into the street."

Sam sat on an open stool next to Randy, who was eating fish and chips. "I thought you said you'd take a mining job," Sam said.

Pete shrugged a slow shrug. "Doesn't mean I won't still drag his truck into the street."

Beyond the bar, some bowling pins erupted, and ladies cheered and cackled.

"So, what'd Swami decide?" Randy asked. "We working this week?" He picked at some fish with his fork, dumped some vinegar on it.

Sam shook his head.

"It's the right move." Chip sighed. "Drowning people's bad for business."

A leathery woman in a bowling shirt stepped up behind the bar, wiping her hands on a rag. "Hey, Sammy. Hey, Chippers," she said, making herself another rum and Coke. She sipped it and patted her thinning orange-dyed bun into place.

"Hey, Rita," said Chip.

"Hey," she whispered conspiratorially, glancing over at Duncan, who sat outside the main circle of Bruce's interest. "Blondie from X-treme is in here. I don't want youse fightin' in here," she said.

Chip shook his head.

"He eats too much on my buffet. Never tips either. I call him Missy. Boy, that makes him hot!" Rita cackled, took another big pull off her drink. "So, what'll it be, Chippers, and my Sammy Whammy?" She pinched Sam's cheek. He'd only been in here twice, but his affiliation with Chip had made him a quick favorite. Everyone knew the more Rita drank behind her bar, the more she became everyone's buzzy aunt. *All my sweet baby sugar pies!* she once declared late on a Friday night, giving out free drinks in exchange for hugs. Tonight she was bowling with her league, drinking plenty, trotting between her bar and her lanes.

"One Coors and two pizzas," said Chip.

"I'll have a Coke," said Sam.

"Sam's being a good boy tonight." She laughed, stepping down the bar and digging into coolers. She chatted up a few other men who leaned on the bar, their heads already sunk down nearly between their shoulders.

"A whiskey too," Chip called after her. Rita nodded. Chip stood and clapped Sam on the shoulder, put some twenties on the bar in front of him. "Pay with that, eh," he said. "I gotta take a leak."

Rita came back and popped open cans, poured Chip a rye whiskey, grabbed the cash. She left it near the register and ran off to the bowling alley to take her turn. The women were chanting her name.

Randy ate his fries. Sam and Pete watched the news in silence for a while. It showed wet farm fields, their furrows filled with water. Pete shook his head in refusal.

"Chip told me Woodchuck's for sale again," Pete said. "You guys gotta keep believing. Keep hoping. It's not over yet. Winds shift."

Sam nodded. "We have some scout leaders coming after the Fourth. Jamboree might still pan out."

"You gotta keep Chip hoping," Pete said. "He's no good without the river, and the river's no good without him. I don't want to live in a Thunderwater where guys like Duncan push out the Chips, and the Sams too. I been thinking about how rivers can work in mysterious ways. And dams can too."

Sam just looked at him.

"I can't make promises, but maybe the river could make it real hard on Duncan during that jamboree. Maybe the river could stay high. Duncan and his guides can't run a high river. Chip can. Woodchuck can. I seen Chip guide that gorge at ten grand. No one can guide that gorge at ten grand. No one the river don't love. River don't love Duncan, or that guy whose truck I'm gonna pull into the street."

"Pete, you're being too bucky tonight," said Randy. "It's early yet."

Pete shrugged again.

Sam whispered now. "Is that really possible, with the dam?"

Pete nodded. Made sure no one was listening.

"There's an old, original bypass in the dam, pure mechanical, no gauges, outflows deep underwater. Only a few of us even know it's there." He looked Sam right in the eye.

Something rose in Sam like water. It felt like the will to fight, or at least go down fighting. And what if the winds *could* change? What if enough money changed hands in that jamboree that Swami didn't have to sell it all at a loss? Pete was right. Woodchuck was better on the water. Sam shifted on his stool.

"Can we really do this—" Sam said.

"*We* ain't doing anything," said Pete. "But like I said. Rivers work in mysterious ways. Dams too. Sometimes we make mistakes at the dam. Could just keep making well-timed mistakes." He glared at Duncan and Bruce as he said it.

Chip returned, took a pull of his beer, and wiped his beard with his forearm.

"Life is good," he said. "It's *good.*"

For the rest of the night, Sam drank Cokes and imagined plots in his mind: high water, rafting reservations changing hands, mining trucks stuck in mud. Chip drank enough after his pizza—nearly a whole bottle of rye—that he started leading river shanties with Rita and some of the locals. Chip sat on the bar and sang a shanty about an albatross, while Rita swayed with him and gave him kisses. She gave Duncan kisses too after he promised, shouted, that he wouldn't fight with Chip and that everyone could get along.

". . . AND THEN SHE DANCED WITH BILLYYYYY!" Chip bellowed, and everyone bellowed with him, even Bruce from the mine. The bowling lanes and kitchen closed, and Rita's transformed into only a dark, smoky tavern. Noise, sweat, spilled drinks. The whole town of Thunderwater was getting tuned up, and there was Chip at the center like an anchor, somehow, with enough alcohol, holding it all together. Pete was right. There was no Thunderwater without Chip, and there was no Chip without Thunderwater. They were the same force of nature, all bluff and sky and river rock. But like all forces of nature, the old was continually supplanted by the new, and like it or not, there was Duncan with his zip lines, and there was NorthSky building its fenced encampment. There was Randy taking too many shots, and there was Pete glaring harder and harder at Bruce. There was Sam, alone, drinking Cokes for the sake of a wife who wouldn't talk to him anymore. And outside, there was the river itself, cutting along its ancient bluffs, its riverbanks filled with Indian mounds and precious minerals.

"I love you, little buddy," Chip slurred into Sam's shoulder, pulling him in close.

"I love you too, Chip," said Sam for the tenth time that evening. Sam had already made Chip give him the keys to the dirt bike, which he'd done gladly and with flair.

"Oh, I wish Moon was here," said Randy. "Where's Moon?! Mooon!"

"Where's my tambourine?!" Rita cackled. She tipped off the back of the bar, and came back up with it. "Now we're gonna do the one about the seahorsey and the mermaid."

Someone lit off a bottle rocket, and it zipped across the bar and popped over the waitress station. No one but Sam seemed to notice.

"Messing about!" bellowed Chip, paddling the bar with a wooden ski he lifted from the wall. "Messing about in boats!"

"Where's my bottle!"

"Where's Moooon?!"

"Where's all my little singing sugar pies! And a one, and a two, and a—"

BOOM.

The floor of the bar shook. Everyone ducked, and everyone looked around as if they'd dropped something. Sam felt it clear as day. And then he heard it again, followed by a big whistling roar.

"Knock it off with them fireworks!" Rita yelled, but the noise seemed to come from outside now. *BOOM. BOOM.*

"Where's Pete?" Randy asked. Sam didn't know.

The roar got louder, and everyone rushed outside to the parking lot.

Sam made it there first and then stopped in his tracks while others rushed past him. The air felt cold and open. There was a deep fog drifting through the streetlamps.

BOOM! Everyone ducked again, and then they saw it. Pete's power wagon, chained up to the rear axle of Bruce's mining truck. The big diesel roared, leaped forward like a whipped mule, the chain snapped tight, and the box of the truck boomed like a kettle. Pete floored it, yanking Bruce's truck from its parking space and raking Duncan's Mustang in the process.

"Hey!" yelled Bruce, pushing past the rest of the crowd. *"Hey!"*

But it was too late. Pete's diesel whistled and roared and shook, firing deep black smoke into the air. All four tires bit through the parking lot, dragging the new Ford out backward and at an angle over the curb and into the street. Bruce chased him. But once Pete's truck had pavement under its tires, it took off like a rocket, noise and rumble and smoke, Bruce's truck shuddering behind it.

The fog swirled and enveloped Pete's truck, and then the enraged Bruce staggered after it.

"This ain't good," said Chip.

Everyone from the bar was howling and hooting again, lighting cigarettes, thrilled at the spectacle.

Randy took off in his blue truck, into the road, after Pete.

Someone fired another bottle rocket after him. It sparked and popped out in the fog.

Duncan shouted about his Mustang, the front bumper crushed in. He started yelling about how someone should call the cops. Rita started yelling about how we don't need no cops. Someone lit off another bottle rocket.

"That's not good," moaned Chip again. "It ain't even July yet." And then he pulled Sam tight under his arm, and Sam was held there by his sea anchor uncle, who smelled like river and deer and pot in the early morning darkness. But Sam didn't feel safe there. He suddenly felt a sinking feeling like anywhere might not be safe, like he was lost in a town that wasn't his own.

Chip passed gas, still heavily draped around Sam. "Oop," he said and gave a satisfied sigh. "A little toot." And then looking back at the empty road, giving Sam a little shake. "That's not *good* what Pete just done."

JULY

ELEVEN

"IT'S THE END OF TIMES," DEBBIE SAID, SITTING IN HER LA-Z-BOY AND frowning in disbelief at the TV in her living room.

"Deb," chided Moon from where she knelt on the carpet with Dell. "The water will go back down."

"Well," Debbie said, and raised her eyebrows and tied another knot into the fleece blanket in her lap. "God said he wouldn't kill us with another flood. That's the rainbow. But what comes after this is what I'm nervous about."

"Don't be nervous," said Moon.

"Hmph," said Deb.

Swami and Moon were invited out with the kids today to make knot blankets and eat lunch. They ate pulled turkey sandwiches with gravy on good, chewy rolls. The trailer was warm and dry and the kitchen smelled like black pepper and butter, and now the cookies that were in the oven for dessert. After lunch they moved to the living room, where Deb had a big box of soft fleece she said she got from St. Vincent's, the thrift store near Ironsford. The fabrics were yellow and pink and brown and gray. One had an animal print, and that's what Dell chose for her top piece. Deb showed them all how to sandwich the two pieces together, make six-inch slits along the edges, and then tie the slits into knots.

"A knot blanket." Debbie smiled. "It's been so damp." Dell beamed at her, plopped down on the carpet next to Moon while Moon helped her cut and tie. Swami chose pink and gray and sat in the rocker. Darren politely shrugged and opted to read a book about small-game hunting, lying on his stomach and flipping the pages, watching the TV. DeeDee lay next to him on her belly, bobbing her head around.

There was a long news special covering the flood. Al Gore was down in the flooded town of Grafton, Illinois. The floodwaters were affecting eight Midwestern states, said the broadcaster, and today Al

Gore and senators were gathering, flying in aboard jets and black he-
licopters. Today's broadcast showed Gore in a green safari shirt with a
wireless microphone, walking with the governor down the main street,
shaking hands, Secret Service men in khaki vests and sunglasses walking along with him. The day in Grafton was sunny. The people were
glad to see him. And then the group arrived at the end of the main
street, big flat-bottomed boats docked right on the yellow centerline.
Gore and the governor got in, and they toured the town by idling duck
boat. Muddy water was right up to the windows of brownstone buildings. Someone had spray-painted *No Wake Zone* on a storefront to miti-
gate damage. A market billboard for sweet corn was nearly submerged.

"Look at how he rides in that boat," Deb had said. "He's all stiff,
sitting right in the middle."

"Well, it's good he's there," Moon said.

"Hmph," Debbie said.

"Not a fan of Clinton and Gore?" Swami asked, smirking.

"Not a fan of any of 'em, don't care what they say," she answered.
"Look at him try to ride in that boat."

There had been multiple press conferences. The flood was all the
news had talked about for a week. Nearly every creek and river in
the entire Midwest was swollen, all tributaries rushing downstream.
The towns next to bigger rivers were affected the worst. Farm fields
were sunk. Seedling corn and grain had drowned and rotted. Debbie
said she'd had to cut a few drainage furrows with her little red tractor
to help her cabbage field drain toward the woods. "Like Venice, Italy,"
she said.

Now Gore and the governor from Illinois were back on shore, discussing the options for disaster relief. It would add millions to the defi-
cit, and they'd have to make that up with other cuts or taxes, but this
was a true emergency and we'd band together and make it through.
These were already the worst floods in over one hundred years. If more
rain came this summer, records would be set. The earth was warming, Gore had been saying, which might mean more major rain events,
melting ice caps, shrinking coasts.

And that's when Debbie said it was the end of times. "Maybe we should change the channel," she said. "Put it on local news awhile." Darren got up from his book to change the channel to number six on the old TV. Moon helped Dell tie another knot.

The town of Thunderwater wasn't flooding so far. Its banks were steep. But the river was high and muddy and closer to the road than anyone had ever remembered it being. When Swami drove the rafting van to town to look at the water levels, people joined her on the riverbank to look at the spectacle, discuss how they thought it was going down. It wasn't, Swami knew. When a river drops, the rocks on shore will have wet bands on them. There were no wet bands. The river was still climbing. As was Swami's inability to pay the bills. The mortgage back home was paid. Woodchuck was *barely* current. She had canceled the property insurance for Woodchuck. And if they had to keep canceling trips—it had been nearly three full weeks now—she'd cancel the liability too. No one knew but her, and she bore it quietly. No one knew about the offer Mr. Blakely made either. Swami tried hinting about it to Chip last week when she drove out to his deer farm with a trailed raft for boat patching. Since they were off the river and couldn't paint the barn in the rain, Swami had the guides patching rafts and replacing leaky valves, retying thwarts into place. They did the work at Chip's place, one boat at a time. He had all the parts and epoxies in his machine shed. The neck of Chip's farm was completely underwater. The culvert stream had made it an island. Chip met her as she waded across, smiling at the ridiculousness of his new island home.

"You know," said Swami, taking his hand as he hoisted her to shore. "You could probably make a mint if you sold this place. *Island* realty."

Chip let go of her hand and tilted his head a moment.

"Seriously, Chip," she said. "You ever think of selling this and retiring?"

He shook his head. "This land is my heart. Where would I be without this place?" he said.

"Florida," suggested Swami, and then quickly changed the subject before he could form a rebuttal. "I brought the next raft for you guys." Sam stepped out of the machine shed down the driveway, lifted his hand in a greeting.

Swami and Sam still weren't talking, connecting. There was just a muddiness between them, as if they stood on opposite banks of a flooded river. Any signs of what came next were shrouded. There was a no-wake zone between them, and that was all. Maybe there could be a slow change back to what was, with lots of time. For the present, Swami busied herself with more immediate concerns, like canceled trips and her camper full of children. Thunderwater's Fourth of July fireworks had been canceled due to rain, which was a deep disappointment to Darren. But they were rescheduled for tonight, and the weather looked promising. Just like in Grafton, Illinois, the sun was shining again in Wisconsin, lifting the smell of puddles from the roads and fields. Randy was going to leave Chip's early to meet Swami and Moon at his mom's this afternoon, and then they'd all drive together to Thunderwater's old ballpark to watch. Swami didn't know if Sam would come. She didn't directly invite him.

"Moon's on TV!" Darren shouted. "Look!"

Darren beamed and everyone leaned in. DeeDee snapped her head up and bobbed it.

"Oh my God," said Debbie in a low voice.

Moon gaped. "They're airing it!" she cried, and then lifted her hands to her face.

"What, Mom, what?!" said Dell.

On local channel six, a brunette reporter held an umbrella and microphone in midconversation with a soaking-wet Moon. Behind them was a chain-link fence, and behind the fence sat the tan work trailers for NorthSky Enterprise. Near the fence, the college girl and an older couple walked a small protest loop in the mud, carrying signs on sticks.

"They tried to put a gate across the base of the road today," said a nearly winded Moon into the camera. "But that road is a *public* road. NorthSky's property begins at this fence, *not* at the road, so we cut the chain and walked up here again. They're trying to keep the River Keepers out. They're trying to keep all of us out of what they're really doing."

"Incredible," said the reporter. "Have you spoken with any NorthSky officials? Have they met with you?"

Moon shook her head and smirked. "They started parking their trucks on the far side. So we'll see them moving about, driving in and out, but that's it. We haven't blocked their vehicles or anything. Not yet. But we want people to know how dangerous this mining operation will be, and that's why we're here every Wednesday and Saturday at noon. And we encourage everyone to come out. Look up sulfide mining and what it really is, and then come join us. You don't have to be a local. This river feeds into Green Bay, to Lake Michigan, to Erie. This isn't just about one small town."

"Incredible," said the woman, looking back at the camera. "And there you have it, Jim. A grassroots effort up here at Thunderwater, residents protesting a multinational mining company. More to come on this. We'll be following the story on channel six. Back to you in studio."

When the screen shifted back to the studio, Moon fell back on the carpet and shrieked with glee. Dell shrieked too and dogpiled on top of her. "I can't believe they *aired* it," Moon said. "I called them and called them and they came out last week. Oh, she was the nicest reporter too. She'll be back again, she told me."

"It *is* incredible," Swami said. "Congratulations, Moon."

"Moon's famous!" said Darren.

Moon bear-hugged Dell and rolled up again, sat cross-legged and smiled, picked up her knot blanket and started tying again. "Oh, I'm so happy," she said.

"Me too," said Dell, and began trying to tie knots on her edge again.

"It's ain't just you," said Debbie. She was sitting still in her chair. She was still staring at the TV with a bit of a terrified look in her eye. "I'm not so sure this is the best idea," she said. "Moon, honey, you're on *TV*. It's one thing to fight your fight, but this is too big. There's a *face* to it now. It's your face."

"Oh, Deb, it's all right. It really is. Everything is legit, and if anything, being on TV will help. There's a story now. Everyone knows. It's safer that way, isn't it?"

"Like I said before, Moon." She tried to take a deep breath. "You fight your fight. I know you will. But it ain't just you, honey. You gotta take care of more than just yourself."

"It's Randy you're worried about."

"It's Randy, it's that college girl, it's these kids. Randy would follow you to death and back, and you know that. I'm just asking that you remember that. I didn't when I was your age either. But life *changes*. It's just you, for a long time, and then it isn't."

Dell held up a knot on her blanket for Debbie's inspection. "How's *dis*?"

Debbie brightened for the child's sake, smiled. "That's good, honey. That's a real good one." She pinched the knot, then petted Dell's head.

"Deb," said Moon.

Deb nodded, still watching the little girl. The woman was genuinely scared. Swami could see it.

"Thank you for saying what you said. I'll remember," she said. She put her hand on Debbie's knee. "I know it. It's not just me."

Debbie kept nodding. Took a rattling breath. Looked at Swami and Dell and Moon and DeeDee. "It's time I show you something. With all that's happening, you should know, if you need it." She set her blanket on the arm of her chair and stood up. "I'm gonna take out them cookies and then I'm gonna show you something."

She walked to the kitchen. Swami and Moon looked at each other, with sympathy in their eyes for the frightened woman. But Swami allowed a quick smile at Moon too. Getting her story on the news was a big accomplishment. Swami felt proud of her, the way she imagined she'd feel proud for a little sister. She admired the younger woman too, her stage in life. It was just about her. Moon could follow her heart wherever it led, and in a way, Swami wanted to protect that for her. Encourage it, even.

And then Deb set the cookie sheets on cooling racks, swept aside a throw rug with her foot, and stooped down and pulled up a trapdoor in the kitchen floor. Darren perked right up.

"Come on down," Debbie said. "I'll show you where everything is. Careful on the steps." And then she stepped down through the hatch and disappeared.

Moon went first, wide-eyed. Darren and Dell followed, with Swami and DeeDee behind them. Swami asked Darren to hold Dell's hand,

and he did. They both had startled, adventure-hungry eyes as they made their way down to the dirt floor.

Debbie stood near the far wall of a small, low-ceilinged room not much larger than a hot tub. Swami stooped. There was one light bulb. The walls were lined with shelves of canning jars, peppers and sau-erkraut and chopped green beans and cooked venison, all snugged together against the old fieldstone walls. The room smelled dry and dusty. The four corners of the room were supported with wooden beams the width of whole pines.

"So here's the original root cellar me and Randy's dad dug before he passed away. We dug it for potatoes and canning. There's about six months' worth of food for two in here. You're welcome to all of it if the time ever comes. I rotate it as I use it up." She tapped a couple of jars filled with light-colored stew meat. "This is them turkeys we got." She smiled.

And then her eyes darted a little nervously among them. "But like I said, this was the original. There's more. And I'm showing it to you because I consider you family, because you're good people, and it ain't just for me and Randy. We got enough for others. But you gotta promise it don't leave this room. Not everyone is good."

"What is it?" Darren asked, thrilled.

"Can you keep secrets?" she asked him.

He nodded. Dell nodded. Swami looked at Moon. She could tell Moon had never been invited into this before either. Swami felt a little nervous now, standing in this silent root cellar, the air so still.

Debbie nodded. "Grab me that little pipe off that wall behind you," Debbie said.

Darren found the length of pipe, an old handle from a floor jack. Debbie took it and turned toward one of the big wooden support beams, fitted the pipe into a drilled hole near the floor. She yanked on it, and the bottom of the beam swung out, and then up, the uppermost part riding on some hidden hinge. Debbie pressed the massive beam up to the ceiling. Darren and Dell backed up a bit. And then Debbie let go of the beam and turned to them and smiled. "We got it rigged up with a dumbwaiter. Darren could open it. You just gotta know how to break it free from the floor with the pipe. The light's right in here to the left."

Debbie wedged herself into the dark gap and sidled through, chuckling as she went. "I'm too fat and old, see?" she called out from the dark. "It's time to show this to some younger folks." And then the gap snapped white with bright light.

Swami peered in as Moon ducked through. There was a whole room beyond the gap, white walls and lots of light, shelves and bins lining the walls. Swami looked at the beam and the fieldstone as she passed through, holding DeeDee very tight to her chest.

The room was nearly as large as the entire trailer. Swami didn't have to stoop anymore. The floor and walls were poured concrete instead of fieldstone. The ceiling was made of metal beams. Bright rows of fluorescent shop lights lit the space. A dehumidifier hummed.

"Whoa," whispered Darren. Dell didn't echo him. She just sidled a bit closer to her mom. From floor to ceiling, each wall was lined with deep shelves and racks. The shelves were filled with sealed five-gallon pails, red jerry cans, plastic tubs, and wooden bins. The ceiling was spanned with painted metal beams. The space was immaculate.

"Have a look around," said Debbie. She looked both nervous and proud, maybe embarrassed too. "Now that you know, this is yours too. Dug out this entire space by hand. It took me twenty years to build it up to what it is now. That and a good freeze dryer."

Swami slowly ambled along the walls after warning Darren not to touch anything. She didn't know what to think of it. She was startled by it all. She'd heard of this but had never seen it. *Preppers.* Her heartbeat quickened. The smell of cookies drifted down through from the kitchen. She glanced at Deb, nervously grasping her apron. The woman was revealing more than her stores. She was revealing her*self.* Swami imagined this woman years earlier, alone with her wall of pines and her baby son, shoveling out a bunker bucket by bucket. It made Swami feel like crying, because she immediately recognized the impulse behind it. The fear and panic, and love too, driving the need to preserve what was hers, these children who came from her body. That the impulse came out like this, as a bunker dug beneath the earth in a field in Wisconsin, made as much sense as it didn't. Swami had felt the need to dig in, to burrow. This woman had literally done it. And had done it for a long time.

There were blankets, cots, batteries, row upon row of buckets of food. Sugar, salt, flour, dried vegetables, dried fruit, powdered milk and eggs, seed. There was a medicine chest with labeled drawers: *Pain Meds, Antibiotics, Tourniquets, Wounds*. In the far corner was a small library: *The Complete Gardener*; *Canning and Fermenting: Basics and Advanced*; *Home Carpentry*. There were mechanics' manuals for tractors and trucks, manuals for investing, manuals for military tactics for each branch of service. There were bins for tents and sleeping bags, water filtration, purification. There was a bench covered in clear bins of brass casings and gunpowder and a reloading press. There were guns. Big guns and handguns and old wood guns and black military rifles. There were hatchets and saws and sharpening tools. There was a bin of children's toys, one of movies, radios, novels. In the center of the room was a water hand pump on a pipe cemented through the floor, a water tank the size of a small car, and a composting toilet. There were four or five gas generators sitting idle and smeared in thick coats of grease. There was a gas mask and a hazmat suit with rubber boots and a hood. When Dell saw the suit, hanging there with its bug eyes, she wrapped her hand around her mom's leg.

"After Randy's dad died, I used the survivor's benefits from the VA to buy a little extra. Instead of one can of soup I'd buy two. Instead of one box of shotgun shells, I'd buy two. I kept that up for a long time. The perishables I rotate, but there's a five-year food supply here for a family. It started for just me and Randy. Then I figured if others came asking I wouldn't have the heart to turn them away, so I started preparing for them too without really knowing who they might be. I guess that means you. You're the family. If you ever need it, it's yours. You know how to get in. The hatch over behind the water tank tunnels out to a rock pile behind the barn," she said. "The rest of the inventory and instructions—planting seasons, animal migration, and such—are detailed in that red binder on the end of the bookshelf."

She shrugged and smiled. "So," she said. "Now you know."

Swami shook her head in amazement. It was odd, and frightening, the idea of locking oneself in down here, and the idea of a world becoming so frightening one would want to. Swami understood the rationale, but there came a point when the impulse to survive became absurd. Survive to what end?

"Who else knows about this place?" she said.

"Chip and Randy," she answered. "And you can tell your husband, of course."

"I—" Swami stammered. "I hardly know what to say."

"Well," she answered, and smirked. "Don't say anything at all."

They heard footsteps on the root cellar stairs, and a moment later Randy burst into the room, a bit wide-eyed and worried. Everyone turned to look at him. Randy looked at them, and then at his mom.

"Hey," he said, and then he relaxed and stuffed his hands in his pockets. He looked at his mom. "You showed them," he said, impressed.

"I guess I did," she said. "It felt right."

Randy nodded, studied her. "It's good, Mom," he said. "It's real good."

"Is Sam with you?" Swami asked. "For the fireworks?"

Randy shook his head. "He's not."

Swami saw Darren's shoulders fall when he heard that.

•••

SAM DOWNSHIFTED CHIP'S DIRT BIKE and took it easy on the throttle as he turned onto the campsite loop at Governor's State Park. It was late afternoon, and the air was damp and cool beneath the green canopy of trees. Swami would be at Debbie's, he knew. When they finished tying the floor on a final raft, Chip turned his attention to his greenhouse, and Randy invited Sam to the fireworks.

"I better not," he said. "She didn't invite me."

"C'mon," said Randy. "Grow a pair, buddy. Come see the show."

Sam wanted more than anything to go sit on a blanket with his family, watch his kids' faces light up green and red and white as the fireworks burst. That was the best part. Sam never watched the fireworks anymore. He watched his kids watch the fireworks. But he still felt the deep sting of shame from that night in the grange hall, the way Swami couldn't even look at him as she walked out. Sam stayed out at Chip's for days after that night at the bar. He slept late while Chip slept off his hangover. Randy and Pete slept it off too, after Randy found him "delivering" the NorthSky truck back to their mining site. Bruce never found out who Pete was, and no one, not even Rita, would tell him who the man was who'd dragged his truck back down the highway. They wanted jobs in this town, sure, but they had their loyalties too. Sam spent the next few mornings walking the woods alone, watching the river, sitting with the silence of the Indian mounds. He'd stand by the deer fence for hours, feeding the herd alfalfa pellets from the palm of his hand.

The night after the grange hall, Chip sat quietly with Sam on the screen porch, watching the fog drift up thick from the river. Chip gave Sam a worried look. It was so quiet Sam could hear the bowl of Chip's pipe crackle as he lit it. *You have to take care of Swami*, he said. *I don't know what exactly, but you gotta try something. It's like a foot entrapment. You gotta get some ropes out, get a plan, do somethin' or it's all over anyway. I know. Hang in there.* Sam knew he was talking about Aunt Mary. Chip lit his bowl again, blew smoke up into the rafters, passed it absentmindedly to Sam, then remembered Sam was teetotaling.

"I can't come to the fireworks," Sam told Randy. Sam was packing a small backpack with a headlamp and some paintbrushes and a jug of water. "It's better if I get some work done tonight. Swami's scout leaders are coming tomorrow. Or they are at least scheduled to. We'll see what the river does. I want to get to the barn and make it go as smooth as possible in the morning."

Randy nodded, shook hands, and watched Sam drive off on Chip's bike.

At Governor's State Park, Sam found the Brave parked where it'd been all summer. The grass had grown tall behind the tires, where Ranger Bonnie couldn't reach with her weed-eater. The rest of the site was tidy: beach towels hung over chair backs, bright plastic buckets nested on the picnic table, the kids' bikes leaning on their kickstands.

Swami had even hung a string of Christmas lights between the camper and a pine. It all made something catch in Sam's throat. He killed the motor on the idling dirt bike and sat a moment. Smitty said the new radiator should be in this week. Sam shook his head. Even that didn't fill him with hope any longer. He'd fix the camper, and Swami would just drive away. But that's what Sam had been thinking lately. He couldn't control whether or not Swami drove away, just like he couldn't control the weather. But he could do what was right, regardless of the outcome. He'd fix the motor because it was right. He'd suffer the shame because it was right. The grand gesture wasn't to win her back. It was to just do the right thing. There were things outside his control. And there was a sad sort of peace in that knowledge.

"Swami?" he called out. He knew she was gone, but he had to be sure. He was deep over her boundary lines, uninvited to their campsite. There was no answer, so Sam dismounted and plucked the Piggly Wiggly bag from beneath the bungee cords on the back seat. He'd driven all the way to Crivitz and back. It was dusk now.

"Hey, Swami?" Sam called again. He knocked on the aluminum side door of the Brave before entering. The camper was empty, and Sam stepped inside. He was *home*, amidst all the signs and smells of his people. There was a load of washed but unfolded laundry on the galley bench, Swami's grain crackers and a wedge of cheddar on a cutting board, a half-played game of checkers, yogurt cups in the sink. Sam rummaged through the cupboard until he found something that would work as a vase. He filled it with a jug of drinking water in the fridge, and arranged the bouquet of roses he'd brought. They looked nice, but two of the stems were badly wilted from their ride near the muffler. He culled them and hid them in the trash beneath an empty bag of granola. It was imperfect, and might even make her angry that he'd been here. It *would* make her angry. But it was right to give her flowers. She had had a horrible summer so far. She'd been through so much. Sam wanted her to have a vase of flowers, as inadequate as that clearly was. Sam stood in the darkening camper and closed his eyes, inhaling the smell of the roses and the washed laundry and sunscreen and sandy towels, the smell of his people. He looked at the unfinished game of checkers.

Darren always wanted to be red. Sam nudged one of the black pieces forward. "Miss you, buddy," he whispered, and then it all felt so overwhelming that Sam had to jog out of the camper, give the dirt bike a good kick, and race away fast enough to feel a breeze on his face.

At the raft barn, Sam adjusted the headlamp and scaled the scaffolding Birdy's grandsons assembled some weeks ago. The barn siding was dry, or at least drier than it had been in a very long time. The face of the barn was painted about two-thirds of the way up. If Sam worked all night, he could finish it, and remove the scaffolding too, and that would make Swami happy, pulling in on the hopeful day of her scout leader trip to a finished barn. He took a breath and minded the present task. He had to climb up three layers of scaffolding, carefully finding his balance as he climbed one-handed, carting a heavy pail of paint in the other.

Sam made it to the top layer, dragged his bucket up, and made his way out to the center, steadying himself against the wall of the barn while the scaffold wobbled a bit beneath him. When he saw the empty beer cans, he put down his bucket.

"C'mon, Randy," he said. He must have been sitting up here with Pete or Moon, drinking and looking at the sky. No wonder this place had run Swami ragged. Managing Woodchuck really was like wrangling cats, stoned and drunk and hungover cats that slept more and smelled worse.

Sam kicked the empties down to the gravel below. Then he turned off his headlamp and looked out at the dark road, and listened to the crickets for a time. Overhead, the moon hung in the sky. A bright white crescent, and the sky was so dark, so devoid of light, Sam could make out the pockets on the crescent's surface, and see the shadow of its dark side too, all of it. The Milky Way sat behind it in a confident stroke of light. Sam felt the weight of the paintbrush in his back pocket. He hadn't painted a canvas in a very long time. The sight of the Milky Way and that moon and the silence made him want to take it up again. But tonight his canvas was this blue barn in a blue moonlit field, beneath bright, bright stars. He'd paint it to its peak tonight, smoothing drips, softening gaps, filling in the rough wood with paint that shone like the wet grass.

He stooped to crack open the tub of paint. The smell of the oil paint overwhelmed the night air. It was a good smell, Sam thought, like turpentine. The farm fields and the smell of paint reminded Sam immediately of a good memory of his mom. It was a few years after his dad died, and many years before his mom became sick. Sam was in middle school, and they drove out in his mom's old station wagon to a pick-your-own pumpkin patch. She got a raise that week, the first in years, and surprised Sam with a set of oil paints and a big art pad with real artist's paper. At the farm, she bought cider and two ham sandwiches and three pumpkins. His mom parked the car in the grass, and sat on the tailgate finishing her sandwich much slower than Sam, while Sam sat just behind her with the pumpkins, trying out his paints. He outlined the bright rows of pumpkin vines growing in the field, the families out there searching through the broad leaves. He painted his mom too in her red dress, the way she looked up in the sun with her eyes closed from time to time, a smile on her face. Sam hadn't been able to capture it all on paper, how he felt proud of her, or how the pumpkins smelled like earth in the back of their wagon, or how the cider was sweet and life felt stable and right at that moment. How could anyone learn to paint that? The memory was so precious it made Sam cry. The way that woman showed up for her son. If Sam had to name the day that had made him want to become an artist, it was that.

Crouched on the scaffolding, Sam clicked on his headlamp, dipped his brush, and set to work on the barn. He took one stroke, and then he heard the fireworks. He couldn't see them over the trees, but he could see the sky light up over Thunderwater, hear the deep bass and some of the faint crackles too. Sam imagined the faces of his kids, and Swami too. He shook the thought from his mind. Next year, he said. Next year. But right now, this. As Sam painted along with the booming fireworks, he realized there was less to paint than he'd expected. Maybe Randy had been painting up here after all. The unpainted peak was about thirty feet wide, arcing up to an apex about ten feet above the scaffolding. Sam could do this, and part of him felt glad to finish it alone like this, out here with the stars and crickets and memories and hopes of a better next year.

When he finished what he could reach, he dragged up a small stepladder. He had five hours until sunup, and only needed about two of them. His hand ached from gripping the brush, and his neck was killing him, but he'd make that peak and then pitch the scaffolding down piece by piece.

The stepladder's legs were just wide enough to straddle two planks. Sam worked his way up the boards, blending in each brushstroke, *blue*, right up to the peak, where he had to go on his tiptoes to reach one-handed. He pressed the final strokes of paint into the grain, dabbed and smoothed it, feeling proud and full of wonder the way he had about that early painting in the back of his mother's station wagon. He felt wonder for all that had happened in between then and now as well. Marriage. The strange and beautiful miracle of children. The arguments. Nights spent sleeping on couches. The loss of his mom. There was so much pain and beauty in it all, but at the moment Sam felt gratitude for the pain too, for having had the privilege of living that too, or of living at all. He was thankful for a hand that could *ache*.

Sam leaned back to look at his work, pressing two fingertips into the wet paint of the wall to steady himself. It didn't matter. He was covered in it, blue like the moon and the sky and the barn and the fields. "Finished it, Swami," he breathed, and made to step back down the stepladder. But as he stepped down, he felt the sole of his sandal slip from the rung, and when he grabbed at the top of the ladder he felt the ladder slip into a gap between planks. Sam clung to a cold metal pipe of the scaffolding as everything tipped. The blue barn fell away from view, fell up, as cold, dark air rushed past Sam like water rushing down a falls.

TWELVE

"MY BUTT'S ALL WET," SAID DARREN, CLIMBING INTO THE BACK SEAT of the rafting van while Swami buckled DeeDee into the car seat.

"Mine too," she said. "Next time we'll bring a better blanket to sit on."

"And Dad," she thought she heard him mumble.

"What's that?" she asked.

"And a pad," he said again, sitting heavily into the seat and pulling his belt on next to his little sister. Swami sat in the back with them, while Randy and Moon sat up front. They idled in traffic for several minutes while the crowd dispersed from the fireworks. It had been a good show, small-town, tall pine trees lit up in the flashes of smoke. DeeDee didn't care for it, so Swami watched the second half from inside the van. All the kids, even Darren, were sleeping by the time Randy eased the old van out onto the road.

Moon turned in her seat. "Big morning tomorrow," she said as quietly as the old noisy van would allow.

"Very big," Swami agreed. "These scout leaders mean scout troops."

"They'll get a helluva ride," said Randy.

"Have you checked the river level?"

Randy put on his blinker and turned onto the empty highway toward Governor's.

"Pete said it's at 6300 and dropping slowly."

"Well," said Swami, "I told them to go ahead and come. If it's one cubic foot beneath six grand, I say we run it if we can. If you can."

"We can do it," Randy said.

"Oh, Moon, that reminds me," said Swami. "I was wondering if I could take your Jeep in tomorrow and you could take in the van. I'll take the kids with me. But anything that can make that barn look a little more adventurous and with-it is good. I'd like to have the scout leaders pull in and see that bright yellow Jeep."

"These are, like, forty-year-old dads, right?" Moon said.

Swami nodded.

"I'll wear my shortest pair of shorts tomorrow," said Moon.

"That'd do it for me," said Randy, grinning through the windshield.

Moon smirked and poked him in the ribs.

Randy pulled into Governor's and drove slowly through the trees. The campgrounds were filling up now that it was July, even in spite of the rain. The old couple who read novels was still there. The young couple had moved on. The other sides ebbed and flowed with colorful tents and different smells and sounds as the days wore on.

"Here you go, Moon," said Randy. "It was good seeing you tonight."

"Good to see you too, Randy," Moon said.

Swami felt, in the back seat, like she was interrupting something.

Moon hopped out and said goodbye. "Just swing by and grab the Jeep whenever you want tomorrow. I'll leave the keys in it."

Moon closed the door and trotted off in the dark toward her small teardrop camper.

"Next stop, Swami's residence," said Randy, putting the van back in gear.

And then just as the van crept forward, they heard a woman scream.

Randy jerked the van to a stop. "You hear that?"

The woman screamed again.

"It's Moon!" Randy shouted, slamming the van in park and scrambling out his door.

Darren woke up.

"What's happening, Mom?"

"I don't know yet," she said. "Stay right there with your sisters for a moment."

Swami reached up to grab the Maglite from the glove box, and leapt from the van.

The light snapped on and she swept the beam through the bushes. When she rounded the corner, she saw Moon weeping and shuddering and Randy holding on to her. Moon's entire campsite was trashed. Her pots and pans were tossed around, chairs kicked over. Her yellow Jeep had dark red paint splashed all over the windshield and hood and seats.

As Swami moved in slowly, she smelled something sour smoldering in the fire pit. She shone her light through the smoke. It was the remnants of Moon's gorgeous picnic quilt.

"Oh no, *Moon*," Swami said, moving toward her and Randy.

Moon cried and shook her hands, folded her arms tightly around herself while Randy moved her toward a lawn chair.

"Sit down a second," he said. "Swami, can you hand me that light?"

She did.

"What is this, Randy? What's going on?"

"I don't know, but I got an idea."

He stepped toward Moon's camper with the still-open door. When he poked his head inside and shone the light, Swami smelled blood, deep and earthy. The entire camper was drenched in it. It wasn't red paint.

All the cabinets had been kicked in, and then Swami looked toward the small sleeping cot, where Randy shone the light. Moon's small flashlight was still shining on the floor, where she'd dropped it. When Swami saw the bed, she nearly screamed too.

She recoiled and staggered back, hand over her mouth. "What is that in there?" she asked. "What was on that bed?"

Randy stood up outside the camper, gave the trees surrounding the campsite a quick search with his light. "It's a pig," Randy said. "It was a pig."

They walked toward Moon, who was still shuddering in her chair and holding her head now. Randy shone the flashlight on it. There was blood in her hair.

"I didn't know what that was," said Moon. "I really banged my head when I ran out of the camper. I'm sorry I screamed. Your kids."

"C'mon," said Randy, giving her the T-shirt off his back to hold against her bleeding scalp. "Whoever did this is gone. It's okay. Let's get you over to Swami's place." Moon accepted the shirt and the help to stand. Randy walked her slowly out of the campsite. "Just some stupid high schoolers, probably. It's got nothing to do with us, Moon. It'll be okay. Watch your step here. We'll get you to Swami's, and I'll go get Ranger Bonnie."

They got Moon back in the passenger seat.

"What happened?" said Darren. "Randy, what happened?"

Swami got back in the seat next to Darren and quickly shut the door.

"Moon got hurt, bud," Randy said, looking at Swami in the dim overhead light. "She hit her head."

Darren looked at the bleeding T-shirt Moon held to her scalp. "She'll be okay," Swami said. "She can rest with us tonight. We'll take care of her."

Randy turned off the dome light and drove to the far end of Governor's to Swami's site. He parked on the road instead of pulling in, stepped out with his flashlight. "Just one second, everyone. Don't hop out quite yet."

"Mom, what's he doing?"

As much as she wanted to lie to him, she couldn't. There sat Moon right in front of her, injured. "Something happened at Moon's campsite while we were gone. We don't know what yet, but someone came and broke a lot of things. We don't know who. Moon got scared and hit her head. Let's just let her rest." Swami didn't have to lie, but she didn't have to spell out every terrifying detail. The image of that pig in her bed, the poor animal. Swami held Darren a bit tighter.

"All right," said Randy, opening Moon's door. "No bears."

Moon took Randy's hand as he helped her step down from the passenger seat. Swami told him to take her right in; there was a first aid kit in the kitchen cupboard.

"I can show him where," said Darren.

"Good, do that," she answered, unbuckling DeeDee's whole car carrier and then lifting Dell to her shoulder.

Moon sat inside later, her hair washed out in the sink and the bleeding stopped. It was a very superficial wound, like a skinned knee, far more blood than damage. DeeDee and Dell were asleep in the bedroom. Randy leaned back against the galley seat with his arms crossed while Swami finished patching up Moon. She noticed he'd been flexing his fists, clenching his jaw while he looked out the window. Darren got his pajamas on but came right back out. He put his hand on Moon's shoulder. "You can have my spot in the bed," he said. "I can sleep on the bench seat."

"I don't want to be any trouble," said Moon.

"Not another word about it," said Swami. "And thank you, Darren. Time for bed, I think, for all of us. Darren, I'd rather you sleep next to Moon, actually, and take care of her if she needs anything. I'm going to stay up and talk to Randy and Ranger Bonnie for a bit."

"Oh, Mom," he said.

She shook her head while Randy led Moon back to lie down. "I'll sleep in the galley tonight," Swami said, and Darren knew there was no use arguing. Then she stooped down and hugged him. "Did you like those fireworks tonight, buddy?"

"Oh, they were great," he said. "Dad would have liked to come, you know. He likes fireworks."

"Next time." Swami smiled a weak smile, then petted her son's messy hair. It needed cutting. "You're getting so big," she said. "You'll be driving soon."

Darren grinned and lifted his eyebrows. Swami hugged him and patted his butt. "Off you go," she said to him. "Be real quiet; let everybody sleep."

Darren hugged her back and turned to plod down the aisle in his shark pajamas. Randy came back, and they met in the hall.

"Good night, Randy," Darren said.

"G'night, little dude," said Randy.

Darren closed the door to the sleeping quarters, and Swami looked Randy in the eye. He shook his head and stepped to the sink to wash his blood-soaked shirt. He washed his arms off too. Swami couldn't tell what blood belonged to that poor pig or to her poor friend. Randy's breaths were shaking, as were his hands. He wrung out his shirt, and twisted it so hard Swami thought it might tear straight through. Every muscle in Randy's lean body was tensed, coiled. He pulled the damp shirt back on, parts of it still stained pink.

"I'm gonna go get the ranger up," he said. "I'll bring her over to Moon's camp, tell her she's okay and staying over here for the night. She is okay, isn't she?"

Swami nodded. "I promise. She just got cut in the door frame. There's no sign of concussion at all. I'll check on her, keep her up for a while to be sure. But Moon's fine."

Randy nodded, and Swami saw his jaw clench again.

"Randy?"

"Yeah."

"That was horrible."

He nodded.

"Do you really think that was just high schoolers?"

"Not a chance in hell."

"But who would do that? And to Moon, of all people."

He looked at her.

"Do you really think it's them?"

"I do. And I'm sure gonna find out." He had such a cold rage about him, it made Swami's heart race. Randy looked flat-out dangerous. Dark as a thunderclap. He was through and through a good man, just as Moon had said. But he was dangerous right now. There was another side showing here. A bunker-full-of-guns kind of side.

"What are you going to do?" Swami asked.

"I'm just going to find out is all. I'm going to go get Bonnie and bring her over, and then I'm gonna find out. I'll have Chip go tell Sam too. Sam should be here."

Swami felt her breath catch, but then she nodded. It was something about the way Randy said it, and what Darren had said too, and the state of that pig in Moon's trailer. Randy was right. Sam should be here.

Then Randy pulled a small, holstered gun from his back pocket and set it on the counter next to the Maglite. "Here," he said, "take my snubby. Just point and shoot."

Swami didn't like the idea. And she was shocked the man had been carrying a revolver in his pocket. "I'm not so sure I want that in here," she said. "Not with the kids."

"Well, just keep it on you, then. It's safe. It won't go off unless you pull the trigger. It will make me feel better."

Swami nodded. "All right."

"It's getting late," he said. "I'll go tell Bonnie, and then I'll park back out here on the road until Sam gets here. You should sleep if you can."

"Thanks, Randy," she said, and she meant it.

"Thank you for watching her," Randy said, nodding back to the sleeping quarters.

"Randy."

"Yeah?"

"Have you ever told her how much you love her?"

He allowed himself the smallest smirk.

"Not yet."

"Well, you should."

Randy nodded, darkened again, and stepped out into the night. Swami sat for a while in the bright kitchen, staring at the small revolver and the flashlight. She stood up and locked the door, locked the kitchen window, and then she turned out the light and sat wide awake in the silent camper, her kids breathing heavily like a little pile of bears. Swami tiptoed into the bedroom and gently tapped Moon's shoulder. She stirred.

"You still awake?" whispered Swami.

"Still awake," whispered Moon. "Where's Randy?"

"He's coming back," Swami said.

"Good," she said, letting her head settle back down to the pillow. "Thanks, Swami."

Swami gave her a pat and slipped back to the kitchen with a pillow and a blanket. She looked out the windows at the moonlit blue, studying all the shadows. She tucked the holstered revolver into her sweatshirt's belly pocket, held on to the flashlight, and then curled onto the cushioned galley bench. She woke only once to the sound of a motor. It was Randy, back with the rafting van. He backed it into the site's driveway, guarding the entrance to the road, and then turned off the motor and waited. Swami sank into her pillow more easily, and slept without waking anymore.

In the morning, Swami woke to the sound of a gentle knocking at the galley door. She sat up quickly from the bench. The shadows were gone outside. The sun was rising through the trees. The rafting van was still parked in the driveway. Randy was standing outside the camper door.

"You all all right?" Randy said when she opened it. His eyes were red.

"Everything's quiet. Were you there all night?"

Randy nodded. "Me and Pete. He's riding shotgun."

"And Sam?"

"Bonnie must not have gotten the message out to Chip's. I wouldn't put it past her."

Swami squinted up at the brightening sky. "Well, you guys had better come in. I'll make coffee. Oh, and here. Thanks." Swami felt the weight of it in her sweatshirt pocket and handed him back the tiny revolver. She was thankful for it last night, in the dark, but she was glad to be rid of it now, in the morning.

Randy turned it over in his hands and slid it into his back pocket. He was still wearing the T-shirt from last night. Moon's bloodstains had browned.

"No time for coffee. If you're all right for now, it's morning, and me and Pete have a place to be." He turned back toward the van and started walking. "I haven't forgotten the scout trip. I'll be at the barn by eight. And Pete washed up Moon's Jeep last night, so you can use it. Bonnie asked us not to clean up the camper yet until they can look it over, so don't let Moon go over there. The Jeep's parked at the ranger station."

"Where are you going?" Swami called after him.

Randy didn't turn around. The coiled tension had already returned to his walk. It was a cowboy walk, the butt of the revolver keeping time in his jeans pocket. He didn't answer her. He got in the van, shut the door, and then tore away like a dog off leash.

•••

ORANGE LIGHT CAME THROUGH THE camper blinds in bands that fell across the small table and sink. Swami didn't want to go meet the scout leaders, but she would. Moon was still sleeping, and Swami wouldn't expect her to raft today. Sam and Chip and Randy would run the trip. She opened the door to the bedroom and watched her sleeping kids for a moment. DeeDee breathed in quick, potbellied puffs. Dell slept with her old baby blanket—tattered on the edges, finger holes poked through it—crumpled against her cheek. Darren slept with his mouth wide open, face serene, just inches from Moon's. If there was any silver lining in this disastrous summer, it was mornings in the camper. Swami loved the half hour where she'd wake in a pile of her sleeping, lake-washed children. She'd just lie there and study their eyelashes, their noses, the small lines in their lips.

Swami sighed and looked out at the brightening dawn. Today was the very last chance to book Woodchuck with enough customers to have a chance of selling it as an operating business instead of a half-painted barn filled with mildewy life jackets. As horrible as last night was, the sun was up now. Scout leaders would be driving up north this very moment. She had to do this.

Swami shut the thin door to their bedroom, made her coffee, and got dressed in the galley. She put on her sportiest clothes, a bright green pair of shorts and a windbreaker zip-up over an undershirt. In the tiny bathroom, she tied her hair back and tried the look with and without a hat. She was going for *I am an adventurous and competent yoga lady who is all about wholesome fun.* She splashed water in her face and rubbed her eyes. She was so tired. Bone-tired.

"Are we fun?" she whispered to the mirror. She waited. No answer. She decided to go with the wide-brimmed hat.

Swami left the camper with a banana and a mug of coffee, and slipped outside into the damp grass and cool air. Birds sang. Leaves rustled in a stiff breeze. She sat on the picnic table. Her tired mind just lumped together the last few days. Bunkers. Fireworks. Decapitated pigs. She thought about bills and canceled insurance. She thought about the way she'd started doing their laundry in the lake to save every penny. She shivered and zipped her windbreaker up to her neck, peeled the banana. Why was she sitting here in the woods, peeling a banana?

The camper door opened, and Moon came out with a mug of coffee. She'd removed the bandage from her scalp, and had one of Debbie's knot blankets around her shoulders.

"How are you?" asked Swami.

"I feel fine," she said. She sat down alongside Swami. "I mean, my *head* feels fine."

Swami filled her in on what Randy had said about the campsite and Jeep, and her plans to keep Moon back from the trip today. She didn't mention that Randy and Pete had gone off early and might cause some sort of trouble. She just didn't have the room to hold that along with everything else. And Moon didn't need to hold that right now either.

Moon nodded. "Thanks," she said. "Why don't you leave the kids back with me today. I can take care of them, take them to the lake, nap. You have enough to do."

"That'd be a huge help," Swami said. "There's three bottles in the cooler for DeeDee—nine, noon, and three—and there's formula in the cupboard if I'm not back before supper. She can try some smashed peas at lunch. Darren can help."

"Smashed peas," Moon said, and sipped her coffee.

"You okay?" Swami asked. "I mean, not just your scrape."

Moon nodded. "I will be. Worse comes to worst, I'll just run away again. I know how to run away."

"Randy's in love with you."

Moon gave a small smile. "I know."

"You could run away with Randy. He could be a cook anywhere."

"I've usually run away *from* men, not *with* them. But I admit Randy is different, which is what makes it so hard on him, that I can't leap."

"Sorry," Swami said.

"Don't be sorry. Ancient history. Onward, you know?" She gave a weak smile, and then the two women sipped their coffee in silence for a time. The wind stirred the trees. The campground was waking up now too, pots and pans, children and parents, the sound of the typical joys and complaints that Swami had grown so accustomed to.

"What about you?" Moon asked. "Are you okay? You and Sam?"

Swami didn't answer that right away. "I hope we will be," she finally said. "I think we will be? But I don't know. We've hardly talked all summer. I better go," she said, standing from the table. "Onward."

Swami grabbed her bag, and checked on the kids again.

"Good luck today," Moon called after her as Swami strode out onto the path toward the ranger station.

A few minutes later, when Swami pulled into Woodchuck, stopped, and then drove slowly up the gravel drive with her hand over her mouth, her first thought was vandalism. Whoever had hit Moon's campsite had been here too. Her second thought was that she hoped Randy and Pete had already found out who did it.

Woodchuck was trashed. Chip's motorcycle was parked out front. Swami pulled the Jeep next to it and turned off the motor. She had thirty minutes until guests arrived, and the damage was worse than she'd realized.

"Chip!" she hollered.

The entire scaffold was crumbled down on the patio. It had torn two of her blue patio umbrellas—stripped the poles clean like dandelion stems—crushed a table and flattened several metal chairs. A dented five-gallon bucket of her bright blue paint had exploded against the retaining wall and spattered its contents up her cedar trees. The blue paint congealed in puddles. Swami crept carefully into the wreckage, jaw agape, body stiff. Ranger Bonnie wasn't going to cut it. They needed real sheriffs up here, and fast. Swami looked up at the barn wall. It was entirely finished, painted to the peak. She just stared at it, trying to put this all together. But when she stepped closer, over a tangle of wooden planks, she saw the beer cans. *Beer cans.* Her confusion turned to a sharp and stony fury. This hadn't been vandals. It had been Sam and his uncle. Painting. And drinking.

Her flip phone beeped in her windbreaker pocket. Three new voice mails had caught up with it while she drove into the signal along the highway. Two messages and five unanswered calls were from Wood-chuck, and one message was from a number she didn't recognize. That one played first. It was one of her scout leaders, calling from down by Crivitz, running late, took a wrong turn but straightened out now. His voice was bright and caffeinated, a vacation voice.

Chip burst from the barn. He held a lit joint in his hand, hobbled through the wreckage. Swami slapped the phone shut.

"Swami!" he blurted, panicked and red-faced, winded. "Why didn't you answer your phone! Sam's hurt. I found him this morning, right here! He broke his leg, or might have broken his leg, is what the medic said. They just took off in the ambulance. I've been calling you and calling you."

"Ambulance?" is all Swami managed to say. She just stared at Chip, shaking her head as he spoke. He was red-eyed and clearly distressed. He kept wincing as he spoke, like something hurt.

"I couldn't take him on my bike," said Chip. "So I called the hospital over in Ironsford. I couldn't even *move* him. He told me he didn't hit his head when he fell, that he hung on when the scaffolding went, but his leg was all twisted back. He was pinned, Swami! Pinned there all night!" Chip lifted the joint to his mouth and took a shaky hit, huffed the smoke out. When he lifted it to his mouth a second time, Swami pulled his hand down, glared at him.

"What happened?" she asked. Something about Chip's panic angered her even more, his childlikeness, his neediness. She was the one who needed people today. Not the other way around. Not this.

"I just showed up early, 'cause it's your scout leader day, and there he was. Oh, Swami, I couldn't even move him. I couldn't lift him out. He yelled so bad."

"But it's a broken leg—they told you this."

Chip hesitated. "Yeah. He's okay, but like I said, his leg was all folded under. He came out to finish the paint last night, and then—"

Swami waved him off. Chip looked ready to cry, and Swami just couldn't bear it.

"Just . . . smoke that," she said, pacing a circle. Chip did. Swami stepped away and looked out at the field for a moment.

"Where's Randy?" she asked.

"Haven't seen him."

"Didn't he get ahold of you last night?"

"No. Why?"

"I'm going to make a phone call. Please start clearing this scaffolding from in front of the door. We'll get as much cleaned up as we can, and when Randy gets here he can blow boats. We have a half hour, tops, until the trip arrives."

Chip frowned at her. "What about Sam?" he said.

"What *about* Sam?" Swami hissed. She looked at the beer cans and broken chairs, the wreck he'd caused. Drunk on a ladder. And now he was laid up in some bed getting fed painkillers by a nurse and eating pudding while they put a cast on his foot. And there was no telling what that deductible would cost them. Swami felt like a dark, cold cloud. And she'd have to fix all of it with sweat and today's nonpaying river trip, if they could even run the river. She took a hard breath and spoke very slowly.

"Chip, we are running today's trip, as planned, and you are going to bend over backward for these guests today and get that scout reservation on the books, or so help me God . . ." Swami didn't quite know how to finish what she wanted to say to Chip, *all* she wanted to tell him, so she poked him instead, in his fat chest.

He looked like he wanted to protest, so she poked him even harder. He took a step back.

"Hey," he said, his brow furrowing. "I get you don't like this place. I get it's been hard for you. But you don't know what you're saying right now. We can't run the trip when Sam's hurt like this." He stood up tall, proud-looking, angry. "We can't go boat when one of the family is hurt."

"Family!" Swami slapped the joint out of his hand before she knew what she was doing. "You *stupid* old man!" Swami spat the words with her whole heart, balled her fists. "You fool! You piece of trash! You are going to start cleaning this mess right now, and you are guiding, *today!*"

Chip's face turned dark red. He leaned toward her for the smallest moment. Swami swallowed. Chip ground his teeth and stepped back. His joint smoldered in the dry grass. When he exhaled, Swami heard the man's lungs—he really was a giant—ebb and flow, grumbling.

"I might be a stupid old man," he said. "But I am not mean. You are. You are as mean as a snake, Swami. And you wonder why Sam can't get it together and run this place. Who could with a woman as mean as you hounding him every damn minute? You've done nothing but cut him down every chance you've had this summer."

"Done nothing. *Nothing!* Says the uncle who unloads a failing company on his own nephew and sits back on his own gold mine while everyone around him sinks!"

Chip frowned at her.

"Oh, I know, Chip. I know what NorthSky offered you for your farm. And I know it's enough you could actually help your nephew out of this mess you conned him into." She hated him. She hated him more than she'd ever hated before. She felt wild with it.

"So that's what you think I—" he started to say.

Swami spat on him. She tried for his face but got his neck instead.

Chip absolutely glowed. Swami heard him growl. He wiped the spit from his neck and then pressed his hand against his chest, winced as if he were fighting back some sort of painful impulse. Then he very slowly turned and lifted a leg over his dirt bike. He gave the starter a kick, and he didn't look at Swami as he revved the little engine away down the driveway.

"Where do you think you're going?!" she yelled after him.

Chip didn't look back at her. He just eased onto the highway, shifting through gears, his overburdened bike leaving a trail of blue smoke on the empty road.

Alone, Swami tried to take a deep breath, but it rattled in her chest. The fields were silent: no bird, no wind, no sensations on Swami's skin either. Swami closed her eyes a moment, and then just left them closed. She stood that way until she heard a car coming down the driveway but couldn't bear to look at it. Chip's words had hit her in ways she didn't think they could. She wasn't mean. She was the *calm* one. She was the *ordered* one, the one that did what others could not, who had to keep it all together. But Chip's words echoed, memories too. She remembered Sam coming out of their old gardening shack, holding that children's bike without pedals on it, a big proud smile on his face—and the way his face changed when she let him have it. She just had to stand very still now, until the words and memories began to settle, hard and cold, like pebbles in a river.

The car's motor turned off. Another car pulled in.

"What *happened*?" asked a man's voice. It wasn't Randy. It wasn't anyone she knew. Swami turned and saw a group of scout leaders, vacation dads wearing neon shorts and neoprene shirts. She stared at them, confused.

"I don't know. We're closed," she said. "I'm sorry, but we're closed today."

After a long, awkward exchange, Swami watched their caravan pull back out, Camrys and Silverados rolling out onto the road, probably to check out X-treme while they were here. Swami watched them go and felt almost nothing, standing in the wreckage, watching Woodchuck's last chance drive away. She stepped through the wreckage and found a gallon of mineral spirits and an old beach towel on a shelf upstairs.

The solvent burned Swami's eyes as she worked. It made her rubber gloves feel cool, even in the heat, while she knelt on a pad of folded cardboard and scrubbed blue paint from the chairs. Swami brushed sweaty hair from her eyes using her forearm, doused the towel in a bucket again, and sopped up more paint. The spills were so thick the spirits just smeared them around at first. Swami scrubbed and wrung and dunked her towel. She picked up the beer cans and chairs. She stacked the planks from the scaffolding frame, which now lay in a twisted grid. She worked on it silently, rectangle by rectangle. Randy never showed up.

All she felt inside was a detached sort of fog, like she could scour the patio all day and night, until it had furrows carved into it, a cave into which she could sink and fume and bite the hand of any who dared approach her. The sun was hot overhead, and Swami needed a break. Her back ached, and her head hurt from the fumes. Inside, she found a bottle of water half-frozen in the back of the fridge. Swami leaned against a cool wooden post, pressed the cool bottle of water against her face and neck. In the shade, she watched barn swallows flit over the back fields, skimming bugs. The water was cool, ice cold, and after her first drink of it she had a very clear thought. It surprised her with its absolute clarity, and surprised her even more when she spoke it out loud.

"I'm done," she said. The words felt like clear water, clear sky, a strong wind. She would not pick up someone else's mess for even one more moment. Not one more dollar. Not one more breath. Swami said the words again, and then stood and walked to Moon's Jeep. She was incredibly hot. She would take a swim now. She didn't even look back at Woodchuck. She drove alone and fast down the highway to a quiet gravel boat landing by the river. At the river she undressed and, perfectly naked, dove down into the water, where it was cool and cold, her fingers raking the river bottom before pushing up toward the air and light.

Treading water, she pushed her hair back and took a breath. My God, that felt better. She dove again and rose again, each time feeling cleaner, freer. She'd never have to see Woodchuck again, and it felt right to leave it in such disarray, for that's all the place had ever been. Chaos.

Swami dove to wash it all off again. She was farther out in the river now, and had to kick her legs to charge all the way to the silty bottom. Swami felt a cool slab of granite beneath the silt, placed her feet against it, and pushed, rocketing up to the surface again. When Swami breached the water a final time, she took a deep breath and pushed her hair back.

As she exhaled, her mouth formed two more words. They came from deep in her past, from before her dad lost jobs and her mom became hard. "Sea lions," Swami breathed. If she could choose to walk away from Woodchuck, and she had, she could choose to walk away from even more. Swami bobbed in the water. She knew exactly what she would do. First she would dry in the sun. Then she'd drive back to camp and collect her children. She'd have her mother sell Woodchuck for pennies, and her house in Chicago for as much cash as it was worth. And then Swami would take the kids and drive west. The camper could rot in the forest. Sam could live in it forever. Swami and her children were going to California, today, to the sea lions.

Swami swam in to shore. An old man was unloading a fishing boat, and Swami walked up from the water without pausing, stark naked and dripping. The old man dropped a bucket of minnows as she passed him. He looked afraid of her, and Swami was glad he looked afraid. At the Jeep, she shimmied into a fresh pair of shorts and a T-shirt from her bag. She got in and began her drive away.

Away.

THIRTEEN

SAM CALLED FROM THE HOSPITAL THAT MORNING, AFTER HIS CAST was set—fractured shin, and the doctor told him he was lucky, given how far he'd fallen, that it wasn't worse. The fracture was mild. Swami didn't answer the phone, but Sam knew it was the day of Swami's big scout trip and that without him there to guide she'd be extra pressed. *Still*, he thought. *Surely the guides could manage without her.* He sat alone on the bed with his leg in a cast, watching the news on TV. Al Gore again, making a phone call to Midwestern governors. He was talking with Tommy Thompson at present. It seemed the whole of the Midwest was underwater.

Chip showed up at the hospital, and then Moon, and then Sam understood. Chip had argued with Swami. Moon had watched her pack the rafting van. "She came back to the campground early," Moon said. "Packed the kids up in the rafting van, and left. She looked wild," Moon said. "Fierce. She wouldn't tell me where she was going. She wouldn't tell me what happened. Dell cried. Darren argued with her."

Moon delivered the news, and Chip watched him from his bedside chair. Sam laid his head back on the pillow. He closed his eyes. The nurse had just given him a second dose of some new kind of painkiller, and his head swam with it, along with the realization. The thoughts came slow, and in sequence, like a line of clouds in an otherwise empty sky.

Sam had painted Swami's barn instead of going to fireworks.

Sam had fallen and fractured his leg.

Chip had found him.

Swami had *left*.

It was so plain Sam could hardly believe it.

"Sorry, Sam," Moon said.

"I'm the one who let her have it," said Chip, looking at the linoleum floor. A nurse pushed a squeaking cart down the hallway outside the open door. "I'm sorry I did that," he said.

"What'd you say to her?" Sam said.

"I told her she was mean as a snake."

Sam groaned at the enormity of the disaster. "And how'd that go for you?" he asked. It wasn't really a question.

"Not good," Chip said.

"Well," said Sam. Another cloud of thought drifted past. It was darker, but Sam let it drift anyway. He just couldn't care anymore about Swami's resentment. He could paint barns, suffer her silence, sleep on porches, break his leg. None if it mattered to her. Swami *was* mean, he thought. Chip was right, and Sam was glad he'd said it. It was weak of him to be glad about that, but his weakness didn't bother him right now either. He'd suffered alone; he could forgive himself alone too, make his own grace.

"Forget it," he said. "You guys want to sign my cast?" he asked.

Chip snorted.

The blue cast went from his ankle to above his knee to immobilize both joints. It looked like a big blue caterpillar. His toes stuck out the top, right underneath Al Gore's chin on the TV. Sam wiggled his toes at Al Gore and felt like laughing.

"Look at my stupid *cast*." He chuckled. "Stupid toes. Look at *that* guy. Talking on his big phone."

"Sam, what'd they give you?" asked Moon.

"Viking something," Sam said, still wiggling his toes at the vice president.

"You got any more?" Chip asked.

Sam stopped wiggling his toes and felt around his bedsheets. "Probably," he said.

Just then, a slim man entered the doorway, followed by a nurse holding his arm.

"Sir?" said the nurse. *"Sir!"*

"Hi, Pete!" said Sam, beaming.

Pete slowly removed his arm from the nurse's grip. "They know me, see?" he said. Pete had a big purple black eye.

"You cannot just walk all over this hospital," said the nurse.

"All right," said Pete, in his gentle, disarming way.

The nurse pursed her lips. "You check *in* next time. You wait."

"All right," Pete said.

The nurse glanced around the room at the hulking Chip and tattooed Moon, the grinning man in the hospital bed. She sighed through her nose and left.

"How's it hangin', Pete?!" Sam blurted. "Sign my cast? My wife is not here."

Pete looked at him. Pete's hair was mussed, part of it pulled out of his braid and sticking straight out to the side, crimped like a lightning bolt. The white of his blackened eye was deeply bloodshot.

"Pete, what happened to you?" Moon asked.

"I heard you were here," he said. "You guys know about Randy?"

"Where's Randy?" Moon asked Pete. She was staring straight at him. Pete's eyes were red and watery. Sam was feeling very confused, but he didn't mind at all.

"He's downstairs," Pete said. "He's beat up. It's bad."

Chip stood up. Moon clapped her hand over her mouth. Sam saw them do this and sat up on his elbows and winced.

"Downstairs, as in checked in?"

Pete nodded. "We drove out to NorthSky this morning, met a few of their crew still up drinking whiskey. They had pig blood on 'em, so we knew it was them."

"Knew what was?!" Chip exclaimed.

"And, look," Pete said, "I haven't talked to no cops. Randy hasn't either, so."

Sam put his finger to his lips and shushed everyone, made sure they knew the plan.

Moon waved him off and walked up to Pete. "Take me down there," she said, turning him toward the door. "Does Debbie know Randy's hurt?"

"No," Pete said.

"This ain't good," said Chip, following them out into the hall. "Sam, we'll be right back."

Sam nodded and watched them go, and then fell back on his pillow. The room was quiet again except for the TV. Al Gore held the big beige phone to his ear, assured the governor of Wisconsin that federal disaster assistance for the ruined crops and homes was coming. *Thank you, Mr. Vice President*, said the governor. *Thank you, Governor*, said the vice president.

•••

THE NEXT MORNING, SAM DROVE out to NorthSky with Moon, and Duncan too. Sam rode in back of the Jeep with his leg propped up. It ached, but he refused to fill his prescription of pain medicine, and signed himself out with just a pair of crutches. He needed his head about him now more than ever. Moon sped the Jeep toward the NorthSky mine site, downriver a few miles past X-treme. It was just past noon, the day and time for her regular protest. She'd spent the whole night at Randy's hospital bed and wanted Sam's help stopping today's demonstration. But when she stopped by X-treme to tell Sally that they wouldn't protest, that they shouldn't, that the town needed to cool off a moment, they found that Sally had already been out all night and all morning, making sure everyone knew what the handful of men at NorthSky had done to Randy, the town's favorite son. Duncan told them this, came jogging out onto the porch.

"Maybe I should come with you guys," he said. "Maybe I can help."

"Sure," said Moon. "Get in."

Duncan smiled and hopped in the passenger seat. "Not that I like you guys," he said with a grin, and then saw Sam's big blue cast. "You were with him?"

Sam shook his head. "I wasn't," he told Duncan. "And the feeling's mutual. Woodchuck is still going to run you out of town."

"Ha!" blurted Duncan, as Moon sped toward the mine property, revving the big motor high.

"Rumor has it there were going to be some investors in town today," Moon said. "Big fish. I didn't want to be out here today."

Duncan's blond hair blew in the wind. "Maybe it's a good day to protest. Let the big fish know what's what."

"Until someone gets hurt," Sam said, and Duncan just rode quietly after that, the river breaking through the trees with its glimmer from time to time.

All last night, Sam had tried to call Swami. She wasn't answering her cell. He called the raft barn and let the phone ring and ring. He called Ranger Bonnie, and asked if she could check the campsite. There was no one there. Sam called home to their landline too, and let it go to voice mail five different times before finally leaving a message. "Swami," he said. "I know you left, and I know Chip yelled at you. Please call Chip's phone when you get this. You don't have to talk. Just call and let me know you're there. Please."

When Sam hung up the phone, Moon walked into the hospital room and said she needed to stop the protest. The sun was just up. Chip had gone out to tell Randy's mom in person sometime after midnight. He had the best chance of keeping her steady. He'd known her the longest. And if they put off telling her any longer than they already had, it would be so much worse. Randy was conscious but heavily sedated. He'd begged them not to let his mom know, not right away. His ribs were busted in, in the front and back, his eyes swollen and right hand broken. He and Pete had confronted the mine employees. Bruce was there, along with four others. Nevertheless, Randy strode right in and thumped the pig head down on their card table, and punched Bruce right out of his chair with a big roundhouse. The others jumped them, and were so drunk they didn't stop. Pete fought what he could, but they knocked him out pretty quick. Pete woke up in the ditch grass next to the river. Flies on his face in the hot sun. He thought Randy was dead.

Moon downshifted onto the NorthSky mine road, sped around the pine curves, and bumped down where the asphalt turned to muddy gravel. There were a lot of tire tracks. Sam knew they'd been bringing in more equipment lately. Big graters and well diggers and pile drivers. A row of several massive dump trucks were parked on low ground near the river. The temporary headquarters was the first bit of land NorthSky was able to buy, marshy and unbuildable. They brought in just enough gravel to park their machines and trailers.

Moon came around the next-to-final bend.

"Oh no," she said.

Cars were parked up and down both sides of the gravel road for a solid quarter mile. Channel six news was there too—two vans. Sam recognized Pete's truck. He didn't see Debbie's green flatbed or Chip's motorcycle, though. Hopefully, Chip was calming her down, driving her into Ironsford, keeping her at the hospital. Even then, thought Sam, it was just one woman. How bad could it really get? Moon was exaggerating. Debbie was a tough cookie, but she wasn't dangerous. No one in this town was truly dangerous. They just seemed that way.

Moon didn't park in the line of cars. She kept driving toward the gate. They rolled up to an old man in an orange cap hobbling quickly down the road toward the mine fence. Sam recognized him from the town hall meeting. He wore a dirty pair of denim overalls, carried a long yellow crowbar in one hand and a can of Coors in the other. He eyeballed Moon as she slowed down.

"Going to raise some hell," he said, without being asked. He was stomping along, and Moon had to drive along with him. "You hear they beat up Randy? These miners from out of town? We'll show them where they *are*. They might have rolled through other places, but they ain't been to Thunderwater, that's for damn sure!" He stopped walking. "Now give me a lift. I'm winded."

Moon stopped the Jeep, and the man got in. Duncan let him have the front seat. "Say, you're that Moon lady from the grange meeting, ain't you?" He leaned on his long crowbar like it was a cane.

"I am," she said.

"Well, lady, you got yourself a protest now. Looks like you were right."

The trees opened around the last bend, and the mine came into view. There had to be well over two hundred people gathered, pressed along the fence, shaking it. They were standing on cars, yelling for the miners to come out of their trailers. Sam watched an old woman rattle a broomstick against the fence. The old man with the orange cap leapt out and made his way into the fray. On the far side of the fence, poor Ranger Bonnie waved her hands at those who threatened to climb it. Her face was bright red. She was begging them to protest peacefully.

Behind Bonnie, the tan work trailers were buttoned up tight, shades drawn, a handful of nice pickup trucks parked out of reach of thrown stones. A cameraman filmed it all.

"Come out here, you rats!" yelled the old woman with the broom. Sam realized it was Rita, from the tavern. It looked like she'd brought out her Saturday clientele. "You mess with my sweethearts, you mess with me!" she yelled, and then joined others in chanting. "Come out! Come out! Come out!"

Duncan helped Sam get out of the back and onto his crutches. Their tips sank in the mud a few inches. Sam took his time, careful to keep his cast out of it. "Man," chuckled Duncan. "I'd hate to be in there right now."

Sam looked at the buttoned-up windows. Someone landed a mud ball against the side of the trailer.

"Please," Ranger Bonnie yelled into a megaphone. "Please, no mud!" Another mud ball spiraled through the air and broke one of the lower windows. Someone inside pushed a couch cushion against the hole. The crowd got even louder.

Sally pushed out of the crowd and came up, breathless, to Moon. She looked sweaty and thrilled. "Can you *believe* this! This is awesome. Moon, you gotta come talk to the news crew! They've been asking for you."

"Sally, no. Randy's hurt. This isn't good. Someone could get *really* hurt here."

Sally looked at her, aghast.

"We've worked all summer for this. What do you want, to send them all home?"

"This *is* their home, Sally. Do you have any idea how many of these people probably have rifles in their cars? This isn't some political rally." She waved the girl off. "Just try to keep them from climbing the fence. I gotta get in there and talk to Bonnie. Maybe she can let me use her megaphone."

With Duncan's help, Sam hobbled after Moon.

"Excuse me, excuse me!" Moon yelled, pressing between bodies. When they saw who she was, they made way, and made way for Sam on his crutches too. The reporter spotted her and began calling her name, but Moon ignored her. She got a spot next to the fence. It swayed on its posts as the town of Thunderwater chanted, "Come out, come out, come out!" Right next to them was the young couple from the town hall, the husband who'd wanted the truck and the schools. He was chanting along with everyone else. His church wife screamed with a bright red face. Sam was doubting his judgment. Something ran very deep in this river town. It was as if the men in that trailer had beat up everyone's own little brother or sister. And up here, you didn't beat up someone's little brother. That and people here just really knew how to fight. They practiced nearly every Friday night at Rita's.

A pack of firecrackers went over the fence and crackled in the mud near the trailer. The old man in the orange hat cackled. Sam could see him trying to light another wick with his silver Zippo, his yellow crowbar tucked under his armpit.

Ranger Bonnie slipped in the mud as she rushed toward Moon and Sam. She arrived at the fence, and the young couple started in on her. "Unlock this fence!" they shouted.

"Oh, Moon, Sam! You guys gotta call this off! I'm here alone! Backup is still twenty minutes away. There's NorthSky executives in there, and they won't come out and talk, and the longer they won't come out the rowdier all these nice people get. Oh, I don't like this. Sir! *Sir*, get off that fence! Get *off*! You gotta talk to them, Moon."

"Toss me your megaphone!" Moon shouted.

Rita poked at Ranger Bonnie with her broomstick through the fence. Bonnie's face got bright red, and she snatched the stick right out of Rita's grip. Bonnie smacked the fence with it from the other side.

"I am a state forest park ranger and interim Sheriff's Department deputy!" she snapped at Rita. "And I would ask that you show me and this fence some respect."

"Gimme back my stick, you woods cop!" Rita yelled.

Moon gave up, pushed through the crowd toward the nearest truck, and climbed onto its hood.

She waved her arms and jumped up and down, cupped her hands

around her mouth and yelled for attention. Only the cameraman seemed to notice. Another pack of firecrackers went over the fence.

And then Sam saw Moon's eyes scan to the back of the crowd, and everything in her seemed to sink. She jumped back down into the mud just as the gunshot rang out.

BOOM! *BOOM!*

Birds flew out of the trees. The crowd quieted and ducked. Ranger Bonnie ducked in the mud and put her hand on her can of bear spray.

BOOM!

Sam ducked as best he could on his crutches. Some people began to run toward the woods, the crowd dispersing enough for him to see for the first time the gate in the fence, padlocked with a big chain. He still couldn't tell where the shots were coming from. He glanced at the trailer and saw the metal blinds snap back shut.

"Debbie!" shouted Moon. "No!"

Sam saw her then, the stout mother marching through the mud in a dress and rubber boots, loading more shells into a pump shotgun as she walked. Her hair was wild, sticking out in all directions. Her face was the color of ash and her eyes bloodred.

"NORTHSKY!" Debbie bellowed. "COME OUT THAT TRAILER!" And then she loosed another round into the air.

Duncan was squatting in the mud now. Everyone had either run off or ducked, or slipped in the mud and just lay there. Sam was the only idiot still standing, holding his cast up out of the mud, frozen.

"Deb!" yelled Moon, and Debbie's eyes shot over so fast and murderous it stopped Moon in her tracks. It stopped Ranger Bonnie too. She dropped her bear spray in the mud and held her hands up.

"LAST CHANCE," she yelled at the trailer. "YOU COME OUT AND LET THE RANGER ARREST YOU FOR WHAT YOU DID TO MY SON!" She shot another round into the sky, and then loaded another shell into the magazine tube. The shotgun had a leather bandolier sling stuffed to the gills with twelve-gauge shells. Debbie wasn't running out of ammunition anytime soon. She racked the slide. "OR I'M GONNA DRIVE YOU OUT!"

The woman's jowls shook as she yelled. She looked like a battle horse, a very mad bull.

The blinds on the trailer bent down a slit, and then snapped shut again.

Debbie's nostrils flared. "NO? ALL RIGHT!" She marched forward, shouldered the shotgun, aimed, and shot through the lock. The lock shattered, and shrapnel from the round buzzed through the air. Debbie kicked the gate, and it swung open. She racked the slide again, topped off her gun. She staggered through the mud toward the trailer, then mounted the steps and paused just long enough to aim at the doorknob. "BETTER BACK UP FROM THE DOOR!" was the only warning they got.

BOOM!

The slug punched the doorknob straight through the cheap trailer door, and Debbie kicked that in too and went in, muzzle high and firing. The darkness inside lit up with the muzzle flash of the shotgun. Rounds blasted holes in the tin roof. Glass broke. It sounded like a desk turned over. *BOOM! BOOM! BOOM!* She fired and fired, and the little trailer shook with it. A fire started, and smoke began to pour out the door. Another blast shattered a length of the trailer's pine siding, and everybody outside ducked again. The smoke thickened quickly, and flames licked up out of one of the broken windows.

Two men came running out, and then two more. The first one tripped on the stairs, and the rest tripped over him, and all four of them landed in the mud. The first four had jeans and Carhartts on. Bruce was with them. Another well-dressed man came out coughing with his hands on his head. He stumbled down next to the other men and knelt in the mud in his nice pants and little shoes. Sam heard sirens coming from the road. He saw the man with the orange hat hightailing it for the pines with his crowbar.

"Uncle Greg?" Duncan exclaimed. Sam turned back to the trailer to see a final man duck out of the smoke. It was Blakely, the man with the money behind Duncan's rafting company. Blakely coughed, had his hands on his head. Debbie had him by the scruff of his neck, shotgun barrel pushed into his back.

The sirens were close now, clearly on the gravel road leading in. He could see their lights through the trunks of pines. Sam hadn't realized it, but a thick black cloud had rolled over, and it was beginning to rain again, big, sparse raindrops the size of horseflies smacking the mud.

"Not one of you move," Debbie said to the line of men.

"You're going to jail for this," Blakely told her.

"You and me both," she said, and kicked him in the back of his knee so he knelt in the mud with the others.

"Uncle Greg?" Duncan said again, much quieter now. Sam frowned at Duncan, for Duncan.

"Bonnie, come over quick," said Debbie. The trailer was barreling with flames now, deep black smoke firing from its windows like a diesel.

"Debbie, no," whispered Moon.

Bonnie crouched over, and Debbie handed her the shotgun by the barrel. "Point this at us," Debbie said. "It's all right, take it. I'm sorry I scared you."

Debbie took the shotgun.

"I didn't set it on fire," Debbie said. "Can't get me on arson. That was him done that." Debbie knelt down in the mud next to Blakely and put her hands on her head like the others. Two squad cars with sheriffs from the next county roared up to the fence. People hurried away. The trailer smoked and roared and popped, sending a whirlwind spire of flames up into the thickening rain. Ranger Bonnie awkwardly held the shotgun and waved the sheriffs over.

Duncan glared at his uncle.

Moon cried.

Sam lost his crutches and couldn't stoop to get them. He put one hand on Duncan's shoulder to steady himself and another on Moon's. They watched through the fence as Debbie looked straight forward while the other men ducked their faces from the stinging rain. Sam watched the woman's chest rise and fall with a deep breath. She lifted her chin as the officers surrounded her, cuffing one hand and then the other, lifting her to her feet in her rubber farm boots.

FOURTEEN

A VERY FULL WEEK PASSED QUICKLY. SWAMI ARRIVED AT THEIR HOME in Chicago on Friday, pulling the smoking rafting van into their paved driveway on an oak-lined street. Swami had had to run the heater on the freeway to keep it from overheating, a trick her dad had taught her with all his old cars. DeeDee lay on her belly now on a blue blanket in the center of a nearly packed living room. Swami sat near her, folding a basket of laundry and placing the items into either a bin or a suitcase. She had one small pile of clothes for each of them, Darren's lightning bolt swim trunks, Dell's bright yellow swimsuit with the purple frills, multiple pairs of Sesame Street underwear, and one nicer set of clothes plus a light jacket for each of them. Winter clothes, along with the rest of the house, would go into storage. Larger items, the couch her parents had bought them, the oak hutch, beds, window treatments, would all sell with the home. Swami's Realtor mother agreed it was a seller's market, but tried to convince her the rental market was good too.

"Why not try a three-month lease first?" she wondered out loud. "Test the waters instead of selling outright. The rent would be enough to cover the mortgage, and then some. Enough for your vacation."

Swami stopped her, shook her head. She was feeling fierce and determined lately, a rising momentum that quietly excited and scared her. "I want it sold, Mom. I want a fistful of cash, a new car, my kids, and two or three suitcases. That's all I want in the world. I need to go."

Her mom exhaled through pinched nostrils. "I just don't want you to make an emotional decision," she said.

"I *am* making an emotional decision," Swami snapped, then collected herself and apologized. "I am making it because if I don't, I'm not sure I'll have any piece of me left. Don't you understand that?" Swami's eyes welled up, and her mother softened. Swami remembered what her mother had once said about real estate, about family strife greasing the tracks, about fast, cheap sales and overpriced buys. So be it.

"And you have to promise me, Mom, that you won't speak a word of this to Sam. This house is mine, in my name. He can have Woodchuck and the camper and what's left of his retirement. But this part is mine, and I need it. I can't have him coming here before I leave. Don't let him know."

"I won't," her mom answered.

And that's the last they spoke of it, and since then Swami had sensed a new sort of resolve in her mother to be Swami's advocate, to accept what was and champion her daughter and grandkids. A storage container appeared on the lawn, along with a staked display with her mother's photo and *Deidra's Crème de la Crème Realty* near the curb, her mother smiling in the photo in her rose blazer and pearls. Swami liked that sign there, the idea of her mother's determined presence guiding the flow of things. It felt so good to have someone on her side. It felt so good to *lean*. Swami's mom discussed plans to fly in to San Diego, take the kids to SeaWorld.

Swami folded a small pair of jeans and placed it in Darren's pile. DeeDee squirmed and lifted her head, then dropped it and lifted her rump instead, trying to rock on her knees.

"Good *job*," cooed Swami. "Are you going to crawl? Rock, rock."

DeeDee straightened her right leg and flopped over onto her back. She grabbed her toes and grinned, then stuffed one foot in her mouth. Swami gave her a pacifier instead.

Darren and Dell appeared in the hallway, grunting and struggling to carry a loaded plastic bin between them.

"Tell me if you need a break," groaned Darren, his voice strained under the weight.

"What?" said Dell, stumbling behind as her end mostly dragged on the floor.

"Tell me if you need a break," he said again.

"Like if I need to wipe my hair from my eyes?" she asked.

"No," said Darren, tugging the bin again. "Like if it's too heavy and you need a break from carrying it."

"I need a break," said Dell. She dropped her end and pushed her hair back.

Darren dropped his side too. "Mom, when's lunch? I'm starved," he said.

"There's oranges in the fridge," she said, rubbing DeeDee's belly.

"Oranges!" said Dell, celebrating.

"I don't want oranges again," whined Darren. "We had oranges for breakfast."

Swami was in no mood for complaints, and her tone showed it. "I am *not* going grocery shopping today. We're packing the kitchen, not stocking it."

"Well, I'm hungry!" he yelled now. "Are we going to eat oranges all the way to damn California?"

"Damn!" yelled Dell.

"Darren!" Swami shot the words. "Dell, don't ever say that, okay, sweetie?"

"Okay, Mom," she said in a sweet voice.

Darren's face grew red.

"And why do I have to pack all my good stuff in storage? My bike even! We're moving without any stuff!"

"I want my Goosey-Bricks!" yelled Dell, angry alongside Darren again. She didn't know which side to be on.

DeeDee's pacifier trembled and she started to cry. Swami picked her up and patted her butt. She bit her lip. "We already talked about this," she said to Darren. "It's not forever. It's just for now." Her voice trembled as she spoke. She took a breath. "We'll fill the gaps when we get there. For right now, Mommy needs help packing for just one car."

"Goosey-Bricks!" Dell spat in defiance, hands on her little hips, her potbelly sticking out. She looked at her brother out of the corner of her eye for affirmation.

"*No*, Dell!" Swami erupted. DeeDee started wailing.

Darren went ahead and erupted now too. "I want to talk to Dad!" he yelled.

"You're de-forcing!" said Dell, defiance on her face, her little fists balled up like her brother's.

"*V*," corrected Darren, "*Vuh. Vorce.* Di-vorcing."

"Go to your *room*, Darren!"

"This house is *not fun!*" Dell shouted.

"She's not going to tell Dad, Dell. She's not telling Dad we're leaving!" Darren said the words as he angled away from Swami and then ran up the steps and slammed his door. The slam echoed loudly in the packed-up house.

Dell cried now too. DeeDee bellowed and shuddered. Swami needed distance, quickly. She set DeeDee down on the blanket—the child flailing her arms in protest, red-faced—and jogged to the kitchen. Swami yanked the bag of oranges from the fridge. She slammed a wooden cutting board on the counter. She began to peel the oranges with her nails and fingers, and when the peels stuck she began to mangle them, ripping the orange in half, peels and all. Her daughters cried in the living room. Darren slammed his door again upstairs, and again. Citrus hung in the air and stung Swami's eyes. She took the next orange and slammed it against the counter, splattering the wall and hurting her hand. She spun down onto the kitchen floor, cradling her sticky hand and crying against the cabinet.

"Mommy?" said Dell in a quiet voice.

Swami turned and saw Dell watching by the door frame with a furrowed brow, her blanket over her shoulder. Swami, still on the floor, opened her arms, and Dell rushed into them. Swami rocked her and wept, then carried her to the living room and scooped up DeeDee too. She knelt, all three of them shuddering.

"We're not divorced," said Swami to herself. "I just don't know what else to do. You can have your Goosey-Bricks, okay? I'll find them. And Darren can have his bike. Let's go upstairs and get your brother."

Just as Swami stood, the living room door swung open and in spun Swami's dad in his Birkenstocks and white socks, balancing pizza boxes and two liters of orange soda and lemonade.

"Pizza!" he called. "Get it while it's hot. Get your . . ." He stopped when he saw his daughter and granddaughters. He stood up straighter, looked around the room.

"Everything okay?" he asked.

While they waited for Swami's mom to arrive, Swami sat on the back porch swing while Darren and Dell kicked an unpacked soccer ball around the yard. The pizza stayed warm in the oven. The picnic table was set with paper plates beneath the oak tree with the lights in it. Darren was sullen while he waited. Swami and her dad each held a glass of iced lemonade that sweated in their hands. Swami's dad had picked a few fresh basil leaves from a clay pot and tucked them in between his ice cubes. Cicadas buzzed in the trees, ebbing and flowing like a single noisy lung.

Swami could feel her dad looking at her. Swami watched her kids. They moved on from soccer and began building a fort out of moving boxes. Dell was inside, just her eyes and blond hair peeking over the wall. She was bossing Darren where to place the next one, pointing with a pine stick scepter. Soon she'd be walled off, alone in her castle. Then she and Darren would knock it down and start again. Swami's dad sipped his lemonade.

"Just say it," Swami asked.

Her dad folded his long legs, his white-socked foot dangling.

"I want you to know I've got your back, no matter what happens between you and Sam. I'm in your corner, your mom and me both. We always will be."

Swami tried to exhale. "But—" she said.

"Are you sure about this? *Really* sure?"

"Dad."

The phone started ringing on the wall near the opened kitchen window.

"Just let me say it all," he added. "California is a *far* way off, and just because you're mostly packed doesn't mean you can't still unpack, if you've changed your mind."

The phone rang again, and the answering machine picked up.

"Dad, I told you I'm going, and I am." She set down her lemonade and hugged herself. "It might not be forever, but I need the winter, at least. I need sun. The kids need sun. I need beaches, and seagulls, and waves, very loud waves, and nothing but the waves."

Her dad nodded. "I get it."

"Mom, the phone's ringing!" Darren called from the yard, frowning with a box in his hands.

Swami nodded.

"I just need you on my side," she said to her father.

"I am," he said, and looked out at his grandkids with a bit of sadness in his eyes, and then he took another drink of lemonade.

The answering machine beeped. *Hey, Swami, It's Sam—*

"I'm going for a walk," Swami said, leaping from her seat. "Can you stay with the kids until Mom gets here? Start without me."

"Yeah, sure I can," her dad said. Swami was already striding toward the side yard, barefooted. She pushed through the painted gate, past the grill and wound hose and hydrangeas, out across the warm asphalt and the smiling, rose-colored Realtor photo of her mom.

A silver sedan coasted to a stop as Swami turned onto the sidewalk.

"Excuse me," said a man, leaning over the lap of his passenger to speak through her window. "This place for sale?"

Swami didn't stop. She wiped her eyes and pointed to the sign and kept going, trying not to fold her arms across her chest as she cried, thankful for the loudness of cicadas.

•••

"YES!" EXCLAIMED HER FATHER, STANDING from a picnic table where everyone sat, holding his arms out wide and beaming. "Uno!" he called, clapping his hands together and sitting again. Swami's mom rocked in her seat to turn and wave at Swami.

It was dusk now, and the strings of Christmas lights lit the yard with a soft glow. Empty paper plates and cups of lemonade sat on the table, a game of cards unfolding between them and a big glass bowl of popcorn. The kids both sat on their knees on the table, hunched over the game in concentration. Swami's mom frowned a pity frown as Swami walked up through the grass.

"We saved a plate for you inside, and the blender's full of margarita," she said. She had a big salted glass in front of her. "DeeDee's asleep in her crib. She had a whole bottle and some avocado."

"Hey, kid," said her dad, watching the game unfold. "How's the hood?" Dell put down a reversal with a mischievous grin. Swami put her hands on her dad's shoulder, thanked her mom. The smell of his shirt and her mom's perfume transported Swami to a lost world, one of neighborhood street hockey and Sunday papers and cupboards full of groceries she didn't have to pay for. She wanted to sink into him, tell him everything, cry. Weep in the grass. Everything was too hard.

"Mommy, I got a *three* and a *seben!*" exclaimed Dell, and Swami was so thankful for her daughter's interruption. The girl held an absolutely massive handful of cards, losing joyfully.

"Se-*ven*," said Darren. "*V, vuh.*" He didn't look at his mom when she arrived.

Darren laid down a red five, and his grandpa groaned.

"You've been getting lots of phone calls," her mom said, with pursed lips.

"Mom."

"Maybe we could just let him know where you are so he can know. I'll bring these plates in."

"Daddy sleeps with Chip now," said Dell, happy to inform the discussion as she placed another card onto the table.

"Daddy sleeps with who?" said Swami's dad.

Swami closed her eyes. Felt the continents colliding. Could she just sit? Could she have a drink? Could she please have a plate of pizza and just watch them play cards?

"Dad sleeps at Uncle Chip's," said Darren, laying down another Uno card. It was a wild card. "Red," he said.

"Darren," Swami begged him.

"Dad and Mom fought all summer," he went on, "because Dad used *retirement* to buy a camper and creamed a deer and then Mom wouldn't talk to him anymore, so Dad started smoking that pipe with the river guides she hates so much. She won't tell me what's in it, but I know it's marijuana."

"Darren!"

"It's true," said Darren, turning toward her now, upset. With his grandparents at the table, Darren held the upper hand, and he knew it. Everything he could say now would hit doubly hard.

"Shh, shh, shh," said his grandmother, but even she seemed a bit surprised by these revelations. "Let your mom sit, honey."

Dell tilted her head toward her grandpa. "And what Dad drinks is *bee-er*," she said. "With *Randy*."

"Stop it, both of you," said Swami.

"Mom won't even let us *see* Dad anymore," said Darren.

Swami yelled now. She didn't try to. It just came. "Stop it, Darren. Just stop!"

"*You* stop it," he yelled back at her. And then he whipped his cards across the table and ran past them all, out the side yard.

"Darren!" Swami yelled after him.

Dell stood on the bench and threw her cards down too. "And I heard Mommy say *shit* in the camper. *Shit! Shit!* You said it, Mommy!"

Dell's grandma scooped her up before she could run off too. Dell did her best to cross her arms in defiance in the woman's embrace.

Everyone looked at the lawn. Her dad just held his cards in his hand. Grandma bounced Dell.

"Excuse me," Swami said, and without another word jogged into the darkness after Darren. Before she knew it she was sprinting. Tears blurred the sky and the sidewalk, so she ran even faster, to outrun it all.

"Darren!" she called, breathless, at the stop sign. She didn't see him. Down the street there was the small bridge spanning the creek they'd walk to sometimes. Beneath it was a little stony beach. It was no Thunderwater, but it was a place to hide, a place for the neighborhood kids to chase a crayfish.

"Darren!" she yelled, pain welling in her body. The whole universe felt made of sand, hot abrasive sand, but if she could just catch up to Darren, just hug him and rock him and cry, everything would be okay. She and Darren and Dell and DeeDee could hold hands and sleep it off, like they had each night in their camper up north.

Swami arrived at the bridge, panting beneath the pines. She scoured the shadows and patches of moonlight. And then she saw him, the small hunched back of a boy hugging his knees to his body on the creek bank. Swami jogged toward him then walked again, stepped down through the weeds. The air and sky seemed so still, the water perfect glass. She could hear Darren's sniffling. He held something shining in his hand, a glint of moonlight. As much as she wanted to rush to him, she didn't want him to run again either, or feel he had to resist her. He was proud as she was, the kind of boy whose crying made him cry.

Swami stopped walking and stood a few steps behind him. Darren turned and saw her, and looked back to the creek again, wiping his face with the sleeve of his shirt.

She waited, then sat near him on the cold sand. He was holding his compass. Swami could just make out the dim glimmer of its silver needle. Darren didn't budge, so neither did Swami. She folded her arms around her legs as her son had, the two mirrors of each other, sitting before the mirror of the black water. The moon, so full overhead, bathed the scraggy bushes and rocks in a light that seemed to mute the sounds of the community, the occasional laughter from a backyard, the suburban owl up in a tree. *Whispering hush*, thought Swami, remembering the children's book Darren used to like and Dell still liked and DeeDee one day would. Swami felt deep love rise up inside herself, a longing for her son. The miracle of his very existence astonished her. And he was so *small*, so easily overshadowed by the busyness of life, and yet he was one of the few things on earth that really mattered to her. Swami felt so inadequate after that thought.

"Darren," she finally whispered. "I am so sorry." She meant she was sorry for getting so wrapped up in this awful summer, for not seeing him clearly, for forgetting about him. She was sorry for the world, the flooding, war, everything that had ever existed that wasn't bright.

"Are you mad at me?" she said.

Darren shook his head. Swami saw his lip poke out in the moonlight.

She slid near to him, and the moment their bodies touched, Darren let his mom hug him and cried. He melted into her the way Swami had wanted to melt into her father moments ago, to just be held. Swami held him, breathed in the smell of his hair for a while.

"You're not having a fun summer," she said. "I haven't helped that."

"I'm just so tired of playing with Dell all day long," he sputtered. "And I don't like being in the house."

Swami waited.

"I don't like how it looks packed up. And my compass broke," he said.

"Oh no," Swami said. "How'd it break?"

"I threw it," Darren said. "When we fought this morning. It won't spin."

Swami started to cry very silently.

"I want to go back to our camper," Darren said. "Can't we just go back to the camper? Why can't you and Dad just get along?"

"Oh, Darren," Swami said. "Come here," she said, and scooped him into her lap. "I'll buy you a new compass, okay? I'll buy you a brand-new one." Darren straddled Swami's legs and bear-hugged her the way he did when he was much younger. Swami hugged his bony, ten-year-old body, kissed his head. The two just stayed that way for a time in the cool sand, silent, listening to the burble of the creek under the bridge.

Darren wiped his eyes with his sleeve and then laid his head on Swami again. "Grandpa let me drive his truck today," he said. "Just up and down the driveway. We went slow."

Swami nodded slowly. "He did?"

Darren nodded.

"Well, driving is good," she said, and thought maybe she should say something about how big he was getting, but that didn't feel true. He wasn't big. He was *small*. All of them were still so small, and Swami resented herself, and Sam too, for not paying more attention to that. She sat with that for what felt like a long time, Darren's head heavy on her shoulder.

"Do you want to set up the tent tonight? It's not the camper, but maybe we could all sleep in the tent together. No more working today, or tomorrow."

She felt Darren shrug. "Sure," he said. He felt heavier in her arms. Swami looked at the swollen little creek. She thought about Thunderwater. Heard the gorge in her mind.

"Please forgive us," she finally whispered, but no answer came. She looked down and saw Darren's face, mouth open, eyes closed, beautiful. She watched him for a very long time. And then she gathered her legs beneath herself and stood carefully to not wake Darren, and walked back into the lamplit street. She would talk to her parents about everything tomorrow.

Swami walked the long way home, hugging her son. The cicadas were going to bed, much quieter now. Mist gathered in the tree canopy. "You ever hear of a back ferry?" she asked her sleeping son. "It's a counterintuitive move," she whispered. "A rafting move. It calls into play invisible forces."

She surprised herself with the memory. She walked up the sidewalk and remembered the gravel switchbacks in West Virginia. She imagined her former self, with brown pigtails and a rafting helmet. She loved how tanned her legs got those summers, how they looked when she pressed them into a thwart to brace for a wave. She imagined that self holding this boy, telling him how good he'd be. She remembered Preacher. Laura. Peaches. Goddess. She hadn't stayed in touch with any of them. She hadn't wondered what became of them for a very long time.

She turned at the stop sign and remembered the way Sam showed up that night on the rock ledge with his bag of pretzels. She remembered how furious she'd been, how serious she was. And she remembered Sam's trembling wrists in her hands. She could still feel them, as sure as she felt Darren in her arms now. Darren was an extension of that time, and of his father, that night on the cliff in a mountain where Darren had never been. He came from that mist, those summers. Preacher once told Swami and Sam that their night on the rock with the snake was a *sign* to them, and they should listen to it, have eyes to see. He told the story of Moses holding his arms and staff aloft during battle. If Moses dropped his arms, Israel began to lose. If he lifted them, they began to win. When Moses could no longer hold his own arms up, someone else held his arms up for him. *So you're saying I should hold on to Swami*, Sam had said, smiling in the campfire light. Swami and Sam weren't really a thing yet, but they were getting closer. *You'll have to catch me first*, she had said, smiling into the fire as Preacher playfully pushed Sam's head, and Sam smiled into the fire too.

Swami felt the warm sidewalk underfoot, and imagined the warm rock ledge. She stood right where she'd stood all those years ago, right where Sam sat. She could look out at the steel-colored clouds, pulled back from the stars, the fog in the canyon. She closed her hands tightly around Darren's body and Sam's wrists. Could still feel them. Could still smell him. And then, years later, to survive, she let go. Sam had let her down more than she'd ever imagined possible. But she had let him fall. That was true too. What would it take from her to pick him back up, to help him? Swami walked up her driveway—holding on, letting go, holding on again, like breath, like a paddle stroke, a counterintuitive move across water. She didn't know what she'd do tomorrow, or the next day. But what she felt she might have to do scared her. She could not think through it any more tonight.

Swami didn't set up the tent in the yard. Instead she whispered apologetic thanks to her parents cleaning the kitchen, and carried Darren upstairs. Her mom already had Dell sleeping in bed in her pajamas. Swami tucked Darren in next to his sister and lay down next to him with her dirty bare feet. And then she got back up and carried DeeDee into the bed too. And then she got up one more time to turn off the humming central air, and she slid open all the bedroom windows so the damp and the moonlight and the sound of frogs could come in. And then she exhaled and rolled toward her children and slept.

AUGUST

FIFTEEN

BANGING AND CUSSING SPILLED OUT FROM BENEATH THE BRAVE. Randy's legs stuck out from under the front, the heel of his cast digging into the grass for leverage. Chip and Sam stood near the picnic table covered in tools and parts, Sam favoring his strong side with his foot in a brace now. The cast came off two days ago. With few trips on the books, the three of them had been able to work on the Brave's front end for the last three days. Sam had picked up the parts from Smitty's with Randy's help.

"What happened to you guys?" Smitty had said, waving out his high school employee to help the two men on crutches struggle with the handful of boxes. "You get into that ruckus out at the mine or what the heck?"

"What the heck," said Randy.

Smitty just nodded, hands in his big coverall pockets.

The whole town of Thunderwater had buzzed with little else for the rest of July. They'd gotten on the news, as a town. Sam had seen the footage. Moon on the hood of a truck, waving her hands, Debbie blasting her way through the fence, flames and rain and mud. Rita had started a fund at the Lanes and Lounge to bail out Debbie. She was staying in the county jail at present. Rita had three of the five thousand dollars. "It's not the first time one of us been in the clink," Rita said. "We'll take care of her. No one's talking." Bruce and Blakely became scarce, but the NorthSky crews were still in town. Rita didn't let them drink at her bar. A divide had formed in the town, as muddy as a river, with most locals on one side and outsiders on the other. A handful of families still wanted the mine and the jobs it would bring, but they stayed quiet about it. Most of the yard signs disappeared. There was tense distrust. Static hung over the small town like it did before a rainstorm. The river was dropping again, but everyone feared more flooding would come.

"What's the latest with your mom?" Sam had asked Randy on their slow drive out to the campsite.

"You know," Randy said, grinning and shaking his head, "you'd be surprised, but she's really all right. She's really going to be all right. Pete hooked her up with the tribe's lawyer. He's a shark. I never pressed charges on NorthSky's crew or talked to the cops. NorthSky didn't press charges on Mom. They wouldn't talk to the cops either. All anyone has is the news video of a crowd, a few gunshots. Lawyer says he can get her off on 'brandishing a firearm,' now that the story's died down."

"She brandished it, all right," Sam said. "How's Moon?"

"She's good. I'm heading to her place after. We're cooking her spicy food tonight."

"Been spending a lot of time over there," said Sam.

Randy smiled, let the big steering wheel slip against his palm. "She's talking me into cooking school," he said.

"No kidding?" Sam said. "You gonna go?"

Randy shrugged. "Maybe," he said.

Beyond the cast on his hand and foot, and a scar where his ear had split, Randy was healed up. He was good. "You should go," Sam told him. "It'd be good to go."

They'd pulled into Governor's State Park. Chip was waiting for them. He had the air compressor from his shop strapped to the back of his bike. He stood up and carried out the boxes to the front of the camper. Unpacked the parts. Since only Randy knew anything about motors, he'd been the one who shimmied very slowly under the camper. Sam and Chip handed him tools so Randy didn't move his healing ribs any more than he had to.

Chip seemed sullen, standing there in the hot sun, swatting bugs. All the woods were swampy. The mosquitoes were bad even in daylight. Chip seemed extra aggravated by the bugs ever since what had happened in July. He asked about Swami a lot. He ate a lot of Tums. He walked to and from his deer fence several times a day, shaking the bucket of alfalfa pellets, feeding the deer with his hand. When the giant old buck, Old Mossy, came to the fence, Sam couldn't be sure, but he thought he heard Chip talking to the old deer. He thought he heard

Chip say something about Aunt Mary, and about Sam. After two weeks of Swami not answering calls, Chip stood up from the kitchen table and demanded they drive down there.

"In what?" Sam asked him. "The rafting bus?"

Chip shrugged. "Randy'd let us borrow his truck, or his ma's truck. A vehicle's not the problem."

"Look," said Sam. "I called Deidra's real estate office. Swami's at home and safe. That's all her mom would tell me, because she'd promised not to talk to me. Swami and the kids are fine. I'm not going down there if she won't even answer the phone. I know her. You do too. Going down there won't help."

Chip relented and slumped into his chair again. "Well, this is the beginning of the real stuff," he said. "Whatever you decide to do or not do next, matters. It *matters*," he said. He sighed. Sam could tell his mind was arguing with itself, circling. "There's limits, though, you know? There's limits to suffering."

Sam frowned at him.

"Never mind me," Chip said, shaking his head. "I'm just a stupid old man." And then he limped out to his greenhouse, pressing his fist against his chest and eating a few more Tums from the bottle he kept in his poncho pocket.

Sam transitioned to sleeping out at the camper. At night he sat alone at the galley table, and then crawled into the bed, which still smelled like his kids and his wife. Every other day, he called home and left a message. He sent Swami a postcard from the camp store. It was a risk, but because it was something they used to do, he felt it might be more right than wrong. In the daytime, Sam limped around the raft barn on crutches, sweeping sand out the door across the stained patio, then into the dry grass. Birdy had come out to clean up the scaffolding. He was more worried about taking Sam and his family bowling than his wrecked equipment. After two weeks on crutches, Sam could hobble in a giant Velcro boot, help Chip with raft trailers, drive the riding mower from Chip's place into town to gas it up and ask Smitty about camper parts. He drove the bouncy old mower down the gravel shoulder, remarking how the summer felt late and strange and empty.

The world slowed down. Sam paid attention to things like the sound of gravel under his tires, the smell of rotting grass in the ditches.

"It's the wrong radiator!" Randy yelled from beneath the truck. His feet twisted and jerked in the grass. The peal of a hammer rang out on metal. Randy snaked out from underneath, wincing, keeping his cast out of the dirt. "Aftermarket garbage!" He swatted gravel from his jeans as he stood and put his crutches under his arm. "Hoses fit, but the mounting holes don't line up."

"I'll call Smitty," Sam said.

"Nope," said Randy, as he instructed Chip to throttle up a small gas generator he had in the bed of his truck. He tossed a tangled extension cord toward the front of the camper. He crawled back underneath with a giant yellow hammer drill, holding it like a soldier would a rifle going to war. The Winnebago started shuddering as Randy wound the drill into its frame, yelling at it over the whine of the drill.

Chip wiped his forehead with a handkerchief and stepped away from the noise. It was August hot. Humid, and far too bright. The whole campground felt steamed. Sam had killed the camper battery twice falling asleep with the fan on.

"You got any trips coming in?" Chip asked, backing away from the drill noise toward the picnic table.

Sam shook his head, hobbled after him. "But there's always hope," he said, laughing at himself. "Woodchuck'll make me rich yet."

Chip didn't smile. He sat down on the end of the table. The boards bent. "I'm selling my farm to NorthSky," he said, and then added, now that the truth had come out, "Selling it to Blakely."

"You're not serious," said Sam.

Chip looked at him and then looked at the grass. Chip nodded.

"Got it!" yelled Randy. There was the *ping-ping* of a hammer on a bolt head, and then the cranking of a ratchet, and then Randy squirmed out beaming. Chip grabbed the heavy drill from him. Randy gathered his crutches.

"Pack it up," Randy said. "I won't charge for the extra holes. It's good enough for the Northwoods."

"It'll run?"

"Fire it up when I tell you and turn your heater on. I gotta bleed the radiator."

Sam climbed up to the driver's seat and turned the key when Randy nodded. The motor grumbled to life, and then found its idle and ran smoothly. In a few minutes Randy had the radiator bled and topped off. Sam left it running with the AC on while Randy washed up in the camper sink.

It was amazing, seeing this expensive camper coming to life again. The gauges all working, the vents blowing ice-cold air. "Man, I owe you," Sam said.

"You owe me twenty-five bucks," Randy said.

Outside, Sam paid him through the window of his old blue truck.

"I'm sorry, Randy, about Woodchuck, that the trips dried up. I wish I could pay you all more this summer. I wish we could all get paid more."

"Don't sweat it," Randy said. "You did what you could. I'm off," he said, with a broad grin, because he was headed toward the woman he loved, and who was clearly beginning to openly love him back. Sam slapped Randy's hood, and then looked toward the running camper, where Chip was enjoying some air-conditioning in the passenger seat, like a big dog. Sam walked over and shut himself in with his uncle. They sat for a moment, letting the vents wash over them.

Chip had his eyes closed as he began to speak. "Blakely stopped out at my place. Cat's out of the bag—now we know he's a land manager for the mine. I *knew* I recognized his voice from somewhere. He was the one calling from NorthSky earlier this summer, leaving messages. Anyway, he told me NorthSky still wants to buy my farm and mine it. To sweeten the deal, he'll direct NorthSky to give you guys top dollar for the land Woodchuck sits on too. The Woodchuck land ain't for mining, but they'll take down the barn and build cheap condos for workers. *Money is money.* That's what Blakely told me."

"What?" Sam said.

"So I'm gonna sell. And you can sell if you want. I recommend you do. Get you and Swami out of this mess. Blakely's coming out to the farm later this week with a surveyor and Ranger Bonnie. She needs to say what to do with the deer permits."

"Chip," said Sam. "I don't want you selling your farm for us. It was our decision to buy Woodchuck. We'll climb out ourselves. You don't have to do this."

Chip waved him off. "It's not just for you. I'm doing it for Randy too—I decided when I saw him in that hospital bed—and for his mom, and for Pete, and this whole town. And I'm doing it for me too. I never imagined I'd be able to retire. Now I can."

"Chip."

"I don't want anyone else getting hurt," he said. "Too many people have been hurt."

"No," said Sam.

"Yes," said Chip.

"Well, what will they do with the deer?"

"Probably destroy them. They are domestic game. They can't be released." His eyes welled up a bit. Chip looked out the passenger window. "You got bigger things to worry about than old deer," Chip said.

Sam tried to imagine his uncle without Woodchuck, without his farm, without his kitchen, where he fried his eggs in his faded wet suit. He'd become like one of those old lions, too old to fight, just enough muscle left to plod off and disappear, or get nailed by a safari hunter.

"There's something you need to know about me. About my life."

"Chip," said Sam. He didn't want his uncle to have to do all of this right now. The days had been hard enough. Everyone just needed rest.

"Your aunt Mary," said Chip, still looking out the passenger window. "She came back once. She tried to come back after she left me, and I didn't let her. I couldn't let it go. Pride ruined the rest of my life." Chip cried now. His big red beard quivered. "I wouldn't forgive her. Do you understand what I'm saying? What I'm telling you?" He looked at Sam with intense red eyes.

"She left you," said Sam, gently as he could. "For another man. It wasn't your fault."

Chip wagged his big head. "And she tried to come back. She stood right at the end of my driveway, by the gate. She cried and wept, and I shouted her away. Your mom saw the whole thing, Sam, your stepdad too. They were over when she came. It's what caused the break between your stepdad and me. He tried to talk me down after I drove her off. I went crazy. I drove him off too. Slammed the gate shut behind everyone. It's why I couldn't come to your mother's funeral."

Sam hadn't talked to his stepdad since the funeral. They'd never been close. Mom was the only reason they'd stayed in touch. His name was Peter.

"Peter never told me any of that," said Sam. "Never mentioned a word of it. Mom neither."

"Because they are good people, Sam. And I am not."

Sam frowned at the gauges.

"He would have let you come to the funeral," Sam said. "You could have come to her funeral."

"He would have. And that's why I didn't. You understand? He would have suffered through my presence, all my wrongs. He would have *held* them. Most people can't do it, won't even suffer when they're the ones who are wrong, let alone when they're in the right. It's why the world keeps burning. I was too proud to come. I went out to the cemetery that night and said goodbye to my sister."

Chip held up his big, rough hands to his face. They shook. His voice cracked. "I think back to Mary that day in the driveway. All I want is to go back and open that gate." And then the palms of Chip's trembling hands pressed together as if in prayer, and Chip started sobbing. He pressed his hands to his lips and turned away. It was frightening, seeing a man this large cry. Sam looked away too. All of Chip's loneliness came coursing out like a river overflowing its banks. How many years Chip felt all this, regretted this, played it out in his mind at night. Sam tried to put his hand on Chip's heaving shoulder, but took it away again. They just sat there until Chip's weeping calmed, and then stopped. Sam didn't know how long it had been. Eventually, though, there was just the sound of the air-conditioning again. Chip dried his face on his shirt.

"So," said Chip, "now you know all of my secrets."

Sam took a breath. He didn't quite know what to do with everything Chip had just told him. There was a sense of betrayal in it, a family drama into which Sam had never been invited. He had to rethink the way he saw his stepfather, and he hadn't expected to have to do that this late in life. Sam wasn't angry about all he'd just learned about his uncle and stepfather. He was just confused about how to hold it.

"Okay," he said. "Now I know." There was a sort of mercy in it. It was a way to hold it. It was plain. *Now I know.*

Chip drank it up, embarrassed, thankful, quiet. He nodded.

"If she comes back, Sam, just take her back. Don't make it about who's wrong or right. Just take her back. Let her take you back."

Sam nodded. The trees outside sagged in the afternoon heat. The campsite was all packed up.

"So," said Sam, "Blakely's coming out later this week."

"Yeah."

"I just wish there was another way," Sam said. "For all of this. Wood-chuck. Your farm. All of it."

"I know you do," he said.

"I want to say thanks," Sam said. "Thanks for teaching me the river this summer. It's been good. The river's been really good."

"It's a bright spot," said Chip.

"Chip?"

"Yeah."

"You want to go boating today? Right now. Let's go put a raft on the water, just me and you. Fun run."

Chip looked at him. His red eyes brightened. "Your foot," he said.

"I'll tape a dry bag over it. It'll be fine. We'll take it easy. One raft from top to bottom, run the whole gorge without stopping. What do you say?"

Chip nodded a big, slow nod. "Let's boat," he said.

"Yeah?" asked Sam, holding his hands apart, ready to clap them.

"Yeah," said Chip.

Sam clapped, put the camper in gear, and checked his side-view mirrors for any remaining lawn chairs. "Leave your bike here," he said. "Let's take the camper."

Sam let his foot off the brake, and for the first time since that night in May, the Brave lumbered forward under its own power. It rocked out onto the asphalt path and roared forward into the bright sun.

"Whitewater!" Sam yelled, rolling his window down and feeling the hot breeze on his outstretched hand.

"Whitewater!" echoed Chip, and then he smiled.

•••

SAM AND CHIP DIDN'T TAKE just one boat. They took six. They each sat with their feet in the river, bow-stroking a raft and towing two apiece. It was a slow and aimless float, quiet, shared by two men with love for the river and a profound sense of defeat. They didn't need to speak to each other about the stone bluffs, the heat, the white pines, the waterline on the rocks showing the river was dropping, or trying to drop, or the level of the line showing a water level around five thousand. They just drifted and churned the bright water with easy paddle strokes. Sam eased his foot out of its dry bag and Velcro boot to soak his ankle in the cool water. A bald eagle roosted on a pine and watched them.

Chip dangled his toes in the water and puffed on a joint, bobbed his head to some silent song, held his paddle like a guitar. Sam tried to envision Chip as an even older man, retired in Florida, hamming it up in some Jimmy Buffett tiki bar. He knew Chip would never go. His uncle would end up burning through all that money in a year or two, or just giving it away, or both. Chip would grow old alone by the river, hunched by his woodstove in winter, the water frozen over. Sam let the thought go. There was almost nothing in his life he could affect or control. Life changed. The river rose and fell. It was okay. It's what *was*. Sam was so tired of fighting against what *was*. Besides, he assured himself, if anyone could live a hardscrabble life of venison jerky and canned tomatoes and wood heat, it was Chip. The man could thrive under a tarp.

As they drew near to Sand Portage, Chip did something Sam found beautiful, and it removed all pity Sam had felt for the man. Chip buckled his faded helmet onto his head, wrapped his old life jacket around his body, wedged his foot under a thwart, and then leaned out and patted the river the way a person might pat the arm of an old friend. Framed in by the pines of the island and the shore, with the glassy black horizon of the rapids before him, Chip was a king, bathed in riches.

Chip had *lived*. As others had spent their best years tied to desks and machines in tan-colored rooms, Chip had been out here for decades, breathing in pine, tasting the river on his lips, shaking his beard, warming himself on silt-colored rocks, a raft guide.

Sam buckled his own helmet and put his foot back in its boot and bag and followed Chip through the bob and sweep of rapids, working with the currents. Sand Portage was big and smooth, rocks buried, with tall rolling waves. They beached on the sand near a small stack of Duncan's boats. Sam shook his head. Of course Duncan had trips today. He had the customers lined up and waiting for the water level to drop. *No matter*, thought Sam. *Good for Duncan.*

With just the two of them sitting side by side, the raft felt light and playful. They did a spin above the falls and dropped down into the thundering gorge. They dug their paddles in fist deep. The hole behind Volkswagen was massive but manageable. Chip leaned way out and let the wave bury him, came up with his helmet cocked sideways, his woolly beard beading water, a massive grin. They eddied out at the bottom, in the big shaded pool, beached next to one of Duncan's boats, and hiked back up, Sam hobbling beneath the forest canopy and the high sun.

They ran the gorge again and again, looping it opposite Duncan, each group depositing another raft at the bottom each time. With their second-to-last raft, Sam slipped out of the boat in the eddy and just floated in the copper-colored water, letting the current of the big pool drift him in circles. His back was tired, and it felt good to let the river hold him. He thought about all the fear he'd had about losing his job, and the outfitter, and Swami too, and how none of those fears actually helped anybody. They only balled him up, made him freeze, prevented him from pulling anything off. And then Sam realized that right now, afloat in the water, he didn't feel afraid of much anymore. Sam watched the top of a pine tree circle through his field of vision.

"Thank you," he said to nothing in particular, or to everything in particular, or to whatever it was that held everything else inside it. Sam washed up on the sandbar and sat in the water. A crayfish scuttled away. Across the eddy, Chip was pulling his shorts back up. He'd just finished peeing all over one of Duncan's green boats.

And then someone hollered from the river where the current came rushing past the pool. "Damn it, Chip!" yelled the voice.

Chip panic-tied his shorts. Sam turned. Duncan came swimming out of the current, with an empty raft overturned behind him. He swam fast to shore, or at least as fast as he could. He looked exhausted.

"Where's your people?" asked Chip. He knew he'd been caught, and decided not to care.

Duncan waded in, shaking his head. He took off his helmet and used it to splash water into the raft Chip had just peed in.

"Sorry for peeing on your raft," Chip said. "Sorry you caught me, anyway. You know how it is."

Duncan was still sucking wind. He turned and sat heavily on his beached boat, pointed at Chip's raft beside it. "Well, I just peed all over that one, so."

"Ha!" Chip said. "That's the spirit. You're almost getting the hang of this now."

Sam waded in and stood waist deep in the water. Duncan grinned.

"Hey, Sam," he said.

"Duncan."

"I'm out here alone today. I'm trying to figure out the water level."

"Pretty hard paddling by yourself," Chip said.

Duncan looked embarrassed. "Well, like I said, I'm out here alone." He wrung some water out of his sodden shorts. "Truth is, I don't have a guide who can raft this at five grand." He looked right at Chip, defiant, "And I'm not too sure I can either. If Volkswagen doesn't smoke me, the Sisters do." He looked back at the water. His overturned raft had nosed itself into an eddy on the far shore. "I'll figure it out. How's Randy? And his mom?"

"They're good," said Chip, and then he winced. "How's your uncle? Heard you guys had a falling-out."

Duncan darkened. "Damn right we did. As of right now, I own only the rafts and the bus. NorthSky owns the property and everything on it. My uncle is a regional land manager for NorthSky. He does have roots up here, so the company thought he'd be the right man to win over locals. It's his job to buy property or secure leases, and make the land profitable until mining can start. The entire time I thought we were building a raft company, he was building a front for NorthSky. The land wasn't even in his name, it was in NorthSky's; he flat-out lied to me. It was all a sham. I don't like being back at the outpost anymore. I still like it out here, though. I still got my boats."

Chip nodded. Sam looked at him. He knew he wouldn't mention the sale of his farm. Everyone up here was just trying to survive. "You know," Chip said, "I like you a whole lot better when you're upset."

Duncan laughed. "Well," he said, "pleased to meet you. Sorry I got in your face earlier this season."

Chip wagged his beard. "It's all part of it," he said.

"You out of boats up top?" Sam asked.

Duncan nodded. "That's my last one over there. Belly up. Suppose I should go get it."

"Pick it up later," Chip said, looking at Sam. He knew what Sam was thinking. "Come on," he said. "We got one more up top. Paddle it with us. I'll show you the angles at five grand."

"Yeah?"

"Yeah," said Chip.

•••

WHEN THE RAFTS WERE PUT up, and Chip left on his bike, Sam locked up the front door and left a message for Swami. He told her about the river, about the working camper. "I miss you guys," he said, leaning his forehead against the wooden post and then hanging up. Then he hobbled upstairs and sat on an overturned bucket between open barn doors out back. The sun was low. Everything was amber. The barn swallows were out, skimming the grass and alfalfa fields, playing, snatching bugs. And then the phone rang. Sam nearly couldn't believe it. He overturned his bucket and limped as fast as he could back down the stairs.

"Hello!" he said breathlessly, and then frowned. It wasn't Swami.

"Yes, this is Woodchuck." Sam made a big reach at the end of the cord for a clipboard and a pen. "You want to what? How many?" His eyes widened. He scribbled furiously, thanked the man, finished the call.

Immediately, Sam called Swami again. "Swami," he said as the answering machine picked up. He was nearly breathless. "Swami, we have a jamboree trip. It's not huge, but it'll help. It's on the books. Please come back," he said.

SIXTEEN

"MOM, WHY ARE YOU DRIVING SO SLOW?" DARREN ASKED. DARREN had wanted to ride shotgun, and Swami let him once they got north of Green Bay and the traffic thinned. He was happy as a peach, watching and asking about all the road signs, holding an unfolded map on his lap with his brand-new compass, leaning over and watching the tachometer rise and fall on the old van. His new compass didn't fold like his old one, but it came in a pack with a signal mirror and a bright orange whistle, and Darren was pleased with it.

"We're going north now, Mom," he said.

Swami gave him a quick nod and a tight smile. She could do this, she hoped. At a rest stop in Wausaukee, Swami saw her kids talking conspiratorially about the roadside ice cream shop across the street. Their eyes flashed disbelief when Swami walked them over and paid for three swirl cones. Swami smiled as Darren and Dell stunned themselves with cream and sugar. They looked like little bears, deliriously drenched in honeycomb. *Olay!* Swami thought, watching the occasional logging truck idle past. And then she thought of Birdy. She'd call him, she decided, tell him they'd finally come bowling. Doing that would give Swami a solid reason for driving back up here, for returning. The rest of it still felt like a river bottom underfoot. After weeks of packing the house, planning her path to the ocean, Swami got Sam's last message and packed the rafting van and drove north, told her parents they'd be gone no more than a week. She wasn't going *back*. But for some reason, the way forward, the way *west*, somehow had to include first driving north. Swami needed to untangle a knot. That's the closest she could come to explaining it to herself.

"I'm driving slow because we're almost there," she said.

Darren furrowed his brow.

"Is that a driving rule too?" he asked.

"Here, it is," she said.

She turned off the road onto the gravel drive. Chip's place. There was the gate. There was the old deer farm sign in the weeds. The culvert was flooded over with water.

"We're here!" Darren exclaimed.

"Where, Darren, where?" Dell said. She'd napped through a sugar coma.

"Chip's deer farm," said Darren. "I think. Right, Mom?"

Swami nodded. The kids cheered. Swami was not excited. This felt like a mistake now. "Wait here," she said.

She stepped out for a closer look at the water. The peninsula was an island. The flowing creek rippled over the stones in the driveway. She stepped into the cold water and felt the gravel. It was still solid underfoot near the driveway's center. Swami waded around. The edges closest to the culvert ends were deteriorating, washing out as the creek rose and fell. The water crossing was up to her knees at its deepest. Swami looked up the driveway. Around that bend, she knew there was Chip's brown cabin, the sagging screen porch, the deer. She didn't know who else might be here—Chip, Moon, Randy. Swami took a big breath. *The sun is warm*, she told herself. *The pines smell very good.* But it was an odd sort of sunlight. A haze of clouds was closing in. The newsman on the radio said more rain was coming, but Swami had turned it off as she drove past sodden farm fields and very full creeks. She didn't need to hear about any more rain.

Swami got back in the van and started the motor again. Her gas tank was down to fumes. She could smell it, the way the old motor smelled extra hot, lean. Chip would have gas in his machine shed. She wouldn't have to hike a gas can back across if she made it to his shed. She looked at the stream covering the driveway.

"Hang on," she said.

Darren held on. He rolled his window up when he realized what she was doing.

Swami eased the front tires in, and then the rear, and when the exhaust sounded like it started to burble, Swami just punched it. The van forded, pushed a big wave out on both sides. The motor roared and steamed. The kids were glued to the windows. Swami climbed the van up to higher ground, and then the motor sputtered and died. The van jerked to a stop and now sat dripping and silent, a very tired horse. Water drops hissed inside the engine compartment.

"There," she said. "We made it, I suppose."

"It broke, Mommy." Dell frowned from the back.

"It did," she said.

Dell unbuckled her seat belt and clambered up to the back of Swami's seat for a better look through the windshield. Up ahead, they could see the machine shed now. Alongside it sat the Winnebago Brave, with its bold teal stripes.

"The camper is here," Darren said. "Dad got the camper running."

"Daddy fixed it," said Dell, smiling.

"Come on." Swami sighed. "Let's see who's home."

Swami hiked up the driveway with her three children, DeeDee in her car carrier. They walked past the Brave, with its new headlights and bumper. They stopped when they got to the center of things, the house, the woods, a few blue rafts stacked in the machine shed. The house and yard were quiet. Swami could see the deer dozing in the pasture beyond the shining black pond. Dell hadn't seen the deer yet. It was part of the reason Swami drove here first instead of the campground or Woodchuck. She wanted Dell to see the deer. It was one small part of the knot.

Chip plodded out from the machine shed, carrying a bushy armful of green plants on his shoulder. He looked covered in greenhouse dirt. The neck of his shirt sagged with brown sweat. Swami knew he kept a greenhouse back there. And she knew what he grew in it. He didn't see Swami standing there right away, but then he turned toward her, toward a small lawn mower trailer half-filled with the plants. Swami's breath caught in her chest. She lifted her chin.

"Chips!" exclaimed Dell, and Chip jumped and dropped the plants and saw Dell and then Swami. And then he turned to run back inside his shed, and then he stopped and turned back toward the dropped plants, and then just ducked and turned again and ran into the machine shed and didn't come back.

"What's he *doing*, Mommy?" Dell asked.

Swami shook her head.

And then Sam walked out, slowly at first, and Chip followed him. Now Swami felt like ducking.

"Dad!" Darren said. And he and Dell ran to him and hugged him. Swami stayed where she was. Sam ruffled Darren's hair and rubbed Dell's back as they squeezed his waist and leg. Sam was sweaty and dirty too. The kids beamed. The adults all stared at one another.

"Chips, you are *silly*," Dell said, giving him a push. Chip smiled a worried smile and stooped down to her level, let her jabber at him about their ride, the ice cream, how they drove the van through the river and broke it.

"I have bags," Swami said. "In the van. Is the camper unlocked?"

Sam nodded. "Yeah," he said. "I mean, yes. It is."

Darren watched them.

"We're here." Swami shrugged. She could hardly speak. Her daughter gabbed at Chip, and Swami knew Darren was waiting to see how his parents would interact. He was old enough to know everything, pick up on every tension, the shame and difficulty of it all. He was also still such an innocent kid. Swami was about to cry. She couldn't really look right at Sam, so she looked past him. The deer in the pasture began to stir, seeing all the humans gathered. A massive buck rose and watched them.

"For the raft trip," Sam said. "You guys came for the jamboree."

Swami nodded, really looked at Sam for the first time in a very long time. He was deeply tan. His hair had grown shaggy. He was as dirty as his uncle. He also looked kind. There was kindness in his eyes she didn't know what to do with.

"I'll help you get your bags," he said. "I'm glad you're here."

Swami nodded again without speaking. Tight little nods.

"Dell, look," said Darren.

"What, Darren?" she said and spun. "Ohhhh!" Dell gushed, a melting affection in her voice. Then she spun back to Chip and grabbed a fistful of his beard. *"Deers!"*

Chip winced from the tugging, laughed at her.

"Oh, can we go see them?" said Dell.

"Is that okay with Mom?" Chip asked. He groaned as he stood again, held his back.

"Yes," said Swami. "Go."

"You want to feed 'em? They could use a snack," Chip said to his great-niece, his big eyes bright and wide.

Dell looked like she'd burst.

"Come on," said Chip. "Darren, grab that white bucket over there that says *alfalfa* on it." Darren sprang to action. Chip quickly stooped and grabbed the stalks he'd dropped and placed them in the lawn mower trailer.

"What's that, Chips?" Dell asked.

Chip shook his head, gave Swami a quick, apologetic glance.

"Just cleaning up the greenhouse," he said. "Come on." And then the three of them made toward the pasture. Dell grabbed Chip's huge hand and skipped. Darren leaned with the weight of the pail. Chip turned back once. "It's good to see you guys, Swami," he said.

Swami grinned and waved. Chip was already leaning down and saying something to Dell, pointing to the big buck.

"Can I take her for you?" Sam asked.

"Sure," Swami said. She'd forgotten she was still holding the heavy car carrier. "She's sleeping."

"Ohh," whispered Sam, and Swami recognized Dell's voice in the way he said it. "Hey, little one," he whispered to the baby, tucking in a corner of the baby-sized knot blanket Debbie had made for her.

Sam looked at Swami. "A lot's happened," said Sam. "I have a lot to tell you."

Swami could tell he was having trouble speaking too. "I do too," she said.

"I'll get your bags," he said. "Then maybe a walk?" Swami nodded, and they walked together toward the van, stiffly. Sam walked with a slight limp, holding the car carrier between them.

"Your leg," Swami said. "You don't have a cast anymore."

Sam shook his head, smiled. "Nearly healed up. Still a bit weak. I still wear the boot most of the time." He handed DeeDee to her and got the bags. Sam went to the van, and Swami watched him try to start it, and then just carry the bags instead. The camper had been thoroughly cleaned, but it still held the smells of their summer, a lingering of Timbrel Lake sand and sunscreen and laundry.

"The old heap rafting van," Sam said, climbing the steps into the galley, hoisting bags in each hand. He dropped them on the galley bench. Swami stood in the galley of the camper and wrapped DeeDee on her chest. She felt the little girl's spine, patted her bottom, looked down at the girl's strawberry tuft of hair.

"So, Chip is selling the farm to NorthSky," he said.

Swami distributed the fabric folds round DeeDee. She was out like a light.

"I knew Blakely wanted him to," Swami said. Swami busied herself a little longer with the wrap than she needed to. She didn't want to look Sam in the eyes in the quiet of the camper. "And I knew Chip didn't."

"Blakely's buying it to mine it," Sam said. "Blakely is NorthSky. Any land he claimed to be buying for X-treme, he was buying on behalf of NorthSky. He's coming out here tomorrow with a surveyor and Ranger Bonnie. She's coming along to see what the state will do with the animals."

Swami looked at him. Sam did have things to tell her.

"Come on," he said. "I'd like to show you something while I still can."

They walked past the machine shed and past the fence where Chip and the kids fed the deer.

"No, Dell," Darren said. "Keep your hand flat when you feed him. *Flat.*" Darren started guiding her hand toward the deer fence, but Dell pulled away from him.

"I know how," Dell said.

Swami smiled, felt a bit of pride rise up in her. She walked next to Sam in the tall grass. *I know how*, she thought to herself. "Kids, we'll be right back," she said.

The kids hardly heard her, but Chip turned around with a big grin. Gave a thumbs-up.

It was getting windy now. The haze of the sky had thickened instead of cleared. A big gust blew the tops of the pine trees. The prairie grass in the pasture moved in green breaths. Swami took big breaths too. Poplar trees shimmered green and silver, their leaves spinning on their stems.

Sam filled her in on everything she'd missed. What had happened to Moon, Randy, Pete, Debbie. Swami stepped with Sam through the wood line, and then over the collapsed wire fence Sam held down with his foot. They walked uphill, into an opening of giant hardwoods. Sam stopped walking, and Swami looked out at the woods. Old, mossy humps rose from the earth. They looked like giant tortoises creeping amidst the trees. They looked to Swami almost like Indian mounds.

"And then I finished the barn," Sam said, stopping.

"I saw the barn," Swami said.

"I wasn't drunk. Moon told me you thought I was drunk."

Swami was looking at the mounds. "Sam, are these what I think they are?"

"It's why Chip wouldn't sell," he said. "That and this place is—"

"Home," Swami said very quietly.

"Sorry?" Sam asked.

Swami shook her head. The treetops raked each other in a big gust of wind. Their trunks creaked. Swami watched them move. She looked at the mounds, tried to wonder what was beneath them, but all she could think about was Debbie and her bunker, and Moon and Randy, and Sam falling from scaffolding, and what she'd said to Chip and what Chip had said to her. It all felt like ghosts swirling up, too much unearthed all at once. Swami imagined mining trucks in her mind, these giant trees thumping down, acidic gravel dams mounded up the way Moon had described. Another gust moved through the treetops. Then another.

"Swami, I am so sorry," said Sam.

Swami looked away, looked out of the woods at the bright fields, toward the kids. She couldn't see them from here. They were feeding deer with their great-uncle, who was taking a break from harvesting pot. Her old pang of frustration rose up, heaped itself on the gravel dams.

"I am sorry about Woodchuck," Sam went on. "About this summer.

I'm sorry I didn't tell you I might lose my job. I'm sorry for falling apart so fast. I am sorry I hurt you."

Swami's eyes tightened as he spoke.

"You did," she said. "You did fall apart. Everything did. It hurt, Sam. It still does."

Sam looked at the ground, then at the woods. Snapped a small twig from a tree. "And things fell apart even more after you left. But they're still here too. It's all still here."

"Sam, I'm selling the house."

"I know," said Sam. He snapped the twig again.

"You *know*?" Swami said.

"Your mom told me."

Swami felt her jaw tense.

"In her defense, I bugged the hell out of her. Look, Swami, I know you're mad, and you might be mad forever. And I just wanted to say that I'm sorry. I really am."

"I don't know where we stand," Swami said.

"I know," Sam said.

"And I don't know what all of *this* means." She waved at the mounds, and then down the hill, where she heard Dell laughing with Chip. "But I am here. And I'll stay through the river trip. After that I really don't know what's next. I'm trying."

"I know," Sam said. He looked right at her. "It's okay not to know. I'm glad you're here," he said.

Swami bit the inside of her cheek. Swami looked at Sam. Those bright, sad eyes. That stupid mop of hair.

"The kids are going to need supper soon," she said.

"I was planning on grilling burgers," said Sam. "And making a cucumber salad."

Swami nodded. "Good," Swami said, because enough had been said already.

They walked back toward the fields, and Swami looked back once at the mounds. They were amazing, and they were here all along. They were here all summer. They were here when Swami was six, when her dad drove them out to California. They were here when she and Sam were learning to be river guides. And now, soon, they wouldn't be? It was too difficult to imagine. Sam held the fence down again, and Swami stepped over it and felt thankful when she moved back into the sunlight, the wind blowing loudly through the waist-high grass as they hiked back. The wind wasn't cool. It was from the south. It added to the heat of the day.

Dell stood by the fence and held out another handful of pellets. Chip stepped away and made way for Swami to kneel next to her. Sam put his hands on Darren's shoulders, squeezed him, gave his belly a pat. "Dell and Darren are gonna make my deer get fat," Chip said. Dell had fed four yearlings and three mom deer already, Darren told them.

Dell stood very still. Now the biggest buck ambled toward them, and everyone grew quiet. A smaller deer moved out of the buck's way. He truly was impressive. Swami watched his muscles work beneath his gray-brown hide. All the velvet was gone from his antlers, and the burnished, ivory-colored rack stretched much wider than Dell could spread her arms.

"He's safe," whispered Chip behind them. "He's gentle."

"Chip," Swami whispered without thinking. She felt mesmerized as the buck approached. "What's going to happen to the deer?"

"What, Mom?" Dell whispered, not taking her eyes off the animal.

Swami looked up at Chip, and Chip looked at Dell and shook his head. Darren saw him.

"They're gonna get fat," Chip said.

The buck nosed down toward the girl's hand. When his antlers bumped the wire fence, he turned his head sideways instead, and with velvet lips vacuumed up the pellets. He had a gray chin, silver stubble, deep black eyes surrounded with brown irises. Darren held the bucket so Dell could feed him another handful. Dell reached out and stroked his nose while he ate, her eyes as wide and deep as his. His white-and-brown tail flicked. Dell pushed her hair behind her ear with her free hand, smiled, petted his nose again. The deer softly grunted and huffed while it ate, and Dell kept making soft sounds, both exhalation and exclamation, and Swami felt something loosen, unknot.

"Oh," Dell said. "*Oh.*"

•••

SAM HAD TO BROIL THE burgers in a pan in Chip's kitchen instead of grill outside. In the time it took him to start the charcoal, the hot wind from the south bowed the trees, the air turned green, and in came the dark bank of clouds, big cold raindrops that stung the gravel driveway. Sam looked up at the dark clouds, and something inside him wilted. For two or three days now, the weatherman on channel six forecasted the biggest rain event of the summer, a twelve-hour downpour. There would be breaks, he said, between thunderstorms and heavy rain, but to expect flooding near creeks and rivers, and washouts. He said to pre-pare to stay home and limit travel during the next night and day.

Chip stepped out of the machine shed a moment to look at the green dusk. He looked knowingly at Sam across the driveway. "Here she comes," he called.

Sam nodded. And there goes the jamboree, he thought. The river would blow out again. He'd lose his trip. Duncan would lose all of his. There was a small consolation in that, but no real joy in it. A fat rain-drop hissed on the newly lit charcoals, the smell of lighter fluid and coming rain filling the air. Chip shook his head at the rolling clouds, wiped his forehead with the sweaty front of his dirty shirt. He looked bushed. After feeding the deer and getting Swami settled, he insisted Sam stay in with his family, said he'd finish the garden himself.

"You sure you don't need a hand?" Sam said.

Chip had been going hard for nearly two hours now. Coming out with more armfuls of stalks of his prized plants, driving the little lawn mower and trailer off into the woods to dump them far away from the prying eyes of Blakely and his surveyor and Ranger Bonnie. The buds he was collecting in a giant contractor's trash bag. He'd hang the pun-gent bounty to dry out of the elements in an old deer blind by the river.

Chip shook his head. "I'm nearly there," he answered, ducking back under cover of the open bay as the rain picked up. "Take care of your kiddos!" he called, and smiled.

It wasn't lost on Sam that something very important was replay-ing for Chip in Swami's arrival. Chip seemed happy, despite how tired he looked. Maybe satisfied. Swami coming up that driveway was, Sam knew, some sort of echo of Aunt Mary's exclusion, history revised rather than relived. There was children's laughter. A meal was being prepared. She'd come back. There was sadness and loss in the green air too. This land, Chip's cabin, all of it was being sold to a man who would never love it. It was too horrible to speak about.

Sam flipped the burgers in the pan and watched the rain beat the glass windowpane. Swami and the kids moved from the screen porch to the living room. They'd be sleeping in the camper, Swami said, but Chip had a much larger table for supper, and running water and an oven that wasn't out of gas. That and the wind didn't rock his little cabin the way it did the Winnebago.

The meat sizzled. The buns were warm and ready. There were sliced cucumbers and tomatoes on the table next to the ring of plates. Sam added a pad of butter to the cast-iron pan, dropped another burger in, and stole another glance at his family. Swami nursed DeeDee under a blanket, sitting cross-legged on the couch. Darren read a book to Dell, *The Wind in the Willows*. They'd been at it awhile and were at the part where the rabbit said something about "Onion sauce!" Dell laughed. Swami smiled. Sam could hardly believe his eyes and ears. She had come back. And it all felt so fragile. Sam didn't say much while they set up for dinner. Swami didn't either. She did ask him, as the kids were digging through Chip's movies and books, what would happen to the deer.

"They'll destroy them," Sam said, quietly so the kids couldn't hear. "They can't just be released because this place is licensed as a game farm. They're basically zoo animals."

"What zoo animals?" Dell asked, surprising both of them, standing beside the table with a giant book in her hands.

"Oh, nothing, sweetheart," Swami said. "What book do you have there?" She walked Dell back to the couch, where Darren sat, watching his parents.

"All right," Sam said, flipping the last burger and turning the burner off. He carried the plate to the table. "Supper's ready." The kids rushed the table. Swami finished with DeeDee and patted her back.

"I'll go out and get Chip," said Sam, while his family started in on the food.

He slipped into a rain jacket on the hook by the door, and went out into the dark and driving rain. The hard gusts at the storm front had passed, and now the rain just shot down in a steady blast. The ground was already so saturated, it could absorb nothing and the rain would run straight into the creeks and rivers. Sam splashed into an ankle-deep puddle at the base of the porch steps, shielded his face with the rain hood, and jogged toward the machine shed.

He shook himself off under the bare light bulb and stepped toward the hoop house door. It was quiet inside. The rain drummed on the metal roof.

"Chip, soup's on, man!" Sam called out as he stepped through the threshold onto the pea gravel. "Give it a break for the night. I can get up early and help you finish." Sam stomped the mud from his sandals and looked up.

The garden was brightly lit with a floor light. Nearly the entire bed of Chip's pot was harvested, the soil raked smooth again, the contractor's bag stuffed full as a pillow with flower buds. Only a few bushes remained, towering all the way up to the ceiling, casting a shadow on the tarp roof.

"Chip?" Sam called, walking around the tall bushes.

And then he saw his uncle. Bowed over in a hump on his hands and knees next to the trash bag, slumped against the boards of the raised bed.

"Chip!" yelled Sam. *"Chip!"*

Sam skidded beside him, put his hand on the man's huge sweaty back. Chip's skin was so pale it was gray. He was drenched in sweat, gripping his chest with his folded arms. Chip looked up at his nephew with terror in his bright red eyes.

"My chest," he said. "Oh, wow." And then he winced and cried out, bowed over again.

"Okay, Uncle," said Sam, quickly looking around for help. "Shit," he said. He was alone. They were in the middle of nowhere. The hoop house walls popped and snapped in the storm. Sam felt dread and ice in his gut. "Okay," he said, his voice quavering. "Okay, Chip. We're going to get you to a doctor."

Chip just nodded.

"How long have you been here?" Sam said.

"Not long," Chip said.

"I'm going to be right back. I'm going to get the camper and Swami."

Chip shook his head. "The driveway," he said, and then something hard gripped his whole body and he arched his back in pain and closed his eyes and couldn't speak.

Sam stood and slipped in the pea gravel and charged back out into the night.

When he burst into the cabin, Swami stood with a slice of cucumber in her hand.

"Chip," Sam told her. "His heart."

Swami ran out with him in her bare feet, charging Darren with the momentary care of his little sisters. In the hoop house, with one of them beneath each of his arms, Sam and Swami were able to walk Chip out into the rain and into the camper and help him sit down on the bed in the back. Sam found a bottle of aspirin in the bathroom cupboard, had Chip chew a couple.

Chip shook his head but ate the aspirin. "I was going to come tell you—the driveway's gone," he said, panting and sweating, leaned forward with his hands on his knees.

"What?" Sam said. But Chip was overwhelmed with pain again. He just nodded.

"What's wrong with him, Dad?" asked Darren, buckling himself in next to his sister. Sam saw fear and worry in the boy's eyes and flushed cheeks. Sam squeezed the boy's shoulder and shook his head. "It's his heart, buddy. We're going to get him help. I need you to look after Dell right now. Can you do that?"

The boy's face pinched. He nodded, took Dell's hand. Sam gently squeezed the back of Darren's neck, gave Dell a kiss. Swami was buckled into the passenger seat, dialing for an ambulance on her cell phone.

"Chip says the driveway's out," said Sam. He leaned over Swami's lap and grabbed a flashlight from the glove box. "I gotta check." Swami looked at him and nodded. Her phone was ringing, and she held it to her ear.

Through the rain, Sam could see the rafting van, but something was wrong with it. He could see its undercarriage. Sam trotted to a stop and shone his light over the van and the scene. The creek had swollen, carved out the driveway, and taken the back half of the van with it. Where the culvert had been, there was now a deep gap, a miniature canyon of caving gravel with a creek along its bottom that rushed through the forest and all its tangled undergrowth before joining the river downstream. The soft ground Sam stood on began to give way. He leapt back and fell, out of breath, staring at the gap blocking their path. It was too steep to climb down. And Chip couldn't get back up the other side. And if someone slipped, the creek was blasting through all that undergrowth, an absolutely deadly tangle of strainers. The old van just sat there, headlights pointed up into the rain as if it were mourning its own demise. They weren't getting off Chip's land this way. What were Sam's options? The rain pelted his neck. He nodded. There was only one other way.

Sam hoisted himself into the driver's seat.

"The ambulance is heading in from Ironsford."

"How long until they can get out here?"

"They said it will take them at least forty minutes in this storm. They'll be coming on Highway Two. I told them to look for a camper with its hazards on. They'll transfer him roadside."

Sam started the motor and put the camper in gear. He roared it out into the muddy driveway. "Call Randy, or Moon, anybody who is closer than an ambulance," Sam said. "Tell them to get a vehicle to the bridge below Chip's. Tell him we're coming down with a boat."

"What?" Swami exclaimed.

"The driveway's washed out. *Gone.* We can't go out or in that way." Sam slammed the camper in reverse, swung the wheel, backed up toward the machine shed, parked it.

"Well, then which way are we going?"

Sam pointed out beyond the field, where the path led past the pasture and out to the woods. "The river. It'll be fast. Try to get someone. Tell him to be at the bridge in ten minutes. If you can't get ahold of anyone, call the ambulance back and have them meet us there. It'll be faster either way. I'm hooking up a raft."

Swami began pressing buttons on her flip phone with wide eyes. She stopped him as he got out.

"Wait, Sam," she exclaimed. "Get a paddle for me too. The wind. You can't paddle into this wind. It's coming straight up, right?"

"The current, though," Sam said. Swami was right. The wind was blowing hard, straight upstream. Even with the current moving down, the rafts skimmed the water, got pushed around like sails. He could make the half mile with just him and Chip, but it'd be a long, slow paddle.

"What about the kids?"

"Bring jackets for all of us. Whatever Chip has." She held the phone to her ear.

In less than a minute, Sam had a raft filled with paddles and vests tied off on a tether to the back of the camper. At the last second, his light fell on a folded tarp, and he threw that in too.

"Hang on," he said. And he muscled the big wheel around in the rain, straight into the rain, and bumped down the farm trail, keeping as much momentum as he could through the wet grass, dragging the raft like a sled. Deer eyes lit up in the headlights, where their pasture went into the trees, while Swami made more calls.

"Dad?" Darren called up from his seat. He was still clutching Dell's hand. "Why are we going this way?"

"We're going rafting, buddy. All of us. We're all going together. It's going to be okay." He caught Darren's eyes in the bouncing rearview mirror for the shortest moment. They were wide.

Sam pulled as close as he could, where a path sloped down to the riverbank beneath trees. The river would be high, but it would be wide open, and the bridge would be an easy landing. He got out and dragged the raft down the wet slope. Leaving it on shore. He arranged paddles. And then he went back one by one and arranged his kids. Darren first, on the floor between thwarts, right in front of where Sam and Swami would sit abreast. Dell started crying in the rain, and didn't want Sam to go back for Chip. But he nestled her into the seat right next to her brother, and unfolded the tarp so they could hold it over themselves. And then Darren put his arm around his little sister while her dad explained how he'd be right back. Her eyes were shining and beautiful and brave in the yellow glow of the Maglite. Sam left the flashlight with them, got Chip into the bow seat. Swami sat in the back across from Sam, arm's reach to all of her kids, DeeDee howling in the car seat she'd hold between her feet and cover with a corner of the children's tarp.

Sam buckled Chip into a vest. "You hanging in there?" Sam asked. "That aspirin doing its job?"

Chip nodded, his eyes still closed in pain.

"Almost there," Sam told him, and snapped himself into a jacket. Swami stood near the back of the raft, buckled up and ready with a paddle.

"Everyone ready?" Sam called back to her.

"Ready!" Swami shouted.

Darren stuck his thumb out quick from under the tarp.

"Okay, Swami, I'm dragging it in!"

Sam dragged the raft by its front strap. Swami pushed from the back. The raft gave suddenly, and Swami jumped in and Sam splashed down in front of it as the boat floated and spun on the rain-pocked river. The river felt much warmer than the air. Sam came up with a gasp, still hanging on, worked his way to the side, and kicked himself up and over, belly up, by the kids. Darren had the flashlight on under the tarp. They looked like two kids telling stories in a tent. Dell looked at her soaked dad with surprise on her face.

"Dell, you keep an eye on Chip," Sam told her. "And stay down low and close to Darren." She nodded at him. "And Darren, do not let her go." Sam stepped around them to the back of the boat.

Swami was already J-stroking the raft out into the current on the left, away from shore. She sat on the left tube, where she always sat. Sam sat down on the right, tucked his foot under the thwart near his smallest daughter's car seat, and began paddling in rhythm with his wife.

"Who'd you get?" Sam called through the rain. He was so thankful there wasn't thunder. DeeDee was calming, and so was Dell. The downpour and darkness were hard enough. And Swami had been absolutely right. A gust of wind and rain pushed the nose of the raft and spun them upstream. It would have taken Sam an hour if he had to make the bridge alone, and that was if he could make it at all.

"Duncan's coming," Swami said. "I couldn't reach anyone else."

This surprised Sam, but he pried the boat and nodded.

"Good," he said. "Thank you, Swami," and he meant it about the phone call, but he meant it about everything else too—for being here, for helping Chip, for bringing the kids back, the family. Swami did a draw stroke to help the spin. And then both of them, without needing to say a word, began paddling into the driving rain. Leaning forward and back in unison, pulling hard on their paddles, adjusting automatically to keep the raft straight into the wind, following the cut banks where the current would be fastest. They paddled like this until their backs hurt and their breath became fast, and then they kept paddling.

In the distance, much too far away to hear the thunder, lightning strobed the miles of storm clouds. In the little bit of light it provided, the river stretched before them, white with rain, one more bend and then the bridge. DeeDee had quieted by Swami's feet. And Sam imagined her under cover of her tarp, snug, wide-eyed, the sound of water beneath the boat and above her too, sheeting across the tarp, her mother's calves on either side of her. In front of DeeDee, the big kids had grown quiet too, Darren's small wet fist holding the front edge of the tarp. And in the bow of their boat sat the still, hunched figure of Chip, big as a river boulder, anchoring the bow to the water. Sam stole a look at Swami. Her wet hair was pulled back in a ponytail that lay flat across her shoulder. Her lips puffed breath and rainwater. Sam realized how much Swami still looked like she had when they'd first met on those flooded riverbanks in West Virginia, and how this was the first time this summer that all of them were together in a boat—the whole family, rafting, husband and wife and their brave, miraculous children. It was certainly not what Sam had envisioned. But here they were. And in the middle of all that rain and trouble, Sam felt thankful he wasn't so alone.

"It's not far now," Sam said.

Swami nodded.

The bridge came into sight, and then came close, and Sam and Swami drove the nose of the raft hard against the sliver of sand still available beneath it. The boat stopped. The rain stopped, coming down in a sheet on either side of the overpass. The river was high enough that the beams were close enough to touch with an outstretched paddle.

Sam made his way forward along the side tube and pulled the bow higher onto dry land.

Duncan came sliding down the sandy path along the side of the bridge with a big flashlight.

"Sam?" he called. "Swami?"

"Here!"

Duncan found them, started to help Sam hoist Chip out of the boat. Swami came out and held the front of the raft.

"How long's it been?" Duncan asked them.

"Twenty minutes, half hour?" said Sam. "He ate three aspirin."

"The ambulance is coming on Highway Two," Swami said. "Pull over and flash your lights when you see theirs."

"Got it. Let's get you up this hill," Duncan said to Chip.

The older man nodded. "Thank you," he whispered.

Chip didn't look good, his face bone pale in the light of Duncan's lamp.

Duncan noticed. "Yeah, man," he said, looping his head under Chip's big arm. "Of course. Ambulance coming. Help's coming."

They carefully loaded the sodden Chip into the passenger seat of the bright green Mustang. Sam buckled him in. Duncan ran around and got in the driver's seat.

"Nice car," Chip said. "Hope I don't—poop my pants in here when I die." He tried to smile but then winced, and his eyes got wide and afraid again.

Duncan fired up the big motor. The exhaust droned.

"You coming?" he asked Sam.

Sam shook his head. "My family. They're in the boat. We'll be at Chip's."

Duncan nodded. Put the car in gear. The brake lights lit the gravel shoulder red. Sam patted Chip's hairy, wet leg.

"I'll see you real soon," he told his uncle, and closed the door. "Thank you, Duncan!" he yelled again through the glass, and then the brake lights went dark and the lime-green Mustang revved away. Duncan drove fast, hazards on, muddy gravel rattling the wheel wells and then the motor roaring hard through its gears once it made the pavement.

The wind kept up, but the rain quelled as they padded home. This time Sam and Swami sat on the middle thwart, with Dell and DeeDee on the floor between them. Darren was willing to be point man, shining the flashlight from the bow to watch for any logs or debris coming downstream. The stiff wind at their back nearly carried them upriver, and it was much easier going upstream than it had been coming down. It was nearly effortless, as if each of their paddle strokes were harnessing invisible power. Sam and Swami glided the raft carefully through the drizzle, across the point bars this time, the river's inner bends, where the head currents were weakest. They could all hear thunder coming through the lull, but it was still far behind them, very far. Sam took a deep breath and exhaled it, realized he'd been holding it for some time. He heard Swami do the same.

•••

AN HOUR LATER, SWAMI STOOD alone in Chip's room in dry sweatpants and one of Sam's sweatshirts, drying her hair with a white towel. Sam told her she'd find fresh towels in the closet, and she did, but now the strangeness of being alone in Chip's room made her pause. She was getting a look at the man. She regretted what she'd said to him that day in front of the barn. Chip slept on a twin bed. The sheets and his whitetail buck blanket were pulled tight; the bed was made. There were a bottle of Mohawk vodka and a glass on the nightstand near the bed. The room was clean but stale, its rough green carpet more sad than dirty. There was one giant pair of white underwear on the floor near the dresser. Swami picked them up with the tips of her fingers and dropped them into the laundry basket with all of their wet and muddy clothes. And then she stared at the picture in a frame on the dresser, twisted her hair under the towel.

Sam came in. "Kids are all crashed," he said. He'd put them to bed together on the hide-a-bed in the living room. With the storms and wind, the cabin would be better than the camper. The worst of the thunderstorm had missed them, and the only sound was the heavy rain on the stout little cabin's roof. Sam's great-great-grandfather had built this cabin. Swami knew that. It felt odd to be in it. She imagined the ghosts of old farmers watching them, along with the ghosts of Native Americans who built mounds in the forest.

"Who's this?" Swami asked of the photo. The frame held a photo of a much younger Chip and a very pretty blond woman. Chip held the woman in his arms, standing in front of a trailered stack of rafts, both of them tanned and lean and happy-looking in short shorts and high socks.

"That's Aunt Mary," Sam said. "And Chip. I called the hospital. They have him. He made it to the ER. I haven't heard back yet."

"I'm glad," Swami said. "They'll be able to help him," she said.

Sam nodded, he and Swami still looking at the photo instead of each other.

Swami studied the young Aunt Mary. She was about Swami's age. Swami wondered what she was like, if they would have been friends. She wondered what drove her away, but she also felt she didn't have to ask. She knew. Swami knew the pain she'd probably borne, and Chip too. It was hard to look at the happy couple in the photo and know what they'd go through, how all that optimism would end up.

"Chip has lived a hard life," she said, looking around the lonely room, stooping to pick up the laundry basket.

"I believe in many ways he has," said Sam. "But I think he's lived a good life too."

Swami looked at the carpet, and then at the little Remington clock on the wall. She felt so tired. Her body felt so spent from the adrenaline.

She was ready to sink into bed next to her kids. They'd sleep late tomorrow. There was nothing to do until Blakely arrived at noon, and Swami was forming new opinions about that, about mines and rivers and land. Her head swam with it all. For some reason, standing there in Chip's small room, Swami remembered what she'd felt like after giving birth to her first child. It had been hard, Darren's birth, a daylong labor, then a full hour and a half of pushing. Afterward, when everyone was warm and dry, Swami felt dreamy, spent, numbed by the tremendous ebb and flow of her own body.

"It's funny, you know?" she said, turning out the light to Chip's room and carrying the laundry into the hall.

"What is?" said Sam.

She set the laundry down outside the bathroom where the washer and dryer were. "Everything." She shrugged. "Good night, Sam."

"Good night," he said.

Swami had a drink of water and crawled under the blankets with her children. DeeDee slept in a crib at the foot of the bed Sam had arranged using an empty dresser drawer and a folded quilt. Tired as Swami was, she stayed awake for some time, listening to her kids breathe. Sam brought his cot inside from the screen porch. They lay apart but in the same room. Swami could look across the dark living room and see him there, the mound of his sleeping bag. Swami watched him, and felt watched, and thought about ghosts. She thought about her parents, and herself as a mom. She thought of the unyielding flow linking one generation to the next, children growing into adults, leaving home, having children, all the letting go that people had to do, all the coming to terms, all the pain.

"Sam," she said, very quietly.

"Yeah," he whispered.

"I have to tell you something."

"What is it?"

"Earlier this summer," she said, "when you lost your job, I really resented you. I hated you. And I know it hurt you. I am sorry."

"It's okay," Sam whispered.

"I am sorry I did," Swami said again.

"It's okay," he said.

"I want you to know I don't hate you. I'm not mad at you anymore."

She watched him, the still, dark mound. Sam's sleeping bag rustled, and he wiped his face with the heel of his hand.

"Thank you," he said.

And then they both lay still beneath their blankets until the wind and quiet creaks of the cabin roof and the distant rumbles of thunder put Swami fast asleep. The rain sounded like the patter of tiny feet, she thought, drifting off. The wind whispered, *Hush*.

SEVENTEEN

WHEN SAM AWOKE EARLY ON HIS COT IN THE SCREEN PORCH, HIS family was still asleep, their mouths wide open, hair over their eyes, cheeks pressed into the pillows and lumpy mattress. Dell's dirty feet stuck out the bottom of the blanket. DeeDee lay curled with her rump up in the air, and Sam gently lifted the quilt back over her. Sam dressed and made his way outside. He checked the phone for messages. There were none. But he already had the news he needed most. He woke once in the middle of the night, pulled the phone on its cord into the kitchen pantry, and closed the door to call the hospital. Chip was fine, they'd said. And a man named Randy and a woman named Moon were staying with him in his room. He'd had a heart attack, but it was caught soon enough and he was fine. The aspirin had bought him time. They'd monitor him for another day at least, and expected him to come home soon. Sam sat on the linoleum floor of the pantry after that, cried quietly with the phone in his lap. Beyond his own children, Chip was Sam's last remaining blood relative. Sam didn't want to lose him. Not yet. Not like that. Sam cried for what Swami had told him too, before she went to bed. He felt relief, but the abruptness of letting go of so much tension all at once confused his nerves, made his whole body shake, like a deer might shake rain off its hide. He sat there until he heard the screen door blow open. Then he rose and closed it, and checked on his wife and kids, and then wrapped himself up and slept until daylight.

Sam stood in the open door of Chip's greenhouse now. The warm air inside spilled through the door, strong as a skunk. He'd need to finish the job this morning before the ranger showed up, and air the place out too. The rain had stopped, and a deep fog had settled over everything. It was a fog so thick it made him wet to walk through it. The last row of Chip's plants were so tall they pressed against the plastic tarp ceiling. Buds the size of grapefruits hung in fuzzy clumps, frosted-looking and fragrant. Sam shifted in the muddy gravel.

"Will he get in big trouble for this?" she said.

Sam startled. He hadn't heard her approach from behind him. Swami wore a rain poncho and held a big cup of coffee in her hand. She stepped in, and her eyes grew wide as she saw the true height of the plants.

"Yeah," he said, and wilted inside. "I'm sorry, but I gotta get this out of here before Blakely arrives. It won't take me long."

Swami stood next to him, offered him a sip of her coffee. Sam took it slowly and told her about the news from the hospital. The coffee was hot and warm and very black. Sam handed the mug back. Swami clasped it in her hands.

"I can help," she said.

Sam looked at her. He was afraid he hadn't heard her right. Swami clearly saw the disbelief on his face.

She laughed at herself, shrugged. "Why not?" she said. "And I wish they weren't coming today. Blakely. I just—I just don't feel like seeing anyone, especially him. And I hate thinking about what will happen to those deer."

Sam nodded.

Just then a horn blared from down the driveway.

"Oh no," Sam said. "They better not have come early."

It blasted again.

"Mom?" Darren called from the cabin door.

"I'm right here!" Swami called back. "I'll be right there." She looked at Sam. "What do we do about the greenhouse?" she said.

"I'll lock it up," said Sam. "Hope for the best." Swami disappeared toward the cabin, peered down the driveway as she went.

Sam trotted down through the wet fog. The sun was risen fully now, somewhere, and a breeze began to push the fog loose. The horn blasted again. Sam could barely see across the ravine. The rafting van was on its side now. What had become a small river flowed right through it. The water had broken the windshield, pushed the back doors open. On the far side of the river, Blakely stood with Bonnie and a man with a tool pouch and surveyor's stand.

"How do we cross this?" he yelled as Sam limped toward him

through the wet fog, rubbing sleep from his eyes. Sam's ankle felt stiff. He hadn't even had his own cup of coffee yet, and here was this guy yelling and honking his horn.

"Morning," called Sam. "You're early!"

Ranger Bonnie waved at him. "Is everyone okay?" she called out. "What on earth happened?"

The breeze picked up now, blowing in from higher ground. The fog started flowing into the river.

"Culvert went out."

Bonnie shook her head in amazement. "I heard about what happened to Chip," she said. "I called in. He's doing fine. Scary!" she said.

"Thanks," said Sam. It was.

Blakely looked impatient. The surveyor was a small man with a beaky nose. He watched the fog moving out, followed it, like he smelled something.

"Oh, hey, guys!" Ranger Bonnie said, waving. "Long time, no see! Hi, Darren! Hi, Dell! Hi, Swami!"

The fog rolled back as far as the machine shed now. Swami strode toward them, holding DeeDee in her arms. Dell and Darren walked with quick steps. Dell waved, but she looked nervous too.

"Hey, Bonnie." Swami smiled. "Good to see you."

"Ah, you too, you too," Bonnie beamed, hands planted on her wide hips. "Looks like you all had quite the adventure last night."

"Chips is safe!" Dell said. "We saved him! We went out in the storm in a boat, and then Darren held the flashlight, and then we went to bed, and then—"

Darren shushed her.

"Listen," Blakely said. "I'm glad to hear Chip is all right. I really am. But since there's no confusion as to anyone's motives anymore, I'd prefer to just get this over with, what Chip and I already agreed to. Surveyor needs some measurements. Bonnie needs to see the deer. And then we'll be out of your hair."

Sam was about to speak.

"How's Debbie?" Swami asked Bonnie. She looked right at Blakely as she said it.

Bonnie looked at the ground. "Oh, that," she said. "Well, that's over, pretty much. Judge will sort it all out. I don't think anyone . . ." She blushed and looked at Blakely. "I don't think anyone's gonna see much trouble out of it really. Don't think anyone wants it. Better things to do."

"Now, you listen—" Blakely began.

"*Hey!*" Sam barked. He was surprised at the heat in his voice, in his veins. Everyone looked surprised. But it had been a long night, and a long summer, and Sam had his family back with him, at least for this moment, and no one was going to talk to any one of them in any way suggesting disrespect.

Blakely stopped, started again. "I would just like to know," he said, in a metered voice, "how we can cross this, and do the inspection, and leave."

Just then a big breeze blew at them, toward the river.

"There's the deer pasture," said Bonnie. "I can probably inspect it from right where I am. No need to cross." She squinted. "That the pasture?" she asked. "Where's the deer?"

The surveyor sniffed the air again. Everyone looked.

Dell climbed very quickly into Sam's arms. Darren looked off into the woods. "Daddy," Dell whispered into Sam's ear, so close he could feel her breath. Swami leaned in toward her daughter too. "Me and Darren," said Dell. "We did something."

Sam smiled. There were no deer in sight. He followed the fence with his eyes. The gate was still open.

"What did you do, honey?"

"*Dell*," hissed Darren.

"There's no deer in there," called Bonnie, behind them.

Swami looked at Sam. Sam looked at Swami. Swami closed her eyes and bit her lip, grinned the most imperceptible grin, the kind only Sam would be able to see. "Darren," Swami said without looking at him. She just put a hand on his shoulder. "It's okay." And then she stooped and kissed the top of his head.

Sam turned so that the breeze blew the hair from Dell's worried face.

"Did you let the deers go?" Sam whispered.

Dell teared up and nodded very fiercely. "Is Chips going to be mad at me?" she asked.

Sam kissed her. "No," he said. "Chips will be very happy with you. He'll be very proud."

"It was so dark, Daddy," she said. "But the deer just came. They followed us. We showed them where the river went across."

Sam hugged her close, kissed the side of her head. "Oh, you brave, beautiful kids." Swami reached out to hold her then, and Sam handed Dell into her free arm. Swami hugged DeeDee and Dell both.

"Excuse us," said Blakely.

And then Swami's face hardened into the glare she used when she was about to lay down her law. She turned around and stepped to the edge of her side of the fresh ravine. She cut a powerful figure in her short shorts and raincoat, daughters in hand.

"You don't," she said coldly, plainly.

"Say again?" asked Blakely.

"You don't come across. This land isn't for sale today. Neither is Woodchuck."

Sam's heart leapt inside him. He put both hands on Darren's shoulders.

"Watch this," he whispered to Darren. "Your *mother*."

Darren grinned.

The surveyor shrugged and began walking back to the truck.

"Now everyone just hold on a minute," Blakely said. "This sale is between me and the owner, and you are not the owners of this property."

"We're his family," Swami said. "And he's in the hospital, so we're speaking on his behalf right now."

"That is *not* how it works," he said.

"Yes, it is," Swami said.

Blakely got hot. Stammered. Looked around himself. Bonnie stuffed her hands in her pockets and ambled toward the forest, smiling. The surveyor already had his tools back in his truck.

"Well, what about Woodchuck?" Blakely asked. "Pure loss, out of business, who else is going to buy it, and for what I am offering?"

Swami shook her head. "What you are offering? As I understand it, *you* haven't been offering any money at all. It's all NorthSky's. You're a snake-oil salesman, no skin in this game beyond getting your employer its pit mine. Do you get a company bonus for all the land you gobble up?"

Blakely turned red. Parts of him were purple.

"And for your information," Swami went on, "Woodchuck has a raft trip tomorrow. We'll be on the river, right beside Duncan."

"This land will be sold to NorthSky," Blakely said. "And you will regret not off-loading your heap of a business while you still could."

Swami just lifted her chin. Glared at him until he couldn't hold her stare any longer. Blakely stormed off toward his Jeep, cussing the gravel he walked on. He slammed his door.

"He's got a dirty mouth, Mommy," Dell said, glaring at him with the same intensity as her mother.

"Yes, he does, sweetheart," Swami answered.

Blakely revved his Jeep and tore off. The surveyor shrugged, waved, and pulled out slowly.

Ranger Bonnie ambled back, hands still stuffed in her pockets, grinning very broadly. "You all need help getting off this?" she asked, looking the ravine up and down. "It's still dumping rain up in the watershed. Dam's going full blast, and they say it's gonna stay that way."

"We're okay, Bonnie," Swami said. "We have boats."

Bonnie nodded with satisfaction, smiled at them all, and walked back to her truck. She turned back just once before leaving. "Oh, and I didn't want to say it earlier, but I know the judge taking Debbie's case. He's old-school Northwoods. Carries a revolver. Word on the street is misdemeanors all around, but I didn't say nothing."

Sam and Swami watched her drive away in silence. The kids stayed quiet too. Sam could tell everyone felt they'd just avoided trouble and didn't want to upset the fragility of that. Swami turned with her girls to the house, and Sam and Darren followed. Sam watched the backs of Swami's legs as she walked, her sandaled feet. He felt amazed by her. It felt like hope and joy and wonder—all things he'd forgotten about through too many weeks and months and years. His thick skin was shedding, and what was under it was good. Sam was falling in love with his wife.

Just as they reached the steps of the cabin, a horn blew again.

They all turned. It was Randy's old truck. Moon was with him. And then another figure, who stepped slowly out and lifted a big hand in the air.

"Chips!" Dell yelled, then dropped from Swami's hip and ran back down the driveway again, driving her little legs as fast as they'd go, waving, jumping, cheering.

•••

THE DAY OF THE JAMBOREE, early, before the trip, Swami stood with her family and guides on the bluff overlooking the river. The river boomed and leapt, muddy and higher than any of them had ever seen it. Swami felt electrified. She'd felt this way since she and Sam had rafted Chip down in that storm, and since she'd turned Blakely away from the creek. The river rose all that day and night. Moon and Randy ferried Chip across and spent the night. The driveway crossing wasn't dangerous anymore. The river was high enough to bury all the undergrowth and strainers now, and most of the rafting van too. Randy and Sam traversed the creek all morning, stringing ropes and then tow straps so Randy could pull the van up out of the water.

Chip watched with Swami and Moon at the riverbank. He stuffed his big hands into his poncho pocket. It rattled with all of his new pills.

"I got nitroglycerin," he said, "cholesterol meds, beta blockers, calcium blockers." Chip's eyes watered. He'd already explained how he checked himself out early. He was trying to come back so he could talk to Blakely himself; he'd hoped Blakely might change his mind, or that the surveyor might find the land worthless. When Swami recounted how she'd sent Blakely packing, Chip cried quietly and sighed a big rattling sigh of relief, and looked out at the river beyond the forest. Swami knew Chip understood her denial of Blakely to mean he should keep his land, that he should never sell it to be dredged or drilled or ground into dust, and that he wasn't obligated to bail Sam and Swami out of their troubles with Woodchuck.

"I owe you, Swami," he said. "Both of you. I don't deserve people good as you in my life."

Randy's old 4x4 bucked a bit, belched diesel as he floored it. The van moaned its way up the wet gravel bank and flopped on its side. Water poured from it as it lay there. A bush with a muddy root ball hung in its exposed undercarriage. Moon cheered at them across the river.

"Nobody owes anybody anything, Chip," Swami said. "Money is money, and that's *all* it is."

"And I'm sorry," he went on, "for what I said to you at the barn."

"I'm sorry for what I said to you too. It's not true."

Chip wiped his eyes with his poncho sleeve.

"Most of it," she said, giving him a smile. Chip smiled too.

Moon had been pretending not to listen to any of this, but now she beamed and hugged them both. "*Real* good energy, you guys," she said, and left it at that, and arm around each of them.

Swami did feel a sort of grace washing over them. There was something new in the air, shaking from the wet leaves of all the flooded trees. The blue midmorning sky overhead seemed a deeper blue after so much rain. Swami could smell pine, and also Moon's patchouli. She'd missed it. Randy stepped from his truck on the opposite riverbank and pumped his fist in the air, like a cowboy who'd just roped a massive bull. Moon smiled even more.

The river rose and rose. Everyone ate. A big carp nosed around a pool of water near the driveway. The kids napped. Chip napped. Sam drove the camper up into the woods near the Indian mounds, onto the highest ground he could find. They'd be gone all day tomorrow, he said, for the river trip. He didn't want it to suffer the same fate as the van. For the length of a day and night, everyone just bided their time, talked quietly, looked out at the empty deer pasture. Everyone knew that Woodchuck's last trip of the summer and maybe even forever was coming, and the river was blowing out, and nobody dared talk about the possibility of canceling, of not rafting the gorge.

Now, looking at the river, they weren't so sure.

Swami had DeeDee packed on her back. Darren and Dell stood wide-eyed, Dell gripping Swami's hand very tightly. It was only an hour after sunrise, and already the day was extraordinarily hot. The rare northbound rains had left behind a wallowing pocket of humid southern air, along with a river that could hardly be called a river. The gorge coiled and boomed beneath them, smashed and leapt against the cliff faces, reweaving itself, erupting against its own white waves.

"What level is *this*?" she asked.

"I've never seen this before," Chip said.

"It sounds like thunder, Mommy," said Dell. It did. The river rumbled like a thunder peal that had no end to it. The falls itself, the river-wide entrance to the rapids, was now rounded off, a massive mud-brown hump rolling downward and beneath itself. The wave train downstream of it was high-peaked and broad, spraying the canyon full of mist and rainbows. And then in the middle of it all was Volkswagen Rock, or what had been Volkswagen Rock. The buried boulder wrenched up the river and then dropped it in a hole the length and width of a bus. Swami just shook her head at it all. She hadn't seen whitewater like this since her training days in West Virginia. But in West Virginia the New River was wide, able to better hold its water. This narrow gorge was now pressed in ways that seemed unnatural.

"It's how the town got its name," said Chip. "There was an old Indian name for it, the way this stretch of river could rise up like a storm. The white settlers couldn't pronounce it. So they just called it Thunderwater." He looked out at the river like a hungry man looking at a feast. His eyes were studying the new ways the waves were moving.

"All the years I've run this, and this is the day I miss. It's so pure, like what it must have been like without the dam. Swami, maybe I could sit with Sam and just do one run."

She shook her head. "The pure river just wants you to watch today." Chip sighed.

"Are we really boating this?" Moon asked.

She looked at Swami and Sam. Sam shrugged. Swami didn't have an answer.

"Well," said Chip. "It'll be fun watching Duncan get tore up out here today." He eyeballed Darren. "Get ready for some carnage, young man."

"He saved your life," Swami said.

"And I'd save his. And I am looking forward to watching him get spanked today."

They hiked down slowly and sat in a clump in the back of Randy's truck, except for the kids, who sat with Moon in the cab. As they drove up the highway in the warm wind, Chip closed his eyes and put his face in the wind, like an old dog, problematic, limping, but good. Swami could smell the sun lifting rainwater from the hayfields.

When they came into view of the electric blue rafting barn in its green field, Randy hit the brakes and pulled over on the gravel shoulder overlooking the fields. They all turned to the cab, and saw it immediately.

"What the hell is *this*, now?" said Chip.

The entire field surrounding the barn was dotted with a rainbow of small tents. Small campfires smoked between several of them, the white smoke drifting up in columns, kids and parents milling about. The tents stretched all the way to the wood lines. There were literally hundreds, like mushrooms that popped up after a rain, orange and red and yellow and green. And then Swami saw it. Parked alongside the raft barn was Duncan's shining green bus. He was out in front of it, waving a clipboard, talking with his arms to a group of dads standing near the camp's edge.

Randy looked back through the cab's rear window, raised his eyebrows. Swami motioned for him to pull in, and Randy kept it on the shoulder, pulling into the gravel driveway very slowly. He parked in the middle of groups of people with beach towels and smeared in fresh sunscreen, three trailers stacked with rafts, two buses, and a handful of poorly parked cars.

Chip frowned at it all.

Sam slid down from the bed of the truck, and Swami took DeeDee through the window from Dell and followed him. Duncan was pleading with the group of dads for patience, saying that they'd get the morning's trip out soon, if they could just tell him the names of their reservations again so he could mark them off on his clipboard. A handful of Duncan's guides scurried about the place, topping off rafts with a hand pump and trying to set vests and helmets and paddles out on the grass in some sense of order. When Duncan spotted Swami and Sam, and Chip not too far behind, he dropped his conversation and ran to them. He was breathless. His blond hair was falling out of its ponytail.

"I didn't know what to do!" he whispered at them. "I'm so sorry, I tried to get ahold of you, but it all happened so fast. We didn't have anywhere to go. Chip, you're okay. I'm glad you're okay."

Chip just nodded and frowned in confusion.

"Duncan, what's going on?" Swami asked.

He took a huge breath. "The *jamboree* is going on, and I don't have a raft company."

"What?!" Swami said.

Duncan looked out at the crowd in exasperation, let his clipboard fall against his thigh. "I've got fifteen boats and one bus and guides who can't raft this water, *and* I have four hundred ticked-off Boy Scouts who showed up last night to a locked gate."

Swami waited for him to take another breath.

"My uncle," he said. "He shut the whole thing down. The NorthSky site was flooding. He took all their equipment and moved it onto X-treme's property and locked the gates. He was livid. Kicked my guides out of their cabins."

"Why?" Swami asked.

"He said without Chip's land, and with all the flooding and trouble, he was pulling the plug on all of it for the season. Locked the gates. He owns all of the property. He always did, and it was always a damn front. All I got is my bus and boats."

Randy limped up with Moon and the kids.

Swami saved Duncan the trouble. "Blakely closed X-treme," she said.

"The state park was packed full," Duncan said. "I didn't know where else to take them, so I brought them here. Your scout troop arrived here twenty minutes ago, by the way, in that red van over there. I asked them to wait. I've been trying to ask them all to wait. For what,

I don't know. I can boat this level, maybe, but not one of my guides can. They are class-three guides, and this is class-five water."

"We saw the gorge," Sam said.

Duncan shook his head. "I may as well just hike the scouts up to the falls in groups and have them jump off the edge. Set up a net at the bottom. To be perfectly honest, I don't even know if I'm insured right now. I don't know what my uncle's doing with all of that."

Swami looked at the red van, the small scout troop gathering by the open cargo door. Laughing Eagle Scouts pulled on fresh aqua socks. A dad closed his eyes and wiped a handful of sunscreen on his face. Beyond them, the tent city gleamed in the sun. Smoke rose. Sam looked out over all the tents too. He nodded, his shaggy red hair falling over the back of his neck. Swami hadn't noticed, or had refused to notice, but Sam had grown lean and brown over the summer, more muscled. All the sun and paddling, all the high-fat breakfasts out at Chip's. He didn't look like the pale art teacher coming off a cold spring term and slushy commutes. He looked strong. Duncan was right. He didn't have a single guide who could raft this water. But Swami did.

"Duncan," she said.

"Yeah." He was watching in despair as one of his guides tripped over an armful of life vests he was carrying. An Eagle Scout helped untangle him.

"I'll make you a deal," she said. DeeDee gurgled and pulled at Swami's hair. Swami caught her little hand in her own and kissed it and handed the girl to Sam. Sam looked at Swami as he took his daughter. He seemed to know, was maybe even thinking the same things. He nodded a small nod of agreement.

"Woodchuck's broke," Swami said. "We've needed a bigger piece of this jamboree all summer, or Woodchuck's over. X-treme needs real guides, or this jamboree is over for you. You need guides, and we need custies." Swami liked the way that last word felt in her mouth. It was so much better than *guests*. She was reminded of a sticker she'd scraped off the bus earlier this summer: *Raft Guides are here to save your ass, not kiss it.* Right at this moment, that sentiment matched her mood quite well.

Duncan nodded his head as she spoke. "What do we do. Just tell me."

"We split this jamboree fifty-fifty, raft them all under Woodchuck's waivers this whole weekend. We double guide every raft—one of our guides with one of yours riding shotgun." Then she went for it. "And we split the jamboree fifty-fifty every season moving forward. That is, if we both manage to still be here. The rest of the regular season is fair game, of course."

Duncan didn't stop nodding. Sam and Chip just watched it all quietly. Duncan's guide had gathered up the vests again with the scout's help.

"Yep," Duncan said, and sighed. Tension visibly dissolved from his body. A broad grin came across his face. He opened his hand wide and shook hands with Swami. "That's a deal. A good deal. The river wouldn't be the same without you dirtbags on it anyway."

"Let's boat!" said Moon. "Yes! But who's guiding? Randy's out. Chip's out. That leaves just me, Duncan, and Sam—trips of, what, six boats. This is going to take a while."

"Eight boats," Swami said. "Throw two on for me."

"Yeah?" Moon said, holding her arms wide, fingers spread.

"Mom, can you guide, though?" Darren asked.

Swami lifted her chin at her son. "Your mother is a fully checked out, class-five, swift-water-certified, West Virginia river guide. Oh, I hold my angle, young man."

"YES!" Moon cried and wrapped Swami in a bear hug. Swami laughed. She saw Sam smile at her, and he kept smiling and put his forehead against DeeDee's forehead.

"Who's watching us, then?" Dell asked. She knew the drill after a full summer of it. If someone was boating, someone else had to watch Dell.

"Uncle Rando can watch you guys," Randy said. Moon let go of Swami and kissed Randy's cheek, put her arm around his waist. He blushed.

"And Chip too?" said Swami. "If that's okay."

"Rando and Chips!" cheered Dell.

Chip sighed, or started to sigh, and then Dell pushed him and he squatted down and smiled at her.

"Big fat Chips," she said, and gave him a hug.

"Who you calling fat?" he said.

Dell giggled.

"Be polite, Dell," Swami said, but neither Dell nor Chip heard her. "Duncan, could I see that clipboard?"

"It's all yours," he said.

"I'll get the barn unlocked," Sam said, carrying his daughter with him. "Darren, give me a hand?" Darren trotted off with his dad, while Swami stepped up to the group of restless scout leaders.

"All right, guys," she yelled, trying out her river voice. It felt good to yell, to bark at them. She'd bark at them all day. "I'm Swami, and this is Moon. We'll be two of your lead guides today!" Duncan motioned for his guides to drop what they were doing and listen in. More scouts ambled out of the web of tents. Swami lifted a page from the clipboard.

"Where's Green Bay?" They lifted their hands. "You're on the blue bus; follow Moon in for your waivers and gear. Where's Milwaukee? You're green bus. Where's Oconto? You're blue."

•••

SAM SAT ON THE LEFT tube and wedged the foot of his good leg beneath the thwart. The other foot was in its big boot. On the right side sat a very nervous-looking guide of Duncan's named Carl. The launch from the beach above the gorge was fast and deep. Ahead of him on the shining river was Moon's boat. Behind him on shore, Sam heard Swami call for an all ready, and he turned back to watch her jog her raft off into deeper water and leap effortlessly into her seat. On shore behind her, Duncan walked his full raft into deeper water. Sam took a strong stroke, and then pried and let the current turn the nose of his boat in a beautiful arc downstream. The river bottom sparkled with copper-colored rocks. The sun was hot on Sam's skin. Cold water lapped at the side of the raft. The gorge roared downstream.

"Forward two!" called Swami behind him. "And two more!"

Swami heard Sam call the same, and pried her ferry downstream. Duncan was in the river behind her, and all four rafts floated toward the falls in a loose string. And then she heard Moon bellow her first command, and Moon's boat disappeared over the end of the falls.

"This is *crazy*," Swami whispered.

"What's that?" said Duncan's guide, Becky. Her face was pale.

Swami shook her head. "You remember what I told you up top?" Swami said.

Becky nodded.

"Good," Swami said, and punched her foot again for a good grip beneath the thwart. High on the bluff, where she and the kids had stood all summer, Swami could now see Randy and Chip and the kids. Darren held DeeDee. All of them waved, and Swami lifted her paddle into the sun, up toward the green pines and the bright blue sky. She'd forgotten what this felt like, this moment before a very big rapid, when you're in the flow, and there are explosions over the horizon and you're now too deep into your approach to turn back even if you wanted to. Swami didn't. Sam bellowed up ahead. The tail of his raft swept with a clean pry and went over the edge.

Sam hooted as the river exploded before him. Down they went, in a fast swoop toward the bottom of the falls. Sam watched the bow press hard into the trough, and then rise up a massive brown wave with a twisting ridge of foam in its middle—up and up. The guests leaned forward to keep their seats.

"Forward two!" Sam yelled. The water was getting loud. "And two more!" Carl panic-paddled next to him, crouched very low in the boat.

Swami was twenty feet from the edge, then ten. The raft rocked forward as its crew took each stroke. The view of the whole river opened up as they crested the falls. The crests and spikes of whitewater looked as tall as young pines. "Forward two!" barked Swami, shaking a wave from her face. They dug in. The wave peaked, and they raced toward a trough again.

Sam draw-stroked now, felt the raft straighten at the next peak when the raft was lightest. He left his blade in the water, flat as a rudder, waiting for a pressure one way or another to let him know what he had to do. The brown-and-white heap of river pillowed over Volkswagen and dove over its own horizon line.

Swami leaned into her strokes. Duncan's guide Becky was keeping it together, eyes downstream.

Sam's raft met Volkswagen, a wave as high and broad as a trailer full of rafts. Everything else in the world had stopped, no noise, no sky, no wind, just this wall of whitewater and his paddle. Somewhere high on the cliff, his children were watching, and his uncle. Somewhere behind him in the canyon, Swami was in it too. Downstream, Moon. The nose of the boat hit the wall, and the wall erupted through the first row of paddlers, water rushing beneath their armpits and over their heads, flapping the black straps of their vests. The first row of paddlers disappeared, then the second and third, and then Sam was underwater.

Swami's paddle flexed when she went under. She felt its blade in the water. She tasted boulders and silt and river, felt the raft climbing out. The raft held, and climbed—and then in a moment of quiet equilibrium, began to level off. Swami felt the stern buck as it lifted her back up into the bright white river, sunlight and noise and air. Becky came up, sunlit, grimacing. The raft breached, flattened, splatted downstream of the hole, shedding water from its tubes and the backs of eight paddlers. The custies rose up again, some of their helmets knocked to the backs of their heads.

Sam yanked Carl, his only swimmer, back into the raft. And he looked up to see Swami standing in the back of her raft. The stern stood her right up. Her boat rode a big wave now, downstream of the hole. Swami roared a battle cry. River water sprayed from her lips, arced from her paddle as she raised it overhead, up in the sun and white sandstone and black pines.

"Forward two!" called Swami, falling back on her seat. The strokes were messy as the crew found their footing again. "And two more," she yelled, flicking her ponytail behind her with a toss of her head. Becky grinned and dug into the water, stunned they'd just made that wave, that a wave like that could even exist. Behind them, Duncan hit the wall and emerged.

Sam took a stroke, then another, and did a quick head check before dropping down into the Island Wave. Swami was a bolt of lightning, a waterfall goddess, a mother of terrifyingly blue-eyed children somewhere up on that bluff full of green forests.

The unstoppable river pulled them around the bend, downstream toward more waves, big and benign. The Island Wave. The Twin Sisters. Terminal Surfer. The rafts rode and bucked. Swami and Sam hooted and whooped. They dug in, wiped their faces, paddled, and drifted until the rafts, all rafts, spun out downstream in flat and shining eddy water.

SEPTEMBER

EIGHTEEN

A FEW EARLY YELLOW LEAVES DROPPED ON THE BLACK WATER. THE floods were over, but the rebuilding wasn't. It was the first time Thunderwater had flooded in over two hundred years. Both Woodchuck and X-treme offered boats and labor in between September's trickle of raft trips. Woodchuck had three small trips after the jamboree. Duncan had a few more. They used each other's buses whenever they needed.

The doctors told Chip he couldn't raft anymore, that a bad swim would stress his heart too much. "Well," Chip told the doctor, "we're all just living in between swims," but he cooperated well enough and altered his diet and took his daily walks. Each day Chip puttered his dirt bike to the trailhead of Piers Gorge with a packed salad lunch and a fishing pole, sometimes taking along one of his books that weren't ruined when his cabin flooded along with everything else. He'd hike up to the falls and sit in the shade and watch the rafts come down. He'd do sun salutations like Swami had taught him. He'd sit in the autumn warmth and eat his salad and fish for bass. "Big bronze ones behind every rock," he'd tell Sam afterward. "And Duncan had *decent* runs today. It's starting to smell like fall out there."

Swami spent her time going back and forth to Chicago with the kids. The house was still on the market. She and Sam had talked about that once, awkwardly, and Sam told himself it was simply a time of waiting, that things were at least better than they had been even if the future was still uncertain. He and Swami were better, but still bruised. Regarding Swami's plans for the house, Sam had seen enough to know what was in his hands and what wasn't.

As the river first rose into Thunderwater and made itself known, it reminded everyone who really owned the valley. "Reservoir's flat overloaded," said Pete, wiping sweat from his forehead while he helped with sandbags. "Every gate's wide open. There's nothing we can do." And then he leaned in toward Sam, smiled. "It's like I said before, rivers work in mysterious ways." The sandbags proved futile. The river came over the banks, a black swell seeping first through the grass and then filling the streets between curbs, filling the basements of the houses in the flood plain. A pink plastic playhouse floated south through the town. NorthSky's worksite downstream was on low ground, and the whole thing washed out. The tan work trailers rose from their block foundations and tumbled downstream. Blue porta-johns were tipped and broken apart. One big pile-driving truck too heavy to float just sank further and further into the muddy bank, the river washing the ground from under its wheels and then drifting it against the sides.

Most of Chip's island went under too. The stick-framed machine shed tilted then collapsed, and the plastic tarp of the hoop house washed into the woods and wrapped around trees. Chip's cabin lost its screen porch, but the bones of the home his great-grandfather had built with thick timber and stacked fieldstone stayed firmly planted even as the water flowed through it. Everything from the kitchen counter down was ruined—beds, couches, the cupboards filled with silt. Windows blew out. The only things that remained untouched were the high built-in shelves with Chip's books and Hallmark movies.

"The whole thing will have to be gutted," he said when the water came down enough for Sam to paddle him over in a raft. Chip shook his head, but then he brightened when he stepped back out into the ankle-deep water where his screen porch once stood. "Maybe it'll be nice like this," Chip said. "Just the original cabin again, fireplace, a wood oven, books. I could get used to that. Slow it all down." Chip's breathing seemed labored as he said it. Sam watched him for a moment, and told himself he'd recommend another follow-up appointment when they got back to Debbie's place. And then a big dark river carp struggled up the driveway in front of them both, its dorsal fin folded over in the sunlight. It swam toward the deer pasture, which had been flooded to the height of a man for days. If Dell and Darren hadn't freed those deer when they did, every one of them would have drowned in their fence. Sam often thought about Old Mossy, imagined him ferrying across the dark river that night, his big antlers flashing in the lightning, stepping to the far shore toward new freedom, cornfields, and orchards.

The only part of Chip's land that was left untouched was the high forest knoll with the Indian mounds and Sam's marooned camper. He was so glad he'd chosen to park it higher up the hill than seemed necessary. The rise with its oaks and mounds looked like an island within an island. The rest of the land around it that wasn't still underwater was swept almost entirely clean. The tall grasses of the fields were pressed flat. The low trees and undergrowth were stripped of every leaf.

"Well," said Chip, wading back to the moored raft. "Here's to second chances."

The floodwaters eventually blew down to Lake Michigan like a spent breath. Sam spent a few days cleaning up sandbags in town. Despite the destruction, it was an oddly positive time. No one had been hurt, and now the sun shone and the whole community was outside and working together, discussing what they'd do and what they'd fix up when the insurance and disaster relief came. Debbie was out on bail too, which lifted and affirmed many spirits. She'd been ordered along with Blakely and a few of his NorthSky men to do a collective thousand hours of community service together. Ranger Bonnie was right—the judge was old-school. Randy had been there for the decision. After the grave judge gave out an armload of misdemeanors and the incredible heap of community service, he eyeballed the whole room. "And if a thousand hours of community service seems too *unusual*, we can hand out felonies today instead. It's easily done." Everyone sat very still when he said that, and then the judge whacked his dented oak table with his wooden mallet and went to lunch. Two days later, when Randy and Sam were coming back from gassing up the camper they'd finally gotten off the island with a temporary forest service bridge, they saw Debbie in her big flowing dress, shoveling dried mud from the curb gutter with a square spade. A solid twenty yards away from her, Blakely shoveled too, sweaty and red-faced. Randy leaned out the camper's window.

"Love you, Mom!" he called to her.

She stood up straight and squinted in the sun. Then she waved happily. "Hey, honey!" she called back. "Love you too!" In the rearview mirror, Sam saw Blakely stand up from his shovel work. Debbie barked something at him, pointing with her thick arm, and Blakely stooped and began shoveling again.

Duncan told them all that NorthSky was done for the season, but that his uncle claimed they'd get back at it next spring, using X-treme's property as a new headquarters. Duncan's uncle stopped talking to him, having grouped him together in his mind with Moon and Sam and all the other guides from Woodchuck. The last thing Blakely told him was a message to pass along. "The only thing you and all the other hippies have accomplished," it said, "is the delay of solid jobs for these families up here. And when you look around this winter and people can't afford enough heat, or good clothes for their kids—or enough money to spend on your damn rafting trips—just know you are the ones who did that, and that's *all* you did."

And then came the dark day, two weeks after Labor Day, when Sam found Chip lying in the brown ferns and pine needles on the riverbank. Sam had been working on barn cleanup, and drove down to the river for a swim to cool off. He saw Chip's bike at the trailhead, and decided to hike up and sit with him awhile, see how the bass were biting. Sam found him tipped over in his usual spot, and just thought he was napping next to his half-eaten lunch. Sam actually chuckled as he made his way down the slope. But then Sam got close enough to see his uncle's face, his eyes open and glassy and unnaturally still, staring out at the bright black river. Sam knelt down next to his uncle on the pine needles, put a hand on Chip's face, cool, waxy. Sam sat down beside his uncle and gently closed the man's eyes. Sam sat there for quite a long time and watched the river while the sun tilted west and warmed the riverbank. The smell of pine and water rose strong from the earth.

"Okay, Chip," Sam finally said very quietly. "Let's get you home." And even as he said it, he knew Chip was already exactly where he'd want to be, the river sparkling orange and black between the broad trunks of white pines, the ground a soft and good-smelling bed.

Seven days later they had the ceremony, and everyone gathered late in the afternoon near the lip of Mishicot Falls. Swami, who had just finished finally closing on their home in Chicago, drove back to Thunderwater with the kids. She let Sam know the news about the house before Sam let her know the news about Chip.

Swami stood on shore with the kids now, and the kids had picked a bouquet of ferns and wild mint and fallen maple leaves on their way up the trail. Dell's lip quivered as Swami and Darren helped her let her bouquet go in the thrumming water. Moon brought Chip's favorite poncho, the one with the belly pocket he liked to wear to warm up after every river trip. Randy brought Chip's paddle. Pete was there, standing quietly with Debbie on a wide, flat rock. Both of them looked out at the water with sad red eyes and their chins held high. Duncan canceled his rafting trips for the day and hiked up to the falls. He nodded quietly to everyone, stood next to Randy under the pine where Chip had died.

Everyone watched as Sam waded out along the exposed rocks above the falls, holding the urn that held his uncle's ashes. Reaching the brink of the falls, Sam looked back at the gathering. Moon cried quietly, her hand over her mouth. Debbie made the sign of the cross over her chest. Swami gave Sam a sad smile and nodded. The summer had been so hard on her. Most of their marriage had been hard on her. Sam wanted better for her, moving forward in life. He still wasn't sure if he'd be invited into it. She really was remarkable, Sam thought, standing there on the riverbank, present, choosing to be here in the setting sun, their youngest wrapped in a bundle on her chest.

Sam stepped to the edge of the falls. The rushing water filled the gorge with its thrum. The sun was golden orange, dipping behind the cedars and maple. The sky overhead was still blue, and Sam looked up to watch two barn swallows flit and twist downstream with their forked tails, light brown bellies above the tea-colored river.

"Off you go, Chip," whispered Sam. "We love you, buddy." Sam let the ash spill into the falls and the air above the falls, the breeze and water carrying it downriver. When he finished pouring, he rinsed the urn in the river and poured it out again. He remembered the feeling of Chip's big shoulder under his hand, remembered his big bellow in the gorge, the way his bare feet dangled happily from the bow of a raft in the flats. Chip would always be here, part of the gorge as much as the gorge was part of him. Sam sank the urn in a crevasse between a few river rocks, washed his hands and arms, and waded back to shore. Everyone had a chance to say what they wanted to say. They all shared a story, or released a memory into the river. And it was done.

When all had said their goodbyes and made their way back down the trail—the kids walking back with Randy and Moon—Swami touched Sam's arm and asked if he could talk for a minute.

He nodded and followed her. She waded halfway out to the falls and sat on a dry, flat boulder. The sky was turning indigo. Swami picked her wet feet up onto the warm rock and hugged her knees. Sam sat on the rock too, not close, but beside her.

"It's getting cold," she said, drawing the collar of her fleece up around her neck.

Sam nodded. They watched the river.

"I'm leaving on Tuesday," Swami said. "I'm taking the kids in the camper out to California."

Sam said nothing right away. This is what he'd been too afraid to ask. Swami had been in Chicago. Sam had been in Thunderwater. An awkward sort of silence planted itself between them. Even the one time Swami took everyone bowling with Birdy at Rita's place, Sam's attempts to talk to his wife all clunked heavily like the balls the kids kept thumping into the gutters. Sam knew deep down she'd sell the house, that she'd be leaving. And that made sense to him. How could they go back to living the life they were living before? It seemed so impossible, and undesirable, but Sam was too afraid to bring up the future because he didn't know if he'd be invited.

Sam turned his face away for a moment.

"But, Sam," she said, "that's not all I wanted to tell you."

He waited.

"I'm taking the kids to California, but after a little while, I'd like it if you came out too."

Sam looked at her. He knew he had tears in his eyes.

"I do need some time, though, to sort things out. I need time out there by myself, just me and the kids and the ocean."

Swami's eyes welled up a bit too. They both looked out at the river again.

"That week of the jamboree," she said, "boating this incredible river. It made me remember things I'd forgotten. And it allowed me to begin to imagine again a future for this place, for Woodchuck, for us. It got me imagining a new vision."

Sam watched Swami watch the river.

"I saw the kids on an ocean beach, seagulls, DeeDee learning to walk on the wet sand. I saw surf lessons, warm air in winters, ripe avocados. And then I saw summers here at Woodchuck, showing Darren the ropes eventually, doing yoga under the pines again. *If* people want to join me, I mean. No more forced yoga."

"That's a very good vision, Swami," Sam said quietly. "Please keep imagining that."

"It seems fragile, though," she said. "I mean, we sort of tried already, didn't we? Look where it got us."

Sam knew she meant the pain they'd endured this summer, along with the uncertainty they still sat in. But then he knew she also sensed another possibility. The summer had also gotten them here on the lip of a brilliant waterfall, sitting together on a warm rock, healing, their family still miraculously together, the river canyon filled with barn swallows.

"Well," said Sam, not rushing his words, "I would like to try again."

Swami's face pinched as he said it. She nodded at the river and cliffs and sky.

"Okay," she said, and then she took a deep breath. "I'm sorry about your uncle," she said. "Chip was good. I'm glad he gets to stay here."

"Me too," said Sam, and he didn't quite know how to ask what he wanted to, so he just asked it.

"When will you know when I can come?" he asked. "Where will you be?"

"I don't think it will take so long," said Swami, and then she smiled. "I will send you a postcard."

"What about school?" Sam asked. "For Darren."

"His dad's a teacher. We can homeschool."

Sam smiled and nodded. "Okay, Swami," he said.

"Okay, Sam," she said.

They sat for a bit and watched the sky turn dark, the big mottled moon rising over the trees.

"Will you walk me back?" asked Swami.

"Yeah," answered Sam.

•••

FOR THE REST OF SEPTEMBER, Sam stayed in Chip's gutted cabin, straightening out Chip's property and Woodchuck too, winterizing the boats and bus with Duncan's help. Eventually, everything that could be done was done. Chip's cabin was just logs on fieldstones, original again, the way Chip had planned. Sam used a pitchfork to lift all the drying carp from the driveway, and planted them in the bare spot where Chip's garden had been. At Woodchuck, the gravel around the patio was raked smooth and the lawn mown short. The bus had a tank full of gas and a bottle of fuel stabilizer and an oil change. The rafts were deflated, dusted in talcum, and rolled up in the barn for storage. Sam even took Chip's dirt bike in to Smitty's for fresh tires and brakes and a full tune-up, plus a luggage rack he'd ordered through a parts catalogue.

And then one early evening, a black sedan pulled up to the cabin. A man stepped out and looked around a bit warily. Sam had contacted a lawyer a few weeks back to see if he could find any sort of will or executor Chip may have left. The man introduced himself as that lawyer. He'd tried to call, he said, but the phones were disconnected. He had some findings to discuss, if Sam had a few minutes. Sam shook his hand and invited him in. There were no more utilities connected to Chip's cabin, which meant there were no more bills either, which felt like a breath of very clean air. Swami had used the sale of their house to pay off Woodchuck in its entirety. They were debt-free, with fifty grand and a camper and little else. Sam used two Coleman camping lamps to light up the kitchen.

"Rustic out here," said the lawyer, removing a folder of papers from his bag. "It's kind of nice."

Sam nodded.

"So, bad news," the man said. "Your uncle did have a will, but neither you nor your wife were named in it."

Sam shifted in his seat. "Who was?"

The man looked him in the eye in the dim light of the kitchen, slid some old papers across the table for Sam. "The most recent will Chip had drafted and signed was in 1978." Sam braced himself. If this property somehow came up on some auction block, there would be no stopping Blakely from buying it. "And in it," the man went on, "Chip named the Menominee Indian Tribe as the sole beneficiary of this property unless he sold it before his death. Because he did not sell it, all rights to this land and cabin belong to the tribe now. I'm very sorry. Because you are next of kin, you are welcome to remove any of your uncle's personal belongings." He looked around the gutted cabin. "But perhaps there's not too much. If you'd like to negotiate a purchase with the tribe for the land and cabin, perhaps I can help. They've been informed of this too."

Sam sat very still. He nodded. Thanked the man. And then he sat very still in the dark cabin for a long time after the man left. Sam thought of the mounds in the forest, the land returning to them after all this time, after being washed by a river too. There would be no negotiation, Sam knew, not with Sam, and more importantly, not with Blakely. The tribe, Sam knew, would never part with this land again. It was safe. Sam smiled a sad smile. The late-summer crickets sang outside. He would spend one last night here on the island, which wasn't his, never was, and that was as it should be.

He invited Moon and Randy and Debbie and Pete out to Chip's farm the next day to collect any belongings they'd like to have. Pete didn't show right away, but the others did. The lawyer was right. Beyond the cabin logs and fence posts and a few boxes of things stored high in a closet, there wasn't much. Randy collected a few serviceable tools and hoses from the mud where the shed was, plus an old .22 rifle Chip had kept over the fireplace. Debbie kept two nice cast-iron pans. Moon just wanted one of Chip's wool army blankets, to sleep in sometimes, she said, or stay warm next to a fire. Everyone agreed that Sam should keep Chip's dirt bike. He also kept the photo of Chip and Aunt Mary from when they started the company. He tucked the photo, along with *The Wind in the Willows*, into his backpack and bungeed it to the rack on Chip's bike. The rest of Chip's clothing and dishes fit in two boxes they'd drop at St. Vincent's.

Pete finally puttered up the driveway in his red truck. He waved at them all, smiled, and shut off his motor, his big husky riding shotgun. He stepped out and shook hands all around, and then he grinned a big grin and reached into the high side of his truck bed. He removed the lid from a crate and very gently lifted out a squirming ball of black-and-white fuzz.

"Check it out," said Pete, cradling the puppy to his chest. "Husky puppies!"

Moon gushed. Bear stood up proudly by the driver's-side window as Pete took more puppies from the crate and they each held one.

"I got too many of 'em," Pete said. "So, in another week or two, when they're ready, they'll need a place to go."

"Sign me up," said Debbie.

"Us too," said Moon, smiling at Randy while he put his arm around her. He and Moon were leaving for the winter together. There was an organic vegetable farm down in Georgia where they'd work for room and board. They were going to learn about an emerging movement called Farm to Table, which Randy hoped to bring back to the Northwoods with his disaster check. Both planned to stay on as river guides in summers.

Sam held his small puppy up by the armpits. It had one brown eye and one blue. It was far more laid-back than the others, just happy to hang there and stare back at Sam. Sam wished Dell were here for this. She'd absolutely melt.

"And, Sam," said Pete, "I didn't come out here to take any of Chip's things, but I wanted to tell you that some of the elders just met, and they all agreed, after I told them what you and Moon did for the land this summer, that they'd draft up some sort of permanent easement to this property."

Sam cradled the dog again. "What does that mean, exactly?" he asked.

"It means that the tribe is going to keep this land as it is now, off-grid, forever, but if you and Swami ever need a place to park your camper, or grow a small garden in the summer, and Moon too, you can do it here. And you can stay in the cabin too."

Sam looked at the land and the cabin, pictured Dell and Darren chasing a husky to the river. He buried his face in the dog's fur and nodded. "Thank you, Pete," he said when he could. "Very much."

In the weeks that followed, Sam fell into a habit of checking the mailbox, drinking his coffee while looking out through the trees to the river, and then hiking the Piers Gorge trail with his new husky puppy. He practiced taking the dog for rides on the dirt bike. Sam used a river strap to secure a plastic milk crate on top of the bike's tank. He lined it with old sweatshirts and harnessed the puppy in to be comfortable but safe. The tiny dog sat gamely in the crate while Sam puttered the bike along back roads. The dog had bright eyes and bright fur with a black raccoon mask on its face. As Sam drove, the little dog peeked over the crate and closed its eyes, its fuzzy black ears feathering in the good-smelling September air. If Sam drove longer than twenty minutes, the dog curled up in the crate and dozed with its fox-like tail over its face.

Sam was glad for the company. Moon and Randy left in Moon's Jeep, and Debbie cried but said it was about damn time too. Duncan sold off his Mustang and drove his rafting bus to Colorado for winter ski work. Sam and the dog were alone together. The river was quiet. They waited.

And then one morning late in September, the mail came. There were three postcards mailed from a PO box in Encinitas, California, on the same day. They'd clearly collected them in their travels west. Sam read them by the mailbox. He read them again while he walked back to the cabin, the puppy trotting alongside him. "Last gorge hike today, buddy," he said to the dog. "We're leaving tomorrow at dawn."

Sam and the puppy hiked to the falls that evening and sat on the riverbank near Sand Portage, watching the black river swoop and break in the rapids, bright yellow and orange leaves floating on it. The husky waded in a shallow pool near the river's edge, pouncing from time to time at crayfish. Sam watched the dog. Watched the sun set. Sam took the postcards from his flannel pocket and turned them over in his hands again and again. The first one they'd picked up in the desert. It had a lone cactus standing before red rocks.

We miss you, Dad, the postcard read in Darren's hand. *The desert is HOT. We saw a rattlesnake! I am helping Mom pump all the gas. Love, Darren.*

The second card had a picture of a hot dog cart with balloons tied to it. It read, *Daddy!* in a massive wobbly scrawl, and then a heart with Dell's name in the middle.

The third card had a picture of a bronze surfer statue, with *Encinitas!* printed in bright blue letters. And on the back, a note from Swami.

Dear Sam,

We're here! I'm ready if you are. The sunsets are stunning, and the air smells like ocean and flowers, just like I remember. We go to this beach by the statue every Tuesday at ten. Darren's taking surf lessons. We will meet you there. Please come home.

We all miss you.
Love, Swami

Sam stood, patted his thigh, and walked back into the quiet wooded path. The puppy splashed out of the river and galloped ahead. Sam ran with him.

The next morning, Sam hung a sign on the blue door of the raft barn that read *Closed until Memorial Day Weekend*. He walked to the mailbox at the end of the driveway, put a postcard of his own inside, and raised the flag. It was a Thunderwater postcard he bought from Ranger Bonnie at the campground store when he said goodbye. The card was a painting of the big wooden musky sign with the pines and bluffs behind it. *On my way*, Sam wrote. *This card will beat me there. I love you. I am proud of you. Love, Sam. Love, Dad.*

Sam straddled the dirt bike and hoisted the puppy into the crate. He gave a final tug to a few straps. He carried a backpack full of clothes.

He had a small tent and a jug for water and a can for gas strapped to the luggage rack. Sam pulled his son's compass out from the neck of his shirt and let it dangle on the lanyard he'd tied—the compass Swami had replaced when the first was broken, and that Darren gave to Sam before they parted. Darren said he wanted it back, though, that it wasn't for keeps. Sam smiled at the compass, then tugged on an orange dirt bike helmet and strapped it under his chin, adjusted ski goggles over his eyes. He felt light. Incredibly light. Last year at this time, he'd already been grading bad art history essays and worse drawings, serving lunchroom duty on Wednesdays, drinking burnt coffee in a teacher's lounge in Chicago. But he wasn't doing any of that. He and his family owned a raft company, free and clear. He was about to road-trip a dirt bike along back roads until he hit the Pacific Ocean. He was going to rejoin his wife, paddle out for surf lessons with his son, hand a puppy to his daughter and ask her to name it. Seagull. Ocean. Hot Dog. Avocado. Whatever she chose would be it.

The puppy was excited, sensed the difference of the day. It stood with its paws on the edge of the crate. Sam stood and kicked the starter. The motor burbled. The dog hunkered down, ready. Sam blipped the throttle, lifted his feet, and rattled down Woodchuck's dusty driveway, the Queen Anne's lace dry and tall in the ditches. He stopped at the driveway's end, and the dust and exhaust caught up to him. He looked back just once, the blue barn squared away and waiting, Swami's cedars standing tall beside it.

"Off we go," said Sam. "Home to the ocean!" He revved the bike onto the empty highway and pointed it west, toward his family. Sam accelerated his way into fifth gear. The motorbike buzzed and hummed as light as a feather down the bright road. Sam twisted the throttle just a little more, adjusted his goggles. The little dog closed its bright eyes, lifted its nose into the westward wind.

ACKNOWLEDGMENTS

This novel, *True North*, is a story very near to my heart. I grew up fishing and hiking a stretch of whitewater named Piers Gorge on the Menominee River, which forms part of Wisconsin's northern border. After a tour in the USAF, I returned home, started college on the GI Bill, and learned to guide whitewater rafts through Piers Gorge during my summers off. Guiding whitewater rivers—learning to yield to the water instead of fight it—has become one of the central joys and metaphors in my life. I love whitewater rivers, and I love the free-spirited people who guide them, the Sams and Swamis and Chips and Moons and Randys one can find stacking rafts and telling river stories at any outfitter on the planet. I really wanted to get this story right. To that end, I owe thanks to many for support and guidance. Thank you to Helen Atsma and the whole team at Ecco and HarperCollins. Helen, you helped me find the spirit and flow of this novel, and I can't thank you enough for your trust in this story. Many thanks to Maggie Cooper at Aevitas, a terrific reader and phenomenal agent, without whom my novels would still be manuscripts in sock drawers. Many thanks to the Ohio Arts Council, whose support helped free up a summer for me to work on this book. Many thanks to Wittenberg University in Ohio, where I very happily teach and write on a beautiful campus alongside talented students and unendingly supportive colleagues. Many thanks to every reader holding this book (and every book) in your hand, for championing storytelling, and libraries, and bookstores, and time well spent with a novel. Thank you, Piers Gorge, for your waterfalls and bluffs and tea-colored water. And all my love and thanks to my family for your companionship and beauty through every sort of waters—you are, each of you, a bright and shining river.